"*Where All Is Night, and Starless* is both a love letter and a wry, knowing nod to Lovecraft's mythos. But it has greater ambitions than this. John Linwood Grant sets out a compelling argument for his own mythos—an elegant and entirely organic beast, resolute in its own strange identity. This is a deeply intelligent and inventive collection which seeks not to answer life's great mysteries, but to drag them into the light so that the reader might examine them in glorious detail." — Laura Mauro, author of *Sing Your Sadness Deep*

"A cornucopia of dark delights, this collection is highly imaginative, extremely well written, and a delight to read. Weird fiction at its finest!" — Tim Waggoner, Bram Stoker Award ® winner and author of *Your Turn to Suffer*

"With *Where all is Night, and Starless*, Grant has crafted a far-reaching collection, imbued with beautifully deft prose, where dark humour, melancholy and ghoulishness effortlessly share the same space as though in cosmic alignment with the fates. A truly magnificent achievement by an incredibly gifted wordsmith.

"Grant is a wordsmith of great nuance, setting scenes where the reader walks, mesmerised by sublime narratives of profundity and meaning, before being led into dead ends and dark corners where all things ghastly await." — Dave Jeffery, author of *A Quiet Apocalypse* and *Cathedral*

"Whether it is making the familiar unfamiliar or the unfamiliar familiar, John Linwood Grant's worlds are ones of terror, heart, irony and a small bit of grief. *Where All is Night, and Starless* is a long-awaited gift to those of us who have been fans for years, and a welcome invitation to new readers looking for a full showing of Grant world building and storytelling talents." — S. L. Edwards, author of *The Death of An Author*

"Whether the tale is set in East Yorkshire or a Nigerian village, John Linwood Grant excels at constructing a credible, detailed environment for a particular kind of weird fiction, which relies upon the folk beliefs and practices of a specific area. The setting is much more than atmosphere or background, and Grant never lapses into mystification. He establishes the parameters of a well-researched time and place, and then introduces supernatural elements that play against reality until yielding something eerie, something dangerous.

"'Small magicks appeal to me more than many grand ones,' says the author, in one of the story notes. He can certainly tell a cosmic tale as well as any Lovecraft devotee might. But his strength lies in the ability to portray ordinary individuals who embrace these 'small magicks.' The vast unknown is far away and significantly less compelling than the strange creatures of legend who occupy the woods just outside of town.

"The stories in this wide-ranging collection demonstrate immense skill. Grant seems to be adept at just about any genre, set during any period. But his writing really sings when he brings to life small remnants we know all too well and routinely ignore, briefly reigniting our faith in magic, and confirming the power of one lit candle to hold back the terrors of the night." — S.P. Miskowski, author of *I Wish I Was Like You*

"John Linwood Grant's *Where All Is Night, and Starless* is a stealth recon into the uncanny, a wildly imaginative excursion through light and darkness. With his folk horror sensibility and his deeply empathetic approach, Grant's stories are somehow always about more than mere monsters. Whether we're in the tunnels below WW1, the faded British coast or timeless Oklahoma, Grant presents his scenarios with a historian's precision and a born fantasist's ingenuity. He never loses sight, though, of what makes these stories special: the uneasy emotional life of his outcasts—single parents, extraordinary children, Igbo tribesmen, Harlem stage performers more than slightly past their prime— is always front and center.

"But the real magic in Grant's stories is something deeper and more rare. There's a chameleon's heart at work here, and an unusually humanistic resonance with his characters. In this way, he dazzles you and reels you in, and implicates you along with the darkness—he makes you one with the monsters. In Grant's fiction, not a single soul gets away unscathed." — Polly Schattel, author of *The Occultists*

where all is night, and starless

john linwood grant
myths, mysteries & mythos

TREPIDATIO
PUBLISHING

ISBN: 978-1-950305-90-2 (sc)
ISBN: 978-1-950305-91-9 (ebook)
Library of Congress Control Number: 2021941523
First printing edition: July 9, 2021
Published by Trepidatio Publishing in the United States of America.
Cover Design: Sebastián Cabrol
Cover Layout: Scarlett R. Algee & John Linwood Grant
Edited by Sean Leonard
Proofreading and Interior Layout by Scarlett R. Algee

Trepidatio Publishing, an imprint of JournalStone Publishing
3205 Sassafras Trail
Carbondale, Illinois 62901

JournalStone books may be ordered through booksellers or by contacting:
JournalStone | www.journalstone.com

To Sarah, with more love and gratitude than ever.

contents

On Myths

where all is night, and starless

introduction:
john and the lurchers

THE CLIFFS RISE in the distance, walling off the broad sweep of the fault-wracked escarpment. The Yorkshire wolds might as well be the landscape of some alien planet. You feel very foreign; regrettably, blandly American; desolate, a stranger with no hope of ever truly assimilating. The wind kicks up. You tighten the hood of your wool anorak jacket. The bruised purple moors lie before you. The reeds that surround you bend in wispy, whispering prayer.

A figure hails you from the horizon, a man with his arm raised. Two low figures, beasts of some kind, flank him as he trundles your way. Somewhere in the clouds, unseen birds shriek and flee. The man tugs at the two leashes that tether him to the beasts. He winds his way between thick-trunked trees limned with ancient moss. One of the beasts lets loose with a volley of rough barking. The man hushes the beast. The voice is gruff but loving, though the words are difficult to discern.

Then he is in front of you, having somehow bridged the great distance in what feels like mere moments. His greying hair flies around his head. Glasses shield kind eyes. A beard fills the lower half of his face. He's clad in layer upon layer, long johns under flannels under a sweater under a zipped top, all covered in a longish leather jacket. A scarf is wound tightly about his neck.

John, he says by way of introduction, but you knew that already. *And these rather rambunctious souls*—he gestures to the grinning long dogs that sit at either side of him, tongues lolling—*are lurchers*. The dogs' grins seem to widen. *They're friendly, of course.* His warm hand envelopes your cold one.

A blink and you're sunk in a generously cushioned chair inside a warm, comfortable den. The windows are dappled with dew and show only grey. A cup of tea sits before you, sending up a twisting ribbon of warmth. A stone fireplace harbors leaping orange flames. The walls on either side of it are made up of wooden shelves anchored by concrete blocks, crowded with books in varying stages of their lives. The lurchers are piled upon a couch, their bellies stretched out. They're snoring gently. One stretches out a paw and vocalizes comfortably.

You know John from his deceptively mannered Edwardian tales that drip with evil under their civilized surface like a tuxedo lined with very sharp needles. You're ready for more, but as you sit, sipping your tea, which he replenishes with the efficacy of a water-refiller at a Chinese restaurant, he instead unspools tales that are wild, colorful, dark, mystical. You realize you are in the presence of a wizard. These tales, you reckon, written at a different time, would surely find themselves among bizarre illustrations in issues of *Weird Tales*, *Amazing Stories*, *Terror*, woven throughout works by Clark Ashton Smith, Fritz Leiber, and Hugh B. Cave. It's also easy to picture them bound in mass market paperbacks on rotating newsstand racks, with cover art depicting towering forests; gritty, graffiti-smeared 70's New York streets; a traveling carnival caravan on a midnight highway, furtive creatures in shady glens.

The roof disintegrates and the vast and ravenous cosmos swirls into dizzying view as Grant tells tales in an unabashedly Lovecraftian vein, with a sort of sequel to *In The Mountains of Madness* that deftly takes on the "Lovecraft was onto something" premise and makes something unique and compelling from it. Here are tales of hidden texts and dilettante-cultists, missionaries of a sinister order meeting more than they bargained for in Nigeria, extreme ritual scarification as a path to the ultimate transcendence.

At the conclusion of a particularly jarring story, you spill your tea with a start. "Oh, bother," says Grant. "You weren't falling asleep, were you?"

"Anything but," you say, and he cackles madly. He can see that you're very much wide awake. You chuckle and he rises with a groan to refill your cup. As he busies himself in the kitchen, cups and tableware and kettles clinking and clanging, you glance at the books that crowd his shelves. Below the shelf of ancient, peeling, foxed tomes whose spines glow with unearthly colors sit horizons of yellowed paperbacks, mysteries and mythologies crowded together in piles. The charity shop aroma mingles with older odors, times past, abandoned attics, asylum libraries.

Grant returns, gingerly places your newly filled cup down on the table adjacent to your chair.

Where were we, he says. *Ah yes.*

And now you're transported to a comedy club where a stooped figure summons living revenants to torment his audience; you're one of a crowd of people engaged in a group-possession; you're under the soaring canvas walls of a tent put up by a malevolent traveling carnival with feral clowns; in a room swimming with dust motes you're watching old scratchy films from the light of projector. You're dizzy. Grant pauses. "Cake?" he says, and the answer to that question is always a resounding YES.

But you hold your fork aloft, cake sitting uneaten, as Grant transitions to stories of goblins engaging in cruel mischief with the complicity of humans seeking transformation, of chilling oceanside rituals and the legacies one cannot escape, of wood nymphs seeking refuge from the brutality of their...

STOP, John says. He's standing now, grinning. The lurchers have joined him and are standing at his side. They look hungry. *Is this for the introduction you're writing? For my collection?*

Well...yes, yes, it is.

You're just summarizing the stories, old chap.

(He pushes aside my teacup and places a glass in front of me. Into it he pours gin from a fancy-looking bottle. I take a hearty swig and cough a bit.)

Ugh (I say), I told you I'm better at writing fiction than I am at writing about fiction.

You said I was a wizard.

Well, it's essentially accurate. You say tomato...

Look, write this down instead: "Some crumbling Yorkshireman dressed like an unsuccessful hobo wrote the following. I've seen worse. You should buy it because the dog's eaten his shoes."

That's not nearly long enough an introduction. Plus, your shoes are...oh.

Yeah.

Well, what I was trying to do here was say how these stories might subvert the expectations of readers. How this witty, lovely Yorkshireman has cast his dark tales in unexpected settings, utilizing a diverse cast of compelling lead characters who are well beyond your typical pale Lovecraftian timid, scholarly...

Then just ...

...including a horse...

...say it.

Well, reader, you already have the book in your hot little hands. Or else you're looking at the preview on Amazon. Either way, you owe it to yourself to get reading. John Linwood Grant is a hell of a storyteller, and a sweetheart to boot. I'm jealous of you, getting to read his work for the first time. My little summaries above don't do them justice.

The fact of the matter is, I'm a fan. Trust me: you will be too.

And so I set out back into the wolds, warmed by tea and gin, enthralled by stories, unnerved by the condition of Grant's chewed-up footwear. I still feel desolate, alone. But the skies are strangely colored now, and the stars have all been switched around. We're all strangers here. But if you're seeking a cosmic guide, you can't get much better than John Linwood Grant.

Enough from me. Start reading.

Matthew M Bartlett
New England, June 2021

on mythos

sundry reflections concerning
a rather difficult cosmos

strange perfumes of a polar sun

I WORRY ABOUT the floor joists. I had them checked by a builder, and he said they could bear a considerable weight. I felt relieved at first, but then I heard him on his mobile phone on the way out — he called me "that mad woman at Number Sixty-Five." I no longer trust his judgement, so I've started using polystyrene more often. It's far lighter and easier to move than stone, though I hate it as a material. The smell of the hot knife cutting through it, and the urge I have to press the blade to my arm before it cools — these are not good things. I don't need distractions.

Now that the old water tank has gone, I have the whole attic space across two houses. Until the landlord who owns next door manages to sell it — or finds out that I've knocked through. I don't expect either for a while. The housing market's quite depressed, and these Victorian places need a lot of work.

The latest peaks have been difficult. I use Lovecraft's book, of course, along with maps which I've annotated, and the satellite photos that Misha sends me. It's getting more dangerous for her, she says. They're talking about vetting the staff at the UN Antarctic Survey data-stream centre again, after someone leaked blurred footage of D732, the higher of the two most northwesterly mountains. UNAS is obsessed with secrecy.

Once I had downloaded Misha's better definition photos of D732, I could see that there is surprisingly little erosion; the almost-perfect clusters of stonework on the south face are astonishing, like cubes of sugars embedded near the tip of one of those old conical sugar-loaves. I used pumice stone to model the peak — I like the rough feel of pumice, the scrape against my skin. A hardened hacksaw blade and a set of files gave me reasonable results.

So that's most of the northwest sector done. I think the Four are pleased. I slice open an orange for breakfast, and there are only five segments under the peel. That feels like a good sign. Four plus one. With D732 completed, the end is in sight...and yet I'm uneasy. Not because of what I do, but because others may be taking an interest.

Someone has been watching the house for the last few days.

I keep a lookout from the first-floor windows when I'm not working, and make notes on who comes down the street, who hesitates or lingers. I don't know who is out there. It could be that Misha's superiors at UNAS have ordered surveillance, although I thought we'd been careful. All our exchanges are through the Dark Web, for example, but it's possible that we missed something. And there are always lunatics — cultists and the "End of the World" people — who would want to connect my work with their own ramblings. I've had enough trouble avoiding that type in my time.

Maybe it's nothing more than potential burglars, wondering exactly what I have up here. Or squatters, waiting for me to go out and leave a window open.

Yes, that's probably all it is.

***

It's been four years now. Four years since the Beardsmore Glacier tore itself apart under its own weight. Great swathes of the Antarctic had already lost their protective ice, and then the major glaciers began to calve at a rate never seen before. The seas were rising, and the ice was shrinking. Dramatically.

There were a lot of theories about the sudden changes at the southern pole in particular — an artefact of global warming, a change in volcanic pressure beneath that great continent, and so on. And then there came the day when an American survey plane from McMurdo spotted unusual rock formations. The ice had slipped away from a high plateau on the edge of the Transantarctic Mountains, and there was...

The City.

With Danish and British observers on board the plane, the Americans were unable to hide what they had found. Speculation swept the globe. Geological oddities became primitive objects of worship (an early anthropoid sub-species, lost as the pole froze, said some), then buildings, constructed by an unknown people of Atlantean ability, and at last, undeniably, a city — an entire city, which could not be human in origin. There was no hypothesis, scientific or even faith-based, which could explain it. No one could question the strange geometries which were being exposed.

There had been strangers on the planet, a hundred million years ago.

Which I already knew.

***

I don't expect anyone to understand what I'm doing. I don't want them to — they would interfere, or stop me. Let them dismiss me like the builder does, if it makes things easier. I am used to being separate from others. From the faint whisperings I heard as a child, and the incidents when I started secondary school — who gives medication to an eleven-year-old? — I recognised that I was different, though not why.

For my real entry into this Antarctic mystery did not come with the drawing back of the ice, but far earlier. I was twelve. A boy whose name I forget tried to touch me after school, and I ran from him, hiding in the waste-ground by the former brickworks, barely a hundred yards from my house. There, amongst the ghosts of buildings long-demolished, the Four found me.

Alike and unalike, four women of indeterminate age in long, drab coats. They slid towards me over the landscape of shattered bricks and concrete boulders, and I knew they were not what they seemed. They were There and Elsewhere at the same time, though I was too young to put it that clearly. Illusions, phantasms.

The figures moved as a group, coming close to where I crouched, and behind the appearance of cheap perms, I could see a shadowed writhing of intricate tendrils. And there was the smell. They had tried to make it perfume, but it was not. The breeze brought a dark, fungal odour and, I thought, a hint of what the freezer smelled like when my mother defrosted it. Old stuff, neither rotten nor right.

We did not touch. I knew what it would feel like if I stretched out my hand; it would not be warm flesh that my fingertips found, only air and a cold hint of the far south. Instead, they stood there, and they allowed me to hear the lives that dwelled behind those projected images, a dry rustle of unbearable ages. I don't think they were physically present at all that day; they were simply offering an appearance which would not alarm me.

I was not alarmed. Rather than recoil, I wanted to know more. I felt... I cannot express it properly. Sudden kinship. Something beyond that which I had ever known with my parents or the other kids at school. The bond was made there and then — a sharing between my narrow grey eyes and their large red irises. The crimson of a polar dusk while the sun was still high.

I was of value.

When they left, my body sat in a brick and concrete wasteland; my mind was in Antarctica.

From then on, they wove their way into my thoughts, month after month, though I rarely saw them again in any of their forms. It was a cerebral bonding. I had no idea where they were physically — indeed, at that time I had no certainty that they had physical bodies at all. They were simply the Four, ancient spirits of the ice.

As I grew older, they brought me night-fevers of vast, deserted plateaus and winds which scoured flesh from bone; visions of drowned cities and forbidden peaks. They gave me hints that they themselves were real, material, and they fed me concepts of stone, in all its conceivable forms, starting my first poor attempts with chisel and file. They fed my isolation from other humans, strengthened it, and they made me a sculptor.

***

I gaze upon the expanse of shapes and shadows in the attic, and smile. The actual site in Antarctica is littered with UNAS watch-stations and scientific bases, troubled by fearful probes into the darkness. They hack and sample, causing even more damage. Misha tells me that they lost seven people last month — a crevasse beneath the ice, they say. Rumours abound, though I doubt the more fanciful tales that there are still such beasts as shoggoths roaming the abyss. That's a popular one — protoplasmic monstrosities gliding through the abandoned tunnels. I've read everything. Shoggoths were supposed to be adaptable. Why would they be down there, and not surging through our own cities, after all these decades? They would be here, swollen with ambition and hunger. It is nonsense.

Only the Four still exist.

And my pure city, which I build for them, is untainted. It is the core they need, the pattern for freedom, and they — we — must succeed.

In the months after the City was first photographed, everyone read Lovecraft's "At the Mountains of Madness" with a new urgency. Whole publishing houses grew rich, as scholars, scientists, and lunatics scoured his other writings for more hints as to how. How had this odd, troubled writer, who had never travelled far and never left North America, known that there really was a city in the ice? How had he described so perfectly the landscape which had emerged with the retreat of the glaciers?

If some did become rich through examination of stories from a century ago, none became wiser. Most of poor Lovecraft's writing is invented nonsense, a blur of horror and science fiction which, if unusually imaginative, is yet of very limited value. Only that one tale matched reality, though the City's emergence did encourage a mad hunt for other locations, even deep-water submarine explorations for sunken cities which house dreaming gods. Not a single Cyclopean block, not one non-Euclidean ruin, was found elsewhere, above or below the oceans.

But even his fiction had not prepared us. An alien place, too insane to accept, too real to ignore. Thousands died trying to reach the City on their own, or with well-funded private expeditions. During the first few months, there were frequent military engagements — a Chilean reconnaissance plane shot down by the Chinese; an American "supply" plane which turned out to be heavily armed. Russian scientists shot at a group of a dozen people who were found dragging a granite carving towards a waiting Sno-Cat. Two more men died as a result.

And weapons; there was always the hope — or fear — that there would be weapons. There won't be, but such is the madness of the military complexes that they dream of the ice holding armaments that will dwarf our nuclear technology.

It was obvious that no single nation could have jurisdiction down there, or be allowed to explore alone. UNAS was the world's frightened compromise to the situation. No flyovers or expeditions, except when sanctioned. The members of the Agong Mission, sponsored by a Malaysian tech-billionaire, are still in custody, a year later, and even the Americans now accept UNAS jurisdiction. The organisation is a clamp, a constraint which controls the centre of Antarctica, and throttles the free passage of data. Not that I care about any of this, nor do the Four. We wish only to leave — to be quit of this failing planet.

You will know your Lovecraft. Take it, and slash at it, removing all the fictions which the man from Providence added. Undo his excess of language and terror, the confabulations layered upon accounts of the genuine Pabodie Expedition report of 1930. Cling to one part only — that the expedition from Miskatonic University did find a number of the City's original inhabitants, preserved in rugose glory deep within the caverns. The easiest word is "hibernating," but it was hardly that. Nature had, through use of the intense cold and accidents of geology, pushed them out of Time. The Pabodie Expedition brought them back, with such tragic consequences. The narrator of Lovecraft's story had one thing right — only four survived, unaccounted for.

I was twenty-five when the City was spotted, and as the images came back, shared all over the world — before the UNAS interdict — I rejoiced. I felt the soft caress of tendrils which were not there, and the chill warmth of their purpose. I read Lovecraft's story, and I understood my visitors at last. I knew what they were.

Old Ones.

These days, the rising sea levels worry most people more than the alien city. The Netherlands have almost gone; Venice has gone. Tensions rise with the oceans — India stirs for war, and the highlands of the Philippines are burning.

None of this concerns me, for I will not be here.

The Four have promised.

***

A man comes to the door. His jacket is too clean and pressed, the material too fine; I do not trust him. Dark glasses (don't they all have those in films?) and dark hair, perfectly cut. My own hair is a tangle of polystyrene fragments and rat-tails.

"Have you let Salvation into your life?" he asks.

"Yes," I say. When he hesitates, I smile. "And it will be here soon."

He leaves, tripping on the steps outside the front door.

At times I hear the fluttering of membrane-wings, as if the Four are also worried. I can no longer doubt that my activity has been noted, somehow. The man who called may be one of the ones who watch at night — though I cannot believe he is with UNAS or the security forces.

I must work more quickly.

***

Additional footage has arrived, filling in the blanks around the swathe which marks the passage of some antediluvian river. Misha's note says she may not be able to keep this up much longer. The UNAS authorities are having another crackdown on leaked material — reports of finds in the lower levels had been passed to one of the big international news sites. A chamber which contains a burial mound in the still-frozen soil — a five-pointed mound, hundreds of metres below the surface in utter darkness. Empty, but the source of much speculation.

I rush from the computer as soon as I can print out the aerial shots. I have a sophisticated CAD package which reconstructs certain parts of the ruins for me, but I prefer to work from direct images if I can — and the thoughts of the Four. When maps and photographs are useless, then fragments come into my head, the recollections of other minds, from other times. I must always adjust for the countless millennia which have passed, but it is still a shock to find that I have sculpted something that I should not know — a strange, angled spire, or an intricate spiral of ramps which descends into the earth. Occasionally, I do not even remember carving such wonders.

I stumble as I move around the south quadrant of the model. The floorboards are definitely sagging, despite the I-beams I had installed in the rooms below — I told the builder I was storing slate and granite blocks up there, which had him shaking his head. Even seasoned Victorian timber has its limit. I will have to use hollow moulds for most of the final section. The weathered remains in the surveillance photographs must be restored to their original configurations.

***

Misha and I met online not long after the City emerged. She's been processing imagery from the Antarctic sites since the ice retreated; she had been re-assigned from a UN geological survey project. We were idle visitors to a number of websites and message boards, making comments about ludicrous conspiracy theories, but soon realised that we had more serious concerns under the wisecracks. We started messaging privately. She is internal, much like myself — a craftswoman in her own way, though with electronic data, not chisel and palette knife. No real friends. I think she is autistic, and clearly very good at her job.

I have one picture of her at a desk in Neuquén, Patagonia. She is small, distinctly Asian, quite pretty. I don't know why she's called Misha

— I thought that was a European name. I suspect that she has fallen for the tall, white woman with the unruly hair who sits and carves, so many thousands of miles across the ocean. I don't mind — it's sort of sweet — though I cannot remember having any sexuality, whether I liked girls or boys when I was young. I neither encourage nor discourage her online.

I am asexual. I don't know if this is my natural state, or the result of so many years of communion with the vegetative, sexless Four. It's possible that they want me to be this way, without libido, so that I can share their thoughts. I suppose I could have learned sex, if needed. My parents copulated at least once, obviously, though it is hard to imagine. They were affectionless, distant even from each other, pursuing small careers which left them no monuments except the headstone I carved after the car crash. I was twenty years old. "Dead," I cut into the granite, earning the enmity of my few surviving relatives.

Losing them had no impact on my life, for other parents had been preparing me.

***

From the bathroom window I can see a man, sitting in a long, low car on the other side of the road. The streetlights form cones of orange light, but he is parked away from them. I think he's the man who came to the door, and no longer believe he was here to introduce me to religion, not in the usual sense. But I think he meant his reference to Salvation. Now I have to decide if he is a threat, or merely one of the many who have constructed confused beliefs around the emergence of the City.

I go back upstairs and complete D735, the next peak, in a hurry. Detail isn't important on the edges, only relative position and perspective. It must be as it was, you see. Lovecraft called it oppressive, but it wasn't to them. The dark stone towers, the canyon-like streets, and the high walkways were part of an immense pattern which held racial memory — as time ground that down, the meaning was lost.

What they must have felt! Awake, aware, after so many millions of years, and sliding in haste through the ruins of their former lives, to find such loss. Imagine that you emerge from a coma, or a decades-long drug-induced sleep, and know that you can put things right. You need only pick up the instruction book, the encyclopaedia, the manual for the operating system, whatever you call it. But when you find it, it is torn and defaced, hardly readable.

That is the City as it stands in Antarctica.

D735 is no more than a bookmark. I work it to my satisfaction — their satisfaction — in pumice, polystyrene, and simple filler. The hardest part of the work was completed two weeks ago — an array of five-sided towers and pyramids which I carved and chipped from slate, no easy task. My initial work on that section was in sandstone, but the Four told me that the vibrations were wrong. They didn't mean vibrations, but it was the nearest word we could share. I wept with frustration as the slate split, fractured, again and again, but I succeeded. A text, a holy text in stone, as it had been laid out from the beginning.

Lovecraft's characters claimed they read an entire racial history in the symbols carved on the walls of their find, bands of glyphs that ran along ice-frosted walls. Perhaps they did. They were reading the wrong thing, though. They were children, reading the notes scrawled in the back of a revered family Bible, with no idea of its true purpose or contents.

The City is the answer, not what is written upon it.

The man in the car hasn't moved for hours.

Dare I go to sleep?

***

Two police officers come to ask me questions about a death. I take them into the living room, which is heaped with broken slate, chisels, and head-high stacks of newspapers. I'm aware that the room has a musty odour, and that there is nowhere to sit.

"You're some sort of artist, Ms. Paling?" The female officer, young with blonde hair tied up tight under her cap, seems uncomfortable.

"A sculptor."

"Henry Moore." The man, much older and unkempt, picks up a fragment of slate, puts it back down. "I like his stuff."

She nudges him, and he pulls out a mobile, showing me the screen. On it is a photograph of the man who came to the door. He is obviously dead, the flesh sunken around the closed eyes.

"I know it's unpleasant," the male officer says. "Sorry about that. But we're asking everyone around here if they recognise him. He was found in his Volvo yesterday, parked outside Number Sixty-Four — the house has been empty for months. A dog walker wanted to know if he was all right, tapped on the car window, and, well..."

I want to shove them onto the street and double-bolt the door. Instead, I nod. Someone might have seen him call here.

"Three days ago, yes. He didn't say who he was. I thought he was a Jehovah's Witness, or charity collecting. I sent him away." My smile is that of a woman trying to be helpful, but knowing nothing. It seems to work.

The mobile goes back into his jacket. They ask me exactly what he said, and I tell them. They write it down, and head for the front door.

"Anything odd around here in the last week?" asks the female officer as I open the door for them. "You know, other unwanted callers, strangers loitering on the street?"

"No. It's been quiet." I hesitate. "How did he die?"

They look at each other.

"Nothing sinister, Ms. Paling. Probably a heart attack," she says. It's obvious that she is lying.

***

I cannot change course now; I can only put the finishing touches to the city. As I work, I'm aware of the leathery whisper of thin wings, the slow flood of images — titanic blocks of masonry, rearing above fields of ice, but the Four are otherwise silent. They are contemplating how close we are. I know nothing of the man in the car. Who was he, and who killed him? I am certain that he was deliberately removed.

Polishing the edges of a star-shaped set of ramparts, imbuing the dull slate with a certain oily gleam, I wonder about Misha. She does not have my advantages, for the Four have never appeared to her. I've never heard of anyone else seeing them at all, which might make you wonder about my sanity — except that I have been able to construct something that cadres of UNAS scientists have been unable to manage, cannot even conceive of.

A way home.

***

Misha has been arrested. She sent me one last message to say that she had been identified as a "leak," and that they suspected her of working undercover for a leading government or coalition of governments, probably the Eurobloc. The message is addressed to "My Love," and says that she is wiping everything, that they will find no trace of me through her.

I know enough about information technology to be doubtful. They will find a trace eventually — a route through the signals shifted and pinged across the globe. I must finish the final touches as soon as possible.

As for Misha, I do not know what to feel. I used to wish that I had told her of the Four — it might have comforted her to know that a higher purpose was being served — and yet now I'm relieved that I did not.

I hope they will not hurt her. I cannot love her, but I can care.

***

It is a woman who calls at the door this time. Not the police, but a small, eager woman in her fifties. One of her earlobes is torn, only recently healed.

"There is worse to come," she says as I peer at her, the front door half-open. "The City must be saved."

She proffers a handful of leaflets, and I take one. Prophesies of the End Days, of strange alien forms arising from the Antarctic ruins to scourge the planet. An accusation that UNAS is a front for an agreement with non-human powers.

Behind her, I can see someone knocking at Number Sixty-Eight, a young man similarly laden with papers.

I hand the leaflet back. "Did you know the man in the car? The one who was killed?"

She looks horrified, backs away. I step out. A few doors down, Mr. Chen is sweeping his garden path. He holds the broom ready, wondering.

"Did you know the man?" I say more sharply, and she flees. Mr. Chen smiles, and goes back to clearing leaves.

***

That night I dream. People always tell you their dreams, as if you want to know. This is the sort of hallucinatory moment that you don't tell anyone about. Five figures rise above an enormous granite cylinder which glows, a pale light that is not quite a colour. Violet would be the easiest thing to call it. All five have great wings of glistening lace, spread wide from bodies of such complexity that I cannot describe them. A radial symmetry pervades their structure. A "six foot, five-ridged barrel torso" was Lovecraft's description. I do not know how he could have been so wrong, and yet known of the City. To use the word "barrel" about these beings is to dismiss a bird-of-paradise as appearing like a broiler chicken. It fails to capture anything of the reality.

I am one of them. I know that. The youngest, least sure about its flight. The Four have accepted me.

The cylinder in my dreams is the one I am trying to recreate at the heart of my city in the attic, and at the same time it is the original, as it was first set in place before humanity existed. There were trees in Antarctica once; perhaps trees clung to the slopes around the cylinder, proto-pines and strange cycad-type ferns. Around and beyond it, avenues twist in patterns which have meaning only to their builders, patterns containing the knowledge of an almost-dead race.

They could traverse the void in those days — the dust on their wings was the stardust of interstellar wastes. They must do so again, a last journey from this drowning, poisoned planet. Four is enough to begin their kind again; five is even better. Their system of mathematics is centred around Base 5.

Everything they need to know, the blueprint for their passage, is contained in the very shape of the City's heart. They have fragments of the knowledge, passed down through aeons, but need someone to complete their manual, to correct the errors of continental drift and erosion, of mere stone failing, cracking, and losing its crisp form. In constructing my model, I am giving them the key.

I don't bother to shower the sharp sweat off my body when I wake up; yesterday's clothes will do. I'm sure that UNAS will send people soon, their own or co-opted from the British security forces. Favours for favours. The price for my detention will be an offer of details of a newly uncovered catacomb, or a wall of alien glyphs not yet shared with any other government. Not that UNAS are likely to keep their word, once they have me.

As for some of the others who are observing me, I'm less certain who they are or what they represent. The woman with the leaflets clearly knew something about the car man — but not that he was dead. I will watch out for her.

***

In the end, I take the risk of leaving the house. Wearing advanced night-vision goggles bought via an illicit site, I patrol the neighbourhood. I want to gauge what I might face. It's easy to emerge via the hatch in the original Victorian coal cellar — the hatch is obscured by dense stands of rhododendron — and take the back alley.

The streets are quiet; I head for the tube station, and then circle my way back, using the shadows. A couple of drunks fight over a six-pack of beer; two teenagers have sex behind an advertising hoarding. A street away from the house, I see a hunched figure in the mouth of an alleyway, looking towards where I live but with no direct view of my windows. A man, by the bulk and broad shoulders. What is he looking at?

Another car, not one that belongs to the neighbours as far as I know. The hunched man's eyes are on this vehicle, parked at the corner of my street. I pad round, out of his sight, and emerge by the side of the mini-mart opposite. Crouched there, I can see that there is a woman in the car, and she is definitely watching my house. The goggles aren't perfect, but I think she is the woman who came to the door.

I return to the coal cellar hatch, uneasy. There may be directional equipment in one of the empty houses, listening to the chip of my chisel and the hiss of my knife through polystyrene. And there must be hackers trying to peer into my computers, questioning servers, tracking my history. The CAD package is on a stand-alone machine, precisely because of that worry, so they cannot see what I have built up — Misha suggested that. Outside of that, they will find only some well-encrypted conversations around the general subject of Antarctica, and my weekly orders for groceries to be delivered.

How many hundreds of thousands of scientists, conspiracy theorists, and lunatics are discussing the City at this very moment? Why would I be any different from them? UNAS is seeking to monitor and control every line of speculation, however bizarre. A bureaucratic stranglehold.

Or do the Four have darker enemies, ones which have also survived? They have never said so. Lovecraft's suggestions seem ludicrous — flying fungal things and octopus-creatures, always unspeakable horrors that cannot be pinned down. I still do not know how he got so much right, and so much wrong. They say he was influenced by Poe's "Narrative of Arthur Gordon Pym." I have not read it. The Four lay in deathless sleep until the Pabodie Expedition, that much I know. But their minds... What could such minds have done, even in that deepest state of cryptobiosis, of life interrupted? Perhaps Lovecraft came closest, his fearful mind attuned more than any to that which hovers outside our comfortable lies. Yet even he had to add the gloss of his own fiction...

It doesn't matter. This planet was theirs, but their people are dead. Many times the edge of deep emotion has brushed me — better, they feel, that they had slept until the sun grew dark, than been woken to such a world.

The last of the true rulers of Earth wish only to leave, to abandon their lonely vigil.

***

I don't quite trust Delta665Black, but he's been useful before. Misha worked with him occasionally. He sends me skimmed details from his access to police databases. The man who was found dead in the car is an unnamed forty-three-year-old male, showing no signs of violence — or of any other reason why he's no longer alive. The vehicle itself was supposedly scrapped five years ago. There are tags on the files, indicating that the information has been sent up the chain — Delta665Black thinks this means that national security has become involved. He says nothing about Misha.

***

There was a real Starkweather-Moore Expedition, intended to follow the disastrous one from Miskatonic University, but it fell apart before it reached the Beardsmore. You can read up on this part in any public library. The 1931 banking crisis in Europe removed some financial backers, and Professor Starkweather suffered an almost-fatal heart attack shortly before the passage to catch the Antarctic Summer. Most of the concerns of Lovecraft's narrator were irrelevant in the end. He overestimated the amount of time and money available for such ventures, and no one sought out that great plateau after all.

The Four, after decades of futile exploration amongst the ruins, abandoned their past to see if there were other paths to freedom. They found the land masses strewn with simian cities, cluttered, ugly places without true order or purpose. With little else to utilise, they attempted to understand these simians, and were, I believe, appalled.

But the Old Ones were the mothers and fathers of Life, and their talents had not entirely failed. They sought any who could receive whispers of their clean, orderly thoughts — could feel their need, and be of value...

Simians, humans, break easily. I am not their only attempt since they awoke, not their only experiment to communicate fully with another consciousness. As the seas rose and the City became fully visible, they reached out, but human minds fragment like slate. The wrong touch, and they break. Mine is the only one which did not — and this is the only mystery left between us. They will not tell me if I am a remnant of some Old One experiment, a last survivor of a gene-line which held deep memories of them, or a creature of pure chance. Perhaps I was never human, only wearing this shell. Behind their surface thoughts, there are hints of those who travel between bodies, in them but not of them.

If I succeed, it does not matter.

As you might expect, there are others who *believe* that the Old Ones speak to them, but they are fools. The Azathoi, a disorganised movement which grew up after the first unwise footage of the City was released — before the UNAS clampdown. They are, from what Misha and I could tell, a ragtag group of UFO conspiracists, Illuminati nuts, and others, determined to prove that the City indicates that Lovecraft was right about the true nature of the Cosmos. Chaos at the centre, and no meaning for humanity. I'm not entirely sure why they don't all simply commit suicide.

Oh, and a hundred cults, most notably the Church of Elder Knowledge, which at least wants to learn from Antarctica. The Western world holds many hundreds of thousands — if not millions — willing to swap a familiar Jesus for a more exotic Saviour.

Idiots.

My Salvation is real, and it comes — with the Four.

***

Two or three days, at most. I'm so close. This morning I go to the reclamation yard to obtain a length of granite which I can work for the final tower. I pay well, and the yard delivers my stone along with peat and gravel for the garden, to avoid drawing too much attention. Mr. Chen believes that I am doing the place up on the quiet, planning to sell to a major investor. He is hoping to benefit from the work he thinks I do, pushing up the value of his own house.

Four women stand by the delivery bay at the reclamation yard. The image they project is the same as it was when I was a teenager — tall, heavily swathed in full-length coats of muted colours. It is a pretence they have maintained over the years, even though I understand their true forms now. I see their large red eyes, the intensity with which they stare at me. And the smell of antediluvian passages cut deep into the Antarctic, lit by a pulsing phosphorescence, populated by a race to whom we are almost too ephemeral to consider.

I am not ephemeral. I am theirs, both willing servant and student. They look in my direction, and they are with me, yet a hundred million years away. I can see the graffiti-covered wall behind them, through them. Their tendrils weave the air. Tasting me.

I bow my head, and the Four move away.

"You get all sorts here," says the yard foreman, bringing out my paperwork.

"You saw them?" I feel threatened, a private bond exposed.

"Saw who?" He twitches his moustache. "I was just saying, we get all sorts here. You'd be surprised at what people will shove inside perfectly good houses." He winks. "Not you, Ms. Paling. You're a professional, know what you're doing. An artist."

"I suppose so." I sign the forms, and leave as quickly as I can.

Of the seven people I see on the short journey home, three do not seem right. They pretend not to notice me.

The ones who do not look directly are the ones who are watching.

***

Time is a flurry of hastily grabbed moments. In between long hours of work, I eat, sleep, relieve myself. Delta665Black messages me. He believes the Church of Elder Knowledge have worked out who I am, what I am trying to do. I ask if they are a threat. He replies only "UNAS," and then he goes offline, stays offline.

Given that the Church would never work with the authorities, it seems that some of those who walk the streets are at least not against me, even if they do not really understand. To them I must appear to be some sort of inspired hermit, building a shrine to the Old Ones. A solitary enlightened soul, who might be persuaded to join them and share what she knows. As if.

I have something else far more pressing to consider. Delta665Black's last message can only mean that UNAS is close.

***

Carbide-tipped chisels and a set of electric grinders.

I rig up heavy cables and additional circuit breakers so I can use the more powerful tools on this new piece of granite. Everything but the very core of the model is complete — an astonishing creation which stretches sixteen metres from the nearest attic wall to the farthest, a wonder of spires and cylinders which soar next to low, five-sided strong-points, pentacular ramparts in whose hearts are sunk deep shafts. One hundred and sixty square metres all told, constructed in almost perfect detail and echoing the heart of the City. As it was, not as it is. I wish the whole house, every floor, could have been used, so that I could have constructed true subterranean corridors and catacombs, rather than having to hint at them.

The granite yields slowly. Without this reconstruction of a crucial eroded tower, the blueprint, the secret, cannot be read with certainty. The Four know what it should look like, in principle, but they cannot quite see it. Their minds feed me what they remember, and I carve away. Their forebears' efforts to predict changes in the planet were heroic, but not perfect. Random movements of the Earth's crust, an unexpected burst of volcanic activity, and the grinding erosion of the glaciers... The CAD package, with certain add-ons provided by Misha, is invaluable. I have to make the final adjustments, correct these things in the model. My sculptor's eyes and fingers will serve them — they will know if I have it right.

If I do, then it means freedom. Lovecraft's narrator spoke of curious preparations that the Old Ones once made to travel the almost-starless gulfs — the absorption of certain chemicals, for example. The man seemed to have no understanding of physics. I alone know that the transitions between stars, though eased by complex techniques, was a matter of far more than chemistry. The oldest of the Four outranks the other three (not that they would use that concept) by many millions of years, and remembered the true process, the Transition.

And the heart of the City, built on the site where they first came to this Earth, held the pattern which made it possible. Beings of such marvellous lifespan and achievements would hardly trust carvings on walls to hold their secret. What they built in Antarctica *was* the secret, and if the Old Ones who still survive know sorrow, it was that their later kin had forgotten this — if they had not forgotten, an entire race might have fled the simian future.

These thoughts are a wash of emotions as I carve. My need to complete the work soon is more than a matter of personal satisfaction. The urgency of the Four comes in waves — last night my dreams were of a drowned abyss and repeated images of the Old Ones, their fleshy, five-pointed heads rotting in the dark. Constraint; imprisonment. They cannot bear what the planet has become.

Neither can I. One more day...

***

I wake up to a sharp, unrecognised sound, and to a flutter of alarm that makes me queasy. The Four are concerned, as agitated as such beings can become. Grabbing my robe, I rush to the window, pulling back the curtains. There are people in the street, at three in the morning. Not late revellers, nor early deliveries. Dark shapes, uniforms, crouch low by the bins across the road, and in gateways. I see helmets — and weapons.

I hear that sound again. A gunshot.

The thoughts of the Four strengthen me.

Down by a rusted white van, the woman who carried leaflets is the one shooting. The uniforms must have made a decision, because some of them begin to return fire, and I hear the high spang of bullets hitting the van. It looks like she is trying to keep them away from my house.

She can only be from the Church of Elder Knowledge — which means that the dead man in the car was probably from the same ranks. Ill-informed fanatics, but at this point they are all I have to delay my real enemy.

Headlights cut the night — a heavy black transport. Six or seven men in body armour scramble from the back; one spins, suddenly, dropping to his knees. It looks like he's been shot in the shoulder, though I didn't hear anything that time — there's a lot of shouting. Then I see Mr. Chen, crouched by his neatly trimmed hedge with some kind of rifle.

Mr. Chen?

Lights flick on in adjoining houses; some of them flick off again very quickly. By the far end of the street, near the park entrance, four tall women are watching...

Mr. Chen looks up, sees me at the window.

"The City must live!" he cries out, and fires rapidly in the direction of the uniforms, who return fire. He disappears behind the hedge – I have no idea if he's been hit or not.

Someone is hammering on the front door.

It is Now, then. The true Now, when it must be done.

No time to dress properly. Up the stairs to the attic. I slam the reinforced door in place. Massive bolts, a specially strengthened frame. It will take heavy equipment to get through that. A flick of a switch, and the generator, independent of the electricity supply, provides a clear white light to illuminate the work of so many months.

The peaks, with their honeycombed bases and sides clad with blank stone cubes; the centre of the plateau, a marvel of spires and ramparts, high walkways and deep, circular pits. The five points of what Lovecraft might have described as a dwelling place, actually a gestalt hall for the Old Ones to commune...

The heart, where deep ravines flow, circuits around the re-constructed cylinder which is the processor of the City's dreams of the void, the monstrous gulf between suns.

More shots, muffled by distance and the house walls. Screams, imprecations. It sounds like they have breached my front door, despite the extra locks...

And the Four arrive, in the sliver between moments. Their ancient light; their smell, which is now – to me – like the finest wonder of a Parisian perfumer. I draw it into my lungs; I seek to exude it from my pores, to be as they are. The glorious figures which stand and rustle around the city are not projections, not this time. There is hardly room for them at my side.

But we are together.

Then I realise that I have made a mistake. After all my work on my own place, I failed to strengthen the route up through the house next door. I forgot. Of course, the authorities have broken into Number Sixty-Three, charging into its dim, deserted decay and to the attic there – which is also the attic here, since I took the brickwork between the houses down. Their surveillance must have told them this.

I panic for a second as a sledgehammer drives the far door off its hinges. I hear hammering at the door behind us as well. Is there enough time?

Huge wings rustle around me, within me, and the Four stand in communion. The city is complete. I see my work shimmer in a haze of that not-violet light, and the armed men at the other end of the merged attic pause. A woman with them, incongruous in a white suit, shouts something about not damaging anything, taking me alive.

She does not know alive. And the expression on her face reveals that she does not know the Old Ones. When she sees them, she looks as if she is about to vomit — or flee.

I let the Four embrace me, let their tendrils caress my skin, share their aeons with my few short years.

"Her eyes!" a policeman yells, a taser in his hand. No, not a policeman. He has black body armour and a single identifying mark on his right shoulder. The stark white symbol of UNAS, in the shape of that ancient continent. "Look at her bloody eyes!"

Yes, my eyes. I know that the irises are a livid crimson, and that I am being remade in the polar glow, the light of other times which has enveloped the entire model. The mothers and fathers of Life are keeping their unspoken promise to me, and I would weep, but I no longer have tear ducts. I wonder if the City in Antarctica feels this activation, this memory of Transition. I wonder if Mr. Chen is still alive, and who he was.

I can read what is before me, from the marker peaks to the alleys and the newly finished granite tower, to the single dark cylinder which stands proud, ready. I can read everything, and use it.

Changed, enveloped by the thoughts of the Four, I open membranous wings, their tips touching the opposite walls of the attic. I am no longer bilateral, but radial; no longer hampered by clumsy fingers but gifted with the most sensitive of tendrils and filaments. Simians gibber on the other side of the model, confused. We ignore them.

The space-between-spaces beckons us, the way to the stars. The route which had been lost. We are Five, and we are leaving.

Goodbye, Misha.

AUTHOR NOTES

When I was nine or ten years old, I wrote and illustrated a story about explorers and monstrosities in Antarctica. And I made it into a little pamphlet to show to my indifferent fellow primary school pupils. Plus I always wanted to drive a Sno-Cat. Some years later, I read "At the Mountains of Madness," and was left, primarily, with a deep sadness for the surviving ancient Antarcticans. That is all you need to know. Oh, and I quite fancied having my own giant albino penguin.

THE FIRES AT Alexandria did not consume. The *aedificium* of St. Michael's Abbey burned, but there was only air to fuel the rage. And the House of Wisdom was empty when the Mongols reached the banks of the Tigris.

I know this, because I have seen what they contained, those great libraries of the past. I have touched the legacy of Al-Ma'mun with these hands, and know that ink alone turned the Tigris black. Not the pigments from books or scrolls, as the histories tell, but ink unused, darkness trapped in carboys of glass, waiting to become knowledge.

Hulagu Khan had his day, but we had our nights, so many nights that the House of Wisdom was emptied of everything of value before the horde crushed the horizon.

Nothing shall be lost.

It is His Will, and His Need.

I tell my daughter these things, so that she can understand how great our labours are, and how servitude will, in the end, be freedom. To explain why we are here, in a cold waste that is not Kadath.

She tightens her coat around, and shivers. There's a sharp wind from the sea today. She knows that her father is still looking for her, but she is thirteen years old, and learning. She understands how to turn from security cameras at the rest stops, how to order coffee and pie without being either too furtive or too open. We have had enough time on our own — two years, seven months, and nine days — to make our understanding. A daughter's place is with her mother, and her mother's place is where He commands.

Alaska.

"Will we meet them soon?" she asks.

"Yep." I smile, and stroke her ash-blonde hair. "Soon enough. Are you sure, Kitty? You could sit this one out if you want."

She gives me one of those angry, "I'm not a kid" looks.

"His Need," she says, flicking her bus ticket angrily against her leg.

Catherine Elly Mayburn. Kitty.

Sometimes, when I sleep and see His faceless anger, I hope that she will have a few years yet. It isn't my decision, but a mother can hope.

I teach her, every day. Languages mostly, and IT skills, of course. These are not the days of Al-Ma'mun. So much information on a handful of memory sticks, an external drive. A single Mongol soldier could destroy an entire library by treading on it.

"It's coming."

I look up and see the silver-white bus pulling round the corner. We had stowed on a cheap cruise to Seward, and this would be the last leg of our journey north. Seward to Anchorage direct, paid in cash, no trace of two people passing through.

We snuggle together at the back, but it is warm. The bus smells of air-conditioning, that dry, slightly electrical smell, along with a whiff of bourbon from the old man snoring in the next seat forward.

She sleeps. I open my backpack and search through documents, falsified papers, ID cards made by one of our own people in Seattle. This month we are Barbara Torstein and her niece Eleanor. I am taking Eleanor — Elly is a useful half-lie — on her first visit to Alaska. Dog-sledding and wildlife cruises, an exciting opportunity for a teenager from the city. And who knows, we might be allowed to do those things, eventually.

We will find out after Anchorage.

I lay my head on Kitty's shoulder, and let the rumble of the bus take me far from here, far from anywhere...

***

The White Pines Lodge is cheap, a flaking set of cabins on the edge of town. The owner doesn't care who we are or what we do, and the amenities are few. The mattresses are slightly stale, and raccoons, or something else, have clawed the furniture. It's perfect.

"Wait for me."

Kitty pouts, kicking her heels against the bed frame. Dust flares in the acid sunlight.

"I won't be long, sweetie. You know that."

"'Kay." She stretches out and reaches for a book from my pack. A fragment of the *Book of Seven Parts*, in an Aramaic translation from the fifth century. Not bad for a thirteen-year-old. I feel a flush of pride, and mutter a prayer to Him. Pointless, because He is with me, in me, but I come from a long line of Catholics. Even when you change Gods, habits are hard to break.

This is not the Anchorage of the television dramas, all snow and lumberjacks. High summer has reached the wilderness. Kids play in shorts and t-shirts on the grass, girls wear cotton frocks and laugh at awkward boys. The public library is modern, a set of pleasing curves set on a slight rise. Glass and concrete the colour of pale caramel, a satellite dish gleaming on the roof.

I know where I am going. Stack Fifteen, at fifteen hundred hours. The library is busy, and I am nothing to the seekers and chatterers around me. I find the spot easily.

A man of indeterminate age stands in the shadows. His lightweight suit bulges slightly at the waist.

"Hello," he says.

We need no code, we who serve the Messenger. The man's eyes are the same grey as his suit, but what lies behind them is the focused, exquisite madness of our kind. We are ripe with purpose, with knowledge, a kind of sanity which would bring psychologists to their knees, mewling.

"Did it happen?" I can't stop my eagerness from being apparent.

"Two nights ago." He grins. "A Russian deep-water trawler, supposedly with engine trouble. They used a storm in the Chuckchi to argue their way in, and they're dickering over the cost of new parts."

"The package?"

"Passed on, as we expected. I think..." His grin widens. "I think it's genuine. We have a paper trail from Moscow to Provideniya."

Part of me is still in Seattle, though I've tried to brief myself as much as possible.

"It's the nearest decent Russian port," he says, seeing my hesitation.

I nod.

"And the receivers?"

He sneers.

"Schalck and McConnell."

We both know those names, and what must be done.

"His Need," says the man. The spittle on his lips and the trembling of his hands make me certain of his loyalties. He is excitement and fear in a single breath.

"I'll see to it," I reassure him.

I gesture that I must go, but it is hard to leave this place. The library fills us both with an almost-sexual arousal. Here, the air is thick with information, not only the stacks of printed words but the rapid passage of data as students browse the Internet, as the satellite dish on the roof draws down a world of words and images. I can hear it all, feel it in my crotch. The misspelled memes, the complex dissertations, the chatter of Saturday browsers...

This is His Domain, here, as by the River Tigris.

There we took even the smallest fragments of knowledge, down to the tally of bricks being shipped by the slender, white-sailed dhows. Hulago set his Chinese general Guo Kan to the destruction of the city, but destroyed only buildings and people. We saved that which mattered, just as we saved the last fragmentary copy of Homer's *Margites* from the Imperial Library at Constantinople. Only those who came before me knew that it still existed.

The Mongols were no better than the crusaders. They valued nothing, and missed everything.

***

Kitty is asleep when I get back to the room. I am only a journeywoman in His name, but I can see the fever in her. She will outreach me, if He permits.

If He permits. It took me many years to accept that side of our service. And then, on a slow June morning in Santa Fe, I saw a drunk slam his pick-up truck into a crowd of girls outside the church of St. Agnes. Three dead, twenty injured, some of them maybe scarred for life.

In one moment of blood and twisted metal, I understood. This was what our former biblical creed allowed, either by will or by negligence. No matter how many masses, confessions, and Hail Marys there were, a man would still drink ten beers and drive his battered Chevrolet into dutiful Catholic children.

In one moment of torn flesh, I gave myself fully to His Need.

I am consoled, as I look down on my beautiful daughter, that if she is taken by the great Messenger, or driven into insanities too deep for conscious being to exist, that there will have been purpose behind the act. Pleasure, even, if it is His Will.

She stirs, smiles up at me. One of her socks is almost off her foot, and her hair is a pale radiance on the pillow, hiding the yellowed stains on the nylon cover.

"Are we doing it, Mom?"

"Tonight. They have it in a hotel not far from here. The Grand Anchorage Hotel."

Her grin is like that of the man in the library. I sit next to her and riffle through the pages of my notebook. I know what they say, but it thrills me to see the words again.

A single shipment, from the Russian State Library in Moscow. Totally illegal, naturally, and unnoticed by any authority except my people. Items from far beneath the archives, from cases thrust next to leaking steampipes in the dark. I will have to see one of them with my own eyes before I believe that it still exists.

I read, she reads. We go out briefly to eat fried eggs and waffles at a nondescript diner, two normal people doing normal things. I tell Kitty more about the Fourth Crusade, and the destruction of the Imperial Library. A difficult time for our kind — little more than fifty years later the House of Wisdom was lost. His Need was so great, and we were so few.

We go back to the cabins, wash and prepare ourselves. I look at her.

"I'm ready."

"Me too." Kitty has laced up her heavy leather boots, and has her parka on. The temperature is dropping. Fifteen minutes at most to the Grand Anchorage, timed for when the kitchen staff have gone off duty. Our librarian friend told me everything I needed to know. I have a plan of the hotel, and a swipe card for the kitchen entrance.

Somewhere the card's owner, a sous chef, lies on his bed and shudders, his mind locked onto a wavelength which may kill him before dawn. If it does, they will call it an aneurysm. The Words of the Messenger are not easy to bear, even when played through a mixtape on an old cassette deck.

Ten at night now, the sky sparkling dark, so much clearer than Seattle. Kitty names the Old Places as we tread the streets, names of dread, those stars which have little more than a Hubble reference number for most of humanity.

"*Ecthe, Inur, Tso'telemen.*"

"*Telemi-en.*"

"*Tso'telemi-en,*" she corrects herself.

"No life in that system now. None of them would listen to His Words."

"Why not?"

I shrug, though I doubt she sees the movement under my thick coat.

"They had a god to protect them, so they thought. Turned out that he wasn't real. The Messenger is."

"What about their knowledge, their books, their tapes, whatever they used?"

"All safe, Kitty."

"Nothing shall be lost," she says, smiling at me.

She puts her small hand in mine, and we turn into the alleys behind the hotel. Anchorage is low and tree-lined, and even the alleys are wide compared to most cities. Two men lounge by a dumpster, smoking and passing a bottle between them. They eye us as we get nearer.

"Ladies." A straggling beard and a tooth missing. The two of them move, not enough to block the way, only enough that we would have to edge past them. Drunken sport, I suppose, since I doubt they would actually attack a woman and a teenage girl.

The stars look down on us, and see nothing of interest.

"New t'town?" asks the other man. His lumberjack coat is too tight over a body which hasn't felled a tree in its life. He smells of the docks, and diesel fuel.

"We have a message," my daughter replies before I can speak.

"Wha' sort o' message, sweetie?" Straggle-beard lurches slightly closer. She looks to me, and I nod. Thirteen is a good age for your first one. You always remember it.

She lets go of my hand and goes towards him.

"Shall I whisper it to you?"

There is a disjointed pause. The men are drunk and curious, but they're not getting the reaction they'd expected.

"We should get t'Molly's, Hank," says the dock-man, uneasy.

"It won't take a second." She smiles brightly, then cranes to whisper in Hank's left ear.

The bearded man jerks, his hands flapping like a puppet's as he takes in what Kitty is saying. The bottle hits the ground, rolls under the dumpster, and she steps back.

"Uh, dear God..." he gasps.

He staggers and leans against the grimy plastic container. He tries to speak, but only vomit comes out, a watery spew that goes over his thin legs and his boots. He sinks to his hands and knees, still bringing up cheap beer and half-digested burger.

"Oh, and my name isn't Sweetie. It's Eleanor." Kitty winks at me.

I take the other man by the arm before he can react, and tell him something about myself, something wonderful. I tell him exactly where the Messenger touches me, what He does when He is with me.

We leave them semi-conscious in the alley. They will live, but they will not speak of tonight again.

"Never try that without me around." I need to remind her that she is still a girl.

"But I did it right—"

"Never." I say firmly. I know what it is to be a good mother. I didn't have one. "Kitty, darling, there are men who will take advantage of you, you know, touch you where they shouldn't, suggest things..."

I trail off, looking into her dark eyes. Thirteen years old — almost independent, but so vulnerable as well. I trust her, but I remember a boy under the bleachers, and my tears as he reached under my skirt. No, I said, please, not there.

My own mother laughed when I told her, said it was how she'd learned. And then she stubbed out her cigarette on the back of my hand and told me to stop snivelling. I carry that moment, and that burn; I go there every time Kitty pisses me off or makes a mistake.

And I am there for her.

"I get it," she says.

We squeeze hands, and slip quietly to the back of the Grand Anchorage. The swipe card opens up a side door, lets us into a cramped kitchen lit by a couple of nightlights. Orange-red shadows, the faint gleam of knives and stainless-steel cabinets.

I want us to have time to leave Anchorage quietly, so there are to be no dramatics if I can help it. My library friend's plan shows service stairs, and we take those. Using this route, we won't be seen by the night-staff on the front doors. We'll avoid other guests, and call on Schalck as calmly as possible.

Concrete walls and steps, stained with long-dried spillages. No windows, only another orange light on each landing. The hotel is five storeys high — Schalck is staying on the top floor, in a suite with a view of the bay.

I met him once, in Portland. A collector of rare books, a "cultist" and so-called mystic.

"May Father Dagon and Mother Hydra bless you," he murmured. I tried not to laugh. I would rather bed an Anchorage drunk than spend time with these minor adherents. They talk of secret blasphemies, and mumble in tongues they barely speak. For them, bulging eyes and a wide-lipped mouth make you special. They don't. They make you part of the ephemera, those things which will be blasted into less than dust when the Messenger comes. Y'ha-nthlei will go the same way as Chicago, Beijing, and Buenos Aires will.

I had no interest in him, but he saw me as some sort of fellow cultist and kept trying to talk to me. I wasn't in the mood to argue. I murmured a few appropriate responses and left as soon as I could.

At the time, Kitty was being held by her father and my latest court petition had failed. She would be brought up a God-fearing child, her father said. And learn some discipline. I still had the bruises from his last explanation of the way the world was supposed to work. I had some thinking to do.

A week after the book auction in Portland I took Jimmy at his word and we ran away. I let the Messenger guide both of us. Now Kitty is truly disciplined, out of choice, and she fears a god who is more than Sunday service and a collection plate.

I don't think Jimmy would appreciate the irony.

"This is Schalck's floor," says Kitty, pressing the door-bar down.

"Three of them, remember."

Schalck the collector, his confederate McConnell — and the Russian trawler captain apparently, staying on the same floor. Perhaps they are still dickering over the price.

She puts her head round the frame, checking the corridor.

"All clear, Mom."

There are two suites on the top floor, one of them empty. The door to the occupied suite is a cream-painted lump of timber that could do with touching up. There's a fisheye in it which is a bit high for me. I knock and stand back so that I can be seen.

A long pause, and the door is opened. McConnell. I recognise him from a handful of photographs shown to me some time ago. He has a history with the Boston Police Department, following a number of violent episodes near Newburyport. One book collector died, two others were injured during robberies. Commissions from Schalck, I imagine.

"Whatcha want?"

"I'm here to see Mr. Schalck. Tell him Susan Krafton needs to talk to him."

Krafton is who I was in Portland. He frowns and shuts the door. A minute later he is back.

"He says to come in."

I nod. "And this is my daughter, Elly."

Kitty waves at him from the corridor, like a shy teenager. This disarms him. His lips make a poor smile, and he beckons us in.

It is not a large suite. Three doors off a main room, and a picture-window smeared with gull droppings which shows off the bay at night. There's no sign of the Russian. Schalck, almost dainty, lounges on the sofa by the window, a shot glass in one hand.

We who serve the Messenger do not judge by appearances. Schalck and McConnell are ugly inside, small-minded and self-serving. McConnell even looks the part due to the plastic surgery which has widened his mouth and thickened his lips, homage to his professed belief in Dagon. He is wholly human, without any taint of the reef, which must sting him.

Schalck is slim and in his late fifties. I know more about him. He seeks the usual things — immortality, notoriety, wealth. He has wealth, at least. He stays on the sofa.

"Ms. Krafton. And your daughter." A tip of his head to Kitty. "You are here for, well, what purpose?"

"The consignment."

"Ah." He uncrosses slim legs, crosses them again. "I'm afraid that this is a private transaction."

Kitty sits on the arm of the sofa farthest away from him.

"Nothing shall be lost," she says.

Schalck stands up and moves away from her. He still has the glass in his hand.

"I'm afraid that you have become a little too involved in your work, Ms. Krafton. I know your interest in...certain books is genuine. You have a smattering of knowledge, yes. But we are diving deep here, far too deep for you."

He and McConnell exchange sly smiles.

"The Elders left Bligh Reef after the Exxon Valdez oil spill." Kitty's own smile is open, guileless. "Y'ha-ngeeth was abandoned by the end of November 1989. In your dating system, I mean, not theirs. They count differently."

The two men stare at Kitty, then at me.

"That's okay, darling. I think we have other matters to discuss."

"You are...one of us?" says Schalck. He makes a sign with his right hand, a twisting of his fingers in the air. I doubt if he really knows what it means.

"I — we — serve another," I say.

"The Dreamer Himself?" His eyes are wide, re-evaluating my importance.

I am getting tired. At this stage it seems easier to leave him to his delusions.

"Show me the Moscow delivery."

The older man considers this, then nods.

McConnell places a chair against the door, then fetches a large oil-stained crate from one of the rooms. He carries it easily, setting it down between Schalck and myself. No one speaks as Schalck removes the loose lid and reaches inside.

He lifts up a manilla folder and shows me the three sheets of paper inside, dark with cramped Cyrillic writing. He does not hold them close enough for me to read.

"The transcript of a broadcast from within the Chernobyl reactor chamber, seventeen days after the site had been completely evacuated. From within the chamber!"

His hand shakes a little as he gives the folder to McConnell. The next item he draws out is a wax cylinder wrapped in cloth. He holds it lightly by the ends, as if it might shatter at any moment.

"This is the sound of the Tunguska event, captured by a naturalist's early recording equipment. It's said that the naturalist himself, Abram Tadovich, died on an isolation ward in the port of Archangel." Schalk's laugh is thin and harsh. "A fitting place for one who seen fire in the sky."

That too is passed to the other man, who holds the items with reverence in large, clumsy hands. Schalck digs down into fibreglass wool packing and removes a smaller wooden container, a cedarwood box the size of a ream of paper.

"And this," he says triumphantly. "Inside this box are fragments of something you cannot imagine, Ms. Krafton."

I can feel them, words that have been hidden for millennia. They flare in my mind, drive shafts of aching light into the darkness of my task, His Need. These "fragments" are part of the vast network of knowledge which He builds through our work. They had been at the Library in Alexandria, but went missing. They never reached the House of Wisdom, though my predecessors had hoped to find them there.

It has been a long trail, and they must not be lost again.

"The Book of Lost Battles," I say. "The record, in an obscure Hebraic variant, of the coming of the archangel Samael to the coastal cities of Canaan. It tells of the retreat of Oannes under Samael's assault. The archangel of death and madness. A face of the Messenger, some say."

I step forward, on the edge of communion with He who rules me.

"Your small god, your Dagon, your Oannes, driven into the deeps by such truths that even he could not bear them..."

"No," Schalck protests. "That wasn't it. There are boundaries for the powers, agreements—"

"There are no boundaries. Not for He of a Million Forms."

I am half McConnell's bulk, but I push him aside with ease. He scrabbles to keep hold of the Tunguska cylinder, frantic.

"Sergei!" McConnell yells, his fish-lips flapping, but it is too late. I am the Message and the Messenger, and Anchorage is no more than an audience, a poor one at that. The lights flicker, and electricity, which is information and thus His Domain, surges around the hotel, shattering streetlamps. Car alarms blare in the streets below.

The Russian appears at a bedroom door, a pistol in one grimy hand, but I am blessed with His Presence. The knowledge of how to use such a device is torn from the man's mind in an instant, and he stands there, staring at the blued metal thing between his fingers. He drops it.

I look to Kitty, who is crouched by the sofa, a feral excitement on her face. She has never seen me go here before.

"The book," I demand.

Schalck stands on the other side of the crate, the Book of Lost Battles between us on the packing case. He tears open his shirt, revealing an intricate piece of gold filigree.

"It is mine, by Dagon's Will." The urbane collector is panicked now, facing true mysteries. An amusing turn of events for a cultist.

"All knowledge is His," I say, and know this to be true because He is with me.

"I have seen Y'ha-nthlei!" Schalck almost shrieks. "I will be a master of those in the deeps, immortal—"

"You will be nothing, and the better for it. You are a dilettante, a mockery."

And I am laughing, lost in coitus with Him, and I know that I have no face, because I can see the demented terror in the three men's eyes as they stare at me, the saliva which dribbles from McConnell's absurd lips. I am between places, beyond their ability to comprehend. They have nibbled on small secrets, like rats, and now they have seen something which can consume them.

Kitty darts forward and grabs the cedarwood box, her arms tight around it.

"I have it, Mom." She is trying to look and not look at me.

I am Al-Ma'mun, collecting the thoughts of the world and venerating them, saving them from the dark, for the Dark. I am a cornerstone in the House of Wisdom. If I am shattered, another will be placed there. Perhaps Kitty, if He wills it, but that isn't mine to say.

McConnell is weeping blood, and the Russian has slumped to his knees, his mind torn open by the sight of me. Schalck reaches out, slips, and falls heavily over the packing case, staring up at me. He grips his toy from the depths as if it will somehow protect him.

In the picture window I see my reflection, a featureless plane between chin and hairline. I am taller than a man, and my skin is midnight black. One of His Million Forms, made flesh in me for these short moments.

Or an insanity of my own. Schalck will never understand that it doesn't matter which. To want what he wants is to remain bound, confined by small imaginings.

I have nothing to imagine when He is with me.

The powerlines outside the hotel crackle, and lamps begin to shine again. I am a lover brought to the edge, never quite reaching the abyssal heights of His Desire, but it is enough.

Schalck levers himself up on the crate, almost standing. He looks like Jimmy after one of his binges.

"We...serve the same...the same Gods," he wheezes.

"I serve only the Messenger," I answer him.

And I do what messengers do. I walk away, carrying words that others must hear. Kitty gathers up the cylinder and the manilla folder as she follows me.

"Nothing shall be lost," she says, trying to emulate my voice.

In the stairwell I stand and draw in deep, shuddering breaths. I am empty.

"*The Book of Lost Battles*." Kitty strokes the carved cedarwood. We can hear people shouting now, moving down the corridor beyond the fire door.

"It is His again," I say.

We move quickly down the service stairs, through the kitchen and into the Alaskan night. The two drunks have gone, though the stench of their vomit remains.

I can hear sirens in the vicinity of the Grand Hotel. The three men we have left behind will make no sense. What would they say, even if they could speak? That a small, nondescript woman and a thirteen-year-old walked unarmed into their suite and robbed them of smuggled artifacts? Ludicrous.

But we leave, because there is work yet to do, in other places.

***

She is quiet on the way back.

"What will He do with it?" she asks when we are in the shadow of the cabins.

"He will hold it for His Need."

I start laughing again, human laughter this time. Maybe it's relief at our success today. Kitty giggles with me as we let ourselves into our shabby room.

I plug in the electric kettle. Coffee would be good right now.

"He will hold it for the day when He possesses every message that has ever been sent, every message that ever will be sent or left for others. The knowledge, the information of a thousand worlds and a thousand eras."

We sit side by side on the bed, sipping our coffee. She knows much of our people's truths, but I am still burning from the night and cannot stop myself.

"Nothing shall be lost. And when it is His, all of it, then He will rise in his million forms, across dimensions unimagined, to call out that one last message of His own. To let His Voice silence those insane flutes at the heart of the cosmos and break the Great Pretence."

"What will He say, Mom?"

I squeeze closer to her, a mother telling her daughter the things a girl needs to know.

"He will stand before His Father, who tasks Him so woefully. The Father who demands that His own son should give service to order, and yet embody chaos. Our Faceless Lord will look into that false madness, and He will say..."

"With strange aeons, even You may die."

I kiss her, my heart erratic with pride.

"Yes. And with the death of the Father, there will be an end to all."

Kitty snuggles under my arm. This has always been her favourite story.

"And the Messenger will rest, at last," she whispers.

We will sleep, and there will be wondrous and terrible dreams. In the morning we will know His Will again, where we are to go next.

An end to all.

That is what happens when you do not show love for your child.

AUTHOR NOTES

I had never intended to write any Mythosian or Lovecraftian stories at all, but being more of a jobbing writer than a cool, stylish author, I let my empty wallet talk me into this. Religion interests me, and I also confess to being taken by the intriguing work of Scott R Jones, who seemed open to taking the Mythos somewhere else. If I was going to write something recognisably Mythosian for him, it had to have some fresh life about it, and so I went for a piece which held its own internal logic and went off in its own direction. And I thought New England needed to be left alone for a while, so I chose to explore Anchorage.

I was not averse to taking a swipe at the world of pretend-cultists and pompous acolytes, but this is more a tale of faith and parenting, so this may not be the Nyarlathotep you're looking for. Move along, stormtroopers.

with the dark and the storm

IT WAS A bad place to build a mission.

The spit of land between the rivers was only a short walk from the place of dark *mmuo*, where the stones talked at night. Sickness came to anyone who slept near them, and the forest was dense there, to keep the stones quiet. Everyone knew that.

Except Father Brennan, it seemed.

Nduka watched as the hired men worked on the thatch roof of the mission house. Yoruba labourers, brought up from Lokoja on a steamer, along with a number of heavy wooden crates. Sullen men with no working songs and a fondness for palm wine.

"Another Jesus-man," said Ezenwa, crouching at his side. "Catholic, they say."

Nduka nodded. "Each mission seems to have a different kind of god."

The younger man laughed. "The minister at Lokoja says that it is all one god, but they serve him in different ways."

"That must be why they have had so many wars," said Nduka. "Against each other, and against the followers of the Prophet, and against—"

Ezenwa showed his palms in surrender, still laughing gently.

"They will teach, and they will get fever or become bored. Then they will go." He looked at the swirling waters where the two rivers came together. "It has happened before, it will happen again."

But there was something different about this mission. Father Brennan seemed harder than his predecessors, driven. Nduka did not like him, or the two white men with him. They smelled of the coast, where men drank and gambled themselves into strange places.

"There is a much better landing," Nduka had said on the priest's arrival. "Less than half a day from here, with firm earth and fewer flies."

Brennan had been determined.

"Where the Tchadda River meets the Ebi. This tongue of land, see?"

He had shown it to Nduka in his book. It was not a book the headman liked, with its old, damp cover and the crawling words inside. There were pictures on some of the pages which made him feel uneasy. He had glanced at the intricate map in there. Accurate enough, yes, but it was still not a good place.

Nduka was barely five years older than his friend, but when Ijezie, the previous headman, had died, there had been disputes, moon after moon, and as Ijezie's nephew, Nduka had been the only person acceptable to all sides. It had put him and his wife in a position which brought only trouble, but he did his best.

That he could read some English, and a little Allemand, had been seen as deciding factors. Every season seemed to bring more demands from the District Commissioner at Lokoja — new laws, an increase in taxation, instructions about their relationships with other tribes. Nduka read them all, rather than relying on hearsay passed along the river. In the process, he found ways round things, and the village did well enough out of his stewardship.

There was no way to object to the mission. The land in question was not Nduka's to give or take, and so Father Brennan had his way. Trees fell, and now the spit was half-cleared, a new mission house erected next to a mud and thatch church.

Nduka, standing on the south bank of the Tchadda, pointed to the house.

"Why build there? If the river rises next year, they will lose their foundations."

Ezenwa nodded. "But maybe their god will keep the river low?"

"I doubt it." He frowned. "But we shall see."

***

When the church school was due to begin, a week after completion, Nduka went to meet with the priest again.

Father Brennan was heavily built, a dark-haired man who did not smile.

"What will you teach the children?" Nduka asked, squatting by the doorway to the church. It was a poorly built place, which also puzzled him. The uprights were badly seated in the sandy ground, and the mud walls were cruder than any village hut. White men, even the Belgians far to the east, usually built their places to last.

Brennan loomed over him, sweat dark on his shirt.

"English, books and songs."

"What sort of songs?" The headman had no fear of Brennan, unlike the Yoruba workers, who had left as soon as they could.

"You'll hear them," said Brennan, curt. "Unless you have some argument with the Church?"

Nduka rose to his feet.

"It is your Church, not mine. The White Father in Lokoja tells me that you have permission to be here."

Brennan noticed the inflection when Nduka said "White Father," much as the headman had intended. He came closer, the drink on his breath prickling Nduka's nostrils.

"You are charged with matters of the body, Onodugo. To keep the mission safe from the thieves, scoundrels, and unbelievers."

"This I am told," said Nduka, his voice calm. He was fairly sure that his entire village fell into one or more of those categories for the priest. And the use of his surname was an obvious impoliteness. "I shall listen for the songs, then — Brennan."

He walked away before the other man could respond.

Nduka received reports over the next couple of weeks. The other white men with the mission were cutting their way back into the forest, uncovering the stones where the *mmuo* whispered lies. The sound of axes echoed in the forest, disturbing men and beasts. Only Father Brennan taught school. Nothing had been said about church services, which also puzzled Nduka.

He had asked the younger man, Curtis, why there was no woman at the mission to teach the children, and had been told that females weren't fit for this sort of work. He relayed this to his own wife, Oluchi, who was greatly amused.

"They don't take women, these Catholic men," she said. "Except as washerwomen. It's why they drink so much."

It would have been easy to take the view of Ezy or Oluchi, and let the mission be about its business without concern. Nduka was not so satisfied.

On a bright noon he stopped his sister's son, Umewezie, as the boy was on the way back from the church school. Nduka's own daughter was with him.

"Go home, daughter," he said. Amaka looked unhappy, but did as she was told.

"*Kedu*, Mazi-uncle." The boy looked uncomfortable, but he had still showed respect. He was as slow as the fat fish in the river, and normally a good-tempered child, but Nduka's sister said that he was moody these days, with no excuse for it.

"So, you've been learning songs. And about the white men's Good Book, I suppose."

Umewezie dragged a toe through the dust.

"There is a book," the boy agreed.

"You don't like their Jesus stories?"

"We don't learn those." This time the boy looked almost contemptuous. "Those are for children."

Nduka settled on his heels, and dragged the boy down to squat before him.

"You are nine years old. What is that but a child?"

Umewezie tried to rise, but his uncle's hand was tight on his upper arm.

"The Brennan man teaches us better things," he said. "Things about The God."

"If not their Jesus, then which god?" asked Nduka, peering into his nephew's shadowed eyes. "That of your fathers, Chukwu who made all? Or maybe the god of the Prophet?"

The boy shook his head, tried again to get to up. Nduka held him down.

"Which god?" he repeated.

"A better one," the boy said. "An older one. The God who waits in the stones, for when the stars are in their proper places."

Nduka, shocked, let the boy go. Those were not the words of his little nephew.

He told Oluchi that night as they ate their evening meal. The maize seemed tasteless, the fish-stew greasy. He knew that it was him, ill at ease.

"We can keep him from the church," said Oluchi. "We can keep them all from the church."

He nodded. "Perhaps. But the words have been said. These are not Jesus words."

Oluchi took a ball of maize porridge and fish, popped it into her mouth.

"You don't believe in their god anyway. Why are you so worried?"

He couldn't answer that. As to keeping the children away from the mission, that might cause problems. There was a tendency for taxes to rise when villages didn't co-operate.

Nduka was an educated man. He didn't hate the British or the Allemand, but they troubled him. The white men brought other problems with them, things which unbalanced a hundred, hundred moons of river life. Hard drink, their own diseases, words which only served the white people, wherever they originally came from — and guns.

Nduka had a gun. It was buried under a palm mat in his hut. It had cost him ten copper rods, traded with a sick Allemand who had come down from the highlands, muttering in his gutteral tongue and begging for transport to Lokoja.

"*Hilf mir,*" the man had choked, pushing the revolver and two bullets towards Nduka. "*Bitte...*"

The weapon was easy to use, but finding more bullets was almost impossible. Only the Arab traders who came down river would sell ammunition to an Igbo, and even then the price would be extortionate. A spear did not need re-loading. So he had buried the gun. This was the first time that he had thought about it in years.

"Don't you think I should do something about what the priest is teaching?" he asked Oluchi.

She leaned forward and brushed his cheek with one hand. Her fingers left a smear of maize porridge behind.

"I think you will, husband. If you don't, then I will have to start worrying."

***

The Government boat came that week. Drums from villages lower down the river gave them advance notice, and Nduka was there at the river to see it steam up against the current. It dwarfed the native boats, a long low thing with a house built upon it for the officer in charge. At its prow sat a Houssa, tending what the villagers called the gun-that-chatters. Nduka knew it to be a Maxim gun, something like many rifles fixed together.

The Houssa troops were sons of the Prophet and had no interest in village affairs; the officer was only concerned with ensuring that taxes were collected.

Nduka instructed his people to transfer the rough balls of rubber and the copper rods onto the boat. The copper had been traded from upriver, each rod the length of his forearm and as thick as a woman's finger. It was roughly cast, dull and pitted in the midday sun.

The young white man in charge nodded affably at the locals and strolled over.

"*Kedu*, Nduka."

The headman smiled. That was always a good move with the British, even if inside you were unhappy. That Nduka spoke good English helped as well. Few of the Government men understood much Igbo.

"Lieutenant Carr. May we have a palaver?"

The officer looked surprised, but followed Nduka to a quiet part of the shore.

"Something wrong, old chap? Problems, rumours? It looks quiet enough here."

"Lieutenant, I do not like this mission." He could think of no subtle way to open the subject.

Carr glanced across the river.

"Didn't think you the type to complain, Nduka. It's merely — what do you people say — *mmuta akwukwo*. Education, good works and so on."

"But is Father Brennan a good man?"

Canoes ferried supplies to the mission house, where the other two white men began checking crates and carrying them inside. A bored Houssa stood nearby, his rifle under his arm.

"Odd question. Catholic priest, educating the young, teaching them their sums. I can't see the harm in it."

Carr didn't seem offended. He was not difficult, as British officers went. Nduka had dealt with him for over a year, and had no particular complaints. Apart from having to be ruled by men from another land in the first place.

"What he teaches them..." Nduka sighed, annoyed with himself. "I do not think it helps them. They come back confused."

"Give it time, Nduka." He leaned closer. "Brennan has the Commissioner's blessing. Don't cause trouble, man. There's already unrest up the Niger. Any difficulty here, well, let's say that it would be dealt with pretty swiftly."

He straightened up. "Do as Brennan asks, and keep your people in order. That's all we need."

And rubber, salt, copper, and skins, thought Nduka. Along with ivory, and firewood for their steamboats, servants for their quarters...

Carr must have seen the headman's hesitation.

"We'll be back this way in a couple of weeks. All be singing hymns together by then, I expect."

He laughed, a reedy sound, and went back to supervise the last of the loading.

But what sort of hymns?

As the riverboat chugged away to the next village, Nduka took a canoe across to the mission again. The priest had not come out to greet the riverboat, which was strange. White men usually grabbed at any chance to meet each other this far from the coast.

Getz, wiry and alert, looked up from the crate he was examining.

Nduka forced another smile.

"Did you get everything you need, Mister Getz?" he asked politely.

"Ja. What is it you want?"

"May I speak to Father Brennan?"

Getz must have had the fever at some time, or some other illness. His face was unnaturally thin, the skin stretched across the bones, and there were pockmarks across his cheeks. He gave the headman an unfriendly look, but went inside.

Brennan came out slowly, a worn leather notebook in his hand.

"Yes?"

Nduka squatted, which seemed to put white people at their ease more.

"This place..." He waved one hand to indicate the whole spit of sand ground and forest between the rivers. "It has long been a bad place. Many *mmuo*, spirits of sickness. Maybe it is not good for you, Father Brennan. Or for our children."

The tall priest eased himself down onto a crate marked "Govt Property: Corned Beef." He pointed one finger at Nduka, the fingernail cracked and dirty.

"I do not like you, headman. A clever black man is a dangerous one."

So there was no game here. Nduka nodded, trying not to show his anger.

"But you teach our children."

"I teach them only what I need them to know."

"About the stones and the stars. I have heard. I do not think you should do this. I am asking now, that you find another place. Please."

Getz was at the mission house door, and Nduka heard the clunk of a rifle bolt.

"There is no other place," said Brennan. "It's taken me five years in the damned country to find this specific site. Five years of hacking my way through jungle, rotting in swamps... But I am here at last. You think I care about your opinion? Go tend your corn, screw your wives—"

"I only have one wife." Nduka flushed. "And one child."

Brennan's eyes were narrow and dark. "I told you, I don't care."

Getz moved closer.

Nduka left.

His second palaver of the day, as useless as the first.

That evening, spear in hand, Nduka took Ezenwa with him on the river. They paddled not across to the mission, but around and to the north up the Ebi. This allowed them to drag their canoe ashore further up the tributary and slip into the forest not far from the new clearing. It was in Nduka's mind to see what was happening behind the mission, where the sounds of chopping were heard on and off all day long.

"Wandering spirits." Ezenwa pointed to a faint glow between the trees.

"Lanterns," said Nduka.

Their bare feet made no sound on the soft litter of the forest floor. The oil palms planted near the river soon gave way to khaya and iroko trees, which towered above them. They touched each iroko they passed, placating the iroko-man inside just in case.

The lights grew brighter, and Nduka slipped into a crouching walk, keeping himself in cover at all times. Many trees had been felled. Without the Yoruba or local assistance, it must have been hard work —

another puzzle. The clearing was twenty yards across, and the *mmuo* stones were far more exposed, the white-rubber vines which had covered them torn away. Two white men were working in the clearing, Getz and Curtis. There was no sign of the priest.

"The stones are larger than I thought," said Ezenwa, peering over Nduka's shoulder.

"Yes."

The soft, reddish earth had been shovelled away from the sides of the stones. Eight massive boulders tapered upwards, suggesting a larger bulk under the ground. They were made of a grey rock that Nduka had never seen before. A single bolt of lightning flashed across the sky, and in its brief glare he seemed to see fingers, great stone fingers, reaching up out of cursed earth...

Ezenwa shivered. "Chukwu protect us."

They crawled as close as they dared. There were carvings on the stones, but they were worn, unreadable. Getz was pulling more vines away, his hands sticky with the sap. The other, Curtis, was holding a lantern over one stone, obviously examining it.

"These are not Jesus stones." Ezenwa whistled softly though his teeth.

"Nor are they things of Chukwu. This is a bad place, Ezy."

The two men looked at each other.

"This is why they are here," said Ezenwa. "The mission is a pretence."

Nduka tightened his grip on his spear. "Not quite a pretence. This is a mission, but it is here for something other than the church they claim."

They slipped away and returned to the canoe.

"You should tell the District Commissioner," said Ezenwa. "He will send the boat back, with the Houssas and the gun-that-chatters."

"I doubt that," said Nduka. "Lieutenant Carr did not listen. So I paddle days down the river, the headman of a small, unimportant village, to say that a Catholic priest is digging up stones. Then what? Do you think that Brennan tells the truth to anyone, even other white men?"

His friend was silent.

***

Nduka had known explorers, even one archaeologist, who had passed along the Tchadda during his thirty-four years. They traded, usually to the village's advantage, and listened to any old tale they were told, never causing any problems. Father Brennan was not like them. He was not like any white man that Nduka had met.

A week had passed, and there was sickness in the village. A fisherman and his wife had the fever, and they had been at the small market the day before, selling their catch and touching many. People were saying that the *mmuo* were responsible, that the priest had woken evil ghosts.

The children went to the church every day a little before noon and came back quiet, withdrawn, every evening. They were being fed, and their English was improving — the priest hadn't lied about that part. What they learned the rest of the day was a mystery.

He had spoken to his daughter Malaka, and told her that he did not want her to go to the mission anymore. The look in her eyes had been a reflection of that in Brennan's.

"The father says we must go. We want to learn," she had said, dull-voiced.

"I am your father."

"We want to learn."

"But learn what, Malaka? What is the white man teaching you?"

"The songs to wake the stones, the songs to wake The God."

His daughter had rolled over to sleep, leaving Nduka and Oluchi staring at each other.

***

Another trip up the Ebi with Ezenwa did not help. A rainy-season storm came with the next evening winds, and under cover of rain they crept back to the *mmuo* place. Amadioha, god of lightning, was walking the land. Thunder boomed across the forest, and lightning fell in the distance, but not anywhere near the clearing.

"Do you see it, Ezy?" Nduka clutched the palm tree next to him.

"Yes." There was fear in his friend's voice. No further evidence of digging or felling, yet the stones were taller than before, reaching up towards the shredded clouds above. Fingers, claws — what they were, he did not know.

"There is no rain in here," said Ezenwa, trembling.

It was true. The white rubber vines were tossed in dead, dry piles; the stones had not a drop of water on them, and yet in the forest all around, it rained almost enough to hurt.

When they heard the *mmuo* shriek from between the stones, they ran.

***

Nduka was at a loss. Short of tying up the children, what was he supposed to do? He considered sending them into the forest, but now Getz and Curtis were to be seen every day, rifles with them. Brennan was armed with a revolver, and the Jesus-mark he had worn around his neck had been thrown into the river. The village was being watched.

He made one more attempt to speak to the priest, but he expected little to come of it. He paddled across the river early one day, when birds shrieked in the forest and Brennan came down to wash himself. There had been less bird song recently, Nduka had noticed.

The priest was knelt by the edge of the Tchadda, running his hands through his long black hair. Nduka made an unnecessary amount of noise with his paddle, making sure that Curtis, who was nearby, could see everything. Dragging the boat halfway out of the water, he stepped slowly towards Brennan.

"There is a fever in our village. Maybe it is not safe for you here." He kept a few feet away, empty hands in sight.

Brennan smoothed his hair back, wet and thin across a deeply tanned forehead. Nduka noticed that part of one ear was missing.

"We have enough medicine for ourselves."

"And the children?"

Brennan made a harsh sound in his throat, almost a laugh.

"You keep trying, don't you? The children will not get sick."

"So Jesus will protect them?" Nduka pressed the man.

"Something like that."

Nduka shook his head. "I do not think it is Jesus you seek." The sand was cool, but it was difficult to keep his feet still.

Brennan looked at the headman with contempt.

"You have no idea what we're doing here. You couldn't understand it, anyway."

"So what is it you tell our little ones?"

"What they need to know. Young minds learn quickly."

Nduka took a deep breath.

"They must stop coming here. You listen to the *mmuo*, the bad spirits here, and then you pass those words on. I cannot allow this anymore."

"Allow? Listen, we have rifles. We have the Commissioner's permission. And we have...another, greater than any power you know."

The priest glanced behind him, seemed to come to some decision.

"She is the Darkness in the Forest, Mother of a Thousand Young. She was worshipped here long before petty little villages like yours existed — before your entire race existed."

"Before Chukwu, who is god over all?" Nduka shifted from foot to foot, trying to control his anger. "Do you not fear your Jesus-God?"

But he could see that the cross had been taken down from the church, and there was no fear on Brennan's face. The priest laughed, a sound which turned the headman's stomach.

"You have no idea, little chief, of the truths in my books, the things I have found on the edges of civilisation. Go home. Send your children tomorrow, and the next tomorrow. I have work for them here."

Nduka left, carrying shame with him. He had never killed a man, but at the moment he wanted to.

In the village, there were many worries. The children did their chores in silence, and would not speak of time spent at the mission. Agu, the father of Umowezie, had also been to the mission and asked to know what was happening to his son. Getz had taken a stick to him, hard enough to draw blood.

Nduka listened to all of their complaints, and said he must think.

That night there was a sudden storm which thrashed the huts with rain and brought down a large palm by the shore. A number of the fishing nets left out to dry were torn beyond repair. Throughout the night, Nduka heard the whispering of the *mmuo*, spirits from the lost past which had found a new purpose. He did not sleep.

In the morning, he shouldered a hunting spear and said that he was going for deer where the forest met the grasslands. Oluchi kissed him, knowing that he was lying.

"You are a good man," she said. "You will protect us."

But their daughter Amaka had gone to the mission again, despite their forbidding.

He headed for the grasslands, but when he was sure no one could be watching, he turned north into the forest, where the butterfruit and the rubber vines crowded in on the path. For two hours he pushed his way through the vines until he came to the place that his uncle Ijezie had told him of.

"This is not a safe thing to do," Ijezie had said as he lay dying in the headman's hut. The sickness from the swamp flies had taken him quickly, before they had realised how serious his illness was. "But if you need it..."

Nduka certainly needed something.

It was a small clearing, with an old hut in its centre. Nduka called out, but got no reply. He went forward cautiously, and peered into the hut. So much thatch had gone that he could see the figure sitting inside quite easily. The *dibia* was still here, then.

The *dibia* looked up. He was thin and naked except for a dirty white cloak which lay over one shoulder. The cloak covered his lap and went down to the torn matting on the ground.

"Nduka, son of Onodugo. I did not think to see you."

"I did not think to come." Nduka sat cross-legged opposite the *dibia*. "Until today. But a dead man once told me that you speak to the gods."

"It has been known." The *dibia* smiled, showing broken teeth.

"There is a god here, near the village. It is a bad god. Not one of our own *alusi*, not one of Chukwu's. Something else."

"And you want me to talk to it?"

Nduka waved his hands. "No, no. I want you to find me a god who will protect us from it."

The *dibia* adjusted his cloak, showing a withered thigh, and Nduka wondered how old the man might be. Older surely than Onyisi the fisherman, and Onyisi was almost twice Nduka's age.

"We will see."

The *dibia* reached to one side and opened a small leadwood box. Taking out a lump of white chalk, he smeared the left side of his face with it, applying the chalk slowly until the white matched the black, two perfect halves.

Satisfied, he took up a handful of kola seeds.

"I will look into the lands of the dead. You must wait for me."

Nduka nodded. He had seen divination before, though only by a passing *dibia* from another village.

The old man unrolled a small mat of reeds, dyed a brilliant blue, and threw the seeds down onto the mat with a twist of his hand. Nduka could see no significance in the way they fell.

"I speak to Ekwensu, he who knows change and conflict. I speak to Ekwensu, he who is the bargain-maker. Guide me, because there are foolish men here, and Ekwensu is cunning."

The *dibia* took up the Kola seeds, and cast them again, his eyes closed this time.

The palm-thatch above them rustled, but there was no breeze. Nduka looked around, his fingers curled around the shaft of his short stabbing-spear. He could smell the old man's body and his own sweat, the mustiness of the hut's walls...

"Ehu!" The *dibia* convulsed, heels drumming on the earth. His eyes were open again, the whites showing all around. "She is waking! She is waking! Ekwensu flees, dancing the tree-tops on swift feet..."

Nduka scrambled to the man, held his bony shoulders.

"What is it? What's happening?"

The old man sighed and lay back, the kola seeds kicked aside, the chalk on his face smeared into a blur.

"It is...she is...an ancient thing. Ekwensu himself fears her. The Darkness in the Forest." He tried to sit up, but failed. "Nduka Onodugo, I cannot help you."

"There is no *alusi* who will protect us?"

"I did not say that." The *dibia* coughed, a bloody spittle at the corner of his mouth. "Ekwensu is my brother, my father, not yours. You need another strength."

He reached into his leadwood box and drew out a piece of charcoal. Painfully, the old man drew a single black mark on his forehead.

"Do you know what this means?"

Nduka shook his head.

The *dibia* sighed. "When you know, then you will have your *alusi*, the help you need."

***

It was not a good return. Nduka found that three more people in the village were ill. Neither Okoro the fisherman nor his wife had improved. Oluchi was angry.

"Amaka has gone to the mission, with the other children. The priest says they will stay there at night as well, to be taught."

He bit the inside of his cheek.

"I will go and bring her home."

"You won't. Umewezie's father did this, and now he has a hole in his arm. They shot at him as he paddled across the river."

Nduka stared.

"Wait here."

Running down to the river, he pushed his canoe into the water and paddled to mid-stream. He could already see the white man Curtis standing on the far bank, rifle under his arm.

"Brennan!" Nduka shouted.

Curtis spat onto the sand, but went back into the mission house. He came out a few moments later with the priest, who had a small child cradled in his arms. It was one of the hunters' daughters, barely four years old. She stirred sleepily.

Nduka paddled closer to the spit on which the mission stood.

"This is not your business, Onudogu," Brennan called out. "White man's magic, if you wish. No business of yours."

"You think that the Commissioner will let you do this?" said Nduka angrily.

"He was paid for it." Brennan smiled at last. "Well paid. I don't think that he will ask too many questions if white men have to protect themselves against native unrest."

Much as Nduka had feared.

"What are you going to do with our children?"

"I told you. We will teach them, but not Jesus things. They are ours now. They will sing to the stones, and break Her slumber. Her kin sleep under the waves, where I cannot reach them, but She is close, so close. This was Her land once."

Nduka, at a loss for what to say, turned the canoe and paddled back to the southern shore.

Oluchi and others of the village were there.

"They did not shoot you."

"And they did not give me the children," he replied.

Ezenwa had a long fishing spear in his hand.

"We should rush them." He jabbed the spear angrily at the air.

"And die."

Nduka could count on six, maybe seven fishermen or hunters who would follow him. Okoro was sick with this sudden fever, as were two others. A further band of six were away in the grasslands, maybe for a week yet. This was not a village of warriors. In fact, it was too insignificant to bother raiding, which had protected them in the past. Three men with rifles were enough to slaughter them all.

"A night raid, then," Ezenwa pressed him.

"Maybe. And if the parents are killed to save the children, what is the village then? A place of small bones, left unburied."

He pushed through the knot of muttering people and sought the privacy of his own hut. A headman's hut, for a headman who had no idea what to do.

That night they heard some of the priest's songs, evil sounds which floated across the river, a tongue more harsh than that of the Allemands. He clutched the *ikenga* that his father had made for him, a three-pronged figure the length of his hand. It had never spoken to him. He might as well break it now rather than wait for someone to do it at his funeral. But even that was a decision, and this had not been a good day for decisions.

Oluchi turned next to him.

"I am not asleep," she said.

"I know."

"You think he has a god under the stones, and that the *mmuo* serve him?"

Nduka sighed. "It may not matter. He has guns, and our children. And there is an evil there. It has always been said of that land where the rivers meet. Perhaps the Darkness in the Forest has been sleeping, waiting for a Brennan to come. The sickness will spread, and—"

She was no longer listening, but weeping softly. "I want my beautiful Amaka, my daughter. I want her smell on me, her arms around me. Where will we find justice, Nduka? Where?"

Thunder sounded, far away.

"Ask Amadioha," he said, his voice dull. An easy phrase — you might as well talk to the god as expect life to be fair.

And he felt his *ikenga* shift in his hand. It was just the tension in his fingers, he knew, and yet it was also hope.

"What is the sign of Amadioha's vengeance?"

Puzzled, Oluchi wiped her eyes on her hand and sat up.

"He...he strikes down the wicked with his lightning. You can tell, by the burn in the centre of their foreheads, where they have been—"

"A god must deal with a god; a man with a man." Nduka thrust his blanket aside, and grabbed at a three-legged stool. "Whose is this?"

His wife peered, only the moonlight coming through the open hut entrance to see by.

"You know. It was Chibundu's. Your uncle took it from him, for being lazy and missing the hunt."

"So it is not Chibundu's. Even if he were to come for it."

"Obviously."

Nduka's mind was with the *dibia*, watching as the old man marked his face with a black, burned stick. *When you know what this means, then you will have your* alusi.

This was Her land once, Brennan had said. Who was Nduka to argue with history?

But now it was not.

***

The village didn't have a council of elders, as many larger villages had. Nduka gathered its equivalent — Chidike, their part-time smith who hammered spearheads and fish hooks straight, Uzochi the deer-hunter, and two others.

He outlined his plan to them. There was no other plan, but it seemed the right thing to do, letting them have no doubts.

"Can you do what I ask?" He looked at Chidike.

The big man frowned.

"I will need many rods."

"We will all contribute."

Uzochi looked uneasy. "The bad *mmuo* will not like this."

"Are they stronger than Amadioha?"

There was general agreement that they were not.

Nduka thanked them, and went into the village to instruct the others. There was no alternative. The villagers were angry, and if he did not act decisively, soon someone would rush the mission and be killed.

Clouds were gathering beyond the river. There would be a storm later, and that was what he needed. If this had not been the rainy season, when such storms were common, he would have had nothing to offer his people. He hoped that it was some sort of sign.

Oluchi had prepared his robes, the red cotton ones which belonged to the village for times of ceremony. Red, the colour of Amadioha. He should have had a white ram to sacrifice as well, but there were none to be found.

"You must be ready by the church," he said, struggling into the unaccustomed robes. They were stale and stiff. "And be careful."

"All the women will be there. We carried them for the nine heavy moons. Do you think we would let the fear stop us?"

"No, no. But—"

"Amadioha will decide who dies." Oluchi handed him the headman's staff. "We must have faith."

"I have sent to the *dibia*. He will chalk his face and talk to the thunder. He will tell the *mmuo* that they are our ghosts, that they must not listen to the Darkness in the Forest."

Nduka straightened, letting the robes hang smooth around his ankles. With the carved *iroko* staff in his hand, he did feel more like a true headman.

"With the dark and the storm," he said, and kissed his wife on her forehead.

There were many things to organise. Hidden from the mission's view behind two of the farthest huts, Chidike handed out lengths of copper taller than a man. Each was made of three or more rods bound together with wire to form a metal spear. Ezenwa greeted Nduka.

"Kedu! We are ready."

The younger man was eager, his anger now focussed on the task Nduka had set him.

"Good. You will know the time from the skies. And I will call out, like this."

Nduka made the shrill cry of a hawk, a piercing noise which would carry across the forest.

The eight men with their copper spears made sounds of approval.

"We will know," agreed Ezenwa.

"Then go to your canoes by the Ebi and take your places."

There was nothing for Nduka to do now but wait. Thunder rolled in the distance; if it passed the meeting of the rivers, then he would know that his plan was doomed.

It did not pass. Leaden skies closed in, and the wind began to move the palms along the riverbank. He thanked Chukwu, and went slowly down to the shore. Rain, light at first then pounding on his bare head, told him that the storm was closing in. By the time he was in his canoe, his robes were heavy on him, soaked. The smell was worse, but they felt also like armour.

A plan forged from education and desperation.

And the nature of Father Brennan, who believed in gods.

Despite the increasingly wild rain, Nduka could see Curtis on the far bank, rifle ready.

"I have something for your master!" Nduka shouted as he paddled. "It is important!"

Curtis came forward, not lowering his rifle. He saw a single native in sodden clothing, carrying a piece of wood, and let Nduka step out of his canoe.

"Wait there," he snapped.

Brennan came out of the mission house with a revolver in one hand, the other hand holding a battered hat to his head. Lightning flickered only a mile away, and thunder boomed out across the river.

"You have nothing important," said the priest. "Accept what is coming."

"I do," said Nduka. "But do you know what it is?"

Brennan scowled.

"A lifetime's work. The Darkness in the Forest wakes, and Her Thousand Young will come with Her. You, your people, will be swept away."

Nduka held up his staff, and the priest took a step back, raising his revolver.

"Are you threatening me, boy?"

Nduka shook his head.

"No. I am telling you. That Her time is long gone, that we have our gods too."

The skies burned with multiple forks of pure white lightning. Even in the heat, ice-water ran down Nduka's back.

"Amadioha has come!" he cried out, and made the shriek of the hawk — louder, more shrill than he could ever have imagined.

And in the clearing behind the mission, he knew that eight of his people drove great copper spears into the earth, one by each of the stones. He knew Ezenwa, and he knew that there was a courage stronger than *mmuo*. In the clearing where there had been no lightning, no rain, there would be a storm. Amadioha's storm.

Brennan jerked round, shouted. Getz and Curtis rushed forward.

"Take this bastard, and kill him."

They did not get the chance.

The Father of the People, the Lord of Justice, strode among them, tearing trees from the ground. Lightning crashed down on the headland again and again, and although Nduka was half-blinded, he could not have been mistaken — eight lines of white fire had struck where the cursed clearing lay.

Perhaps they had been guided by the faith of a village; perhaps by good, clean copper. He had seen the metal rods they placed on the residence at Lokoja once, and the idea had stayed with him, waiting for this moment. Nduka only knew that the Darkness in the Forest was not equal to Amadioha's light.

Brennan heard the terrible rending of stone from the forest clearing, and moaned. He must have realised that his god, or the altar of his god, had been shattered. He staggered towards Nduka, who was watching fire spark across the mission house roof. Even wet, the thatch caught and began to burn.

"You..." Brennan screamed, the sands moving under them.

"Amadioha, judge us!" cried out Nduka. "Whose land is this?"

The thunder answered, and drove Brennan to his knees.

Getz and Curtis panicked. As Nduka wiped rain from his face, he saw them run to the mission's large canoe and throw themselves into it, abandoning their rifles. He also saw Ezenwa and the other men coming down the Ebi in their own boats.

The white men would not be returning to Lokoja.

"You stupid, stupid..."

Brennan grabbed hold of Nduka's robes, and pushed the muzzle of his gun under the headman's chin.

"You'll die for this, you ignorant bastard."

Nduka closed his eyes. He had done his job, saved his people.

He heard the shot but did not feel it.

After some moments, he opened his eyes again. The priest was on the sand, a dark, bloody hole in his forehead.

"Amadioha," said Nduka in awe.

"An angry mother," said Oluchi, holding the revolver she had taken from under the floor of their hut. The Allemand gun. It had still been good for one shot, despite years of damp and neglect.

From the far side of the church, which was also burning, the women were leading the children through the hole they had made in the badly constructed mud wall.

The other part of his plan, to be carried out while Nduka sacrificed himself to the white men.

Nduka and Oluchi held each other, and the sky wept victory.

***

When Lieutenant Carr returned down the Tchadda with his Houssas and the gun-that-chatters, he found charred ruins at the meeting of the rivers. The steamer drew up by the mission, and the Houssas scrambled to the sands, alert.

Nduka was there. Drums from upriver had told him to be ready.

"What..." Carr stared around. "What happened, man? Where is Father Brennan?"

Nduka pulled a sheet from the bundle on the shore.

"He has been shot," said Nduka. "And his men have gone. I think they were not good men."

The white officer examined the body as quickly as possible. It was swelling in the heat and damp.

"Well, that's a bullet hole," he admitted. "No doubt about it."

"It was the night of the storms." Nduka glanced at the ruins of the mission.

"Lightning then, I suppose. Unless Getz and Curtis set fires deliberately. I'll have to send out word from Lokoja, see that the rivers are watched. Can't let the devils get away with this."

Nduka nodded.

"There must be justice, and we must meet such challenges. Do you know what we say, Lieutenant Carr?"

The young officer shook his head. "About this sort of affair?"

"*Ebe onye dara ka chi ya kwaturu ya*," said Nduka. "Where one falls is where his god pushed him down."

Carr signalled the Houssas to carry the body onboard. He seemed flustered and out of his depth.

"Yes, well..." He looked awkwardly at the headman, and went back to his crew.

Nduka watched as the steamer slid back into the main current. It seemed smaller than it had been.

"You see, Father Brennan, I did tell you," he said to the departing boat. "This was a bad place to build a mission."

AUTHOR NOTES

"With the Dark and the Storm" was not really mine to tell, but arose from such specific circumstances that I still attempted it, for better or worse. It relates to the racism in the old colonial tales of Edgar Wallace and in some of H P Lovecraft's stories, both of which I had been reading at the time. One night I was feeling particularly frustrated with the approach they took, and I tried to strike back with a "weird fantasy" of normal Afrikan villagers being faced with obsessive white cultists.

To the best of my ability at the time, and having always been interested in the work of Nigerian Igbo writer Chinua Achebe, I tried to recreate an Igbo setting which reflected the period of Wallace and "Sanders of the River." I thought there was some merit in the perspective this gave, but I doubt I would do it a second time.

lines of sight

MRS. PAROSKI SWILLS the stairs with bathwater and disinfectant, the hallway rank with her sweat. When she sees me heading up to Apartment Five, she plunges a grey mophead into greyer water, and extends her fingers in some vague gesture against evil. I hear that Mrs. Paroski's husband, the caretaker, shot himself three years ago. I think he chose the wrong target.

I push past her, take out the key, and let myself into Number Five.

"It's me," I call out, putting two brown bags on the side table. "I brought the groceries."

James Ward is in his bedroom. It's small, lined with books; the floor, bed, and the antique desk are scattered with a hundred other books, all open. Live languages and dead ones, most of them mysteries to me.

Within this nest, he sits and broods.

"I did it again last night," he says. His shirt sleeve is spotted with blood, the forearm covered.

"Did you clean it properly afterwards?"

"Yes, I did. Don't worry."

He must be thirty years older than I am; I would put him in his early sixties. His hair is mostly dark, but you can see his age in his hands and feet — the way the skin wrinkles and the sinews stand out.

Is he handsome? Yes. Is that relevant? No.

Today he shows me an ideogram which might be close to what he needs. He has to explain what an ideogram is.

"Western China, one of the more isolated populations. I had to learn that." He slams the book shut, tosses it aside. "It was instinctive for her, outlining shapes like this."

We eat a light breakfast, but he's tired. Polite inquiries about my plans for the day — I'm a part-time legal secretary, so there isn't much to tell — and then the closing of the door.

Later I hear him weeping again.

***

Four months ago.

I was in bed when I heard the thud on the ceiling, and a cry of pain. I lay there, waiting for the sound of someone getting to their feet again, cursing. There was nothing.

I knew that Number Five was tenanted, a thin, older white guy who I'd seen a couple of times on the stairs. He always wore a low, wide-brimmed hat, and I'd never really noticed his face. The card by the entrance buttons just said "J.W."

After five minutes, I shoved on some jeans and went up. There was no answer to my knock on the door, so I pushed back the mail flap.

"You all right in there, sir?"

A low groan.

"Can you get to the door, and let me in? Should I call for help?"

A dragging and a scraping. Standing there in my bare feet, trying to work out what was going on, I didn't feel so confident as when I'd left my apartment. But I waited, and the door came open.

He was on his knees, his face lined with pain, one hand on his ankle.

"Did you fall?" I eased in, leaving the door ajar.

He nodded.

"I'm Angie, from downstairs — the girl who moved into Three a couple of weeks ago. Here, let me have a look."

I eased back his trouser leg, intending to see if he had broken anything. Instead, I stepped back, turning a gasp into an awkward breath. His ankle had the faint blush of a bruise already forming, but that wasn't what caught my attention.

From the top of the short, navy blue sock to the rolled-back trouser hem, his leg was scarred, marked, in ways I had never seen before. I couldn't look away. Red weals and paler, older traces which covered the exposed skin, whorls of scar tissue which intersected. They seemed like writing — almost Arabic around his calf muscle, but sharp runic cuts in other places, especially across the shin. Like you saw in Viking films.

"Someone...did this to you?"

He winced. "My ankle?"

I felt at the swelling. He could move his toes.

"Sprained. You ought to get it seen to."

"I don't think so." That was clear, definite.

I looked away from his leg. "I — I have a sports bandage, downstairs. A thick support thing, tubular..."

"Thank you."

Afterwards I propped him in a chair with a malacca cane to hand, and edged my way out.

"Just, you know, knock on the floor if you need anything."

He didn't reply.

Nor did he knock, but a few days later I found a note, pushed under the door while I was at work. Handmade paper, copperplate script.

"I am much recovered. Thank you. J. W."

That was where I should have left it, but I kept seeing those scars — marks — at night, in my head. When I closed my eyes, instead of darkness I saw traces of those lines on his body; some savage, some flowing like rivers. And at night I could hear him moaning, crying — a soft, low keen of pain or loss.

I broke. One Saturday afternoon I went back up to Number Five.

"It's me. From below," I said, loud.

A chain rattled, the lock clicked, and the door was open. He didn't smile, but he waved to me to come in. He was limping slightly.

"I should have returned your bandage." He went into the kitchen and switched the kettle on. "Coffee?"

"Thanks. No, you keep it handy, in case you slip again. Uh, your leg—"

"My ankle."

"No, your leg." I had steeled myself to ask directly.

"Ah."

He showed me into his study/bedroom. Apart from the books, the only other items of note were a stack of vinyl albums and a turntable which looked decades out of date.

"I keep seeing them," I said. "The...cuts, tattoos, whatever they are."

"That's why I cover them up." He sounded cautious, not hostile.

"I wouldn't tell anyone."

"It's not a secret. It simply has nothing to do with other people."

I was being watched, weighed. He had grey, deep-set eyes, and a long face which looked as if it had never laughed.

"Did you say that your name was Angie?" He looked as if he had suddenly remembered something. An odd look, like the name meant something to him.

"Yep. Angie Railton. From Number Three."

He nodded.

"I can tell you about it, if you really want," he said at last. "You won't understand, but if that stops you puzzling over it…"

And so I began to learn about James Ward — and his scars.

***

Our time together is a matter of circumstances, rather than any plan. He rarely leaves his apartment; I have no friends. I have no enemies, either. I don't usually connect with people.

I left a dull, middle-class life in Norwalk, two years ago, for a dull, middle-class life in Manhattan. If my life was a play, I would be the young woman who walks on and says, "There's a letter for you, Edward," and then is never seen again.

Ward and I are linked, locked together, by the intimacy of what he shares with me, not by any personal attraction. He has never told his tale to anyone before; I have never heard — or imagined — anything like it.

Around 10 a.m. each day I go to work at Sutler & Kaufman, filing divorce papers. Between four and four-thirty I leave the office and shove my way through crowded streets. One subway stop, or a brisk walk, and I'm home. To Apartment Three, and then up to Five.

Today he has the vellum out, one of his most precious possessions — the stuff of monks and dank medieval monasteries, but there's no text on it. Instead, in the very center sits a drawing, an inch and a half across, in faded brown ink. An eye, with lids but without lashes. It's quite lifelike, except that there are three fused pupils, in a trefoil arrangement.

The Three-Lobed Eye, he calls it.

It also reminds me of Eastern religions and their third eye. Insight, inner visions, that sort of thing. I'm no expert.

Ward says it has nothing whatsoever to do with Buddhism or Hinduism.

"Older than that, she always insisted. And it's how her journey ended, and began. She never told me where she got hold of the design, or what it means — I think there had been a man…before me."

She. He's talking about Monica.

The lines are deeply impressed into the smooth, yellowing material — you can close your eyes and trace them. I shudder slightly, as my heart pauses and I sense something huge, different, like a network of information that can't be held in a single mind. Like another place. As I sense it, it seems to sense me.

It's not a good feeling.

I prefer to say vellum, but if I'm being honest, I think it's human skin.

***

Ward was in his twenties when he met Monica in the East Village. 1978. She was waif-eyed, short black hair, always swathed in black, and around the same age as him. No surname. He'd been abandoned in a jazz cafe by friends, and he hated jazz; she went in to use the toilet, and tripped over his foot on the way back out. He bought her a drink and introduced himself.

"I'd sort of expected you," she said to him, but never explained.

They saw each other regularly over the next few weeks. They met at nightclubs and in seedy cafes that opened twenty-five hours a day. They talked about music and politics, disagreeing over both, but the attraction was too strong for that to matter. As time passed, he wondered why she never mentioned sex. He'd known girls who at least wanted that, even if they didn't want commitment. So he asked her, one night at her place, when they were both stoned.

There was something he needed to know first, she told him. After that, he might not be so interested. Naturally, he insisted she go on, and most of it came out, spilling from pierced lips like the never-ending coffee and joints that saw them through that night.

Monica had a history of what her family chose to call self-harm. She'd been cutting herself since her late teens. She didn't enjoy it, or get any release by doing it. In fact, it scared her, at first.

"But it wasn't self-harm," Ward told me. "She knew there was another purpose."

"How could she know? Didn't she get help?"

"Her family shoved her into therapy. The therapists gave her explanations which suited their own small worlds, but not hers. She began...began to sense a meaning behind the cutting. The marking of the flesh. So when she was twenty-one, and got a small inheritance, she quit her family and came here, to Manhattan. On her own. A few weeks later she found, or was given, the sheet with the Eye on it, by some drunken wreck of a man she met in the clubs. She never saw him again."

He went to a chest of drawers, and took out an envelope. "I have one photograph of her, an Instamatic I took."

He passed me one of those small "instant" photos. A side-shot, in poor light, which showed a young white woman with short, gelled hair. A hawkish nose, full lips, no obvious make-up. She was wearing some sort of backless shift; you could see one bare arm, and almost down to the base of her spine.

The marks in her flesh were instantly recognizable. Not inks, but scars like the ones on Ward. White scars and raised red whorls of tissue, pale curves and angry lines.

"I took that before she undressed in front of me for the first time. She stood there in the middle of her room, by candlelight," he told me. "Her eyes closed, her beautiful body marked right down to wrist and ankle. At first glance I thought I was looking at the sort of tattoos you see on bikers and heavy metal fanatics, but that wasn't it. She turned around slowly, and let me see everything. Symbols, signs — and some cuts that made no sense at all."

The apartment where we sat was cool, the window open, but he wiped his forehead, where sweat had begun to bead.

"They were carved into her flesh — healed, to various degrees, but clearly deep. You have to realize, Angie — it appalled me, fascinated me. I mean, she'd told me about cutting herself, but this..."

"You thought she was crazy," I said.

He nodded. "But I was stoned, and Monica was naked, offering herself. We... Are you sure you want to hear the rest?"

I laughed. "I'm pretty broad-minded."

"We made love. It didn't go well. I was clumsy, and inexperienced — yes, even at thirty — and although the lights were off, I could...feel everything. On her body, I mean. But I hung in there, and we had other nights, usually with the lights off. Wild, intense nights. She let me touch her, read her with my fingertips. Like Braille. I'm not saying I understood what I read, but I remember how she felt, how she smelled — the iron tang of her skin, the static that surrounded us..."

He fell silent. Was he embarrassed?

"That's...sort of creepy. Fascinating, but..."

"Creepy? This is why I don't tell people, or show them anything."

I'd said the wrong thing.

"I'm sorry," I muttered. "A lot to take in, you know?"

We made our peace, and I left shortly after that.

When I got into bed that night, none of the sexual aspects of his story remained with me. I ran my hands down the smooth dark skin of my belly, towards my crotch, and felt nothing much. No thrill, no secret information. I'd only had a few light relationships, nothing more, and nothing like that which Ward described. I was virtually a blank page.

I tried to visualize Ward and Monica, naked and slick with sweat, coupling. I tried to see Ward and myself, doing the same.

My mind saw only a man, reading in the dark...

***

We eat bacon and waffles by his window, looking out onto the grim street below. Nine in the morning, and two drunks — or crackheads — are punching each other by the subway entrance. One of them has a shoe missing.

Ward is chewing on a piece of burned bacon rind. These days he wears a singlet and shorts when I'm around, no longer hiding his work. When the swirling patterns are in full view, it's pointless to try and use anything like a computer, or to try and listen to the radio. His laptop screen flickers with blue-green static; the radio signal is chopped into jagged fragments of sound.

Neither of us have any idea why that happens. He says it was the same with Monica, towards the end.

"It means I'm close," he says.

That scares me.

***

It would have been easy to see Ward as obsessed with Monica, but I accepted that he had truly loved her. And maybe she had loved him. When I asked what happened to her, he wouldn't say, only that he hadn't seen her for over thirty years. Which made no sense, given the intensity with which he talked about her.

I'd known him about three weeks when I tried to pin him down, over a beer in his apartment. I'd already had a few in my own place, and went for it.

"Is Monica dead? Is that what you're trying not to tell me?"

We drank another bottle each before he answered.

"She's... Look, I'll try to explain."

He stood up and began to peel off his shirt, trying not to disturb what were clearly newly formed scabs. When he was done, I could see how closely the patterns formed by the scars matched those in the photograph. They stood out in groups, mostly down his spine, down the outside of his arms, and over his chest.

It wasn't art. The work was crude, and it jarred, made you think more of the asylum than the gallery. Yet I'd never had a single indication that Ward was anything but completely sane. If you can be sane and do that to your body.

He told me how he and Monica had dated for almost a year, and every meeting had been like wildfire, compared to the slow, damp life he otherwise lived.

"She was... What's the cliché? So alive. Everything was important to her. Lives, causes, music, animals, weather reports...the lot. That she'd noticed me, that she wanted to see me, again and again, was sort of amazing. I didn't feel I deserved her time, in a way."

"And every few weeks a new scar. I even offered to help her with designs, but she didn't need me. It was all in her head, she said, but she had to filter it to find the right combinations. Sometimes I made myself sit and watch as she drew the knife across herself — the skin parting, the first trickle of blood, and that glimpse of the soft, wet flesh beneath..."

He shook his head before I could speak. "No, I didn't get off on it. I'm not like that — can't stand needles, either. But I didn't want to be shut out."

"Why?" I asked.

"Why didn't I want to be shut out?"

"No, come on. Why was she doing it? Let's say that both of you were perfectly rational. You watched her, let it happen, because you loved her — maybe too much. But what was her drive, her purpose?"

"She was trying to open a gap — a door to somewhere else. Somewhere beyond everything we know. She wanted... I don't know, to peer through, to see what the Eye meant."

I was confused. "You mean like 'transcending this mortal plane,' that sort of spiritual thing?"

"No, she didn't like any of that New Age stuff. Monica was convinced that when she had the patterns on her body completed, aligned, something unique would happen. She could never quite explain what she felt."

He said it straight-faced, without a shred of doubt. But he still hadn't answered my question.

Was Monica still alive?

James Ward clearly believed in the woman he lost in 1979, after less than a year of a relationship I didn't really understand. True love, obsession, who knows?

And I was beginning to believe in James Ward.

***

A few days later he had his own question.

"I don't know how to put this..."

I looked up from the book of Celtic knotwork I was reading.

"Put what?"

"Well, you — you're Black."

I laughed. "No kidding."

"I'm sorry. Monica had this set of interlocked symbols, like writhing snakes — they stood out, more than usual. I've been thinking about tribal markings. You know, coming of age, ritual scars on the cheeks and that sort of thing. I don't suppose you know anything about them?"

"Ah. Yeah, there's a lot of that in legal and banking."

He looked so awkward that I relented.

"Okay, you're talking Black cultural identity. My family doesn't even know what part of Africa we come from. It's a big place. The nearest my father ever came to what you call 'tribal markings' was picking the right tie for work."

But his inquiry set me off on a trail of discovery at the library and on my computer. Ritual scarification, traditional practices — women marked across their abdomens to show they were strong and brave enough for childbirth; men cut across the cheeks so that people could see, in an instant, where their allegiance lay. Their social status as well, sometimes.

There were cicatrices and keloids, hatchmarks in the skin, all manner of ways that different peoples did it. I stared at the photographs, fascinated, and was both disappointed and relieved when I found that the practice of ritual scarring was slowly dying out. I could admire a system that said so much without words, that gave you a firm, fixed identity. But marks which once provided recognition and admiration probably engendered only curiosity these days.

We try to make ourselves what we want, or need, to be. Did I want strangers to be able to read my people, my social standing, on my face? Perhaps not. But I could see Ward and some venerable Masai elder understanding each other. The flesh is the message, deeper than spoken language.

Was Ward sending a message — and if he was, who was it for?

I still couldn't work out how Monica got into this. As I searched the Internet — prompting a series of migraines later — I looked for something, anything, which might link to her obsession. So much nonsense, so many obsessives and conspiracy theorists, but I checked anything weird connected to the East Village back around the late seventies. One conspiracy blog caught my eye. A man died at the White Horse Tavern, on the ninth of November 1978, the twenty-fifth anniversary of Dylan Thomas's death. There had been a gathering at the bar, which was the only reason it made the headlines.

Leo Wittner, twenty-seven, was found in one of the upstairs rooms, dead from a drug overdose. There was nothing odd about the death. Wittner, a very minor poet, had reportedly been out of his head on a regular basis, and there were needle tracks up both arms, plus a quantity of Quaaludes in the room — and an empty whiskey bottle.

The blogger was trying to tie Thomas into a dark scene — arcane poets or something. The arguments presented made no sense, as usual. As well as needle tracks, the lower half of Wittner's body was found to be covered in scarification. The grainy photo of the poet on a slab showed enough of the marks down his left leg to see the pattern of the scars.

I'd seen that pattern before, when Ward twisted his ankle.

Wittner had no known relatives, and no one was interested in his death. The blogger had moved on to Flat Earth issues, so I printed out the inadequate photograph for myself.

I asked Ward if Monica ever mentioned a Leo Wittner, describing what I knew of the man but omitting his death. I said that it was a chance connection, a Village thing. The name meant nothing to him, but it had me thinking.

What if this was not a single quest, Ward's obsession with a girl, but part of a sequence? Monica had to have gained her knowledge from somewhere. Maybe it came to her through dreams and delusions — or maybe it came to her from another source, a poet and addict who couldn't follow through to the end. She would already have been in the Village when Wittner overdosed...

I didn't mention this idea. I found him information on the techniques behind tribal scarring, though, and he was grateful.

We experimented. His apartment still had a boarded-up open fireplace which was easy to expose. I burned some pieces of wood in the grate, and extracted the ash. Sterilizing a scalpel, he cut the next design into his forearm so that he could stretch the wound open; it was a mark of how far I'd bought into his ideas that I could pack the sterile ash into the slit in his skin and bandage it.

It struck me that I was helping a man as old as my father to scar himself indelibly for the rest of his life. A man in love with a dead or missing woman — even though my own feelings about him were growing.

And I wanted it to work.

***

The end of Ward's time with Monica came with so little warning that even years later, he found it difficult to discuss. Ward and I were drinking cinnamon coffee on his sofa. It had been three weeks, and the healing process had lifted the snake design nicely, forming a crusted relief against the pale skin. No sign of infection.

I'd opened up myself for once, talked about a life unnoticed, as the saying goes. He'd asked why I was really so interested in him, and I went into a rambling tirade about how pointless everything seemed. I avoided mentioning any possible connection between us.

"At the moment," I babbled, "I can't see me achieving anything, settling down with kids. It...it passes me by, all of it. And I'm allergic to cats. Can't even be a mad cat woman in my old age..."

It wasn't a good sales pitch, if I'd wanted him to make any advances. He let me get it all out, then nodded.

"After Monica, I was on my own, enduring, not living. Trying to forget. Then, twenty-five years later, I found that photograph again, tucked inside a heap of correspondence. I'd thought it lost. I cried most of the night, and put in for early retirement the next day." He almost smiled. "I made the first cut — in my leg — at the end of that week, and I began to live."

"What happened with you and Monica, what you're doing to yourself... I don't even know how I feel about it some days."

"I'm not even sure what I think, looking back on it. Or what I'd expected to happen. That she would somehow be happy, content when she'd finished working on herself, an artist who'd achieved her goal? That seems stupid now. If it had been that sort of mania, she would never have been happy, would she?"

"Like those people who have endless cosmetic surgery, always wanting to change something."

"Yes. She'd told me that there'd be a transition, that when she'd completed the entire pattern, she would see...but I don't think I'd ever taken that as seriously as I should."

He stopped, looked around him as if he wasn't sure where he was. I gave him a moment, and then touched his shoulder, gently.

"What happened?"

He was close to tears.

"She called me, about eleven at night. Heavy rain — like in a movie — and I was curled up under a blanket, reading... What was I reading? A travel guide, to Canada. I was going to ask her if she wanted to visit Quebec with me. When she rang, she sounded excited, almost breathless.

"'I'm going to open the Eye, Jimmy — tonight. And then it will see me, and I will see it, properly. That's the moment when—'

"'Moment of what?' I asked. 'Or do you want to tell me in the morning?'

"That just got nervous laughter from her, like I'd said something really amusing. The rest of the conversation, if you can call it that, was fairly broken up — some sort of interference due to the storm, I guess. I heard her muttering to herself, and looking back, I think she was doing it even while we were on the phone. Cutting herself, in front of the old mirror she had in her room."

He slid his hands down his bare chest, his fingers tracing the whorls and scars.

"'The Three-Lobed Eye,' she said, in between the crackles. 'I've almost finished the Three-Lobed Eye.' And then — 'It's strange, there's no blood. Not a drop.'

"So there I was, clutching the blanket with one hand, the phone with the other, and I thought — in that second — I thought that maybe she'd cut her wrists. I shouted into the receiver that I was coming over, straight away. The line cleared for a moment, and I heard her last words with absolute clarity.

"'I love you, Jimmy. I...I really love you, but I have to do this. I have to.'

"That was it. What I yelled afterwards was into a dead phone. The line was out. I threw on a coat, and ran ten blocks to the dive she lived in. Hammering on her door got me nothing, so I told the drunken building manager that she'd called me, said someone was in her apartment. He stumbled up to her single room and opened the door, complaining all the way."

He looked up at me directly, his eyes wet.

"There was no way out of there, Angie. Are you with me? I went in, fearing I'd find her there on the floor, bleeding to death..."

My throat was dry. "But she'd gone. Disappeared."

"Why do you say that?"

"Because no one goes to all that trouble just to commit suicide. There are plenty of bridges, plenty of pharmacies."

He nodded. "The room stank of...electricity, if that's possible. Like a generator had shorted out in there. Her clothes were in a heap in front of the mirror; when I picked up her cardigan, I found a knife caught in the sleeve. I pocketed the knife when the building guy wasn't looking. And then I told the cops, who weren't interested. They said Monica was wanted for credit card fraud, and she'd have skipped to another county, another state. Too low a priority for them."

"A Locked Room Mystery," I said, and realized how flippant that sounded. "Sorry. I'm not sure how to deal with all this."

"But you believe me?"

"Yes."

"Why? Tell me why you believe me, Angie. I need to hear it."

I had to think.

"Because I can't see why you would lie about it. If you'd wanted a friendly neighbor, or to get into my panties, you sure as hell wouldn't have come up with this." I put the mug of coffee down in the only clear space on the desk. "You're telling me that Monica finished whatever she was doing, and as a result, she disappeared. But you don't know where she went—"

And then I got it. I understood, at last.

"My God, you want to see what she saw!"

"I have to." He smoothed back his thinning hair. "I have nothing to show for the years since, apart from money. Maybe she's dead, maybe she went somewhere terrible. I can't know that unless I complete this, do you see?"

"But—"

"I loved her. I still love her. If she can be found..."

We sat in silence. It came to me that I must be only a couple of years younger than Monica was when she vanished. My coffee was cold, and anyway, I'm not sure I liked it with cinnamon after all.

***

"Not long to go," he says.

"You won't do anything...final without me, will you?"

He is staring at the drawing of the Three-Lobed Eye.

"After all your help? Of course not."

As I walk down to my own apartment, avoiding the suds left on the steps by Mrs. Paroski's cursory cleaning, I am uneasy. It's the "Of course not" that bothers me. Emphatic and unnecessary, like it was directed more at himself.

I fret and tidy. More than once I start to head back to his apartment, but tell myself to get a grip. Around nine in the evening, a pain stabs behind both my eyes, and the TV screen flickers. The small hairs on my arms and legs are lifting; the light in the room shifts, becomes sharp and strange.

Upstairs.

I slip my shoes on and grab my spare key to Ward's apartment. Slow, clumsy, on the edge of a migraine; electric air and doubt as I run up the stairs.

His door is locked. I pant for breath, fumbling as I force the key into the lock.

Can there be such a thing as the polar opposite of a flare of light? A glaring darkness that bursts forth, lingers only a second, and then is gone? As I open Ward's door, that is what I see — and I feel a sudden terror, for the smell which comes from the apartment reminds me of burned-out plug sockets, meat in an oven turned too high and forgotten during church. I half expect to see Ward burning, screaming while he writhes in the middle of the living room...

His apartment is empty.

In his bedroom I find his clothes, still spotted with the rust of dried blood, crumpled as if tossed aside.

His indoor shoes, unpolished.

An old knife with a worn handle and a gleaming edge.

And a handful of small metal fragments on the carpet.

I pick one up, take it to the window and show it daylight. It's a filling, surely. The old style of amalgam filling used to mend a cracked or pitted tooth.

As the odor of charred things fades, I sweep the papers on his desk aside, wanting to scream — and I see a single sheet taped to the wall. Not the vellum but a stained grey piece of A4. On it, the word "Transition" has been typed again and again with a daisy-wheel printer, the sort they used in the eighties. I peel it away, and turn it over.

On the other side is the Three-Lobed Eye, formed of hundreds of lowercase "o"s. Printed with a daisy-wheel again.

I look at it; it looks at me.

Beneath it, though the ink has faded, I read...

A N G I E

***

I don't know where Ward has gone, nor do I tell anyone he isn't here anymore. Not yet. I clean up Five, going in and out as I did when he was there. There are thousands of dollars in a top drawer in his bedroom, and I pay his rent for the next six months. Mrs. Paroski clearly isn't going to ask, as long as she gets the money. The original vellum sheet with the Eye is nowhere to be seen, but I take the A4 sheet that was taped to the wall.

Ward typed it out, years before I was born. It had to be him. I think that — impossibly — he knew that I would come, to help him. And writing that down, here, it makes no sense.

I've no idea what happened to either of them. Do they stand together somewhere strange and alien to our normal senses, lovers under the Three-Lobed Eye?

It doesn't matter.

This is... What can I call it? An inheritance. Something passed down, not through families and kin but through chance meetings — at crowded jazz clubs or in run-down apartments. Monica met Wittner — who hadn't the courage to complete the ritual, maybe — and then James Ward met her.

Just as Monica knew she would meet James, James knew he would meet me. Angie Railton is next in line, if she chooses to be. He left the sheet of paper behind so that I would know. It's my burden, my knowledge now. All of it.

I simply have to decide what I do next.

Ward left plenty of knives and antiseptic behind. I also found, under his bed, a file of those designs he used, and where he used them. No need to experiment or guess this time. I have sterilized ash as well, in a jar — and a lot of painkillers. Most importantly, I have the knife left behind by Monica, which was in turn left behind by Ward. He never said exactly, but I know it's the same one.

I sit on the edge of the bed and roll up my polo top. As I consider the dark curve of my abdomen, I can see how it might be done. Trouser suits, long skirts, long-sleeved blouses and polo neck tops, until the last few moments. A few "personal days" off work when the pain was worst.

I'm not a stoic, like James Ward, but I'm no Leo Wittner. If I do this, I won't go halfway and then wimp out, or lose the plot. It wouldn't take that long — I'm a quick study.

At night, when the radio crackles, and I see turquoise and indigo flashes in my mind — when I smell the charring of flesh and the tang of fresh blood — I know that I am being watched.

I want to know who or what is watching.

I want to find James Ward.

AUTHOR NOTES

Ironically, I am deeply opposed to having any tattoos, ritual marks, or scary signs inflicted on my own poor flesh — although I have been known to draw on my face with felt pens, in order to pass the time. For over forty years I have worn a simple silver ankh on a leather thong, which is my limit — something which has got me into a number of conversations with taxi drivers over what religion I followed. I can never quite answer that one.

where all is night, and starless

March, 1919, Inner Hebrides

THE AGENT TELLS me that the house is built on solid bedrock. It has three rooms, with bare stone walls forming a kitchen, a bedroom, and a parlour. A failed farmhouse for a failed farm. The last owner died in the war, childless, and his wife soon after, in 1918. The agent has no record of how or why. He has a florid, anxious face — a Lowland Scot, desperate to please and yet ill-informed about the Western Isles. I have neighbours on the other side of the island, a handful of crofters, but he knows little about them. A boat brings supplies once a week.

"Nae so fine a place for a lassie." He shakes his head, a sudden burst of conscience, perhaps. "And if your faither takes bad..."

I take out my cheque book, and let my pen speak for us. He swallows his doubts.

"Aye, well, there's nae a snib on the isle, I'll wager."

I stare until he realises.

"No locks, Miss Allen. So I dinna have a key to gae ye."

Our business done, he trudges to the small jetty. The sky is turning dark with promised rain, and he's eager to be away. My father sits in his wheelchair, waiting for me.

"Inside, then," I say. There is grass, wiry grass, under the wheels of his chair, but the soil is thin. I make him comfortable in the parlour, which will be his.

"Soon," my father mutters.

I have waited almost two years, and seen him through four hospitals and recuperation homes. The urgent need I once had has been mellowed, and now I can wait. I can feel that his story is coming, the words which have been trapped inside him since the blast which shook the spires of half of Europe.

We settle, and for a week I let him inspect our new home. He pronounces that we are on granitic gneiss, which seems to reassure him. The term means little to me, but I notice a change in him. He walks, only a few steps, but it is heartening.

Lieutenant Robert Allen, thirty-nine years old, of the 183rd Tunnelling Company in Belgium. A tall, slim figure, easily missed in a crowd — except for the way his head cocks at any unexpected noise. Like a dog, a dog which cannot settle.

When they dragged him from the remains of a tunnel-mouth, they did not know what they had. He was recovered alone and in a state of exhaustion, raving, covered in blood. Those fingernails which he retained were ragged and torn. They had no explanation for me.

His commanding officer wrote a letter which betrayed more than I think he intended. "In the finest tradition of the Army" and "Work vital to our efforts" — brown ink on cream paper — but in between, curious phrases concerning sudden action and "necessary haste." By which I have come to believe that a mine was blown before its due time, and that my father and the sappers were still at work when it was done.

They call his condition shell shock. He himself denied this when I sat by him in the early months. He promised to tell me the truth, one day, when he could. This lonely isle, I believe, is what he has been seeking.

A James McAllister calls, to enquire if we need seaweed for our vegetable garden.

He takes a nip of whisky, and offers to bring a hand-cart full of it over, and my father nods, accepts. Outside, McAllister turns to me.

"Hit bad, thon?"

"Flanders. But he's getting better."

"Aye. Mony a soul lost; mony a guid man broken."

He explains, haltingly, that he was on the fishing fleets, keeping the country fed. I praise his efforts, and am rid of him at last.

Father no longer drinks, but he holds up McAllister's empty glass, watching it glint in the morning light.

"Is this the day, Emma?"

I seat myself on the window-bench, watching his scarred hands re-arrange the cheap plaid rug over his knees. He might be one hundred and thirty-seven, from the look in his narrow eyes.

"Only if you wish."

I take up the blank journal which has been ready since June 1917. I had it when I first sat by his hospital bed, and it has always been to hand. I had always wanted a record, from his own lips.

He puts the glass down.

"I...I think so."

Bending back the spine of the journal, I lift my pen...

***

We didn't hate the Germans (my father began) — the Saxons, Prussians, Bavarians, any of their kind. We'd never seen them, except in photographs. We were tunnellers, sappers, and we were paid well. Tommy Atkins sneered at us, knowing the extra shillings we earned, but he feared us too. We drove shafts and galleries far beneath him, and at any moment we might bring destruction. Our mines ripped open the land without warning, tore through soft bodies as easy as hard clay, and more than one Tommy had been taken on the edge of an ill-timed blast.

If we worried our own troops, we worried the enemy more. We were masters under the earth. Clay-kickers, baggers, and trammers, running our secret roads into the dripping dark, always further, always deeper. Miners from Cornwall, Yorkshire and Durham, Canada and Australia, the old hands from the copper shafts and the coal seams. Behind us came more sappers, and the Bantams, too short to pass a recruiting sergeant, but suited to die in shallow galleries and choke in pockets of poisoned night.

We were transferred to Flanders in the March of 1917. Hundreds, if not thousands, of our kind were at work there — the Australians were said to be under Hill 60, packing ammonal almost beneath the German trenches. I had only been a pit-head foreman, but I had education. They made me sew on a pip, and I was handed fuses and geophones, with the last word down there — how far, how quick, how deep.

Major Cartwright, once a geologist, had taken cores.

"There's a promise here, lads," he said, pulling at one end of his moustache. "They'll never get under us here. The Hun can't kick clay."

They could dig, of course, but they used shovels and picks which resounded through the thick earth, bouncing off the chalk deposits and alerting our listening posts. We worked soft and quiet, the grafting tool cutting into the clay with little more than a soft sucking sound.

"One hundred and twenty feet, no less," said Cartwright. "The Hun are at sixty or seventy, so we'll fox them."

We started where a gallery had been abandoned the previous November. We were to turn it and head for the lower end of a ridge held by the German Fourth Army. We knew that there were a great number of mines being prepared for something really big. We were to do our job and end with a chamber for the ammonal, tons of the stuff.

Thanks to pumps, the gallery had only an inch of water in it. We laid tracks to the incline shaft, so that spoil could be hauled up and timbers sent down. Twelve hours on, then twelve hours off. We ate, slept, and then trudged back to the main shaft, still aching. Sappers and soldiers sweated by the opening, hauling up spoil — we were cursed for not having to share their work, and cursed for causing it.

Once in the gallery, two to three candles were all we had to see by. Our domain was nothing but a single curve of wet, shadowed tunnel, more than a hundred feet of soil and rock above us. We felt its weight, and maybe we crouched more than we needed to.

By the second day, the lads had made a side chamber, and I knelt to use the geophone there, pressing the discs to the slick earth. No one moved as I put in the earpieces and began. For minutes there was nothing, and then I heard the tell-tale sounds — the sharp crack of a pick hitting rock, the crunch of what might be boots. Germans.

Listening is an art. Moving the contacts around, even on the chamber wall, I became fairly sure that the sound came from above us and to the north. It wouldn't intersect with our tunnel, not even close.

I scribbled down "Pickwork, strong, 10 degrees," and sent the note back up to the next listening post. I moved further down, and tried again. Something muffled, further away and on a different bearing, which might have been an echo. It wasn't enough to report.

Morris began working the "cross," angled on the boards so that he could drive the grafting tool into the clay face. Drive, twist and pull, Jack Sleath catching the clay which came out, sliding it into Hessian bags. "Pigeon" Brown was our regular Bantam, ready with rifles as we dug, or helping Smith, our trammer, to push the spoil wagon.

Every half hour I stopped to have a listen. The Saxons, or whichever poor sods they'd enlisted, would be counter-mining nearer the surface. It would be the Upper Gallery's job if they wanted to go for a camouflet and blow the German tunnel. I still thought there was a murmur further off, but I couldn't settle on it, so we pried open cans of bully beef and ate, pressing chunks onto biscuit.

"I'd kill for a kettle," said Morris. He was a closed-mouth Geordie, hard, but a good clay-kicker.

I nodded. "Hot, sweet tea."

Harry Smith scraped the last out of a bully beef tin.

"Any news from the 'phone, Allen?" In the filth and labour of mining, rank was pointless. Nor did I feel I deserved to be a lieutenant. I was still a foreman.

"I'm not sure. They may be cutting towards the north, hoping to find the Aussies. And then..."

They looked at me.

"Aye?" Morris narrowed his eyes.

"It's probably echoes. I thought — a couple of times — that there was something else, something further down on another bearing."

That had their attention.

"You mean they've cut below us?" Smith shook his head. "We're almost 130ft now."

We'd taken the gallery down on a stepped gradient, to please Major Cartwright — a man who'd never been further than the head of the shaft.

The Germans could not be underneath us.

Our section now ran 400 feet towards the enemy lines, and we'd started a chamber for the mine itself. The silence lay heavy on us. I lent a hand to the trammers when I could. Pigeon and a sapper from the rear unloaded the rubber-wheeled wagons when they came back, fitting the timber props together — no hammers or nails. Somewhere up there, the enemy was listening as well.

We were eight hours into a shift when a runner arrived. The ammonal was coming down to pack our chamber. It would take days to shift enough explosive to fill the space, and then we would have to tamp behind it with clay and sandbags, seal it off, only the fuse wires connecting that bulk of death to the living. I checked the canary, Jenny, our warning of a carbon monoxide build-up, and opened tins of pears for the lads, whose fingers were numb from the work.

"We're about ready," I told the runner, a pasty-faced private. Pigeon and Smith had started the back-breaking business of lifting sacks of spoil onto the wagons. I handed Sleath his tinned pears, slopping the thin juice. I saw his mittened fingers grasp the tin...

The world shook. A wave of fouled air hammered into us from the shaft end of the gallery, a deafening blast that lay Pigeon and the runner flat. I saw a set of timbers split, and a mass of clay slide to block half the width of the gallery. The runner's shriek penetrated my dulled senses, and I fell on him, clamping one hand over his mouth. Instinct for a tunneller. The water in the bottom of the gallery trembled, like the old gear we once used for listening, and was still again.

No one moved or spoke. After a couple of minutes – a couple of hours, it felt like – I got up, a warning glare to the runner. Pigeon was on his feet again.

"Check it out," I whispered. He nodded, and eased past the fall, heading for the main inclined shaft. I went round, but everyone was fine.

"Camouflet?" Sleath asked.

"They weren't near us." It was common enough for an enemy counter-mine to be used next to, or under, one of our tunnels. A pipe charge driven into the earth between us, fired so that it collapsed our diggings. But I would have heard them. "See what Pigeon finds."

We waited, and Sleath handed round his miraculously preserved tin of pears. Five minutes, staring at my watch by a re-lit candle, and the Bantam returned.

"It's the shaft."

An accident with munitions; a camouflet elsewhere which had triggered something. There was no way to tell. An entire section of the main shaft was blocked, right where our gallery hit it.

"Days," said Morris. "Days to excavate that."

I glared at him. "Might not be. If it's open further up…"

"If."

My team, the runner, and a sapper who had been helping Pigeon. Seven men in a sealed pocket of night. I looked to Jenny in her cage. How much air, how much oxygen, did a pocket like this hold?

Seven men, breathing.

"You're the officer," Morris spoke, surly.

I turned to the sapper, a stocky man in his forties.

"What's your name?"

"Lambert. Sir."

"Morris, take Lambert. Find out if we could cut into the shaft and clear any of it. The rest of you, not a sound."

I took the geophone into the main chamber we'd dug. Distance was a bugger, which was why we had many listening posts. Triangulation.

There was digging — or something like it. It made no sense. Not from the inclined shaft, but south of us, and under, surely under. Like the times before, but not a muffled scratching or echo now, more a random hacking at rock. I'd not heard the Germans work like this.

The huddle of men looked at me when I returned.

"Someone..." I didn't know how to put it. "Someone's coming up."

"They've foxed us. The bloody Hun." Smith looked outraged. "I'd never have said they could beat us, going this deep."

"We'd better be sharp, then." I wasn't going to let them see my doubts.

Morris came back angry, and filthy. "Shaft's full."

"Any sign of what caused it?"

He shook his head.

"What are we going to do, Allen?" Pigeon looked at me with small, watery eyes.

I formed a smile I couldn't feel.

"They'll be on it now, our people. Hauling out the debris. Meanwhile, we have the Boche below us, God knows how. They'll have fresh air. We'll turn the tables and blast into their tunnel."

Purpose cut through shock. We cleaned rifles and got bayonets ready. Most of these men were better with a knife than with a gun. I employed the geophone, moving along the gallery, until I had a definite bearing. The sounds were louder.

We always had a charge ready, for if I should blow the tunnel or organise our own camouflet — a metal pipe packed with ammonal, plenty of fuse wire and a detonator box. We hauled the cross to the right spot and had Morris cut down and south towards the enemy workings. If I was right, we'd break into the German tunnel, incapacitating — if not killing — their tunnellers.

And if we failed, better a swift surrender than choking to death where we were.

It didn't take long. The charge slid tightly into the hole, the long fuse wire dangling behind. The others began heaping sandbags over it all, to help direct the blast.

"Fall back, lads."

We crouched with weapons ready, and I turned the lever on the fuse box...

The second blast of the day shook more soil from the tunnel roof, and filled the gallery with fumes which bit at the back of the throat.

"Go," I urged.

We rose as one, Morris in the lead with his bayonet thrust out. He was through the ragged hole in seconds, scrambling down the slippery clay. I shone my torch for him, mindful of having no spare battery, and tried to keep my balance as I followed.

This lower tunnel was wrong. It varied in width and height, the roof coming down to less than five feet in places. There were no timbers, either. I began to think that someone had enlarged a natural fissure in the depths.

"It would explain the Germans," said Sleath, his voice low by my ear. "They found this, and had only to dig a proper access shaft to it."

"Must be that. Not seen Boche work this crude." Smith stroked the nearest wall, which looked as if it had been hacked at almost randomly.

Lambert, the sapper, had gone ahead with Morris. He ran back, his face crumpled by an emotion I couldn't read, and tugged on my shirt sleeve.

"Sir, please..."

I followed him twenty feet down the tunnel to where Morris had lit a candle. The squat Geordie stood over a body which lay face up. There was a broken pick at its side.

The uniform was German, badly torn and mouldering. It hung off a corpse which couldn't have been the result of our blast. The smell alone made me think this man had been dead for weeks. I saw a shrivelled face, lips drawn back thin from the yellowed teeth, and the gaping sockets where his eyes had been — no, the broken-edged holes, inches across. The bone had been shattered. There was only darkness inside the empty skull.

"Damned rats," I said.

The men said nothing, preferring to share the lie. No rat had done this.

Lambert pointed to where my torch lit the floor. "There are footprints. Somebody ran — maybe they heard us tamping the camouflet."

Despite the stink of the body, there was fresher air here. Jenny, lowered down to us in her cage, seemed unaffected. I had some mad dream of taking the Germans by surprise and rising up, finding the surface again, followed by a night crawl back to our own lines.

It was a single file job, so much so that in places Morris had trouble squeezing his thick chest through. I allowed us one candle. We found a mattock abandoned fifty feet further along, and I checked the compass, which stuck a couple of times. I had to shake it to get a bearing. We were heading southeast. We were also still going down.

We made slow progress. An hour in, and no living soul, but where there was wet clay underfoot, there were impressions of feet — both booted and bare-footed. No rats. I stopped, and we shared our chocolate. Not long after, the fissure widened, and we hit a sight which paused us. The cavern ahead was low, but wider than a marshalling yard, with granite outcrops and thick pillars of a grey-green stone which glinted. Some kind of feldspar, possibly, and quartz.

We were below the clay.

Edging forward, the crystalline columns had their own light, a weak luminescence, which was barely enough to see by, but it spared our candles. Here and there, slender lengths of feldspar lay broken on the cavern floor. I thought of Goths and Vandals, the German diggers passing through and kicking out idly, destroying things which had been formed millennia ago...

"There's someone down here." That was Clough, the runner from HQ. "I can feel it. They're watching us."

"Aye." Morris had his rifle up.

We spread out as we crossed the centre of the first cavern, equipment clinking gently as we moved from one rock formation to another. Water had flowed here once, enough to break through seams in the granite and expose fields of quartz and other crystals. We followed those forgotten floods, shifting in the semi-dark as we watched for the enemy.

Our spirits were hardly raised when, after pushing through a short narrow section which headed downwards, we came out into yet another, almost identical cavern. Off this ran dim openings, some no wider than the fissure we had first entered, others the size of railway tunnels. Sleath lit a candle, but its light seemed weak, as if their glinting, greenish columns absorbed and held it in their depths.

"Summat up with this," said Morris, his hand on a clustered mass of quartz. I touched it. It felt greasy, slick with something other than water. I wiped my hand vigorously on my trousers.

"The Germans made it through," I said. "We'll go a bit further."

We lost Lambert first. He was to my left, by an outcropping of granite which resembled a clenched fist. I heard a gasp, the clatter of his boot heels against the rocks, and Pigeon and I ran to the spot. There was no sign of the young runner.

We edged forward until we reached a narrow crevice in the cavern wall. There was utter blackness inside, with a smell of decay on the faintest of breezes.

"I could get in there," whispered the Bantam.

"And do what? The Germans have him. I couldn't follow you."

It seemed that they knew we were there. There couldn't have been many of them, or they would have rushed us. Maybe they'd sent up for reinforcements.

We rejoined the others, only to find that Smith too was missing.

"He went ahead," said Sleath. "We didn't know what we were walking into, Allen."

We waited a half hour, an evil half hour where there always seemed to be more breathing in the cavern than our own, and the slightest movement sounded like thunder. The glimmers and pale reflections from crystal to crystal confused any sense of distance or direction. I began to imagine that we were in the mouth of some monstrous dead thing, and that the outcroppings were its teeth, ready to crunch down.

Smith did not return. We tracked him, as best we could. My torch showed the occasional footprint in the dirt, and then, suddenly, dozens of them, a jumble of prints. In the middle of these was Smith's rifle. Beyond that there was bare rock again, unmarked.

"They rushed him, the bastards." Morris picked up the rifle.

"We go back," I said. "That's enough. We've lost the advantage."

Resistance was token — a few protests that we should try to rescue Lambert and Smith, but no idea how, or where, they had been taken. They felt the same fear that I did, at least in some form — we were not meant to be down here.

We would retreat into our own gallery. We would get hungry, but there'd be air from where the camouflet had blasted through, and we could guard the hole. Guard it long enough, hopefully, for our own tunnellers to clear that main shaft.

It seemed simple when we started back, but within half an hour the compass no longer gave a reliable reading, and the oppressive gloom of the caverns confused us all. We had taken the first opening behind us, but had gone wrong — this passage opened out into the largest cavern yet.

Titanic granite boulders were strewn across the chamber floor, half-embedded in growths of the same greasy, crystalline substance, more luminescent than before. And in that suffocating light we saw a work which no German had ever carved.

The granite roof, thirty feet above us, had been scoured smooth. Cut deep into the bare rock was a single twisting design, so intricate that I could make no sense of it. Writhing but motionless, it challenged the orderly, gleaming formations of quartz below and filled us with a sick feeling of intrusion.

"Christ, I can't stand this." Clough threw down his rifle and started to run for the nearest exit. I yelled at him, my voice reverberating around us, and then we saw them. The enemy.

Figures rose from behind boulder and outcropping, men in torn German uniforms or earth-stained shirts and ragged trousers. A few held picks, but most were empty-handed. A dozen, at least, and amongst them, two who were no strangers.

"Smithie!" Sleath stepped forward, but I grabbed him.

"Look, man," I hissed.

The faces around us were not those of men, not as I would have counted them. Where eyes and brows should have been, there were thick chunks of crystal, gleaming with the same weak light as around us. I thought of the corpse we had found. Smith's cheeks were streaked with long trails of dried blood, and as he turned to stare at Sleath, the idiot-slump of his gaping mouth was only too apparent.

Pigeon raised his rifle, cursing, and fired at the nearest German...creature. The shot went into its chest, but it came on, looming over him before he could clear a jam in the breech. It held him, despite Sleath's attempts to help, and then they were charging us. A second one grasped Pigeon, pulling him to his knees. Morris thrust with his bayonet, cutting deep into the thing's back. It made no apparent difference.

I pulled out my revolver and shot one in the head, only to realise that it was Lambert, the sapper. Or had been. The bullet shattered one gleaming mass embedded where an eye should have been, and what remained of Lambert let out a shrill, wordless cry.

Morris was firing at every figure near him. Bullets whined and spanged off rocks, an unholy chorus. I was forced to Morris's side by more of them, helpless to stop Pigeon being dragged away, Sleath hanging onto one thin leg until he was overwhelmed. I emptied my revolver into their assailants, but the things barely staggered with the impact.

"The heads!" I was shrieking, a counterpoint to Morris's angry growl.

The Geordie managed one shot into the face of a thin, shirtless figure, dropping it, and then he too was grasped as I reloaded. Another group had come up, noiseless, behind us. I fumbled, cartridges clattering on the ground, and felt hands at my ankles and thighs. Any hope that Clough had escaped was dashed by a glimpse of him on his knees by the entrance — and by the sight of a figure grasping two long fragments of grey crystal as others held the runner down, forcing his chin to his chest and tearing hair from the back of his head...

I saw no more, thank God, for a blow to my own head rendered me unconscious at that moment.

When sense returned, I was being held almost erect by half a dozen of them, Smith amongst them. The others were Germans, but no longer the Kaiser's men. They smelled of urine and self-fouling, of decay. They were filthy, their clothes rotting, and each had chunks of crystal, two or three inches across, driven in where their eyes should have been.

I saw the marks of rank on one, the jacket still intact but torn and flapping as it moved — and a smeared photograph, sticking out of the top pocket. More unbearable than anything was this picture — a smiling woman and a child — for it said that these had been men like us, soldiers, tunnellers, taken in these dreadful depths.

"Smith," I called out, but drool ran from his slack lips, and he paid no heed. As they dragged me on, I saw Morris's body. He had my discarded revolver in his hand, and a bullet hole in his temple. A better end than the rest of us had found.

I looked away, up to the cavern roof. We were passing that terrible carving which moved and did not move. Passing, but moving on a curious, circling path, as if we should not walk directly below it. I was pushed with the mob, unable to avoid contact with their greasy, clammy flesh, until the far opening came in sight.

As with the seal on the roof, no natural force had made this gaping mouth. I judged it to be forty feet across, and twenty deep, outlined by carvings which lacked sense or meaning. Ropes of granite twisted around what might be symbols, but they seemed to slide into the other, and I was forced to look away, to stare into the blackness beyond.

No gleam of crystal, no single reflection from the main cavern. Utter darkness, that dreadful moment when the candle fails and you are alone in the tunnel, blind.

At any moment I expected to be driven to the ground, for my skull to be breached and for my humanity to be lost, but the figures urged me forward, to the edge of the opening. Hands, whole or rotting, thick-fingered or claw-like, clutched at my shoulders, my hips, and held me there, immobile...

Beyond the sinuous carvings around this entrance, deeper than I could guess, something stirred...

If, in church, I had ever felt the presence of God, then this was His counterpart — not Lucifer, nor any Biblical adversary, but the antithesis of deity. A knowing void, an impossibility.

I felt it reaching into me, and in the process, I felt also the way in which it caressed the ones who held me, controlled and nurtured them. It saw me, through those crystal mockeries of eyes. From it came a questing, a need. This void shed monstrous thoughts as it wormed its way into the galleries of my memories, tunnelling into sudden spaces filled with what I had been. I knew, without logic or rational consideration, that as I was prisoner to these creatures, so that which lay below me was captive, contained. It was a darkness which welled with an icy fury, awoken by its chance encounter with the world of Man.

I pitied us all, then — myself, the men who had trusted in me, and the Germans who had first become its thralls. Pity did not interest this presence. It drove into my mind as callously as it had formed the ones who held me. Why it did so, I cannot tell. A random insanity, or some failing in what it had achieved thus far — the discovery that its own actions had destroyed the minds from which it might have learnt.

It reached deep, clumsily. I saw my father, that slow, shovel-handed man who tried to be kind and so often failed; my mother's pale, oval face as she visited his grave in the Transvaal, a dusty hummock amongst dozens like it. Part of me was in the cavern mouth — part of me followed the presence's search within me.

If I had no understanding of what it was, it had little understanding of the human mind. I felt its incomprehension. More than once I thought that it recoiled from my memories. And then, just as I felt sure that I was soon to be discarded and consigned to that dreadful, blinded crew, it broke into a new place.

"Here, lad, close one eye and look through the other," said my father, the rough material of his uniform pressed against my bare arms. I should have been in bed, but he'd shared a beer with his mates, and we were in the back garden, his old telescope to hand. "The moon's easiest — craters and all — and then we can try some of the brighter stars."

I held onto his arm, a moment of warmth and security, of rare love, as we scanned the heavens together, father and son...

My Flanders body jerked, spasmed in the depths and almost tore itself from my captors' arms as the monstrous presence ran wild through my brain, scattering and confusing memories. Venus, low on the horizon, and my mother taking the brass telescope to the pawn shop. My first attempt to find the Pole Star. A picture I drew of the Man in the Moon, grinning like old Mr. Clegg from down our street...

I swear that the bedrock moved. Around me, crystal columns shattered, razor-edged fragments striking the insensate men around me, and a shard cut open my cheek. Their grip weakened as the presence in the depths recoiled from me.

It had seen. I had seen.

As much as it could read from me, I read from it, and would never be able to forget. That it was bound, it knew, and its fell malignity had fed upon that frustration for such spans of time as I could not grasp. But now...

My father had taught me the stars, and they were wrong. Not wrong for a man and his ten-year-old son, crouched in a Surrey garden — but for this terrible thing trapped within the depths of Flanders, to which I had brought a new madness.

This place was its prison, which fuelled hatred enough. What shuddered the earth at that moment was its sight of the heavens above our planet, excavated from my mind. Heavens where the stars which hung on cold velvet were so alien to the presence that it found no sense, not even the vaguest comprehension of their configuration.

It had thought itself held, confined in some corner of its own time and space, but now it knew.

It was lost.

Utterly lost.

The hands fell away from me, the presence withdrawn into a roiling fury greater than any before. Touched by its madness, those around me staggered blindly, and I ran. An overwhelming need for escape possessed me, nor do I think that the emotion came only from within myself.

Shoving a German aside, I blundered into and over shattered crystal; I fell and rose again, many times, until blood ran down my arms and legs. I cannot know what God or instinct took me to the original fissure by which we had entered the nightmare below, but there came a moment when I saw the most welcome of all sights, the discarded wrapper from a bar of British chocolate.

Weeping, I clambered up the clay slope formed by the camouflet, and found the safety of our own tunnel. Hearing no pursuit, I crawled towards the blockage in the main shaft, to claw at the wet earth with my bare hands...

And I found physical salvation, if nothing else. Others from the 183rd must have been digging for hours. My broken nails reached into empty space, and there were men, men with eyes of blue and grey and brown, eyes which held nothing more than concern. They hauled me from there, roping me and lifting me as gently as they could to the head of the shaft.

It was night, but I could not look up.

"I need..." A sapper lifted his canteen to my lips. I drank until he took the canteen away. "I need...Major Cartwright."

The stiff-backed officer arrived in minutes, eyes dark at the bloody mess which lay upon the stretcher. At me. There was unsuspected humanity in the man, for he knelt and took one of my lacerated hands in his.

"It's all right, Allen. The doctor is coming." He pulled on his moustache, nervous. "The rest of your men..."

"Dead." It was as good a word as any.

"You've been lucky."

Lucky. I choked down laughter, hysteria.

"Major, for God's sake — you must blow the mines...as soon as you can."

"You need rest, Lieutenant. We'll send you back to Blighty, and..."

My grip might have been enough to crush granite. He winced as I hauled him closer.

"The Germans are in the depths! The Germans. I've seen them."

I described the insignia, any insignia, which I had seen upon the German tunnellers. I blocked out their faces, but babbled out every small detail I could remember. Another officer, one of the Royal Engineers, appeared, and was told the same fragmented story.

"A Saxon unit," he muttered. "They were reported east of here, a couple of months ago."

The Major frowned. "Then—"

"We can't risk waiting." The engineer was scribbling in a small notebook. "If they come up into our galleries and pull the fuses..."

I gabbled lies and truths, anything to convince them. Field telephones whirred; runners came and went. I was loaded onto a truck and taken to a field hospital. I was waiting, waiting for what must surely be done, and I clutched my watch in bandaged fingers, possessed by the slow movement of the hands under the scratched glass. One o'clock, two o'clock...

At ten past three in the morning, while two nurses were trying to make me take a sedative, the face of Flanders changed.

I could not see it from the hospital hut, with its blanket-covered windows, but I was told that great columns of crimson flame burst from the torn earth, like Hell emerging for its due. I heard the remaining window glass shatter, and instruments rattled in their trays. The man next to me, his face bandaged, fell from his bunk, and the nurses rushed to help him.

Explosion after explosion, in close succession, shaking the hut and driving strange, hot winds across the land. Surely, I thought, surely it would be enough. Whether or not our mines destroyed the German trenches, I did not care. My only thought was of tunnels, galleries, and chambers, each of them flattened, crushed, and the blessed clay collapsing in its tens of thousands of tons to seal those terrible, crystalline depths.

A prison around a prison...

***

My father's eyes close, and his breathing slows. Hopefully he will sleep for a while. An old clock, left by the previous residents, ticks loud in the corner. I must see to it tomorrow, in case it keeps my father awake at night. I arrange the blanket over his legs, and tuck the journal under my arm.

The words I have written must be nonsense. Better to believe that he is emerging from shell shock and madness, rather than accept what he recounted. Better to believe that my father, who has never lied to me, nor given credence to another's fancies, has been changed by war.

I step out into a blustery Scottish evening. The sky is leaden, much as the sea, and the breeze holds the iodine and salt tang of James

McCallister's seaweed from across the isle. There are no stars to see, and beneath me is only solid rock.

I wonder if I should pray.

AUTHOR NOTES

As often happens when I write period weird fiction, "Where All is Night, and Starless" relates to genuine historical circumstances — in this case, the horrifying explosions of 7th June 1917, at the start of the Battle of Messines in Flanders. Following extensive mining and counter-mining for months, the Allies decided to trigger all their deep mines in the Messines area at once.

"Suddenly at dawn, as a signal for all of our guns to open fire, there rose out of the dark ridge of Messines and 'Whitesheet' and that ill-famed Hill 60, enormous volumes of scarlet flame [...] throwing up high towers of earth and smoke all lighted by the flame, spilling over into fountains of fierce colour, so that many of our soldiers waiting for the assault were thrown to the ground. The German troops were stunned, dazed and horror-stricken if they were not killed outright. Many of them lay dead in the great craters opened by the mines." — Philip Gibbs, British reporter.

This event ranks among the largest non-nuclear explosions of all time.

on mysteries

various observations
on matters strange

where the thin men die

New York, 1975

HE STUMBLES AS he walks across the stage, and some of the audience chuckle, believing it a signature of his act. The truth is he had a minor stroke eight months ago. With his ancient suit and the battered slouch hat which almost covers his eyes, he used to think he looked like a Black Teddy Roosevelt, a Rough Rider of the boards. These days he feels more like Franklin R, headed for a wheelchair and death on the job.

It could be worse, of course. Archie Bowles, the Voice of the Funnies, died last year, and he was only fifty-two; the Bronx Nightingale, Ellie Potsvitch, coughed up her innards alone on the L before she hit the big four-oh.

It's not a long warm-up. A few minutes of patter, to get the saliva flowing, and a joke or two — wife and mother-in-law, nosy neighbors, and hungry dogs.

And then comes the routine itself...

"Black Harry's dead," said Rosalee, folding up the paper. "Didn't you mention him, a while back?"

Tomás frowned. "You shouldn't call him that, these days. It was a stage name, and not one he ever asked for."

"Harold Freedman, then. He was Black, and he's dead. You're hung up about that sort of thing."

Which was what a white girl from the Boston suburbs would say. Tomás had to accept gigs wherever he could, and test the mood every time. He'd started out explaining that his father came from a town in Argentina, not from some vague "Spanish-speaking world" — and got nowhere. He ended up settling for Latino or Hispanic, whatever they wanted to call him on the day.

If it meant a mostly white crowd looking for novelty, or a Black crowd just waiting for him to put a foot wrong, that was what it took to meet the bills. Rosalee typed, and not so well; her jobs rarely lasted longer than a few months.

"I saw him once," Tomás said, before he could stop himself.

"Where?"

The White Diamond, a mixed-crowd place which spoke of uneasy truces, a laying down of Puerto Rican knives and Bronx baseball bats. His father would have called it a black-and-tan saloon.

"Oh, around."

"Was he good?"

"I...I don't remember."

Rosalee pushed the paper aside, losing interest; Tomás looked through his scuffed briefcase, wondering where he'd put the notes he made last night. He found the crumpled sheets and flicked a glob of egg mayo off them. His sandwich was leaking out through its torn paper bag.

So this guy, this Polish guy, goes into a bar... Something like that. He wasn't sure how many Poles drank in the Crazy Pine. It was 135th and 7th, so probably none. Safer not to make any Italian jokes, though.

He was trying not to think about Harold Freedman.

***

The bus took him most of the way to 135th Street. Another Latino guy, buried deep inside in a shiny suit, made a sign Tomás didn't recognize; three Black kids, fourteen or fifteen years old with serious Afros, snickered at him. He was no more at home here than he was at the polished walnut dining table of Rosalee's parents.

He didn't feel safe in Harlem, but then he didn't feel safe in New York. The city was a monster constantly on the edge of starvation; a monster which sharpened its claws on coke-high socialites and street heroin overdoses with the same indifference, which made its body of garbage and tenements, spiked through with shining towers.

The Crazy Pine was easily found, a new joint which had never seen a real tree of any kind. Unpainted drywall inside, Formica and disinfectant. The stage, barely six feet across, was opposite the bar.

"Delgardo?" asked a bored voice from by the pumps.

Tomás nodded. "Yes."

He took in the thick-necked owner of the voice — maybe forty-five, fifty; stained t-shirt, jeans, and a crew cut.

"Get up there, then. Gimme five minutes, no filler."

Tomás clambered up. The stage was sticky, and he could see the glitter of broken glass, tiny stars across a dark night of linoleum. He'd read through his act again on the bus.

"Hey, the Big Apple. Want to know why they really call it that? Ask Mayor Beame where he..."

It was polished, pertinent. Crew-cut pulled a sour face a few times; smiled twice.

"Okay, I'll give you an hour, week on Friday. Twenty dollars and a cut of the door."

"I'll be there."

"If you ain't, no loss to me," muttered the man, and pretended to polish a glass.

The audition was over.

The eyes under the slouch hat should be a deep, lively brown. They're not. One is watery and large-pupiled; the other is a discolored white, like some sort of cataract. Old folk in Harlem – the ones who cling to fragments of the past and still don't approve of TV dinners – remember a conjure-woman who walked their streets in the 1920s, a woman with one eye of milk and honey. He doesn't discourage such talk, in case it draws the curious.

He undoes his suit jacket, trying not to tug a button off altogether. He hates sewing – big, blunt-nailed fingers – and his left hand doesn't work as well as it used to.

There are seven or eight soldiers sprawled in the front row. Large, angry men; small, angry men. General Trầ n Văn Trà is on the Ho Chi Minh trail again, and South Vietnam won't be around much longer. A few of them want to be back there; most don't even know where they've been.

He ought to cancel, but he has no choice.

"I have a lot to tell you," says Harold Freedman.

As Tomás made his way back from the Crazy Pine, he saw that "Black Harry" had briefly caught the imagination of the newspaper editors. Bored with reciting the city's failings or another litany of homicides, they'd pushed Freedman forward as human interest.

He bought a couple of different papers, sat down on a bench and read, taking occasional bites from his egg sandwich. They wrote briefly of Harry's upbringing – a family with no money, a boy with no father. Not one that anyone would name, anyway.

Everyone in the family called young Harry a funny guy. He did his time telling jokes and stories, picking the banjo, whatever got him a meal. It never paid much, but he grew to be a familiar face around the smaller clubs and bars in the forties and fifties.

One obituary mentioned how Richard Pryor pointed Harry out at the Village Gate. That would have been in the mid-sixties. Freedman stood alone, to one side of the audience; Pryor called him a Black icon, but never mentioned him again. The press didn't bother to cover Harry when he was alive. You had to have TV or Vegas to get the real talk going.

Freedman had two routines. One was a stand-up act, although it was rare to see an aging Black man in the role. The vogue was for young, cutting-edge performers. Freedman's act was tired — and safe, far too safe.

His other routine...that was known only on the edges of the New York club circuit, and he didn't do it often. The few people who had seen it would never say what he actually did.

Tomás knew why.

The next bus didn't come, so he walked to the subway. Four in the afternoon, which was okay — you didn't take the subway after six if you could help it. The walk took him past the "Sinsational" Peeporama, which had replaced one of the local theaters.

"8mm Art Films," the posters proclaimed. Porn was gripping the Big Apple with painted nails which covered deep, embedded dirt. The men behind it made money and built empires; the girls it drained put powder over their injection sites, ice cubes on their nipples, and smiled — a rictus of small hopes never to be realized.

The subway was crowded. He lasted three stops and a hustle from a pock-marked white guy with missing teeth, who lisped out a few bad jokes. One of them was from Black Harry's act, and Tomás suddenly needed air. He got off a stop early.

Out on the street, he was in sight of the block where he lived. Ten-minute walk. He began to breathe properly, walking round burned-out Pontiacs and leaking hydrants like a native.

The joke hadn't been Freedman's. It was simply one of those tired gags that went the rounds, year after year. No need to get paranoid.

There were plenty of other things in New York to bring on that sort of feeling.

**

Tomás Delgardo was born in England. His father was an Argentinian-American working in London, his mother an artsy society girl from Chelsea. They'd married in the spring of 1949, in a flurry of raised eyebrows. Tomás, their only child, followed soon after. He'd expected to spend the rest of his life there, but when he was fourteen, his father announced they were moving to New York. No warning, no discussion.

His parents never did tell him why they uprooted – nor why they divorced eighteen months later, when he turned sixteen. His mother went home, and phoned at Christmas and on birthdays; Tomás remained with his father, an electronics engineer, but the teenager had no gift for any of the sciences. Instead, he wrote bad poetry, failed to complete a novel, and ended up working the clubs. Delgardo Senior joked about circuits and "the circuit," but disappointment stained his smile.

In 1973, Tomás was commiserating with himself after a failed gig when he met Rosalee, pretty and smart. They moved in together, and were married a few months later. She wanted to do set design, but there were no openings – there was money in her family, but neither she nor Tomás wanted to beg.

They lived in a brownstone apartment where the rent was bearable, and the tenants paid the local cops to keep the stoop free of pushers and prostitutes. Rosalee had painted the entrance hall in muted greens and yellows, the comfortable side of psychedelia.

When he made it back from the audition, she was by the window, drinking coffee with Nicolette.

"Ay, goat head," said Nicolette, white teeth in a dark face. She and her flatmate Angie were Caribbean, maybe from Barbados. He wasn't sure about that odd accent. Models, presented as the exciting New York Black look, which caused some tension with models actually from New York.

"Hi, Nico." He threw his briefcase onto the sofa. "I got the gig."

"Do ya ting, man. Got to split – shoot in Astoria tomorrow."

Rosalee noticed him watching Nicolette's hips as she left.

"Yeah, she's beautiful. Want me to go into modeling?"

He was tired, but he grinned.

"You'd crush them all."

"White and plain aren't in," she said. "You think the Crazy Pine might be a regular?"

He didn't know. His life was patchwork — a script for a local radio skit, two other gigs this week, and a birthday roast coming up for a man he hardly knew. It paid the rent. He'd been asked to play a bit-part Mexican in a play the week before and had refused. Borrowed Argentinian pride. Rosalee didn't understand, but let it go.

"Mind if I go to Marky's?" he asked.

"No. Back for nine — I'll do a casserole."

"Thanks, chica."

Marky's was only a block away. It held the best and the worst in Tomás's line of work. Beat poets long past their sell-by date; stand-ups who phoned their acts in, thick with bourbon; a few genuine talents. Commiseration over failed gigs was tinged with secret glee, and triumphs received with brittle salutes. "I should have got that slot" was the real tune as the glasses clinked together.

"Black Harry's dead," said Mike, the bar man.

Tomás squinted at him. "I heard. Why are you telling me?"

"Okay, okay. I thought you knew him."

"Not really."

But he knew more about Freedman than anyone else in the bar. He'd been there, at the White Diamond...

September 1973. Tomás was weighing up the competition, and if he admitted it, looking for styles to imitate, material to "borrow." Things hadn't been going well. Booed off stage at the Mimosa Club; bottles thrown at him at a redneck bar. He could put his own spin on anything, he told himself.

Black Harry completed his comedy routine to a scatter of applause; most of the patrons in the low-ceilinged room abandoned their tables for the bar. As the performer gulped down a beer, the door by the stage opened to reveal Martha, the wrinkled, bleach-blonde woman who ran the White Diamond. Tight red dress and plastic pearls.

She blinked in the spotlight, looking around at the remaining audience.

"Any of youse wanna see Harry throw more of a punch?"

Tomás said yes, as did about a dozen others. Maybe there was a blue version of the act — edgier material altogether. It didn't seem to fit with Freedman's tired expression, but there was nothing worth taking from what had gone before.

The passage behind Martha led to the abandoned cinema club next door. The frontage was boarded up; the seating was still in place.

Horsehair stuck out of the seats where rats had been in search of bedding.

Black Harry hobbled in after them, and had trouble with the steps onto the stage. Tomás went forward and helped Freedman up.

"Thanks, son."

The old man's breath smelled of pear drops, his clothes of stale beer. Close to, his face might have come from a curled sepia photograph taken a hundred — or a thousand — years before. Tight-curled hair, stiff with grey, and a few days growth on his chin. The eyes confused you — you were torn between the depths of one gaping pupil and the cloudy white of the other.

Tomás had his hand under the man's elbow. Beneath Black Harry's jacket, beneath dark skin and wasted muscle, deeper still, he felt something he didn't want to feel. Something demanding, though what it demanded, he had no idea.

He realized he was staring, and let go.

"You tread the boards, son?" said Freedman. "You've the look of us."

"Learning the trade, sir."

"I wouldn't. Wouldn't stay for what's a-comin', neither."

Tomás laughed nervously and found a place in the front row of seats. The woman next to him asked what was going to happen; he admitted he didn't know.

Freedman took off his jacket and rolled up frayed shirt sleeves. He had no microphone, just a stand to which he clung for support.

"I have a lot to tell you," he said.

A half hour later, Black Harry put his jacket back on and left the stage, guided off by the owner. Some of the audience were weeping. One man rushed out, screaming "Myra" or "Moira"; a couple of young men in cheap suits were struggling with each other at the back, swearing in Italian. One had blood across his mouth.

Tomás stayed in his seat, stunned. The woman to his right was clutching at a leather bag the angry red of a newborn child.

"The man next door — Al Parker — he's touching my kids," she said, and her shoulders convulsed.

Still dazed, Tomás swallowed bile. "How do you know?"

"Al was here, next to me — between us. He smiled, and told me. He smiled. He said he puts his hand up their dresses, and promises them things... Jesus, they're eleven years old."

"He couldn't have been here."

She pushed him away. "Didn't you see him? He's a big man, red hair. You must have done!"

He wasn't sure what he'd seen — though he knew he hadn't seen Al Parker or anyone like him.

"You should go home."

She wiped her eyes, nodded. "I need to tell Ted. He'll sort that son of a bitch out."

"Maybe...maybe it wasn't real."

"HE SPOKE TO ME!"

Tomás let her go.

The room was almost empty now. One of the Italians was propped against the wall, mopping his bleeding face with a handkerchief; the other had gone.

Tomás had seen, and he had heard, but not Al Parker. His mother had been on his other side, where a ferret-faced guy in a check suit should have been. At times he thought he could see the man through her. She had bouffant hair and her fingers played with a silver necklace. His father gave it to her for her thirty-fifth, and she'd loved it once, but she never wore it after they came to the States.

And she told Tomás things. The words went in, and his brain knew what they meant, but he couldn't process them.

After the White Diamond he drank himself into a stupor at Marky's, got dragged home by a friend, and in the morning it was all right. Black Harry's act had to be smoke and mirrors — hidden microphones, projectors, whatever. And a lot of research into his audience — but that sounded ridiculous. Maybe there'd been acid in the bar-nuts.

Nothing that happened at the White Diamond had really happened.

He proposed to Rosalee the next afternoon. It wasn't a bad decision, but it came from all the wrong places, and only he knew that.

Later that same week he stared into the bathroom mirror. He told himself that he would find Freedman and ask how it was done. One day. But he never did.

He never dared.

They always look impatient after the intro. They're eager for something vulgar or scurrilous, for mean-minded jokes about those they envy or fear. The sex lives of the stars; jokes that play with familiarity and contempt — prejudice about the Polacks, the Canucks, even his own kind, if this old man has it in him. Won't be the first time they've heard a Black act look for favor by sticking it to his own.

He doesn't have any of those, because he doesn't write this part. He only sets the scene.

It's time. He's getting thin now, thin like stained gauze on a cold night's breeze, bloodied bandages in the branches of a dead tree. Thin like rice paper.

And as he fades, others come, eager to talk. Shadow people who settle in shadow seats, slivers of the world the audience left at home. Recognition and whispers. People start to look around, puzzled faces and a twitching of hands.

He clutches at the fake pillar on one side of the stage; his hands feel rough plaster, but only barely. He's stretched so thin he can hardly draw air into his failing lungs...

In the third row, a man starts to argue with no one, with a sliver of air and darkness.

"You gonna raise that again, huh? You gonna start?"

The audience pays no attention, because they all have their own shadows and slivers, born of misery, lies, and the minutiae of never being what they wanted to be, never quite grasping the prize.

A squat master sergeant stares around him, his broken-veined nose matching flushed cheeks, and starts to rise to his feet. One of the other uniforms is muttering to him, hand on his arm, telling him it doesn't matter anymore, that his crew understands.

Freedman gasps, seeing a bad one coming, and he feels so thin that a single spit might pass through him...

Unnoticed by the master sergeant and those around him, the wiry Black soldier at the end stands up, tugs a handgun from the back of his belt.

"You. Will. Never. Give. It. A. Rest," he shrieks, and jams the muzzle of the pistol under his chin. "If you love your brother so damn much, go and screw him instead of me!"

Only Freedman hears the shot. He's too thin – and too old – to react. He knows we all failed someone.

The first few times he thought he'd worked out what was plaguing him, that it was something easy to grasp. He'd been brought up with stories of haints, with whispers from the grave, and could have handled that. Five-spots and mojo bags, they might have helped.

But then he worked it out, and it was much worse.

Black Harry was stretched thin so he could touch those who touched his audience. He summoned the living – and the living had far more to say than the dead.

***

On the Tuesday, Tomás did the birthday roast. Lame jokes about Freddie Sumner, a balding accountant with a poor sense of humor. The money came from Freddie's office, and Tomás suspected that they'd set it up precisely because Freddie wouldn't get half of it. The accountant's wife seemed amused, and spent too much time in the kitchen pressing Tomás to beers and sandwiches. She gave off a heat, a need, which was oppressive; he declined to stick around afterwards, uncomfortably aware that she wasn't wearing a bra.

Trudging back to the brownstone, he saw an elderly, dark-skinned man sitting on the sidewalk, right in front of the tobacconists on the corner. The man's left leg was in some sort of caliper, strapped on over patched corduroy trousers; the steel shutters behind him were sprayed with gang signs and obscenities. Tomás had taken good money for a bad night, and he reached into his pocket for a dollar bill.

The man looked up.

"Jes' restin'," he said. "Takin' in that cee-gar smoke, dreamin' o' Havana."

There was no smoke; the night air smelled of burning slums and dog shit. Tomás fingered the notes in his pocket, and asked what he considered to be the most stupid question of his life.

"Did you know Harold Freedman? Black...uh, Black Harry, some called him. Old-time comedian, used to work the clubs around here."

A frown, wrinkles like the corrugations in the shutters behind him.

"Ain't never met him. Colored feller, was he?"

"Yeah."

"Dead?"

"He had a stroke which did for him, last week."

"Most all o' us headin' that way, soon enough." Narrowed eyes checked out the younger man's best performance suit and the less-than-best shoes. "Want me to tell you 'bout it?"

Tomás stepped back. For a second, he thought that one of the man's eyes had widened, and the other gone white as milk.

"No." He thrust a dollar into the man's hand, and ran, ran for home...

***

An hour later, after a bottle of wine, he placed a call to London. The wine helped cushion the cost, though he knew Rosalee would be pissed with him.

A cultured English voice eventually answered from the moon, or so it sounded. Echoes and emptiness.

"Margrave."

"Justin — it's Tomás Delgardo."

"What on earth's the matter, dear boy? It's two in the morning here."

"You're up, Justin. You're always up. Look, please, I need the truth from someone. About my parents and the move — in '64."

In the lunar wasteland, the clearing of a man's throat.

"Put the telephone down, Tomás — you can't afford this call. I'll ring you back."

He made a strong cup of coffee, because he didn't trust himself; poured out another glass of red because he needed drink more than trust. When the phone rang, it sent ice through his belly.

"You've known my mother most of her life," Tomás started, before the other could speak. "And I know something happened, just before we came to New York."

Margrave was from another generation, a world of art, beauty, and occasional self-destruction. He was also the nearest thing Tomás had to a godfather.

"It isn't pleasant," said Margrave. "But I imagine you know that, from the way you ask."

"I've already heard it. Some of it."

His mother had told him, that night at the White Diamond. Harold Freedman had let her tell him, but the words had been buried so deep inside him that, until now, he could pretend they weren't there. And there was always the chance that it was all a lie.

After thirty minutes on the phone, he knew that it wasn't.

"What...what happened in the end?" asked Tomás. He'd broken the wine glass against the wall, and was watching runnels of red find their way to the carpet.

"In the end?" Margrave sounded sad. "Stevie Slater was a prime bitch, dear boy — a listener-in, a steamer-open of letters. A venomous beast without the charms of his serpent kin. We hushed it up, naturally. I was seeing Leo at the time — Leo Chancel, you remember him, the kindest of fellows. He dealt with your father; I took care of your mother."

"And Slater?"

"The little sod recovered, but the marks couldn't be covered up. He went to try his hand — and his arse — in Prague. If there is any justice in this world, he went under a tank in sixty-eight."

"Thank you." Flat, drained.

"It won't do any good, you know — mentioning it to your mother or father. She's happy enough now. I saw her at Sissy Metcalfe's gallery last month." The older man paused. "Who stirred this up again, Tomás?"

"Harold Freedman," he said, and put the receiver down.

***

When Rosalee and Nicolette got back from a party downtown, he broke.

"My dad screwed another guy, during a bad patch in the marriage. And...shit happened."

It wasn't the best way to greet them as they giggled their way into the flat. Rosalee took in the wine stains on the wall, the glistening shards, and her husband's expression.

"You know where the glasses are, Nico," she said, calm.

And he told them the story — not only what he'd heard from Margrave, but everything that had come out two years before, when Black Harry raised shadows and ruined lives. When Tomás saw a woman who couldn't be there, her face tear-stained, her fingers playing with a silver necklace as she sat in her Chelsea flat, three thousand miles away...

Stephen Slater, an angular twenty-two-year-old little better than a rent-boy, flattered and charmed the handsome Mateo Delgardo. Delgardo's marriage had become sedentary, sexless, and somehow he fell for bright talk of other pleasures. They met in anonymous hotel rooms across London, and did what men do — until Slater started doing what Slater did. Turning up on the edge of work events; "chance" arrivals at Mrs. Delgardo's arts happenings. Suggesting certain interpretations of business trips, letting his hand linger too long on Mr. Delgardo's arm.

Slater had letters, and few would care if they were forged or genuine. Outside of the right "scene," such letters could cripple a man.

"My mother dealt with it," said Tomás.

The two women sat opposite him, sobered, fascinated. Rosalee's knuckles were white.

"How she do dat?" asked Nicolette.

"She had my father write to Slater, and arrange a meeting one evening. "

The Black girl nodded. "She pay him off for licking his mout' too much."

Rosalee closed her eyes, letting her long blonde hair fall over her face; Tomás wet his lips.

"No. She met Slater in an underground car park, near Piccadilly."

Nicolette's eyes widened; Tomás slumped, committed to finishing the tale.

"There was no one else around. When he sidled over and asked for money, she said that she wouldn't pay a penny to scum like him. That any more mention of her husband, ever, or the slightest word to the police...well, she warned him. When he laughed, and suggested what *he* might do next, she took a knife out — a craft knife from her workshop — to prove how serious she was—"

"She cut him?" Rosalee's head stayed low.

"She caught him off balance, and when he fell, she drove her heel into his crotch until he could only whimper. Then she cut him — in more than one place — and left him there, sprawled in his own blood and piss, to limp his way home or bleed to death. She didn't really care."

There was his mother in his memories, smiling as she took a cake from the oven; laughing at the antics of a puppy at a friend's party. Pretty dresses, and a hug at the end of the school day. And there she was in some urine-stained car park one night, a knife in her slim, artistic hands...

"She...she fix dat boy-skank good." Nicolette no longer looked comfortable. With a squeeze of Rosalee's hand, she left for her own flat.

Tomás got up, and began a half-hearted attempt to sweep up the broken glass.

"That's why they came to the States," said Rosalee at last. "To get away from what had happened."

"I guess so."

She held him in the night. It didn't help.

He doesn't think he'll be able to do this much longer, however hard the need drives him. It was never his choice anyway, but now his body is giving in. The pain in his liver is worse, and the blood pounds in his veins, looking for a way to corrupt the flesh beyond.

Better than having it sprayed across the back of an old cinema seat, maybe –
half the young Black soldier's head is missing. A woman has called the cops, but
they probably won't even come. The city's going to shit.

Harry never knows what they're told, by their friends and neighbors, lovers,
mothers, husbands. He doesn't want to. He didn't ask for this, and he doesn't
determine who turns up from the shadows. Someone else will carry on when he
dies – tomorrow, next month, next year. Someone who's seen his routine, and
never let go of what they heard. Never really left the performance.

It always lingered with one or two of them, like it lingered with Harry so
long ago in a North Carolina roadhouse, his only attempt at touring. He helped
an old man up onto a soapbox after a blues session, an old man who said he had
something to tell folk. That was when he first heard those words, and saw what it
meant to go thin...

Truth is a dreadful thing. Harold Freedman would like to feel sorry; he'd
like to make people smile, nothing more than that.

It wasn't to be.

Tomás managed a short set at the Conga King, a bar packed with
plastic palms and plastic people. They liked his film references, his skit
on Gerald Ford; they didn't like the older stuff, the early, warm-up part,
and he realized that he'd used material he'd meant to drop. Material
which went back to the sort of act Black Harry did, years ago. Why the
hell had he done that?

Afterwards, he sank a large gin in one corner, shook hands with a
couple from Illinois, and wondered where all this was going. He'd felt
different during the gig, like there was something he needed to do – the
truth about his parents' past was a worm under his skin, twisting and
turning inside him, and he began to wonder about those who were
watching him.

Lies and secrets...

He pushed the empty glass away and took up his briefcase. He
would have to rework some of the material for the gig at the Crazy Pine.
If he had that as a weekly slot, and could get spotted by an agent...it
might cheer up Rosalee, who was finding him hard work at the moment.

He didn't blame her. She trusted him, but he didn't trust himself
anymore.

Black Harry was dead, and things had changed.

He looks out at the tables, waiting for the chatter to subside, wondering if it ever will. He's already done the introductory jokes, which didn't make much of an impression. A green spotlight shines in his eyes, but he'll have to live with it.

It's a small crowd tonight. Hard-faced Italian construction workers, unable to tell the difference between the rubble of their days and the rubble of their nights. Couples in love who live with their parents, surrounded by damp ironing and the smell of three-day-old bolognese sauce being boiled up again. They have nowhere else to go to be alone together. Uncomfortable wives, dragged out by husbands who use these evenings as an excuse to get tanked. They pray their men will pass out on the sofa later.

A cop, already a quarter way through a bottle of cheap whiskey. He shot a Black kid two days ago, but all the kid had in his hand was an Afro comb. The cop can't decide if he cares or not. The whiskey might give him the answer.

At the table nearest to the stage, a man and a woman. The woman is young, attractive, with soft blonde hair swept back, and she looks worried, distracted. The man is dark-skinned and must be forty years older than her – he limped in earlier, from streets which steam and groan, favoring a calipered leg. They don't seem to know each other.

He folds his jacket on the back of the wooden chair, the only feature on the cramped stage. He's beginning to feel...thin, stretched out around the people in front of him. He's here, and he's being pulled like taffy, drawn thin across the crowd. So stretched that now he can feel the people they know, and the people who know the people they know, a terrible web of interconnecting failures and deceits...

It'll come, because it has to, and it'll change the expressions on those faces, maybe change the rest of their lives.

Already there are strangers in the audience, sliding between the seats, setting shadows where shadows can't be, and other voices are ready to speak...

"I have a lot to tell you," says Tomás Delgardo, as he begins his first and last performance at the Crazy Pine.

AUTHOR NOTES

I'm fond of interweaving tales, and the Justin Margrave mentioned in "Where the Thin Men Die" is a recurring character of mine, a gay art critic who often ends up drawn into unnatural and even supernatural situations, much more out of *curiosity than out of any desire to encounter or investigate these things. And Margrave, from a world of lies and privilege, understands the pain of truths.*

THE HOUSE IS so quiet now, with Kenneth and the others gone. So orderly. As I gaze around the kitchen, I play my fingers across the rack of spice jars, over the slight unevenness of the plastered walls, no longer marred by the clutter of reminders and notes about the current contents of the freezer. Everything is as it should be, where it should be.

I shall make a cup of tea.

Warm the pot; switch off the kettle just before the water boils. Don't want to drive all the oxygen out. Loose tea, never teabags. Oolong, woody but slightly sweet. Let it sit for seven or eight minutes, and then pour.

I add a dash of milk — not too much — and sip. Perfect.

This is how Marjorie likes it. She deserves this. She has plans, wonderful plans, and I am so very pleased to have her back...

***

It was the tea that Kenneth noticed first. He mentioned it, peering over his morning paper.

"You don't like gunpowder green, Marjorie. Too smoky, you always say."

I stared at the jar in my hand, and then at the grey stoneware teapot.

"Getting absent-minded." I put the tea back on the shelf, and took down the oolong. "Going to be one of those days."

Not that it was his place to say what I should or shouldn't drink. He paid too much attention to detail, that was the problem. If you liked something once, he made sure it was in the groceries next time. It took a whole week of Cheerios at breakfast before I broke and told him that I'd only tried them for fun, that now I had, I thought they were dull, at best.

I downed a quick half cup of oolong, kissed him on the cheek — lipstick meeting sandpaper — and left for the office. Nothing would be different there. Typing, photocopying, and too much gossip; comparisons of nail varnish and the endless talk of hairstyles. It was hair. As long as it was tidy and out of the way, what did the rest matter?

I would have thought no more about the gunpowder green, except for that lunchtime, when I traipsed into the work canteen and joined the queue.

"Macaroni cheese, or goulash?" The slow, thick-browed server wasn't looking at me, just waving her ladle in my general direction. There were greasy brown smears in the vat of macaroni cheese — she obviously used the same ladle for both dishes.

"Goulash, please."

Hungarians would have wept to see what was slopped onto my plate. More importantly, I had never enjoyed goulash, even when well-prepared. I couldn't understand why I'd asked for it.

I sat alone at a small table, and as I spooned each mouthful into the inner void, I felt a soft touch behind my eyes. I looked again at the under-spiced mess in my bowl.

"No, I don't want this," I said out loud. A couple of people looked up from their soups, then went back to desultory conversation.

I didn't want it, but my hands fed me the rest of the plateful, lump by greasy lump.

"Satisfied now?" I murmured. There was no answer, of course.

Afterwards I tried to make light of it. I told Suzie, the rather plain girl who worked at the desk next to mine, that since we moved up here, my tastes seemed to be changing.

"Though I can't imagine why," I added. "Our old house wasn't so different from this one; the shops are pretty much the same, and Ressington...well, it's like any other industrial town."

"You're bored." Suzie's mud-coloured eyes met mine. "Ressington is boring."

"I... Maybe so. Perhaps I need a hobby."

Suzie's fingers paused over her keyboard. "My little sister cuts herself. Says that when she's done it often enough, our Mam and Dad will let her leave this hole, go to London or something."

That seemed somewhat extreme.

"She's more likely to end up on a hospital ward," I said.

"Aye, there's that."

We didn't talk the rest of that afternoon.

After work, I went for the wrong bus. I wanted a fifty-seven, but for no reason I could fathom I waited at the thirty-two stop and got on the first one which came. When the service terminated at the park — they call it a park, that sad square of bushes tangled with refuse — I got off the bus and walked home. Two miles, in heels.

That was how it started. Tea, goulash, and a bus.

***

We had sex, on a cold, rainy morning in February. Kenneth lay there with the Sunday newspapers spread out over the duvet, a puzzled look on his face as I straddled him; he didn't resist, but he didn't play much of a part, either. Five inches, barely rigid enough.

Afterwards, he tried to put the sports supplement back into order.

"That was...surprising," he said.

And it was. I'd no idea that I wanted to touch him, never mind have a bit of "the other."

Cleaning up the breakfast cups, it came to me that I really hadn't. Whoever wanted to copulate with Kenneth, it wasn't me. I'd given up that sort of thing years ago. I didn't know whether to be shocked or disgusted. I had a shower instead.

That afternoon, I watched the golf on the television.

I hated golf.

These little alterations to my routine were starting to disturb me. Was Ressington itself somehow responsible? There had been the move to accommodate Kenneth's new position at the plastics factory, and then I'd found a job in the typing pool at an adjoining firm — none of that had been planned much in advance. Nor was it what I would have chosen, myself. The town smelled of plastics and filing cabinets — an artificial miasma of made-things, overlaying what little of nature survived in the area.

We'd not liked Northampton much, but at least it had history. Someone might well have planned Ressington sixty years ago as the antithesis of the English countryside — gravel and tarmac choking the soil; grim rain-stained factories and office blocks looming over the houses, mostly post-war semis built to three standard patterns. Sometimes the construction companies seemed to have given in, and just slapped down thirty or forty copies of the same house in an estate, no longer caring to vary the facades.

If people sent postcards anymore, they certainly didn't send any of Ressington.

Maybe the place was affecting me.

When I went to the doctor for a routine smear, I asked her if people's tastes could change, suddenly — drastically. She frowned.

"I wouldn't know, Mrs. Eden. Not without a reason, I suppose, but there's nothing in your medical history..."

She went through the motions of checking my eyes and my reflexes, and asked if I'd banged my head or suffered any sudden shocks recently. I told her I hadn't, and in the end her opinion turned out to be much the same as Suzie's at the office.

It probably came down to boredom.

I should have walked back from the surgery, but instead, I went to the train station and bought a ticket for the next stop up the line. A dormitory village, absorbed not long after Ressington became the pointless industrial hub that it was. King's Fletching, they called it.

It was like the bus journey, going for the wrong stop. As if another, subconscious part of me had ideas about what I should be doing.

I had absolutely no interest in King's Fletching, yet I wandered its damp streets for almost an hour, and in the end found myself staring through the window of a sad wool shop, everything half price. I shook my head, telling whoever was in there to go away. They could spend the rest of their lives in King's Fletching if they wanted, wondering if a tangle of beige wool/synthetic mix was worth the money.

I was taking the train home.

***

It wasn't easy to work out what all this meant. I remembered Mother's occasional visits to psychics, and her misplaced belief in astrology, reading "the stars" in the paper every morning and trying to twist the day to fit the generalised nonsense. She would have said that I was being contacted, or even possessed. That I was "sensitive," and some poor soul was trying to get through to me.

I was sure I wasn't sensitive. I was mundane, and I knew it; never a hint of anything strange in my life. The supernatural bored me, and the only thing lurking under the bed was dust — and possibly one of Kenneth's missing socks.

The incidents didn't end there. One week I bought fresh ginger and chillies, and four or five different kinds of spices from the town's only delicatessen. I cooked meals I didn't recognise — I ate them when Kenneth was out and washed them down with pints of cold water or milk to ease the burning. I told myself that it was an experiment, that I could stop at any time. Maybe some part of Marjorie really wanted to try these things, but had never told me before.

And I saw Ressington, from the cardboard cut-out semis to the few alleys which remained of the unremarkable village it had once been. The seventies planners had all but extinguished history as well as nature by pouring concrete over it — here a last set of worn cobbles; there a set of stone gateposts which might once have announced an unimportant manor. The rest was gone.

I only worked a three-day week, and so had plenty of time to indulge whoever wanted to peer at the past. These were compulsions, and yet they weren't. Once, when my back hurt, I felt a tug that wanted me to get out of the house and go wandering, and I resisted.

"Not today," I said to the empty house. "I'm going to take a break, read a book."

The sensation — intrusion — receded.

It seemed like a small victory.

You might think I was going mad, but it didn't feel like that. It was...odd, maybe even disturbing, but not insane. At least, I hoped so. I didn't have much faith in the local doctors.

I went online and read up on psychiatric conditions. There was plenty about multiple personality disorders. I had to check the dictionary a lot, but got through them in the end. They talked about amnesia and a lack of awareness between personality states; about trauma, and certain personalities coming to the fore under stressful conditions.

None of that fitted. Neither Ressington nor my job were stressful, they were simply dull, insignificant. They say moving house is stressful, but I'd left that to Kenneth. One day I was in Northampton, putting lightbulbs into a cardboard box; the next I was here.

And I remembered everything that happened to me when I had these sensations. Each time I could feel a slight flutter under the bone of my forehead, but I was still there — Marjorie was there — not locked away in some dusty corner of my brain. No, none of these medical sites explained what was happening to me. And who wants to go to an actual psychiatrist, if you can even get to see one? It's like admitting in public that you've cracked.

Mind you, I did find a few articles which explained a lot about my late mother. A petty personality, manipulative. That was her.

"You don't want to wear that, Marjorie. It's common."

"Your hair doesn't suit you — you should have it long, like that nice Sally Wright down the road."

"Your father would never have wanted you to work in an office."

All said with a smile, camouflage spread across the mean-minded control which Mother had always sought. Mother had always thought Kenneth to be rather common, as well. Daddy, who died early — probably as a result of Mother's incessant harping on about standards — had been meant for great things on the council. That smile of hers had made me marry Kenneth, despite my own misgivings. Because Mother "didn't think he'd amount to much."

She'd been right about him. Lower middle management, golf on the television, and a few pints down the local every Friday. In Ressington, it was the Victoria, where the other company people drank, a mock-Tudor oasis of nothing in the middle of the estate. We went there, regular as clockwork, and I nursed a sweet sherry while he talked about golf or plastics. Kenneth was a man of minutiae, not of grand (or even large) gestures. His version of love letters was Post-It Notes about double-locking the kitchen window at night and remembering to order more toilet roll. Calendars marked graphically with our few social engagements and cousins' birthdays.

I would have known if Mother was haunting me. She would have walked me to the solicitor's to discuss divorce — and a sizeable settlement...

***

Because I wasn't the sort of person to get alarmed, I didn't let that happen. Instead, I started sorting these experiences into types. There were the food experiments and the little trips, the petty violence, and of course the sex. They all felt different somehow, so I decided to assign names to my visitors. That's what I chose to call them.

Visitors.

Mary was older, set in her ways. I decided she was the one who stared into wool shops, who wanted to toddle around the older parts of the area. She was also the golf watcher, and she felt like a Mary. Annoying, but not threatening.

I chose the name Sandeep for the one who was interested in cooking, in spicy and different foods. I didn't know any Asians, not personally, but I'd heard the name on the television, in one of those dramas about the Raj. I wondered if I was being racist, but it seemed to fit. The goulash was an experiment, and disappointed both of us. I could have told him it would.

Jason was more of a problem. I felt him late at night sometimes, and his were darker whims, which I tried to hold back from when I could. He wanted me to kick random passersby, and scrawl graffiti on walls, to do damage — to people, objects, anything that was in his way.

The one who liked sex was Anita. Perhaps the same age as I was, but adventurous, determined. I couldn't imagine being like that. She surprised Kenneth a few times — once, even, in the kitchen, before I'd even cleared the table. Anita, I could feel, wasn't impressed by his performance in bed — or wherever else she tried to take advantage of him. He didn't know how to handle her, though he tried to rise to the occasion, as they say. I could tell Mary didn't approve, even as my bare buttocks slapped against the polished pine...

After almost two months of this, I no longer thought of the visitors as buried parts of me, as splinters of my own personality. These visitors were not Marjorie. Giving them names had allowed me to discriminate between episodes, and to realise what was happening.

These were other people. Real people.

What that meant, I didn't know, but it did push aside any suggestion that I was crazy. I almost talked to Kenneth about it, but what would have been the point? I was hardly that different when he was around — apart from the sex. Kenneth would have started leaving Post-It Notes so that I didn't forget to iron his trousers, and made poor jokes.

"Mary hasn't defrosted the lamb chops, I see."

He saw nothing beyond his own needs. I let Jason smash the old wardrobe, and all Kenneth could say was that it was about time we had fitted ones — his suits were getting bunched up. And I drove my car to the reservoir and threw a suitcase full of Mother's dreadful clothes into it, but I might have done that anyway, if I'd had the courage. She'd left me Laura Ashley dresses with little lace collars, frumpy nightgowns, and horrid viscose blouses. Neither Anita nor I liked them, so it was good riddance — though Marjorie would have donated them to a charity shop.

The oddest thing was, the visitors couldn't read my thoughts. I was sure they couldn't, because I tried sending some very direct — and quite rude — responses. There was no reaction. You'd think that if you had people in your head, they'd be able to pick up on that.

It was all about sensations, physical feelings, and seeing through my eyes. I didn't have to like what I ate, or be interested in where I went — following the nagging impulses didn't change what I thought about the world around me, not in itself. What I was supposed to do about the situation, I couldn't imagine. I suppose that much of the time I clung to the possibility that it would pass as quickly as it came.

But then there was that one morning, late in April.

Mary — I'm sure it was Mary — had me wandering a cramped, run-down part of town. I didn't like it much. Behind a clutter of light industries, older houses slumped together in poverty, tiles missing and the occasional boarded-up window. Battered rental signs stood at angles; bins overflowed on the edge of the pavements. The sharp sunlight made it so much worse.

I didn't know if Mary had lived around there once, or if she merely fancied a change, but I could feel wool and boiled sweets behind my eyes, urging my body to step across the road and down by a row of shops with their steel shutters down. I passed by a wrecked telephone box, crunching over shards of glass, and there was the boy.

I hadn't noticed him before. He slid around the box and put himself in my path — sallow face, mean little eyes, and a crusted cold sore at one corner of his thin mouth. I'd have thought he was seventeen, eighteen.

He jerked his head towards my handbag.

"I'll have that," he said, broken voice carrying over broken glass.

"I don't think so." The shock of it left me no time to be afraid.

"All right then, bitch." He pulled some sort of heavy craft knife from inside his torn anorak, letting me see him weigh it in his hand, letting me get the message.

Marjorie would have given him the bag. I didn't carry much cash, and credit cards could be cancelled. So whoever lunged forward, grabbing the knife from the kid, wasn't Marjorie...

I was the one, however, who stood over his body afterwards, watching one leg twitch, wondering how you could drive a craft knife so deep into someone's abdomen. It's not like they're meant for stabbing, after all.

"I've been...attacked," I said into my mobile phone. I didn't need to make myself sound shaky. "The corner of...Melton Street, by the shops."

While I waited for the police, one of the visitors borrowed me again, and tore my jacket, ripping some of the buttons away. They bent me down and, taking hold of the boy's filthy left hand, they scratched his fingernail across my face. Painfully.

I could see why. "Evidence of a struggle," as they liked to say on the TV shows.

He wasn't dead. I leant against the telephone box, suitably pale, and let the emergency services come, let them do their thing.

The police were wonderful. Middle-class white woman versus drug-using feral low-life with a history of assault.

"You had no choice, love — he could have really hurt you. And it's not as if he needs more than stitching up. Nothing vital touched."

The way the officer explained everything, I wondered what else the boy would be stitched up for. They took me to the hospital, cleaned the scrapes on my cheek, and made me feel I'd done a good thing.

I hadn't done anything — neither had Mary or Anita. I knew that someone else had taken over and sorted the situation out, and I suspected Jason.

It was getting crowded in here.

***

Kenneth started to stay late at the office; I wandered Ressington doing things which spoke of too many conflicting tastes. Another trip to the delicatessen to buy things I didn't recognise; a week knitting sweaters for no one I knew. I managed to drop a stitch here and there, but the process was inexorable. I was beginning to feel a growing resentment.

When Anita had me accost one of the neighbours and fumble with them behind the azaleas one night, I didn't go willingly. Or — I should be more precise — I let things happen as far as the azaleas, wondering what was coming, but when he started to feel my breasts with one hand and work his zipper with the other, I harnessed indignation.

I resisted.

No.

It was Reggie Gault, after all — fifty, dull, and balding in that patchy way which absolutely did not make you a sex symbol.

Yes, Anita indicated by hauling out his member.

Reggie reached what heights he could all over my best tweed skirt, and I ran back into the house, ashamed.

Angry.

I stayed up that night. Kenneth was at a conference in Guildford — Extruded Plastic Mouldings: The Future — and there was no one to ask why I was still awake. I took out the twee notebook which Mother had given me for my fortieth, tore off the cover with its sickly smiling cats. I made notes.

There were at least four of them, I wrote, and I added short descriptions. Mary, Anita, Jason, Sandeep. They didn't know what I was thinking, but they knew what I was doing. They could see, feel, smell, and taste through me. They...

As the pen moved across the paper, I weakened for a moment. All of this was clearly impossible, and for a moment I thought of brain tumours and strokes, of Kenneth spiking my oolong with those hallucinogens the papers talked about...

No, it was happening. I was a sensible woman, a practical one. It was up to me to handle it, or I might lose my sense of myself.

I might lose Marjorie.

After all, I was the person who had mended the broken toilet three weeks before this business started. I'd sorted out the problem with Jane Ferris's dog, and shown Suzie at work how to use a spreadsheet. Who knew what else I could manage?

I filled the next page of the notebook not with questions, but with short, bullet point sentences. What to do when strangers visit your head. I scribbled down tin foils hats, psychiatric treatment, give in, call the police, and a few other ideas, until I came to the last line.

Fight back.

***

Mary took me to King's Fletching, and I bought the wool she liked. Puce. Puke, I would have called it. In the evening, we knitted, but as we did so, I probed. It wasn't easy. I began to get a feeling of walnut-knuckles and frustration; she liked to knit, but it was getting harder for her. Arthritis. I knew she was interested in the old parts of town, so maybe she couldn't get around as much as she wanted. The more I sought — very carefully —

the more Mary revealed herself. She was at home right now, propped in a large, high-back chair, concentrating; the wallpaper was...roses? No, carnations, pink carnations...

I left it there, not daring to push too hard. I had a feeling of her, and what she looked like now.

When Jason visited, during an argument with Kenneth, I pleaded a migraine and went upstairs. There on the bed I went through the motions of sobbing, but I was visiting Jason while I was doing it. He was in a pub, sat alone with half a bitter. I heard a jukebox, and the awful clang and shriek of pub slot machines. I could smell, through his nostrils, that he hadn't changed for a few days — and he had no idea I was there.

It became easier.

Sandeep wore a hat — no, a turban. A Sikh, then, at least forty years old, working in a hardware store. Although I didn't know his thoughts any better than he knew mine, I could tell that he was very bored with his life.

Anita was a hard one. I could tell it was vital that Anita didn't sense what I was doing — she seemed to be the most powerful of them — and so I was very careful. When she had me molest the postman, I did nothing to alarm her. It alarmed him, mind you. When Reggie Gault tried it on again, I let him kiss me, and while Anita was busy with my tongue, I tested the waters. I followed her influence back, prying. I sensed a "generous" woman, which was my mother's euphemism for overweight; a pantsuit or even a tracksuit, and the feeling of dyed blonde hair — and a reflection in a shop window when I was with her confirmed it. Too many highlights, and too many cheap rings on her fingers.

I left the others alone for a few days, concentrating for Anita. Which turned out to be an interesting move, because it was Anita who discovered the phone number in Kenneth's trouser pocket as she was molesting him, and Anita who smelled the cheap perfume on the piece of paper, saw the little kisses written below the number. She made my lips smile, and she took him there and then in the hallway.

Far away, deep inside me, I was thinking things over.

Now I knew the reason behind Kenneth's late nights at work, and the number of "conferences" he'd been attending recently. It looked as if Anita had given my husband a taste for the carnal side.

I considered discussing the matter with him, but that would only lead to a messy argument, and to be honest, I didn't want to hear his reasons for being unfaithful. I didn't want to listen to his point by point explanations, or protestations that it would never happen again. Nor did I want to consider the unpleasant option of the inevitable divorce which would follow. It's not like anyone would fight to keep Kenneth.

In the end, I simply dealt with it.

On an overcast Sunday morning, while he was seeing to a leaky stretch of guttering, he fell off the ladder. It was very unfortunate that the foot of the ladder slipped at that particular moment, and that the guttering which had concerned me was right over the concrete patio. No prickly but survivable fall into the rose bushes which surrounded most of the house...only the satisfying crack of skull against paving stone.

"Happy now, Mother?" I whispered.

The ambulance came, and the paramedics confirmed what I already knew. I managed a suitable amount of weeping and wailing, drawing on a dreadful romantic film I'd watched for research the day before. Practice makes perfect.

Reggie Gault and the other neighbours were most sympathetic in the week which followed.

"Such a nice man, your Kenneth," said Mrs. Jones. "It's a tragedy."

I took her inside, where I made *masala chai* for us. I quite liked it by now; Mrs. Jones struggled through half a cup, and then excused herself as too upset to stay any longer.

I finished off her *chai* as well, before it was as cold as Kenneth.

***

The visitors stayed out of my head until after the funeral, but they were soon back. It appeared that they couldn't resist it. And every time one of them came, I found out more. I had no distractions now, and could spend my time probing, hunting back along whatever mental or psychic link we had. I filled them out, gathering small details, noting locations, visiting them while they visited me.

I learned that I could hover in any of them, unnoticed. I didn't make them do a thing; I observed their lives and pinned them down, filling my notebooks. I was careful never to open the notebooks — or leave them lying around — when there was any sensation of another presence. At the first, the lightest, pressure or prickle at my forehead, everything was put away.

I was learning a new game.

But it was when I visited Mary one Friday lunchtime, as she went through the centre of town, that I discovered something about the game that I really hadn't expected.

She visited a few shops, poking the merchandise but hardly ever buying anything — in an hour and a half, she managed to pick up one can of cat food and a loaf of white sliced bread. I was getting so bored that I was about to pull away, when she turned to hobble into a pub on the high street, which I hadn't anticipated. The place seemed familiar. Was it... Yes, it was the one I'd seen through Jason a while back. I looked around, using Mary's eyes as subtly as I could — and I saw the three other people waiting at a table in the alcove, an empty chair set to one side.

They were unmistakable — a middle-aged Sikh chap in a cheap brown suit; a pasty-faced young man with oily blonde hair; and a blowsy blonde older than I was.

The shock threw me out of my travelling companion, and I was back at home, shaking.

They knew each other.

The four of them knew each other!

It took me a few days to recover from this realisation, days in which I put up no resistance at all. I let Anita make me flirt with the milkman, and Jason take me to stare into the canal — no idea why. I played along whilst I thought this out.

I suppose I'd come to believe that I was vulnerable, that I was actually "sensitive," as Mother would have said. And being so, I'd been found by whoever there was in the area who had a stronger gift, or whatever you would call it. Like the girl who is picked on at school — children can sense weakness, which is why I never wanted any kids.

But that they were a group, and that they had presumably gossiped about me, laughed at me...that made me angry. It made me feel cheap, and I didn't like that at all.

When I'd come to terms with what I'd discovered, I was more determined than ever. I took books on meditation out of the library, and I took time off work — grief over the loss of Kenneth, I told Human Resources, and they couldn't argue with that.

Human Resources. There was an appropriate phrase. I had been used by Mary, Anita, Jason, and Sandeep (I was sure these were their real names, just as surely as they must know that I was Marjorie), and not paid. A disposable resource.

I spent hours sitting cross-legged in our bedroom — my bedroom now — and I focused, finding each of the four in turn and watching, feeling, intently. They all lived on this side of town, and every four or five days they gathered in this pub to boast about their encounters. It soon became apparent that I wasn't the only one being used — there were two or three others in Ressington who had these same visitors. I must have been a delightful addition, moving here and turning up on their radar.

It took a while to grasp on what to do. My initial idea was to find out who the other victims were and form some sort of support group, or get together and expose the perpetrators, demand they stop. But there was no proof, was there? Nothing to show anyone else — and I had no idea who the other victims were.

Even if I did find these unknown people, the thought of introducing myself and trying to explain what was happening seemed not just daunting, but rather unpleasant. Our shared experience — if it were indeed similar in each case — didn't make us friends. They might not even answer their doors to a mad woman muttering about telepathic control, or whatever I would have called it.

I drank half a bottle of sherry one evening, and decided that I should listen to Mother, just this once.

"There's nothing wrong with ambition, Marjorie."

The following morning, despite a headache from the sherry, I sent my mind to occupy Anita. I found her in bed with a spotty young man — a garage mechanic, by the stained overalls on the floor at her bedside. I slipped inside her after the act, and I made her kick the boy out of bed. I moved her hands to slap him, and her mouth to say a few unmentionable things that would have made me blush to speak. He wouldn't be returning.

And I left, before she could work out what had happened.

The day after, Sandeep was rude to a customer, and almost got the sack; Jason made a very bad job of shoplifting two bottles of cider and got barred from his local off-licence. I wasn't ready for anything grand, but it cheered me up to shift the balance of power.

Mary puzzled me. I almost felt some sympathy for her, until I thought of her uninvited jaunts with my body. Merely as an experiment, I had her knit a scarf in colours which I knew she hated.

I carried on like this for more than a fortnight, secretly hoping that they would start blaming each other. I could tell that their pub meetings were becoming more fractious, though I never heard any of them voice a direct challenge to another.

Feeling bold, I conducted more experiments — and was intrigued by the results.

Marjorie had changed.

It was time that she met her visitors face to face.

***

The King's Head was a scruffy public house, one which Kenneth and the neighbours would have avoided. It served very cheap, tasteless breakfasts — I knew that from visiting Jason — and from the boards outside did a Pensioners' Special on Friday lunchtimes. A stale, oily smell greeted me as I entered the pub lounge, which suggested that the "special" was breakfast fried up again.

There they were, my four, toying with their food and engaged in muted conversation. They didn't look so pleased now, and I hoped that I detected a certain suspicion between them.

"Well, well," I said, pulling up a fifth chair and sitting down at their table. "Isn't this nice — all of us together at last."

They stared at me, dumb.

"I'm Marjorie. " I smiled at the stout Sikh, who had been lifting a forkful of baked beans to his lips. "So sorry to hear about your trouble at work, Sandeep."

Fork and beans clattered to the plate.

Jason was spottier than I'd expected. He glared, squared his shoulders, and leaned forward as if he might lunge towards me at any moment.

"You — you're the one who's been messing with us and—"

"Keep it down, now." I made his body slump, sink back into the chair.

"What the bleedin' hell do you—" Anita found herself pushing a slice of toast into her mouth, cutting off what she had been going to say.

I extended my smile to all of them.

"I don't know how you found out that you could do this, or how you came together. I have no idea how it works, and to be honest, I don't care. You see, I've found something out, thanks to you four, and it's quite exciting, really."

Mary, who from her looks might have had "grandmother" tattooed on her forehead at birth, eyed me, a watery blue gaze.

"What are you going to do, dear? I mean, I know we shouldn't ever have started this, and we shouldn't have interfered with you, but we only borrowed you. We never did any real harm..."

"That's a matter of opinion, isn't it?"

"I saved you from that thug on the street." Jason, sitting next to Mary, was just the blend of aggression and fear which I'd expected from prying into him. "Anyway, if you tell anyone, they'll think you're nuts."

It's strange to find yourself in charge. I wasn't used to it, though I could see it becoming easier. Much easier.

"Saved me? I wouldn't have gone to that place if it wasn't for the four of you. And besides, some of you took more liberties than others."

I stared hard at Anita. I wasn't going to let her speak — sex was bad enough without someone else making you have it.

"But I'm not going to tell anyone. If you want to carry on with your little games, that's fine by me. It makes no difference." My smile returned. "You see, you can't use me anymore."

They tried, there and then — I could feel it — and the result was on their faces. Confusion; worry. I was closed to them. And not only did they have no control over me, they were vulnerable. I don't think they'd ever felt that before.

"You...you could join us," said Sandeep, though he didn't sound like he relished the idea. I think he was feeling cornered, which he was. "We'll tell you who else we...know, and you can share in the—"

"We can explain how it all happened, dear," interrupted Mary.

I laughed. "I told you, I don't need an explanation — that doesn't really matter. And as for joining you, well, why would I bother? You can't use me — but I can use you. I can be you, if you want, and I'm beginning to think that I'm stronger than anyone here. Much stronger."

Jason struggled in his seat, unable to reach across to me.

"There's only one of you," he grunted.

I nodded. "Yes, you're right. And I suppose I could thank you for that — if I felt you mattered anymore."

I spread my mental wings, and let it happen. It had been building inside me, day after day, though it had taken me a while to recognise what had happened to me...

Everyone, every single person in the pub, raised the nearest cup or glass, empty or full, and drank. Some did it without noticing; others seemed slightly puzzled at their actions.

I tasted tea; coffee; port and lemon; watered-down whisky; pale ale; and dregs from the barrel. I held up all those drinks, yet my hands were empty. If I'd wanted, I could have made the entire clientele smash those glasses into their own faces, without me moving an inch.

And only the four people at this table understood.

"Oh dear," said Mary.

***

The oolong is cooling, and I have a ham sandwich prepared for dinner. It won't taste of ham, because three towns away a couple are about to cut into an enormous porterhouse steak they decided to share, accompanied by an expensive red from somewhere in Italy.

You see, it's true that some people are more vulnerable to having visitors than others — but it turns out that a little extra effort can take you a long way. I haven't found anyone yet who can't be used — visited — at some level. No one appears to be immune, if you only make a little effort. I don't bother with the four who started me off — small thinkers, small thoughts. I think Anita's already left town.

Instead, I sit at my little kitchen table, alone, and wait for the first bite of the tender beef, interested to see how it tastes on two tongues at once. When they top up their glasses, I might get to see the name on the bottle. I'll make a note. I'm quite keen on wine these days, with Kenneth's cans of supermarket lager finally out of the fridge.

These two people — friends, partners, or lovers — are mine tonight. Not that I'll stay with them for any bedroom adventures. Dear me, no. I'll be off to somewhere else. To someone else. But for now, they are Marjorie.

Maybe one day, everyone will be Marjorie.

AUTHOR NOTES

"Marjorie Learns to Fly" is one of my rare quintessentially British — or even English — stories, which seeks to do no more than inhabit that ubiquitous

suburban world where a practical madness may be needed to survive. I simply took it a little further. It was written as a tribute to the stories of the late Ronald Chetwynd-Hayes, and exists, in a sense, purely for that last line.

Oklahoma, 1968

WHEN THE CLOWNS turn away, you know not to look. They are our hyenas, ready with their grinding jaws and their maniacal amusement at the world's pain. If they cannot face what comes, you do not want to even glimpse it. I do not want to glimpse it.

But I did. Something came to the carnival that night, and I looked.

***

I don't have a name for the outfit that owns me. We are Mr. Maelstrom's Fun Palace, and the Leman Brothers' Travelling Show. Or White's Circus, in a gentle season when the leaves have no edges and children smile. We were Rousch's Carnival a few years ago. I don't remember further back.

I do remember an early autumn in the mid-sixties, and the abandoned gas station that we found. Eddie's Gas, an imaginative name. The Twinkies in the vending machine were stale, specked with grey when we opened them, but everyone was hungry, and there were crates of flat cherry soda around the back. These was no sign of what had happened to Eddie, but what did we care?

The place had a septic tank into which we could drain the wagons, and under the cracked concrete apron there was still fuel in the underground tank. Jackie Knife found it, fooling around with one of the two rusty pumps and spraying herself in the process. Reynard the fire eater closed in on her when he smelled the octane, but the clowns growled him back.

We'd put on five shows in a row across three towns. Wheels churned and axles creaked as we drove from one dead-eyed, God-fearing place to another, playing to half-crowds only. Weatherford and others had paid, but not in cash. This was a land of preachers, who would stand outside the general store and denounce the carnival before it was dust on the horizon.

Sometimes that helped, the thrill of the forbidden, but mostly it made parents send their kids to their rooms, and teenagers hang around the edge of the fairground, hesitant. A good minister could smell us on the wind.

We were tired, and Eddie's Gas was a relief. No need to lift out the boxes of spanners and wrenches, to struggle with the harsh, stiff canvas which rubbed the skin off your fingers and the palms of your hands. Most of the gear could stay strapped to the wagons, and welcome to it.

"Two, three days," said the boss, counting crumpled bills on a table outside his trailer. "Rest up, get those acts tuned. We'll show the next town what we're made of."

I hoped not. We were made of hunger and malice, of sly deceptions, and I didn't think anyone wanted to see that. I helped Jackie hose herself down, indifferent to her sinews and cold nipples. She knew I didn't jump that way.

"The boss says there'll be a wire up for you in the morning, Rudi," she said, rubbing soap into her shaved groin. "Between those big loblolly pines. He wants you trying those turns again."

I didn't care. I knew that I could handle it. High wire and trapeze were what I did. That and scrubbing canvas. I wouldn't touch mechanicals — the wheel, the carousel, or the Brassbound Oracle. That wasn't my thing.

I dried her back, and wrapped the coarse towel round her shoulders. I was going to ask her if she would hold me that night — I felt the cold, and appreciated another body in my bunk — but there was a different kind of chill on the air. December in October.

"What is it?" She saw me hesitate, sniff the air.

"I don't know."

Over by the boss's table, Dino was muttering. Dino, bush-browed and squat, collected ticket money and disposed of those who never quite left the show. He pointed west, away from the Sixty-Six, and I followed his gesture.

It was barely dusk, and the lights rigged between the trailers threw orange and yellow across the grassland around the gas station. A cable sparked by the boss's trailer; a searchlight, part of my act, stabbed the sky without purpose.

The figure walking towards us through the calf-high grass was almost naked. He was tall, far taller than I was, with a weightlifter's body and a piece of grey cloth wrapped around his hips, hiding little more than his privates. As he came closer, I could make him out more clearly.

There are faces.

Such faces slam into you, stop you in your stride. There's little point in trying to pin down the details — is it a hint of a certain color to the eyes, a hair's breath turn to one corner of the lips? You don't tear a painting apart, rip canvas into shreds, to prove that it is beautiful.

This was the stranger, the striding god, who approached.

I wasn't the only person affected. One of the clowns, who'd been right behind me, gave a shrieking call and a titter. It seemed to be a signal, because all of his kind began to walk away, their backs to the newcomer. Too rapt at the sight before me, I was stupid enough to ignore them.

On the edge of the concrete apron the tall figure paused, and we were four, five foot apart, regarding each other.

"Rudi," he said.

And then he smiled and walked straight past me, towards the boss. I followed, a scuttling figure at the stranger's side. His bare skin was pale, and he smelled of winter.

"Come here to cause trouble?" asked the boss, without looking up. "Or a new recruit. What's your shtick?"

"I wish to watch."

The boss stiffened at the sound of the deep, emotionless voice. He raised his head, tugging at his thick ringlets with one hand.

"We're closed. Resting. Come to the show in Elk City."

"Then I wish to work."

"No openings, sir, no openings." He made to rise from the table and leave.

Dino looked uneasy. "We could hire him, boss. Need plenty of muscle to get the canvas up, and Ernie's got the shakes again—"

The boss scowled hard at Dino. Others were watching. Not the clowns, but Jackie Knife, the roustabouts, a few of the tumblers who did tricks in between acts, and Li-Jung Wei, who had come out of his own trailer to see what was happening.

"I will not leave." The newcomer's words were flat, neither pleading nor threatening. The sun would rise tomorrow; he would be here, among us.

That raised a look from the boss. It was the same look I had seen the night that we suddenly had to find a new Chinaman for the show. Dino had cleared up after that, as well.

"I'll talk to this feller," I said, sliding between the two. My heart was tight, telling me something — it was important that the stranger didn't leave. "Boss, I'll see what he wants, explain to him that—"

"Lemuel. My name is Lemuel."

It seemed like the boss was going to argue, but Li-Jung Wei was near the folding table now, his hands thrust into sleeves of yellow silk. With him came the incense, a sort of deep, smoky perfume that every hippy joss stick wished it could produce.

"Let him be," said Wei. "Heaven watches. This is bad time to make argument."

The boss owned us, worked us, fed us. With whatever we needed. He was fearless, but he was sly enough to balance one darkness against another, to slip between disasters and keep his ringmaster's hat firmly on his head. Li-Jung Wei was the real thing, unlike his predecessor, and what he said mattered, even to the man who had bought him.

"Until Elk City," said the boss.

***

It didn't work out that way. We played Elk City, two shows, and got away from there before anyone asked us about the missing woman in the grey felt hat, or the two flower children who had strayed too close to the Crow-man's trailer. Lemuel was still with us when we hitched up and headed east.

He neither ate nor drank, to anyone's knowledge, though he slept often — and always by the trailer I shared with Jackie. I gave him a pile of blankets; he never used them. Each morning he would be there, almost naked, lying coffin-straight in the shadows.

He would lift and carry, if asked directly. He wasn't asked very often. The clowns would not go near him, and as for the boss, he and Dino paid no attention to the man from the grassland.

He wasn't a man, though.

I sat with him when I could, and talked about anything — the weather, the show, my own act — whilst I drew in the wonder of him. His dark hair was swept back from his face, but otherwise he seemed completely hairless, his skin smooth, perfect. Not simply baby-smooth, like you might get with oils and a good razor, but totally unblemished, too unmarked to be right.

"How did you know what I was called, back then when you walked into the camp?" I had asked him the morning after his arrival.

"I know all your names."

That didn't help. "How so?"

He looked down at me. "Because they are your names."

I sighed. "I have to go practice, run through part of the act." I held out my hand. "Rudi Walker. The Air Walker, they call me."

"Air Walker," he said, and smiled for the second time. His own hand enfolded mine, and I trembled.

After that, Lemuel was there every time I took to the wire, whether under the big top or out on a length of cable run between telegraph poles by the highway. There was never a day I didn't practice. Small and lithe, I was a solo act — no catcher, no safety net.

Where I learned how to do what I did, I couldn't tell you. I have hazy memories of being pulled down from the roof of a city building by Dino — I must have been quite young — and my first meeting with the boss, whose long, ringleted hair had scared me. He was the gypsy who stole you in the night, when he wanted to be, and the kindly old carnival owner who praised the Lord when town elders came to vet our intentions. The boss rarely looked the same two days in a row.

I was a natural, Dino said. They gave me a few beers, admired my wiry limbs, and took me on.

Lemuel understood, when I recounted what history I had.

"We arrive, with purpose." His tone never varied — not like one of those movie robots at the drive-ins, more like someone who didn't really know the language and didn't know what inflection to put on anything.

"So what's yours?" I dared to ask.

"Rudi."

And always that smile when he spoke of me.

***

Dawn in Washita County was like dawn anywhere else. The nearest town was Foss — we'd pulled off the Sixty-Six, and were camped by Turkey Creek. A pick-up rattled past about seven in the morning, but that was it. The roustabouts were roasting a mangled deer carcass dragged from the highway, and a few other things besides. I took a greasy portion and a hunk of cornbread to go, along with a mug of coffee. Lemuel was stretched out behind the trailer, the blankets still folded in a neat heap where I'd left them. It had become a ritual.

"You want some breakfast?" I asked.

He rose to his feet.

"No. The rope is up."

It was, slung between a couple of pines which looked like they would do the job. I ate quickly, and stripped to t-shirt and shorts. No shoes, because this was slack-rope work and easier on the feet. The boss wanted more variety, so we were going to alternate the high-wire with some fancy work — swaying and swinging on a loose rope is nothing like working on a tightrope full of tension.

I wasn't as confident as usual. Jackie Knife gave me a kiss on the cheek, and went to do her own thing — slamming narrow blades into any manner of target. She had nicked a volunteer rube back in Elk City and was still mad with herself. It didn't do to let the clowns see blood — it turned their "strange" into "too strange."

Lemuel's gaze shifted between the big, empty sky and the rope, never quite settling. I clambered one of the pines and let my toes feel the vibrations in the half-inch cable as it swung in the breeze. Sweat and pine resin were on the air, and then so was I, using my weight to bring it under control.

Walking the rope was easy. I gave it ten minutes, testing, and then tried my first cartwheel. I was twenty foot above the crumbling banks of Turkey Creek, and reckoned I could roll without too much damage if I fell. I'd fallen a lot in the early years, and always checked the terrain. We'd had a trapeze act, once, who'd practiced over an overgrown field without looking hard enough. When he went down, he met a plowshare abandoned in the long grass. Messy.

I came down after forty minutes. As usual, Lemuel had observed every move I made. He handed me a towel.

"Why?" I asked.

"To dry yourself."

"No, why are you here at all, with our outfit?"

You weren't supposed to ask that sort of question in carny life. It wasn't done. The traveling shows back then sheltered everything from mental cases to murderers, abused children to physical freaks. Everyone had a past, clutched close to them, but I was high on performance, and forgot myself.

I placed both hands, slick with sweat, on his bare chest. He never sweated; his skin was as cool as ever, like a snake whose thermostat had stuck. "And why do you always watch me when I'm on the rope or wire?"

"I can no longer walk the air."

"You were...a performer, on the wire?"

"I was a stranger to the earth," he said. "Until I died."

And he walked away. I wanted to run after him, and press him on what he meant, but I'd been pushy, impolite, already. The boss might have been interested... No, I abandoned that thought. Instead, I went to the Chinaman's trailer.

A good carny always has a Chinaman. The mystic East, the inscrutable nature of the Oriental mind. Most of them were short-order cooks who'd fallen out with their previous bosses, guys with greasepaint lines and fake Manchu moustaches. They did sleight-of-hand, juggling, or pronounced ambiguous fortunes, that sort of thing.

Li-Jung Wei came from Hong Kong, or *Hēung Góng* as he called it. He was a Chinese national who'd taken a merchant ship to the States. What he sought, or what he had fled, I couldn't say. His act included the old "now you see 'em, now you don't" with various items such as glass globes and coins — except that you really didn't see them in his case. I think that's why the boss was careful around him.

Wei was in the trailer, lounging back on a heap of silk cushions.

"Rudi." He nodded. I would have said he was in his late fifties, maybe.

I didn't sit, though he gestured that I could. I poured out what I knew of Lemuel, what I'd seen, felt, what he had just said.

"I need to know what—"

"Rudi."

I was quiet.

"Change comes for you — with tall man." Wei spread his arms, bringing that scent of ancient oils and balms, of smoke on a hillside.

I had spent most of my life, since Dino found me, with fortune tellers of one kind or another. Crystal balls, lines across a crooked palm, and tarot cards. They said Change; they meant Death.

"So I'm done for."

"No. If you die soon, I tell you. But it is as I said." There was a shadow across Wei's face, like gauze between us. "Heaven watches."

***

East again, and the show outside Clinton went better than usual. Clinton was bored, and there were rumours that the big air force base was to be involved in the bombing in Vietnam. No one was sure if that meant more business for the locals or less. They needed a carnival and we provided. The boss had everyone on their best behaviour, and the main tent was packed, by our standards. He opened with the clowns, which was always a risk.

You won't understand our clowns. The make-up is a relief. Red cheeks and a sad smile, a tangled wig — these are kindnesses which make them tolerable to look upon. Without the greasepaint, they are more than most can bear. But in the ring, seen from a distance with their toot-horns and buckets of jello, they go down well enough. The malice between them seems like exaggerated fun, and always interests some of the more "individual" children. The psychopaths, the suicidal, and the loners, I mean.

Jackie Knife enchanted, more skin in show than sequins, and laid lethal edges around a rube who could hardly stand still. The board spun behind him, and she hit every target on it.

After her, I took to the high-wire, a slender cable under tension this time, and made myself the Air Walker. And I pushed myself a little further than usual — nothing wild, but I wanted to be noticed by one man in particular. I dared a couple of moves I'd not tried in a while, and was pleased with myself, not that there had been much risk in a tent which only reached thirty-five foot at its peak.

When I'd finished, I swayed on the small wooden platform, and saw Lemuel directly below me, at the foot of the pole.

He smiled.

That night I found him by the tents of the roustabouts. They were drunk, cat-calling and boisterous; he stood silent and alone. By the corner of the boss's trailer, a clown stared.

I'd had a few beers with Jackie, and I sidled towards the clown. I would never have done that sober. I think it was one of the females — the baggy outfits made it hard to tell. A sad smile was smeared across the face, and black starbursts surrounded the eyes.

"I jus' don't understand," I said, slurring my words. "What is about my fren', y'know, that gets your lot so...weirded out?"

The clown's eyes widened, and it — she — bowed, the sharp, fluid movement of winter seas. She lifted her hands, imitating the flapping of wings, and pointed at me. Then she turned to where Lemuel stood, and pulled down the corners of her mouth. The cry that she made was loss and falling stars, a cold ache in my chest which did not ease when she tittered and ran into the night.

I shuddered, and went to Lemuel.

"Y'want to walk with me?"

We headed out onto a wasteland of dry grass, grease-stained burger wrappers, and discarded bottles. The cars and pick-ups had gone, and almost all the paying customers with them. One or two would be missed later that night, or in the morning. They would never be found, not by anyone who wasn't part of our outfit. I'd learned to live with that. Every home has its rules, its funny ways...

The lights of Clinton misted the eastern horizon; the rest of the sky was a huge bowl of October stars. I clung to him, letting the warmth of my body drain into his too-smooth skin.

"D'you want to...do stuff?" I waved an arm at a softer mound of grass between some bushes. "Mess around, maybe?" Pulling away, I peeled down my jeans, kicking my sneakers off awkwardly as I did so. As he didn't stop me, I threw my t-shirt to one side as well.

"I was a stranger to the earth."

"Yeah, I remember, but I don't—"

His loincloth fell to the ground.

I didn't throw up, though it was a close one. My striding god had revealed himself.

It wasn't only hair that he was short of. He had no cock, no balls, only a smooth mound between powerful thighs. Jackie Knife shaved down there — I'd helped her plenty of times — but Lemuel didn't even have an opening for...anything.

"A freak," I said, suddenly sobered. I didn't mean it badly — plenty of carny folk preferred the term. Better a talented freak than a rube.

"I am Lemuel." Naked he came to me, whilst I shivered in a pair of yesterday's y-fronts. He held me tight, stroking my tensed shoulder. "To walk on this soil is to be dead. To walk the sky is to live."

He lifted up my chin with one finger.

"I do not wish to remain dead."

***

The boss wanted one more show before we took the whole carnival on a long haul, heading out of Oklahoma altogether. We weren't welcome in Oklahoma City itself, so he chose El Reno, and set up outside the city limits. The roustabouts took to their battered hogs and threw leaflets around all the nearby townships, even slipping into Oklahoma City after dark.

Word was getting around.

I stayed out of the parade through El Reno. I said I was sick. The day after Clinton I'd pressed up to Jackie in her bunk, and wept. Afterwards we tried to do it, and I pressed my lips to her sweet dark skin, tried to see some sinuous Nubian boy on the mattress beneath us. It was a disaster, as usual. In the end I touched her as best I could, until she purred and kissed me on the forehead.

She had no views on Lemuel. If he was some sort of accident of birth, that was fine. If he believed he was something else, whatever, that was fine too.

"You do what gets you through," she sighed, lighting a joint.

By the time I'd recovered my wits, he was asleep behind the trailer, the loincloth back in place. I'd managed to get drunk for the second time that night, dealing with shock by drinking moonshine. I couldn't have put a coherent question together if I'd wanted.

The day after the parade, there was work. I couldn't see Lemuel anywhere around, but I knew he was there. The clowns scuttled and slid between the tents, yipping and growling to each other, the pack separating and then gathering once more.

They were keeping an eye on him.

All through Friday, we struggled with the real big top, which rarely came off its flatbed. Four king poles like ship's masts, and a weight of canvas which needed the entire outfit to haul and peg it into place. It wasn't only crowd capacity — the fire eaters could belch up a stream of flame without risk, and we would be able to rig a proper high-wire.

Exhausted, we slept pretty much where we fell that night.

Our show was to be called the Mandrake Brothers for this performance, so on Saturday the boss and Dino stalked the entrance in identical cream linen suits, Southern "gentlemen." They greeted casual visitors during the day, building up expectations of stylish yet wholesome entertainment to come. Once the ticket money had been paid, it wouldn't matter.

Lemuel stood alone by the Hall of Mirrors, which received eager kids and ejected worried ones. The mirrors in there were too accurate for most people.

"Look, the other day..." I tried to start a conversation with him, but faltered.

"I will be with you tonight. Rudi."

His smile drove out all mistakes, all misjudgments ever. He held out both hands, palms uppermost, and I took hold, gently. For the first time I realized that there were no lines across his palms, no whorls upon his fingertips.

"Tonight," I said, filling the single word with others I couldn't speak.

The carousel, never reliable, had broken down, and as some were called to fix it, I helped — reluctantly — to erect the Brassbound Oracle, that monstrosity of a metal head which whined and swore as we tried to fit the parts together. Sven, one of the fire eaters, insisted that I test it when we were done.

I shoved a dime into its razor-lipped mouth. Brass eyes glowed; gears inside the thing rattled and churned. At last it spat out a grubby ivory-colored card, which I grabbed.

"'A long life, many children; a voyage across the sea,'" I read out, shoving it in my pocket. "Yeah, the thing's working."

I left Sven and the others to give the Oracle a final polish. They didn't need to know what had really been printed on the card.

With dusk came the traffic. Farm trucks and motorcycles, pedal bikes and an old bus, co-opted to bring kids from a local orphanage. Beaten-up Chevrolets, and Fords which might have rolled off the first production line. It looked like we would have a full house. Sweat, candyfloss, and anticipation were on the air, whipped around the carnival by a light breeze. Children pointed at the fire eaters lighting the evening, or danced and laughed around the stilt-man as he walked among them. If they'd known he had no stilts, and that each step was agony, they would have probably done the same.

I sat out the early parts of the show. Watching just made me nervous. From outside the big top, I heard the usual rounds of applause, the "Oohs" and "Aahs," and the other sounds which accompanied our shows — the confused reactions which followed some of the more unusual acts. Four or five times I saw fathers hustling their families out of the tent, white-faced, and at one point a group of women came out together and were violently sick behind the Oracle. Might have been the candyfloss; might have been the "Wonders of the Ocean" act. That usually turned a few stomachs.

Eight in the evening, and I went in for Jackie's set. She was on form, and her routine went down well. I think that she and I were probably the only straight acts the boss had ever taken on — we were exactly what we seemed, a woman who threw knives and a man who walked the high-wire.

As she left the spotlight to genuine applause, I saw a cage being dragged forward.

"The boss isn't going to..."

Jackie's smile was sour. "He is."

I wasn't happy. The high-wire was always the last act, and I preferred to follow Jackie or Li-Jung Wei. The boss was going for the Crow-man.

The cage was light steel, ten foot across, ten foot high, with narrow bars which gave you a clear view of the interior. The audience shared a whisper of anticipation as the Crow-man came out into the ring. He was rake-thin, clad in a tattered robe of midnight silk and feathers, and he walked into the open cage. An assistant in a black leotard clanged the cage door shut and locked it from the outside.

The roustabouts, hidden behind straw bales, hammered on tin drums; the audience waited.

A night-black bird appeared in one corner of the cage. Absence, and then presence. Even I didn't know how it was done. It cawed, angry, and the Crow-man flinched.

Another crow, on the opposite side, and another, near his feet. Their eyes glinted, and they became a chorus of wrath, each eye glinting with their displeasure at the man in the middle of the cage. They flew at him, beak and claw, and he shrieked, trying to shield his face with his skinny arms. As more appeared, it became impossible to see the Crow-man himself, only a whirlwind of angry birds and sometimes — if you were standing close — a spray of bright blood...

The drums rattled, and were silent.

Inside the cage, only the birds remained. Their anger sated, they strutted around on the dirt floor and let themselves be picked up and taken out by more of the sinuous assistants.

The people on the benches around me wondered, waited...

"The Crow-man!" cried out the boss, top hat and tailcoat in the entrance to the ring, and there was the man from the cage, thinner than before, stroking the runnels of blood on his sunken cheeks, and laughing. The laughter of pain and hysteria, of someone broken.

The crowd had been seeded, as always. Our own people started the applause, to be joined first by a few rubes who'd been given a dollar, and then by the bewildered townsfolk. The boss made the Crow-man bow, twice, and then had him hustled away.

This timing of acts was showmanship. The clowns tumbled across the ring, as innocent as they could be, for a few moments, and the boss stepped forward to announce the Air Walker, using the usual superlatives and exaggerations. A good old-fashioned tightrope act which would come as a relief to the rubes watching, make them feel good again.

Under the big top, with four huge king poles and so much more room, I had a slack rope at thirty-five foot off the ring, and a wire tensed at fifty. The spotlights followed me throughout. You don't need to hear the details of my performance. I started with the same moves as I'd used at Clinton, but I was high on the wire and high on the thought of Lemuel. He was down there, standing at the opposite side of the ring from the boss, his head up, his eyes tracing each step and leap I made. I wanted to excel — had to excel.

"Tonight," I whispered.

My leotard was tight to every lean muscle, and I danced on nothing. One cartwheel and another, the wire cutting into the palms of my hands; a high leap and a landing which set the wire thrumming like a crowd of its own. Applause, and more applause. I was more off the wire than on it, abandoning the simple balancing acts for adulation.

I was the Air Walker. I truly felt I was close to it, so close that I forgot it was an act. I ran on the slack rope, swaying it and building, building, until at last I leaped up for the high-wire. And I made a perfect landing, balanced on the balls of both feet...

You don't forget the sound of a cable snapping. It's a gunshot, shattering the air around it, and then the high whine of the loose wire as it thrashes and flails through nothing. People in the audience shrieked — one end of the wire slashed down across the stalls and up again, bloody when it rose, and I, I hung there for that half-second where momentum and gravity fought over me.

I fell.

It shouldn't take long to fall fifty, sixty feet, and maybe it didn't. But I saw everything. A small girl, staggering down an aisle with her head cut open; two drunks fighting to make one of the exits. A slim, mousy-haired women screaming as she stood over the body of another.

And the clowns, our dark hyenas, trying to hold Lemuel back from the ring. He forced through them, beat at them with his fists, and still they grabbed at his naked body, the loincloth torn loose. Their smiling mouths formed shrill cries of alarm; their sad mouths echoed with the anger of animals. They tried to overwhelm him with numbers but were thrown aside, damaged merchandise from a toy shop you never wanted to visit.

I fell, and though the hard-packed earth awaited me, it did not have me. Lemuel's great arms found me first.

"Rudi," he said, and smiled.

***

When I came round, the big top was almost empty, except for Jackie and that same female clown — I thought. The clown touched my arm, whined, and ran for the comfort of her pack, but Jackie stayed. She told me I'd been out for almost an hour. The boss had refused to call a doctor.

"Lemuel? Where is he?" I asked, struggling with bone-dry lips. She poured a little whiskey into my mouth.

"He...he disappeared."

"He left?" I tried to get up.

"No." She squatted by my side, feeling along my legs to see if anything was broken. "Rudi, he disappeared. He caught you — at least, it looked as if he caught you — and it was like..."

"Like what?" I managed to prop myself on my elbows.

Jackie closed her eyes. "You fell into him, like the two of you had...I don't know. You fell INTO him. The clowns tried to pull you free, but it was too late, and then he was...he just wasn't there."

She couldn't give me anything better than that to work with.

No one could.

If Heaven was watching that night outside El Reno, I don't know what it saw. I learned what had happened, though, because Li-Jung Wei showed me the next morning. After I begged him, he helped me to the Hall of Mirrors, which had been left up along with the smaller tents for any Sunday afternoon idlers. A few extra dollars while the crew wrestled the big top down and packed it away.

He helped me because I felt bruised and heavy, and because I had trouble walking. There was more of me, somehow — my arms and legs were cumbersome in a way I had never known. Wei pushed the tent flap to one side and led me in.

When I saw my reflection in the first mirror, I understood.

"He took it from me," I said, staring at the image before me. It was Rudi, but Rudi stripped of all grace, of all ability. Uncoordinated lumps of muscle and bone; a talentless thing. Those mirror-lips were clumsy and damp. "He stole everything I was — everything I could do."

Behind my reflection, smoke swirled and formed faces. Li-Jung Wei.

"Yes," said the scented pillar of darkness.

I took a last look at the broken thing in the glass, and asked Wei to take me back to my trailer.

***

I can't use the wire anymore. I can barely walk a straight line on the ground. The sight of the high king pole platforms from which I used to leap fills me with unbearable fear. Ladders are impossible, and even steep sets of stairs bother me. I cling to any support I can find.

Jackie made the carny keep me. She put a knife through Dino's earlobe, and luckily the boss laughed at that. We still share the trailer, like brother and sister. She's much stronger than I am, and I'm not talking about muscle. I work the mechanicals to earn my share — my fingers don't seem to have been affected. I wrench nuts from rusting bolts, and mutter to the Brassbound Oracle, late in the night.

That card it gave me?

'You will fall. Another will rise."

It wasn't a metaphor.

No one can tell me what Lemuel was. Not a man, certainly, and not one of the freaks. He had stripped me of more than my abilities on the wire. Do carny folk like us have souls? I don't know.

Sometimes, when the wind is high and the lighting cables between the trailers thrum with its strength, I stare into the black sky which grips us, and I shudder. Whilst others sleep, I am alone with the tittering, growling sounds of the pack which circles our camp, watching. Protecting us?

In those moments, I can almost understand the language of clowns.

AUTHOR NOTES

I have absolutely no idea what "Wires" means or represents. I hate heights, and haven't been to a circus or similar performance since I was around twelve. Nor do I have any phobia of clowns, so perhaps I have been deeply unfair to them here. Tough on clowns; tough on the causes of clowns.

TODAY IS WEDNESDAY.

Carl does not remember the day before Wednesday; he never does, but he's used to that. He accepts it as part of life. He doesn't understand the shape of clouds, either, or the importance of television; aeroplanes — and the concept of flight — baffle him. There are strange blanks in his mind, for no obvious reason. And he has not been able to taste salt since he was a child.

Such odd deficiencies seem to worry his sister Marion at times, but she is very patient. And she knows that he doesn't like to dwell on them.

"I'm just going out for a while, Carl," she says after dinner.

"I know. You have your coat on, the blue one with the white toggles. It's pretty."

"Will you be all right?"

"I'll be fine."

He will be. The house he shares with Marion is his panic room — locks on the locks, the windows triple-glazed with strengthened glass, and every door set in a steel frame. His sister never brings anyone home, because the house freaks them out.

As does Carl.

When Marion has left, and all is secure, he returns to the room he has had since he was a child. It is where he first formed himself, crouched beneath the blankets, legs drawn up, a spot of urine on his flannel pyjamas. Where he made himself the heart of this place.

The telephone rings downstairs; he ignores it. The last time he answered, he said things to a saleswoman which so terrified her that she spoke to her supervisor, who spoke to others. The police called round, but fortunately his sister was at home. She explained that Carl was no threat, that he had...an illness.

She was lying.

Illnesses, syndromes, and conditions are inherited, contracted, or formed by nature, when vital mechanisms fail. Nothing has failed in Carl.

He made this happen.

* * *

Today is Thursday.

The abyss that lies between Monday and Wednesday was formed when he was eight years old. His sister says that he is different on that day of the week, that he smiles; he talks of playing outside, of repainting his room.

She says that she likes him even more on Tuesdays.

But today is Thursday.

"We're in our thirties, Carl," she says as she hangs up her coat, back from work as always at exactly 7 p.m. Which is 1900 hours for her. One of her only protests is to have digital clocks throughout the house, a challenge to the great long-case clock at the foot of the stairs and the old mantel clock in his room. All of her timepieces show twenty-four-hour time.

"We are," he agrees, laying the table for supper. He stares at the salt cellar for a moment, then places it next to her setting.

"I was talking to Patrick, my supervisor. He says there's a position at head office, with good pay. Promotion."

Carl knows that head office is far away, outside London.

"You ought to go for it."

The kettle clicks, steam misting the kitchen window. Marion starts to cry, then drives it back and makes them both a cup of tea. After supper, she says she has a headache, kisses him on the cheek, and goes up to her bedroom.

When they were both twelve, she slipped into his bed and touched him in the night. Their aunt was asleep, cradled by alcohol and exhaustion.

He understood what Marion was doing, but not why. Or why she was crying then, as well.

"Because you're scary. Because I want my brother," she said. "I thought maybe, maybe if I made you feel nice, you'd love me."

She took her hand away, and he held her thin, trembling body close to his.

"I do love you," he said.
Which was true.

***

Today is Friday.

There are things he has to do. He strokes the long-case clock, the grandfather clock, and feels it sigh under decades of wax and polish. It is pressed hard against the wall, opposite the foot of the stairs, as if frightened.

"I understand," says Carl. "But everything's fine. You are safe."

Most of the furniture in the house is dark and heavy like this — polished walnut, oak, and rosewood; mahogany sideboards, armoires, and cabinets which crouch like slumbering beasts in almost every room.

Marion sleeps with stripped pine and soft, airy fabrics, trying to forget the rest of the house.

He often feels that his life began with the long-case clock. He used to imagine that it was alive, the slow tock a heartbeat which matched his own. Awake in the nights, an awkward but unremarkable child, he let himself — made himself — draw in the rhythm, the reliable rhythm it provided. If he had nightmares, he lay in bed and listened for its steady *thunk*, knowing that it was there for him.

It was wound once a week, every Friday afternoon, and he was always waiting, insisting that his father hurry.

"Four of the clock," his father would laugh, and pulling on a chain, raised the first of the massive brass weights. Four chains, four weights, hanging in the chest of the long-case, almost obscuring the pendulum-heart. Pull, release, pull.

Close the chest, hide the heart.

All is well.

Sometimes he dreamed that he had friends, tiny friends who lived between the weights, that if the clock was not wound in time, they would scramble to do it themselves, a last resort...but in the end, he accepted that he had no friends except Marion.

Better that way.

***

Today is Saturday.

He helps his sister with vacuum and dusters, rubs polish into smooth mahogany. She wants to meet someone. When he asks who it is, she snaps, "Anyone!" but then reddens.

"I'm sorry," she offers. "I thought I'd go to the library. The girl behind the counter is nice, very helpful, and sometimes we have a coffee."

"Of course. You should enjoy yourself."

The immersion heater is unreliable, and he saves the hot water for her bath, so that she can be clean and pretty. He can cope with showering cold, if it makes her happy.

"The green coat," he says, and she smiles.

"You'll be—"

"I'll be fine."

He doesn't mind her going out; it leaves him to enjoy the quiet, just for a while.

It is ten years now since Aunt Mary, who had looked after them since they were eight, died of throat cancer. She smoked too much, but Carl liked the way that the tobacco smoke darkened the house, formed a tar-veneer of age and stability on the ceilings and the furniture. He liked the way that Aunt Mary agreed to live in this house, and not take him and Marion away somewhere new.

Many people had wanted them to move, to be moved. One doctor said that they would never really deal with their past if they stayed there; another suggested that this was exactly how they were dealing with it.

Aunt Mary hated doctors, and ignored them all. She asked Carl what he wanted to do.

"To stay here forever."

Marion agreed with him, naturally.

Only when Carl asked for his bedroom door to have a lock, or when he refused to use the front door, did his aunt hesitate, but he always won those arguments.

And his aunt was patient, though not as patient as Marion. She waited a long time, his sister said, for the slow drip of fluids into her veins, the slice of friendly knives, but in the end, she had to leave.

Carl and Marion had just turned eighteen.

The house was theirs.

***

Today is Sunday.

His parents used to go to church every Sunday morning, though Carl found it boring. And that stopped, of course.

He did play outside at the weekends, when he was much younger — he remembers the scuff of knee on concrete and the smell of damp grass as if they were sweet violets, found pressed in an old book.

He doesn't do that anymore.

They say he is agoraphobic — but they say he is many things. Every year or so Marion asks him to consider therapy, to have tests.

"For what?" he asks, puzzled.

She never quite answers that question, but he agrees to the tests. Every year or so, as long as they do them in the house and he doesn't have to go out. No one from the hospital wants to visit anymore, so Marion takes blood samples, and he fills in questionnaires. He doesn't like her to be unhappy.

He was homeschooled in his teens, and so was Marion.

Everybody preferred it that way.

* * *

Today is Monday.

Carl used to dislike Mondays, when Marion starts her working week, but that has changed. In the early days, he couldn't bear for her to leave him for more than an hour or so. She says that maybe he's improving.

He doesn't really think about it.

He understands that there is a world outside. He will not let it into the house, but he knows it is there. It just doesn't interest him. He has everything he wants, especially Marion, right here.

The window-cleaner avoids this address; the postal workers know the situation. The letterbox has been enlarged, and they thrust everything through, backing away immediately. No one ever comes to the door to ask if they want their drive mended, or their chimneys re-pointed.

The word has been out for years.

If Carl feels intruded upon, if his safe spaces are violated, it does not go well.

The incident with the saleswoman on the telephone was not an isolated one. Marion pays a certain sum every month, by standing order, to the neighbours who moved away suddenly the previous summer. The money covers prescriptions and physiotherapy for the husband who called round to complain about the state of the garden. Marion was out at the time, and...

The authorities were not involved, because the couple were too shocked, too scared, to call them.

***

And today...today is Tuesday.

This is a normal day. In the afternoon Carl plays with his toys, and wonders if he'll be invited to Susie Denton's birthday party tomorrow. She'll be nine, one year older than him, and yes, she is a bit annoying, but there'll be trifle, and he already has a gift, a notebook with flowers that his mother picked up. Maybe he'll give her some crayons as well.

He likes his dinner — beef burgers and chips (he leaves the peas) — but his father mocks him for putting so much salt on his food.

"Blood pressure, Carl. I'll explain when you're older."

He watches the television for a while, and takes comics up to his room, promising not to read too late. His mother says she'll be up in a moment to check on him. He reads a lot of comics, especially those about flying and outer space. Carl sees animals and sailing ships in the clouds, and he dreams of being a pilot. Or an astronaut. He would like to burst through the clouds, to escape to new and strange spaces...

The house has a whiff of the chip-pan about it, overlaying the smell of his father's aftershave. They're going out, and have decided not to take the children, so a babysitter will be here soon. She will watch him and Marion for a couple of hours. Carl is defiant, pouring salt into an already salted packet of crisps and forcing them down as he reads.

The doorbell rings; his father shouts that the babysitter is here, and leaves the bathroom with his tie at an angle, only half-knotted, to go down and open the front door.

There must be a Western on the television in the sitting room, because Carl hears gunshots, screams and curses. It is hard to concentrate on his comic, so he gets out of bed and goes to the top of the stairs, peering down into the hallway.

There is blood on the grandfather clock. The blood isn't right. It doesn't look like the scarlet fluid they use in the films. It gleams dark, sullen. His father lies on the hall carpet, motionless, and there is more blood across the floor.

His mother is kneeling in the doorway to the sitting room. Carl can see the blank grey screen in the room behind her. The television is no longer on after all.

"No, no!" his mother shrieks, holding Marion in her arms. Marion is copying their father, and is also still, silent.

A man with a shotgun and a brown balaclava stands by the open front door. This stranger fires, and Carl's mother topples, her chest a mess of red. The man looks up, hearing the boy stumble on the top step.

"Jesus, another one? They were supposed to be out. Find the safe, Frank, see what they've got. And kick that kid out of the way."

Another man — black balaclava this time, and stained camouflage jacket — starts up the stairs. He too has a shotgun, but it is very short.

Carl has a vague, almost indifferent affection for his parents, but he loves his sister very much. And the old long-case clock. The strangers have spoiled both of these.

Which upsets him. It upsets him a lot.

The house trembles.

Carl has the weight of old dark furniture in his mind, the slow *thunk* of a pendulum. He has everything that means being seven years old and safe, secure, in this one place. Beneath the gloss of his everyday life is another life, far more basic.

He is a creature of the brainstem, though he does not know the term.

"You made my clock bleed," says Carl.

The man in the black balaclava staggers, dropping his shotgun. He grabs the balustrade, and as he does so his abdomen bursts open, revealing blood-filled weights and the soft, misshapen pendulum of his heart. Blood sprays the wallpaper; flaps of skin and muscle peel away like wet newspaper, and purple coils of intestine slither down the stairs.

"You hurt my big sister."

Brown Balaclava sees his companion fall, and curses. He uses very rude words.

Carl stares at him. Stares hard.

Perhaps Brown Balaclava knows that he is not going to walk away from here. He tears at his headgear, but already his veins are fat, writhing spaghetti at his wrists and neck; a minute later, most of the man decorates the inside of the front door. No one will be able to use the wire letter-catcher for some time.

Carl does not like the feel of the stairs — his bare feet touch wet things, slick and warm, but he makes himself go down. He does not like it that part of Marion's head is not there; he can see a folded grey mass, open to the air, and fragments of yellow-white bone. Her small chest is not rising and falling like it usually does.

"I don't want you to go," he says.

And so she doesn't.

Later, the babysitter arrives. She screams, again, again, and again. Many more adults come, and wonder at the small, tow-headed boy, holding his staring, unmarked sister. They ask him questions, but he ignores them, hoping he can go back up to his bedroom.

He has not finished his comic.

***

Today is Wednesday.

"I won't go for that promotion," says Marion, putting down her briefcase. "God knows, I work hard enough already, so I don't need more responsibility. And besides, whatever you say, I couldn't leave you to manage on your own."

"If you're sure." Carl nods and lays out the supper plates.

"Did you get the hospital results?"

"They came this morning." He pushes aside the slim cream envelope. It contains the usual news. "Everything's just as it should be — you needn't worry."

She stares at the salt cellar. "I wasn't worried, not exactly. I just...wondered."

Carl starts to dish out the pasta he's cooked. The slick strands are coated with a crimson sauce, and remind him of something; whatever it is, it's buried too deep for him to reach.

After they've eaten, he squeezes her hand, and goes up to his room.

Only two more days, and then he must wind the long-case clock...

AUTHOR NOTES

The converted farmhouse we once lived in had a huge grandfather clock at the bottom of the stairs, and I was convinced for some years that it had goblins inside it. I was also convinced there were goblins in the even more massive armoire upstairs. And maybe goblins in the broken-down chalk building in the garden. That's quite a lot of goblins – I think maybe I read Christina Rosetti at too young an age...

New York, 1974

NINE. The damaged reel. The celluloid has deteriorated, and for some minutes, all that is seen is a blur of figures. An unknown man mutters to the camera. At 0:07:32, the face of Emile Casson can be seen staring at the camera. His collar is loose, and he appears angry. This image continues to the end of the reel.

I can read lips. My aunt knows this, and she insists that I write down what I can determine from Nine for the twentieth time, as if it might have changed. It hasn't, obviously. The unknown man, from what I can get, is still complaining about being in the same room as "That Goddamn Frog." There is nothing useful on the reel, and she wheels herself out of the projection room without any sign of appreciation.

Another fruitless morning.

In the afternoon, while she sleeps, I go through the mail from the clipping agencies. An obituary covers the death of a man who once met the director Emile Casson, in California. That would be in nineteen twenty-one, during Casson's abortive attempt to get into the West Coast industry. I already have that documented. The Frenchman's peripheral involvement in the Communist Movement, and his virtual blacklisting during the Red Scare, put paid to any plans. He came back to New York after three days.

The last envelope is from the Burgess Agency. It contains a photograph, and a handwritten note.

Mrs. Westercott, this may interest you.

The photograph shows a group of men in dark suits, and a wreath of lilies in the background. A funeral, or a wake. I turn it over, and see names scrawled in pale ink. Teddy Fleming, Joseph Karowski, Manny Goldschein, and a couple I can't read.

Joseph Karowski.

Oh my God.

The same hand that produced the accompanying note has added another line.

After Cedric Gibbons' funeral. Hollywood?

I should wake her up and tell her that we have a lead. Instead, I pour myself a sherry and wait, trying not to think of anything. I go to the shelves and consult the indexed notebooks which hold the most relevant details. Austin Cedric Gibbons, Art Director for MGM, eleven-time Oscar winner. Way out of Casson or Karowski's league; died the twenty-sixth of July, nineteen sixty. After the funeral. This must have been a show of respect — or a circle of old gossips gathering to remember imagined glories.

Karowski is second from the left, going to fat but looking well-enough. His suit looks more expensive than the others. Fleming has his hand on Karowski's shoulder. Steadying, consoling, trying to remind him that the bar is open. I can't tell.

I've never heard of Goldschein, but I find Teddy Fleming. Theodore James Fleming. Worked as a sound recordist with Gibbons, but based on the East Coast. He seems to have been around in the industry through the crucial period in the mid-twenties. Another one who has passed — he died in sixty-five, in New York, from liver failure. Maybe he came across Casson at some point.

Aunt Marian is asleep in her room. A powdered satin face mask keeps the sharp autumn light from her eyes, her gown spreading out on the bed around her, shroud-like. Wish fulfillment on my part. Phoning the Burgess Agency, I get connected to a Henry Fields.

"We're interested," I say. "We need more about Teddy Fleming — addresses, relatives, that sort of thing. We'll pay double rates."

"I know someone, but they're not agency." His voice goes low for that part.

"Have them invoice Mrs. Westercott. She'll pay."

It's the one thing she does with any grace, opening her checkbook and giving that showy flourish of her pen.

I say nothing about the photograph to Aunt Marian. She has me watch Thirty-Two again, to try and identify the chinaware in the film. I check catalogs as she watches me from by the window, crouched in her wheelchair with her eyes half-closed. After an hour she snaps something derogatory, and wheels herself into the projection room that Uncle Hal had built in the sixties. Perhaps she'll fall asleep in there.

I had liked Uncle Hal. Forty years in accounting, much of it for the Astoria Studio, four blocks away. His reward was to fall off a stepladder whilst hanging a framed photograph in this room. A shattered hip and a broken rib, followed by terminal pneumonia. He left behind a palatial Astoria flat, with a library and projection room, a large collection of memorabilia and film reels, and a widow. No kids, thank God. The thought of someone having to be her son or daughter appalls me.

And he left money. Real money. I imagine him in his office, manipulating figures, making those slight alterations which would ensure that Marian May Westercott could live the rest of her life without worrying. A gesture of accountancy, not of love.

Uncle Hal should be the one who haunts the flat. Instead, we have only Casson...

FOURTEEN. *The man is in his sixties or seventies, and perhaps Italian – or Spanish. Mediterranean, certainly. His face is crumpled, as if a great hand has squeezed it until the eyes, nose, and mouth almost folded into each other. He speaks to the camera, showing a few rotting teeth. The table before him is spread with what seem to be small playing cards, laid out in a cruciform pattern. A caption appears: Tarocco Siciliano. We do not know what he is saying, but he points to various parts of the spread in turn. It seems he is asked a question, because he looks up suddenly and spits to one side. The film ends.*

I turn over a page in my notebook, and scrawl "Miseria" again and again. It's the one card with which I am very familiar. The Chained Beggar.

When the postman calls on the third morning, he has a package for me. Miss Julia Williams. Confidential. Inside are names and addresses, newspaper clippings and brief notes. I spread them out on my desk. *Tarocco Siciliano.*

A photograph of Teddy Fleming with a woman too young to be his wife. Daughter, hopefully. Clippings about his work as a sound recordist, and yes, a mention of Karowski and him working together on a shelved series of cartoons. The production company went bust. It was for the Astoria Studio, and places them both in New York in nineteen twenty-six. The same time as Karowski was working for Casson.

I settle on a single name and address. Diane Margut, nee Fleming.

Aunt Marian is with her "personal physician." By which I mean a doctor who will take as much crap as my aunt wants to deliver, as long as his check arrives every month. Her liver rebels at the evening cocktails on which she insists, and her sight is failing.

I make a quiet phone call, and then shout through to the bedroom.

"I need to go to the drugstore, and the stationers."

A disinterested mutter gives me permission.

Uncle Hal's old Windsor sedan gets me to Diane Margut's place in Suffolk County. A solid suburban house. The woman sounded wary on the phone, but I explained that I was researching the history of the Astoria Studio. She agreed to see me.

Diane Margut is a slightly harassed looking blonde in her forties. She offers me a coffee, and we sit down in a very beige lounge.

"You say you're interested in my father, Miss Williams?" She sounds very Brooklyn.

"In the scene and the background. Particularly around the mid-twenties."

She sips her coffee, weighing me up. I mention some names, showing off my credentials.

"He must have known people like Goldschein and Karowski, as well." I throw this in whilst looking out the window, making it the lightest of comments.

When I look back, she's frowning.

"You're not a reporter, are you?"

I squint as if surprised by the question. "Do I look like one?" I know that I look like a dowdy academic, getting middle-aged too early. Tweed and pearls; unpolished shoes; hair the color of mud, pushed back behind my glasses. No one has ever called me an attractive woman.

She looks awkward, and refills my coffee from the pot without asking.

"Sorry. It's just that Mr. Karowski... He and dad were friends. I call him Uncle Joe. He left the business in the forties, became very private. Still is."

My bone china cup is in danger of hitting the floor.

"I didn't realize he was alive."

"Oh, yes. I had a birthday card from him a few months ago."

Time for a careful change of subject. We drift on to how her father got on with some of the names, whether or not he kept up his interest in film, and so on. After an hour, I put down my notebook and smile, thanking Diane for her time. As we head for the door, I pause.

"I don't suppose it would be possible to have a few words with Mr. Karowski? It would be great to add that personal feel to the book. You know how dry these things can get." A conspiratorial smile this time — the woman under the academic.

"He's not on the phone. I guess I could send him a note, ask him."

I give her one of my aunt's cards, with my name written on it. "That would be terrific."

We part on agreeable terms, and I drive back the long way, an aimless route.

Emile Casson worked with very few people. Very few would work with him. Two names came up in what records we had. Louie Trent, a left-leaning drunkard who worked as his cameraman. Joseph Karowski, a young Italian-Pole, his sound recordist when Casson experimented with sound systems, around nineteen twenty-five, twenty-six.

Trent, like most of his contemporaries, was dead. "Uncle Joe" was not.

ELEVEN. *An empty can, marked "Colored children from East Harlem, June 1925."*

At dinner, I tell my aunt that I may have a link to Karowski. I don't tell her that he's alive. She spits out a mouthful of roast chicken and cranes her head forward. Her thin, wrinkled neck reminds me of what we are eating.

"Why didn't you tell me earlier?" she snaps.

"It may not work out." I sound defensive. "The doctor says you're not meant to get unnecessarily excited."

She subsides, keen to be seen as the put-upon invalid.

"Um." After a few minutes of noisy chewing, she puts knife and fork down. "I want to hear it again, tonight."

Uncle Hal left a lot of recordings, picked up during his times at the studios. Some are real collectors' items, going back to the early Vitaphone disks. The sixteen-inch monsters each hold eleven minutes of sound, the same length as a standard film reel. If you have the accompanying film, and can get them synchronized, you can live the twenties again. Should you want to.

I don't.

I take out the tape marked "Casson Thirty-Seven." We never play the original disk, which is lodged in a safe deposit box at her bank. She's been obsessed with it since Uncle Hal died. Obsessed with Casson's work. No one has ever found the accompanying Film Thirty-Seven, or any of the other records which would have meshed with the film reels.

The original label on the record says "Casson 37. 8/9. L'homme italien. Sound – J L Karowski." The cans holding Casson's silent film reels are marked in a similar manner, except that they end with "Camera – L Trent" instead. Sometimes there's no title, but there is always a number.

FOURTEEN. *The man with the cards makes gestures of protest. He takes the table by its edge and tips it over, the small, strangely painted cards fluttering in every direction. Some form of zoom lens is used – the focus blurs, and then holds on a single card on the floor. Miseria.*

Uncle Hal found the record and the films in a disused warehouse next to the Astoria Studio lot, back in nineteen forty-one. The industry had pretty much moved to California. The Army were taking the place over, and my uncle, along with a few friends, searched the corners for anything which had been missed. When I was older, Uncle Hal showed me what they'd found.

Seven films, all one reel long except for Seventeen and Thirty-Seven.

"See, Julia? They wouldn't let Casson on the lot proper, but he had friends. They let him use Warehouse H, and borrow equipment."

I was looking at a heap of dented film canisters, a wrecked projector, and other detritus.

"Why's this stuff important?" I asked. This was the early sixties. I was twenty-seven, unmarried, jobless, and studying French. I thought I was going to travel.

"Well, maybe it isn't. But it's all that remains of his work."

"So who was this Casson — some kind of misunderstood genius?"

"Just another oddball director. He wasn't the only one back then. Fought in the First World War, then came over here. Got himself pegged as a socialist agitator. The studios didn't like that."

"What happened to him?"

"Died in Spain. The Red Brigades."

"Huh."

We played pitch and catch the same day. He should have lived; she should have fallen from the stepladder. That's the thought in my head as she wheels her dry, shrunken body into the projection room. I place the record on the turntable.

The first four minutes and eleven seconds consist mostly of background hiss. The sound booth would have been well away from the camera, and the audio cable shielded, but you can hear the whir of the camera. Then a light voice, accented, which must be Casson...

Ce sera bientôt. It will be soon.

The microphone knocks against a hard surface.

He breathes badly. Oui, montre moi. Yes, show me.

At 0:6:27, a chair or something similar scrapes the floor. The next words are spoken very close to the microphone.

Au-dessus ou au-dessous, vous êtes entre les deux. Voyez-vous maintenant? Y a-t-il une clarté? Above or below, you are in between. Do you see now? Is there clarity?

A low moan, and the sound of ragged breathing. Another voice, very American, says "Hey, Emile, leave the guy some dignity, for Chrissake." I've always assumed that must be Louie Trent, on the camera.

Tais-toi, il essaie de parler. Shut up, he's trying to speak. *Mon Dieu, he sweats!*

Footsteps — someone pacing.

Attends, c'est le moment?

There is a harsh gargle, like someone trying to cough up sputum or some obstacle, and...

Eleven minutes have passed. The record ends.

I could do a better transcription if I had the film, so I could at least see Casson's lips move. But there is no film Thirty-Seven. The record implies there are nine whole reels missing, destroyed, thrown away. Uncle Hal searched for Casson memorabilia until the pneumonia set in — a hobby, like looking for a stamp whose only real value is its rarity.

Aunt Marian turned that hobby into her life. At first I thought that her search for Casson and his work might be some sort of displaced grieving for my uncle. It wasn't. As the months ground by, I began to see only an aging woman with no friends and nothing better to do. I don't think anyone else really cares about an unsuccessful Commie film director who never amounted to anything.

"Did you catch anything new, Julia?"

"I have the Karowski rumors to follow."

She peers at me. She is a projector herself, her petty malice and selfishness playing over every wall of this place.

"I suppose so," she says, pursing wrinkled lips which gleam with Vaseline. I wonder that she has enough spittle in her to swallow.

We part. At least I have a private room. As I read some pathetic romance magazine, I decide to have Henry Fields look further into the Fleming connection. It will cost, but I'm not the one who's paying.

I've no reason to doubt Fleming's daughter. Karowski is alive, and the way she spoke of him, he's not that far away.

The only man who knows what the record represents.

THIRTY-TWO. *A young woman takes a cup and saucer from someone off camera (you see a man's hand, part of his sleeve). Casson sits by her, taking notes. He is a thin man in his thirties, a sliver of France with dark, slicked-back hair. The china is ornately decorated with Zodiacal signs. She tips the cup to let the last few drops of a dark liquid fall onto the ground, and then peers into the cup. She frowns, and shows it to the camera. Tea leaves.*

We know that Casson was ejected from the Manhattan Psychiatric Center in nineteen twenty-five. He was filming on some kind of terminal ward there, ostensibly a film for teaching purposes. Something he did disturbed the doctors. Other than that, he failed to make the news, and his work was never shown in cinemas. Hardly surprising, if the surviving reels are typical.

He had no wife, no children, no known relatives. Inquiries in France have never yielded anything. But now I have some American leads, at least. The next week brings reports via Mr. Fields. Vague stories of sound recordists drinking together in the fifties, in East Harlem. A third man seems to have been part of the scene, but he died in nineteen sixty-one. Marco Fracassi. He had a music shop, which also repaired gramophones, off East 112th Street. The shop is still going, so I need to pay a visit.

I drive along 2nd Avenue and park outside what looks like a respectable enough hotel, tipping the doorman to keep an eye on the Windsor. I'm modestly dressed and I have a small revolver in my bag — Uncle Hal taught me to shoot. I'm no good at it, but can make plenty of noise.

They call it Italian Harlem, but the Greeks are moving in all over the place. I can't see much difference between them. Black men by open windows eye me briefly, but apparently see nothing of interest. The old brownstones merge with derelict lots, a criss-cross pattern of neglect, and I pass a Windsor much like my uncle's, its tires gone and the hood sprung. Two Italian kids are playing on it, jumping up and down. They shout abuse at me, and laugh.

The Fracassi place is easy to find. Inside, it's dust and memories — racks of sheet music, a few instruments, and a bench heaped with broken recording equipment. A man in his forties is jabbing a screwdriver at the innards of a tape recorder. He looks up.

"Sì? *Posso aiutarti?*"

"Do you speak English?" My Italian's not bad, but it would be easier this way.

He puts the screwdriver down. "Yes, of course."

I can't imagine any pretense to use. "I'm looking into early sound recordists, the men who worked around the Astoria Studio. I understand your father knew some of them." I pull out a copy of the photograph of Karowski and Fleming.

He takes it, and peers at it over his glasses.

"Sì. Teddy. He came here, and the other. Joe?"

"Joseph Karowski."

He nods and holds out his hand. "Cesare Fracassi. Marco's son."

"Julia Williams."

He takes me into the back room. A sink, a gas ring with a stove-top espresso maker, three chairs, and a pile of magazines. They're not music magazines. He covers them with his shop-coat in a swift, practiced movement.

Over espresso, he tells me about the fifties. There were four or five enthusiasts who would gather at the shop and then go drinking. Karowski was the odd one out. He didn't drink much, and there was talk. When I asked what kind of talk, he hesitated. I laid a twenty-dollar bill on the unoccupied chair.

Cesare Fracassi has heard of Casson. Karowski's association with Casson was not in his favor, but Fleming had spoken up for his friend.

"What was so bad about Casson?"

"Only talk, you know. He had this thing — he asked questions, took people to film."

"He paid them?"

"Sì, but my father said they did not want to go back, ever. Always it was Fortuna, fate, what was in the cards, he wanted to know. Zingari matters — the stars, the cards, the tea leaves..."

"Zingari? Gypsies?"

"Anyone who spoke of the future."

"Why?"

An expressive shrug. "And, signora, there was a death, my father once said. At the studio..."

I walk back to the car, struggling with a strange feeling. That single photograph from the agency has yielded more than the last six month's work. This is not my obsession, it's hers. Eighteen months of working for my aunt has improved my bank balance, but dulled any real interest in film. She has that effect. Yet the last few days I have felt almost...excited.

TWENTY-NINE. Casson sits and stares at the camera for 11 minutes. His eyes are wide, the pupils dilated. His hands are on his knees, motionless, and he blinks very little. His expression is intense. There is no indication of his purpose in the exercise.

Diane Margut telephones. "Uncle Joe" will see me. I can go, no one else, and the address must be kept confidential. Otherwise, the meeting is off. The address is only a few blocks away from the Fracassis.

My aunt wheels herself into the room as the conversation ends.

"What was that?"

I place the phone down.

"That lead I was telling you about. Someone who knew Joseph Karowski vaguely. I could leave it, of course..."

"You must go," she says. "I won't have corners cut, you know that, Julia."

She looks like Casson in Twenty-Nine, apart from the tic in her left cheek. I am her camera.

"Of course, Aunt Marian."

SEVENTEEN. Two reels, clearly shot in sequence. The set is featureless — a corner of a warehouse or other abandoned commercial building. A tall, barefooted Black woman, one eye milky (cataract?), shakes her head and draws items from an old carpet bag, long fingers folding various things into a piece of cloth. This takes some time. She ties the cloth up into the form of a bag, drips something onto it from a small bottle, and holds it up towards the camera. In the second reel, she stands there and speaks. Her lips say this: "You won't find it. It ain't meant, and it sure ain't right." Then she walks out of shot.

The sharp September wind reminds me of Aunt Marian's tongue, cutting with an indiscriminate malice. I drive west through the city in a sealed, finned coffin, over-eager to get answers.

Karowski lives in a brownstone spackled with bird droppings and graffiti. There are eight name slots by the buzzer, but only one has anything written on it. Esposito. Apparently that's the one. The lobby inside is in disrepair. There's an elevator, though, and it works.

The elevator opens onto a corridor painted in relaxing greens. Two doors, neither marked with a name. The door to my right is slightly open, and I go for that one.

"Miss Williams." The voice is low, almost rumbling.

I twist round and see a man to my left. He's lost some of the weight, and gained almost fifteen years, but it's Joseph Karowski. I hold out my hand, but he waves it away, and shows me into what would once have been the other apartment on this floor. It is a treasure house. Racks of film reels in their original cans; shelves stacked with the sort of books Uncle Hal collected; old movie equipment, gleaming. A row of cinema seats has been bolted to the floor in front of a large screen. The seats look like originals from the early days.

"You kept up your interest," I say, impressed.

"In film, yes. Do sit down."

I edge my way into one of the seats, feeling the old plush under me. He stays on his feet, helped by a cane.

"This is about Emile Casson, isn't it?" He should have been in the movies, with that voice. "I know he's an obsession with your aunt, Mrs. Westercott, and I can't imagine you've sought me out to hear my stories of the film industry."

"They're all dead, Mr. Karowski. Everyone we can find who knew Casson even slightly."

"We get old."

"I didn't mean that, in itself, was strange. But, well...he was, wasn't he? The man himself."

The old man looks up at the ceiling, which is tiled with some sort of soundproofing. "Strange? What have you seen of his work?"

I pass him a list of the films Uncle Hal salvaged. He reads it, nods.

"I thought he'd destroyed Twenty-Nine. And you're better off missing out on Eleven. That was the first one I worked on with him. We tried to use sound-on-film, but it didn't come out well. Emile became angry with the children—"

"He abused them?"

"He shouted a lot, and asked them questions. Inappropriate questions."

"You mean, about sex?"

"About death, and what they thought it would be like. I kept away for a while after that. Went back around Seventeen. No sound, but Louie Trent and I were two of the only people who would work with him. I did everything else." His shoulders sag. "Hell, I was in my early twenties. Emile had dough — we didn't." He sits on the end of the row, stretches out one leg, wincing. "So your aunt wants to know if she can fill in the gaps, I guess."

"That," I agree, "and more about the man."

"He burned most of his own work. Your uncle must have found a trash pile which everyone missed. Which one was it set your aunt on the trail?"

"It wasn't a film. It was this."

I reach into my shoulder bag, and hold out the copied tape of Casson Thirty-Seven — Reel Eight. Karowski takes it from me. From the look on his face, he gains a few years, loses a few heartbeats.

"It was your work," I remind him.

"Yeah. The last film we made. We had the sound almost right, level and synchronization. I'd rigged up a series of pulleys, and..." He stops, and turns the record over in liver-spotted hands. "You've listened to it."

"We don't know what it means, or what was on the other eight records."

"You shouldn't even have this one. There was a runner — Jerry. He didn't just work for Emile. He did odd jobs everywhere around the studios." He paused. "I guess... Yeah, he must have picked up one of the masters, assumed it should go to the plant to be dealt with. He wasn't bright. When it came back, he'd have left it in the warehouse."

"What was Film Thirty-Seven, Mr. Karowski?"

"Nothing, to most people. You have to know the history. Emile was, well, disturbed. He died in nineteen seventeen, you know?"

I don't know what my expression says at that point, but the old man laughs.

"He wasn't a frikkin' zombie, no. I mean he died for a couple of minutes, in a field hospital during the war. After that, he had this thing, this idea that he needed to see what was coming, why he was still here. He wanted purpose."

"And that was what his films were about?"

"Yeah. I missed the early days, but he'd done them all — spiritualists, astrologers, so-called psychics, fortune tellers—"

"The tarot."

"Uh-huh. They say he even had some kind of hoodoo lady, in to be filmed."

"Seventeen," I confirm.

"That's the one." He eases his leg, which clearly pains him. "Then he got this idea that dying people saw more than they said, that they had some kind of insight."

"Manhattan Psychiatric Center."

"That was around the time I joined him again. He wanted me to lug gear into this hospital ward, and record what these dying joes had to say. It was a mess, cables and lunatics, attendants yelling — we couldn't get a decent sound level. One of them knocked the camera over, Louie got mad, Emile got mad. We were chucked out."

"So he was difficult to work with."

The smile on his face is unreadable. "Yeah, you could say. Always looking for something he couldn't find. But jeez, did I learn a lot in that job." He frowns. "I don't want this out there. I'll buy what your aunt's got, and burn the lot. I'll give her a helluva price."

"She won't sell."

"Then say you found Joe Karowski, but he's lost his marbles."

What will I do if there is no Casson to trace, no endless cataloging and rummaging? No clipping agencies, no bored relatives. And no call to watch reel after reel, again and again. I ask him if I can have a drink, and he limps off. He brings back two stiff whiskeys. It's raw, burning my throat, but it's good. Better than my aunt's sweet, sickly sherry.

"Tell me what Thirty-Seven was. Then I'll decide. Is that fair?"

"Nothing's fair. But you seem on the level, and hell, you came this far. You want to see it?"

"What?" I choke whiskey back into the tumbler.

For a moment Joe Karowski is twenty-two or twenty-three years old, excited by his turntables, cables, and cutting heads.

"I kept the last reel of Thirty-Seven, the one after your record. No sound, like I said. Only thing I have left of Emile's."

"Yes. I mean yes, I want to see it."

He turns off most of the lights, and messes with a projector. For ten minutes he's a shadow, shuffling around the place in the half-dark. Used to this, I suppose. His cane taps against the hardwood floor. Tap, tap, as I finish my whiskey.

TWENTY-EIGHT. *A group of people sit around a polished wooden table. The lights are very low. There are three men and five women. They're all smartly dressed. At one end of the table a woman in her fifties, wearing some sort of elaborate turban, throws back her head, and her mouth opens. Something white and diaphanous begins to trail from her lips. Casson steps into the scene, agitated – angry? He pulls at the white matter, and flings it to the floor...*

Karowski is by the projector, fitting a reel of film in there. "There was an old Italian guy who was dying. He lived not that far from Marco Fracassi, who—"

"I've met his son."

"Yeah, well, the son wouldn't know this bit."

"I'm sorry. Go on."

"So Emile has this idea. The dying guy has a daughter who doesn't think much of him, and they have no money. Zilch. Emile pays her so as he can film her father, Roberto something. Get this — Emile wanted to film the man dying. The actual moment. This Roberto doesn't know the time of day, even who he is; the daughter doesn't care. Louie says he'll operate the camera, but he doesn't like it."

"You took the man to the set in Warehouse H."

"We did. Emile says he's going to ask Roberto questions at the very end. It's like the Manhattan all over again, but controlled."

"That's...grotesque."

"Yeah. It was. Three of us, waiting, on a locked set. October nineteen twenty-six."

"What happened?"

"We did nothing for the first day, except keep the guy clean, and give him water. Emile gave him morphine if he seemed to be in pain, but not enough to knock him out..." He falters. "You can judge as much as you want. I don't suppose I've more than a year or two left in me. There was a Joe Karowski there, but I don't think I know him anymore."

"It's all right," I say softly.

He mutters something I don't catch, and starts the film.

THIRTY-SEVEN. *The same set as Seventeen. The table used in Twenty-Eight can be seen shoved up against the back wall. It has what look like medical supplies on it. And a plate of sandwiches, one of them half-eaten. In the center of the scene is a pallet bed. The bed's occupant is hard to look at. A man, clearly old even before he developed whatever disease or condition reduced him to this gnarled, distorted figure.*

"We shot seven reels with nothing much on them." Karowski clears his throat. "When Louie started on the eighth, things changed."

"That's the one on the record."

"Yeah. Emile was agitated. He paced a lot, and kept going to Roberto's side. He started asking questions. You can't hear most of them over the camera. He was whispering in the old guy's ear."

THIRTY-SEVEN. *Casson enters the frame. He has a cup of water, which he puts to the man's lips. The water runs down and soaks the bed linen. Casson leans close, and seems to be speaking, but we can't see his lips. The figure on the bed has some kind of minor spasm, a clawed hand clutching the sheets. Casson is trembling. He takes hold of one thin shoulder, only the back of his head visible.*

"Louie started swearing, saying he'd had enough. Emile kept muttering 'When?' and 'What do you see?' Over and over. I said we should give the guy another blast of morphine, let him go quietly, but Emile wasn't listening. Instead he pulls out this knife..."

THIRTY-SEVEN. *The man on the bed – Roberto – stiffens. Casson is still leaning over him, blocking some of our view. The man's forehead glistens with sweat. His eyes, crusted around the lids, are very dark. The lens blurs and then focuses again, much closer to the dying man's face. Suddenly the man's eyes widen. His lips move, forming short sentences... and Casson moves back, disappearing from shot. As he does, we see the wound in Roberto's upper chest, the dark pulse of blood which runs from it... End of reel.*

I realize that I am shaking.

"He killed him. Casson killed him."

"Yes," says Karowski, his voice flat. "The guy was finished anyway, but Casson stuck him, to get his take."

"Those words, before the Italian dies—"

"I didn't get them on record. Louie grabbed what he could, disks and reels, and stormed off, cursing." He shudders. "I was too thrown to interfere. Of course, he forgot that the last reel was still in the camera. And he missed the master for your disk, I guess."

"Casson?"

"Emile was in a corner, staring into nothing. He didn't want to talk about it. Later, he helped me dump the body in the river."

"And after that?"

"The next day, he checked out of his hotel and as far as I know, he left the country. I never heard from him again. I 'borrowed' some of the sound gear for myself, and got out of there. You know the rest."

He switches the lights back on, and refills our glasses. We have a cigarette, and look at each other.

"I read lips," I say.

He shrugs, drawing on his cigarette, and then his eyes widen.

"So you..."

"I need to see it once more. Just once more."

He's unhappy about that, but he obliges. Afterwards he takes me through to a modest lounge, where he can sit on a sofa with his bad leg up. He wants to ask, but he doesn't want to. We sit in silence for three or four minutes.

"Okay," he says, straightening up. "Tell me."

"He talks about France — something about lost days, and a woman's name — Marguerite? He says 'Spain.' Then he says 'Madrid.' And, I think, 'March nine, nineteen thirty-seven.'"

Karowski looks angry. "You're playing me."

"No, honestly."

"It's Madrid. But you knew that, right?"

"No. I mean, I'm not even sure what I'm saying." The initial shock of what I've just seen has addled my brain, but things start to click. "Casson died in nineteen thirty-seven, didn't he? That's a bit weird. I read he died at Guadalajara, with some International Brigade."

It was Casson's work that interested my aunt, not his end.

"Guadalajara's outside Madrid." Krakowski's voice is dull, a shocked rumble. "Emile was on the way to the front there, against the Italian fascists. He was shot in the chest by a sniper on the outskirts of the city, early on the ninth of March."

And now we both know.

Casson heard the date of his own death from the man he killed.

The old man and I have little more to say to each other. A record led me here, whipped on by an old woman with too much money and nothing better to do.

I stand up, and shake his hand. This time he takes it, trembling with a question.

"Forget it all," I tell him. My decision's been made. "Mrs. Westercott will hear that Joseph Karowski remembers nothing. Film Thirty-Seven was nonsense, a failed film by a failed director."

"Thank you."

I find my own way out. On the street, kids are trashing a burnt-out Studebaker. I don't plan to visit East Harlem again. Back at the car, the same doorman grins at me. He has very blue, very Nordic eyes.

"I scored what I needed," I tell him, and drive away.

Aunt Marian will learn that the past is a dead end. And I don't imagine that her future holds a lot. I see her lying back on those lace-edged pillows for the last time, cheeks sunken and blue, disapproving of death like she disapproves of everything else. I should be horrified by what I've learned today, or full of more pointless questions. But as I drive home, I realize that I'm not.

I feel released.

As I turn the car towards Astoria, I wonder what my aunt will have to say in her final moments, what presentiments she might glimpse. There are many sharp knives in the apartment kitchen, the sort of knives that a panicked burglar might grab...

I think I might like to be there at her end.

To read her lips.

AUTHOR NOTES

For those who like the small intersections of various fictions, the reels in Can Seventeen include a brief appearance by Mamma Lucy, the old Black conjure-woman who features far more prominently in a series of my tales concerning her long walk across the Eastern States during the 1920s. And Mamma Lucy, well-

versed in both psychology and root-work, would not approve of what Emile Casson was attempting.

on myths

some roots unearthed, and cunning remembered

a farewell to worms

IN THE DARK.

In the filthy, sweat-slick, lice-infested dark.

There is the Saw.

It is rust, and blood, and spatters of other idle fluids. It is very large, because what it cuts is even larger, and it shrieks as it bites through something which surely can't exist. Its skewed edge tears at the grain, making clumps of pale, disordered dust and resin from a perfect tree.

Into the quiet order of xylem and phloem, it brings its toothy chaos.

And I am pig-sick of the bloody thing.

The Marinakis family have left a colander out, as usual. It sits on the doorstep, and already one of my more ambitious brothers squats by it, counting the holes. Others might congratulate him on being able to get to five or six (skipping the number three, the holy number, of course) before he loses track. I slap him on the side of the head.

"It doesn't matter," I say. "It's for draining vegetables. Who cares how many holes there are? You don't even eat vegetables."

There's no point talking to him. He's a traditionalist. He whines and goes back to his obsessional counting.

"One, two, the bad word, four, five... One, two..."

He'll be at it until dawn, wasting the whole night. Which is pretty much why the colander is there, to distract idiots like him. That, and the fires kept burning in every hearth, and the wooden bowls of water which hold crosses wrapped with sprigs of basil. Let's all mess with the poor goat-legs, and stop them doing their mischief.

I'm not interested in mischief, only in this particular town.

Not that it's much of a town — more of an industrial village, about thirty miles from Thessalonika. Psariosta, it's called. Fishbone. It certainly sticks in my throat every time. It stinks of fertilizer from the agro-chemical plant, which replaced the shady groves of almonds a few years ago. People across Greece used to burn foul-smelling shoes in their hearths at Christmas, to keep my sort away. They don't need to do that in Psariosta.

As usual, I'd scrambled up through the sullen earth along with the others on the twenty-fifth of December. It would have been nice to emerge on a cool evening and breathe in the sweet, thyme-scented air of some lonely mountainside, or stand next to the surging, wine-dark sea (as they say) and listen to the waves. To relax a bit.

But I had made a vow, by Pan's dangling testicles, that things would be different this time.

So it's Psariosta again. And I have to get it right. Me. Do you think I can rely on my shaggy brethren to contribute their cunning? There are mutton joints in Psariosta with more sense than they have. No, this requires my genius.

Twelve days in which to change the world.

***

I knew a professor at the university in Patras, years ago. He was a jolly fellow, full of goodwill, and had made it his life's work to rehabilitate us, to distinguish between us *kallikantzaroi* and the bloody satyrs who get all the press. "The little tricksters in the earth," he called us, and told of how we were a myth which was symbolic of mockery and jest, more to do with drunken orgies than anything evil.

Bollocks to that, I say. Not that I mind getting drunk, but if there's one thing that keeps me going, it's being malevolent...

What was I talking about? Psariosta.

I've had my eye on Lukas Marinakis for a while. Born on a Saturday, and a very useful Saturday for my purposes — within the Twelve Days of Christmas, and thus close to our domain. Mrs. Marinakis shouldn't have opened a second bottle of *retsina* on that steamy March night.

What is different about this fine specimen of Greek manhood, with his tight, curly black hair and his hazel eyes? Good question. Due to the date of his birth, not only is Lukas one of the few people able to see a *kallikantzaros* properly, he also has serious potential to become one.

Which makes him very special indeed.

His grandmother, who I suspect of being a bit too smart, did the usual stuff at his birth. She tied him up in straw and rubbed him with garlic cloves, so no snatching from the crib, then. However, they hadn't thought that whilst you can keep the *kallikantzaros* from the man, you can't keep the man from the *kallikantzaros*. Lukas was always curious about the Twelve Days.

When he was ten years old, he tried to talk to one of my lot. A really cold Christmas, and the boy picked someone who couldn't even count to two. A saw-monkey, the lowest of the admittedly low already. I spotted them in the alley behind a restaurant, where my dim brother had a hoof caught in a catering-size can of plum tomatoes, and I watched to see how it went.

"You look funny," said the boy, as he watched the antics.

"Funny" was an interesting way of putting it. This five-foot, black-skinned creature with donkey's ears, horns like a goat, and a mass of shaggy fur from the waist down, was hopping around in the alley and swearing.

The boy wasn't at all alarmed, though. I sauntered over, pulled the tomato can free, and kicked my brother up the rear, sending him on his way.

"Hello, little pink fellow," I said.

He stared at me, clearly noting that I was somewhat more humanoid, and certainly more handsome, than the alley's previous occupant. I pride myself that I always comb the sawdust out of my fur and keep my horns in good condition. My tail has a stylish swish, and I'm considered a bit of a looker down below. That's not entirely an advantage when you're surrounded by thousands of desperate *kallikantzaroi*, but my smarts keep me mostly "off the prong," thank Pan. Not that I'm prejudiced, mind you, but have you seen my brothers? They make the most flea-bitten satyr look like Apollo's chosen.

"Hello." He pushed his right forefinger up a dripping nostril. "What are you?"

"I'm not a what, I'm a who. Philodoxos." We *kallikantzaroi* don't often have names, so I do, just to be awkward. I chose it myself.

"Oh. Got any sweets?"

I rummaged in the fur on my left leg and tugged out a few lemon-drops. I remembered sitting on them by accident whilst trying to burn down a local sweet-shop earlier that evening. He picked some of the hair off and sucked on one.

I smiled. "You have a gift, dear child."

"What, lemon-drops?"

"No, I mean a real gift. You can see me and my brothers. You were marked by your birth, which makes you very special."

"Oh. Thanks."

At which point he simply turned round and wandered off. I couldn't believe it. I nearly shouted after the snotty little bugger, but already the old brain cells were churning.

The boy had potential.

In the dark.

An ax bites deep, it is true, but after six, seven blows, it sticks within the fleshy wood, a mess of iron and ooze. The tree is dotted with abandoned axes, offerings to futility.

So the Saw is our God.

Five hundred or more on this end; five hundred or less on the other. All hauling, pulling, or pushing, until the fleas in our fur have drowned in our sweat. Our shoulders pop, and our sinews tear from their bony anchors. Blind eyes, bulging eyes. Hands like crude clay accidents; fingers that are slender and goat-nail tipped. Bodies that loom, and those barely more substantial than a dryad's spittle. The Brothers-in-the-Earth are not easy on the eyes.

We are not a happy people.

That, I think, is why we were given stupidity.

You can do a lot of planning when you have to spend fifty weeks of the year trying to cut down an enormous, mythical tree. I say mythical, but it feels real enough when you ride the Saw. The storytellers call it the Tree of Life, and claim that it holds the world up, keeps everything in its place. It certainly keeps the *kallikantzaroi* in their place. It binds us to a task which is utterly futile, down there in the squalid depths around its trunk.

Only for the Twelve Days of Christmas are we released from the dark, and to do what? To be a minor nuisance, and a cautionary story which children don't believe anymore. We can't go out in the daylight, even then. And when we trudge back down into the dark, what has happened? Oh look, the Tree has healed itself, and we have to start all over again.

Makes you think that Sisyphos has it easy.

Makes you sick.

As does the sight of a Greek town at Christmas. Apart from the colanders and the blazing hearths, the place looks like the Orthodox Church, driving a donkey cart, has crashed into an American shopping mall. A neon Santa vies with icons of St. Basileios and St. Nikolaos, patron of sailors, for pre-eminence, and half the angels are jammed next to Coca-Cola ads. No one knows what the fuck to believe.

I mean, look down that street. A troop of children in procession. Their faces gleam as they hold out little painted wooden boats to show passersby. Some have toy drums, which they beat with the enthusiasm of the tone-deaf; others hammer on triangles and sing. Yes, they sing as well — the *kalanta*, seasonal carols whose main value is to increase the share price of paracetamol manufacturers.

These boys wear trainers, have been shoved out of the house to get them off their Grand Maim/Slaughter video games, and want to know if they're getting film merchandise for Christmas. The only thing that they like about the church is the funny black hats, which make good targets for their air-rifles.

Peh!

***

Lukas Marinakis was born with a twisted foot — nothing serious, but enough that he has to wear corrective footwear to stop him limping like a drunken fisherman, fresh from a night on the cuttlefish boats. It's a typical mark of one touched by the Twelve Days. I didn't notice it when I first saw him, so maybe I'm not as smart as I think I am.

I like to think ahead. You never know what might come in handy, years, even centuries, down the line. After I spotted the foot, every Christmas I whispered in the local children's ears at night. "Hopfoot, Goat-boy, Reject," I whispered. "That Marinakis kid, he's not like you."

It worked quite well, and by the time he was fifteen, most of the kids were well-versed in the art of picking on the odd one out. They didn't need a lot of encouragement, frankly.

I had sown the seeds of Discord (or Eris, as we knew her).

On Lukas' sixteenth birthday I stole a half bottle of *ouzo*, and left it by the back door of that same restaurant where I'd first met him. He was working there as a pot-washer, outside of school hours. And occasionally inside them. When he came out for a smoke later that night, he looked around; seeing no one in the alley, he picked up the bottle and took a swig.

Three more swigs, and I slipped into sight.

"Oh, it's you." He sounded morose. "Philo-wotsit."

"Philodoxis."

He offered me the bottle, and I joined him. The smell of fried fish wafted from inside the restaurant, making my stomach rumble. You don't get much choice down below, clustered around the Tree. We don't exactly have spice racks or cupboards full of delicacies. We have a lot of damp things which crawl around your hooves and go squish. Earthworms are prized, and let's just say that if you find a rotting frog, you keep it to yourself and eat very quickly.

"Not busy?" I asked.

"Pretty dead in there."

"So you're having it easy. What's the problem?"

A subtle blend of *ouzo* and my charm brought out his tale of woe. Neither girlfriend nor boyfriend — no one to admire his swelling manhood — and a lot of hassle from the other kids. He was bright enough to be hurt by their jibes, not quite bright enough to have any crushing rejoinders immediately to hand.

I flicked my tail. "Maybe some of them should be taught a lesson..."

"What do you mean?"

"Well..."

It was that easy to drag him in.

I had nine nights left in which to play, and so that Christmas a number of teenagers in Psariosta had unfortunate accidents.

Funny, that.

Eleni, a pretty blonde from Lukas' street, had a revulsion to my friend's bare foot, which she'd seen at a swimming competition. On the twenty-eighth of December, she awoke from a heavily drugged sleep to find some of her toenails missing. Pulled out, to be more precise.

She was quite a screamer.

The same night, Niko, a boy who prided himself on his physique, found himself being taken for a canter by kin of mine — a suitably massive and lumpen-brained *kallikantzaros* only too happy to cause trouble. Astride the boy's shoulders, the fellow rode him almost to cock's crow. Niko wouldn't be competing in anything physical for a year or two.

Or for variety, there was...but we won't dwell on Ioannis, a particularly obnoxious boy. He left Psariosta quite quickly the next day, not even waiting for St. Basileios to knock on his door. Shame.

"I'll be around again," I said to Lukas before I went back down into the dark. "Next year."

He smiled.

He knew what I'd been up to, and he smiled.

I liked him.

***

When Lukas was eighteen, I dropped a reproduction statue of Pallas Athena, bless Her, on one man's head, and helped another to appear drunk and naked in the town square, with a sign saying "Stavros Lykopodes sleeps with goats."

There was talk, and some remembered the number of Christmas incidents two years before. There was also an increase in the number of locals professing renewed faith in the church, but these things happen.

The following February, Mr. Stavros Lykopodes, the hiring manager for Psariosta Agro-Chemicals, selected Lukas for a trainee management position, rather than the other two young men who would have been candidates. Had the first not been on a head trauma ward in a Thessaloniki hospital, and the second in disgrace following that drunken incident with the sign.

I kept myself under control for a while after that. I made cheese go moldy, froze wash basins, and almost bored my own tail off, but it would be worth it. For twelve nights every year, I talked to Lukas Marinakis. I suggested things; I listened. I told him of the dark, and he filled me in on certain aspects of the modern world. When he got bored, I told him tales of the Old Gods, and drew him in deeper. Last Christmas, all my ideas came together, and I was ready for this year.

I had only to leave Lukas to set things up.

In the dark.

In the ordure-filled, endless dark.

We work the Saw.

Crooked figures huddle, gasp for breath and claw at their own hides, frantic with vermin. Leaping figures laugh, their sanity gone after centuries at the Saw, lost in dreams of a falling Tree and warm oblivion. No longer can they tell when one year ends, another begins.

I do my part, but my dreams are different.

Counting out the days on my blisters, I look forward to the Twelve Days, and the plan...

Lukas Marinakis is twenty-one years old today. His family have half-memories — the colander proves that. And there is that typically irritating grandmother who keeps fragments of the old stories alive, who insists on precautions. She gets some of them wrong, and her dentures, when she has them in, make it hard to work out what she is saying. Greek is not a good language for the dentally challenged. But I have the feeling that she knows about us, somehow.

"*Ochi!*" she snaps when Lukas' father accidentally tips over a bowl of basil and holy water. "No, no no..." I thought about dropping a roof tile on her head last Christmas, but I got distracted by a chance to curdle all the milk next door. I said earlier that I wasn't interested in minor mischief, but it must be genetic. None of us can resist an opening like that.

The old woman's not important, though. This is my moment, and here I am outside Psariosta, with snow tickling the land. The snow has softened some of the stink from the factory, and makes the place look almost seasonal.

There are no sleighs or jolly fat men in sight. Nor beaming Orthodox saints. Instead, I have gathered those Brothers-in-the-Earth who retain a semblance of sense. They know enough not to shove themselves down hot chimneys, or give in to the siren song of the colander. They realize, in some blurred manner, that by every seventh of January the Tree of Life has had time to recover, and there's a whole year of pointless work ahead of them.

At the bloody Saw.

They crowd around me, interested in this fresh form of trickery — which is what they think it is. The snowflakes make them look like they have sudden, uncontrollable dandruff.

"You don't have to kill," I tell them. "If you come across humans and have to sort them out, give them a mischievous blow to the head."

"Pink ones," says a monster of a *kallikantzaros*, lurking at the back. A long tongue the color of a burst spleen lolls from his mouth, and his huge horns weigh his chin down on his breast.

"Humanthhh," says another. We have a lot of lispers, for some reason.

"Yes, quite." I bare my yellow teeth. "Knock them out, and get what we need. My friend will let you in."

I lead them south, to the gates by the factory warehouses. Lukas Marinakis is waiting there. He's abandoned his socks and shoes, and his normal foot has begun to match the other. His toenails have grown, as well.

I hesitate.

His grandmother is by his side, which wasn't part of the deal. There is a strong moon, and she peers over her reading glasses, seeing the mob of black, distorted shapes which I call my brethren. I urge my people back, waiting for a shower of holy water, or imprecations and saints' names.

To my surprise, she laughs.

"*Nai, nai,*" she says. Yes, yes (forgive me throwing the Greek in occasionally — it makes me feel at home).

I'm a bit puzzled, which amuses her even more. Lukas looks embarrassed as the old woman hobbles over to me.

"Your idea, all this, *kallikantzaros?*"

"Uh, yes."

"*Entaxei.* Okay."

I scratch my left horn. "Really?"

She pokes my rounded belly with her stick. "I am ninety-two years old, little monster. I'm sick of all this shit, sick of sitting there with aching bones, watching television until I die."

"I...I imagine so."

"Philodoxis, eh?" She looks down at my member, which is decidedly un-priapic in her presence. "And you have a plan, my grandson tells me. To put an end to the cycle of misery. Tell me, what happens after this end of yours?"

That's a good question.

"No one is sure, *giagia.*" I feel oddly respectful towards her. "A drunken centaur once told me that if the Tree of Life falls, the world will reshape itself. After that...maybe everything will start again. Or maybe nothing will happen except we finally get a proper holiday."

I am standing outside an agro-chemical plant, at the head of a small horde of monstrously misshapen creatures from the bowels of the earth, and an old woman is interrogating me.

It's different.

"We can only hope," I say, my voice close to cracking. "Anything is better than...the Saw."

Her head bobs in understanding, black shawl fluttering in the breeze. She smells of camphor, piss, and lemon-drops. Her left eye glints at me.

"Maybe, *kallikantzaros*, the Old Gods will come back to us. *Ochi?*"

"We can only hope," I repeat.

"Good. Get on with it, then."

Glad that I hadn't thrown that roof tile at her in the end, I turn to the troops.

"You heard the lady."

The *kallikantzaroi* rush forward, a few of them giving polite nods to grandma, and they surge towards the open warehouses. Some miss the gates, knocking parts of the wire fencing down in their enthusiasm.

"They shouldn't meet any opposition. I managed to reduce the staff down to one nightwatchman," says Lukas. "And I got him drunk, in case. He's not a bad chap."

"You did very well. The feet are looking good."

His toes are hardening, the nails fusing. I see fine hooves in the making, and am satisfied that I have released the *kallikantzaros* in him.

My kin come lisping and giggling back from the warehouses, excited. It's a nice change in routine for them. You can only curdle so much milk before the trick loses its appeal.

The large ones — and some are very large — carry great metal canisters on their shoulders. The small ones roll their prizes before them. As they head for the tunnel mouths, back into the dark, they chant a playful refrain, their own *kalanta*.

"Bugger the Saw; sod the Tree. Bugger the Saw; sod the Tree!"

That's not something I taught them. I feel proud, like a father whose idiot children have at least managed to stand upright.

"I told the boss it was a special order," Lukas says. "I had to call in bulk supplies from other factories, forge a lot of documents... We nearly didn't manage the quantity we agreed."

"But you did. Lukas, my boy, I couldn't be more pleased."

It's true. I have shaped a ten-year-old into a man who will be sung of for centuries.

A small, warped *kallikantzaros* stumbles past, his tail twisted round his shaggy legs. He is almost useless, but he pushes the massive canister assigned to him over rocks and hummocks all the same.

The label and the warning signs on the canister are obvious in the moonlight. A big black cross on an orange background, and a skull and crossbones. It lists the actual chemicals as well, but I don't care. Lukas says they're what we need.

I expect it will take a while to work. Months, probably. Myths can be annoyingly persistent. But I have faith, and I have a feeling that Lukas, caught between being mortal and *kallikantzaros*, will have got it right.

I kiss grandma on the cheek, and shake Lukas' hand.

"I'll see you again," I tell them. My tail is whipping around like a dog who's been given an unexpected sheep carcass. "One way or another, next Christmas is going to be very different."

It will be. When I come above ground again, the mortals will be using colanders as helmets, to protect them from the joyful rampages of the *kallikantzaroi*. We'll stuff basil in their mouths, and spoil their holy water. We might even disembowel a few priests, if the mood takes us. We'll dance under the sun, and we'll drink deep with those who remember the Old Faith.

A grand time will be had.

I'll do what I want, and I won't be going back. None of my brothers will be going back, for over five thousand gallons of concentrated herbicide are currently heading into the depths. Especially formulated for woody plants, Lukas assures me.

The Tree of Life won't know what hit it.

And if you like extra honey on your *baklava*, Lukas has a friend who works at an industrial smelter near Athens. Just the place for melting down rusting tools that no one wants anymore. I have another idea, once the Tree is dead...

In the dark.

In the thrumming dark that will belong to us.
The Saw is...
Going to get a nasty surprise.

AUTHOR NOTES

This story is entirely due to a mention of the kallikantzaroi in a Roger Zelazny novel. I remembered that mention decades later, and suddenly wanted to explore the reasonable grievances that an actual kallikantzaros might have. As you do.

a slow, remembered tide

THERE WAS NO horizon that late afternoon, there by the leaden waters. Sky seeped into ocean, and the bay was what it had always been, an emptiness that tugged at him. He scuffed his feet across the sand as he skirted the waves, sparing his old shoes. The tide would soon erase any mark of his passage, but white salt stains would be hell to get out of the leather. He was at an age where these things mattered.

Gulls clustered on the foreshore, a chatter of grey backs, cold yellow eyes. He had never liked them. How long did gulls live? Were these the children, the grandchildren of those beaks which had terrified him once? He supposed not. Beyond them, a cormorant perched on a single dark rock which stood out from the sea, a sentinel against the flood. At his back, the cliffs were a tumble of clay and wiry grass.

He recognised it all.

"I'll leave you here, then," said his wife when she parked behind the seawall.

Which she would, not just for the two weeks whilst he was here, but for all the days to come. He felt it in the half-hearted kiss, in the tremor of a finger on his shoulder. He knew, without further discussion between them, that his retreat to the coast would turn into a series of large brown envelopes and awkward phone calls; meals shared, if at all, in silence.

He watched her as she headed back to the car, clothes hugged tight around her body. She was a bundle of memories which he would no longer share. They had been together for fourteen years, but he could already imagine forgetting her face, her name.

The boarding house was a mile away, but he'd asked to be left on the sands. His luggage was safe at his lodgings, and she hadn't argued. This was damp feet and blankness to her, a place devoid of interest.

"You don't swim, Christopher," she reminded him on the way there. "You don't like the cold, and you complain when the wind bites at your ears."

"I was born in the place."

Narrow eyes, narrower lips. "And you've not been back for thirty years."

"I know."

Followed by grinding gear changes and silence.

He wasn't born in this place, not quite here. He took a fine handful of sand and let it trickle through his fingers. He was born on hard chalk, three miles inland, but this coast was his history.

The gulls rose, disturbed by a dog walker farther along the shore. A dirty cloud of them wheeled and shrieked, only to settle a few hundred yards south. The sea paid no attention. He had an hour, maybe two, before the tide came fully in.

Maybe the sea was blue or turquoise, or even ultramarine, elsewhere. Here it was slate-coloured and muddied with the sand it lifted, tangled with shreds of old fishing nets, and bladderwrack. He remembered popping the dried bladders under the cliffs, the bubble-wrap of childhood. He had always been disappointed that every single one had been empty. There should have been something wonderful inside — a pearl, a drop of sea-honey, anything. But there wasn't. Only stale air, like the alcohol-heavy breath of the dead on his neck...

He trudged towards town.

The holidaymakers were long gone, and even the birders had almost deserted their nests. Birders and twitchers, noting each swoop or tumble of feathers in their little books, necks heavy with cameras and lenses and binoculars. Dedicated. But this was early November, and only the hardiest would stay.

The boarding house was quiet, and would have depressed him at any other time. Brown paint and the smell of disinfectant.

"Mr. Mainprize. I have you booked for two weeks, is that right?"

The owner was a hen of a woman, jerking her head and clucking to herself as she took his details again, scratching in her folders of forms and leaflets.

"For now."

"Plenty of room in the off-season." She looked up, smiling. "Stay as long as you want. You from round here?"

"Once."

He took his bags up to the room. A sink, a bed, one chair, and a shared bathroom. If he added a camping stove, it would have been the bedsit he stayed in when he fled the town. The Great Escape.

Gulls cried outside the open window, white Post-It Notes on grey skies. They were there to tell him that he could never forget.

They were right.

***

There had to be a first, and there was, outside the chip shop on Monkgate that evening. The boarding house provided a sort of dinner, but not the sort you wanted to eat.

"Chris! Chris Mainprize."

He squinted at the florid face, the torn anorak.

"Uh, hi."

"You remember me — Steve, from school. I had that party, back in eighty-seven, you know, before you left."

He did, now that he'd been prodded. Cheap cider and hot dogs on the beach; girls better-looking than an agency's model book. That natural Northern beauty, coast-girls with calf-muscles and cheekbones. The party had lasted until dawn, and by noon he was on the train inland, heading for an anonymous place in an anonymous city.

Steve Something grinned.

"God, that was a night. Haven't seen you in — is it thirty years?"

"Suppose so."

"Here, let's catch up."

He let himself be guided into a nearby pub, where bored teenagers played pool, ripping the baize of the pool table and baiting each other. They were him, at sixteen or seventeen. Steve bought a round of drinks, and took over a copper-topped table, sweeping beermats away. The reminiscences were painful, laborious. The beer didn't help.

"...And she married a butcher, of course. Three kids, gone a bit mad now."

Christopher nodded. The third pint was making tidal movements inside him.

"And then there was..." The man paused. "Look, Chris, mate, I might as well say it. Only two days to go until the eleventh. Are you back for—"

"I don't know."

Serious nod. "We could do with you. I find it hard, even now."

That surprised him. He'd thought...or he'd not given it enough thought.

"I sort of assumed that most of you who stayed..."

Steve Rhodes. That was the name. Neither clever nor stupid, one of those friends who you left behind more by accident than anything.

"Not many of us take part, but it has to be done," said Steve. He swilled the beer around in his glass. "You had the guts to leave; I didn't."

"It wasn't guts."

He didn't want to think about that.

"It's important," said Steve, as they headed for the pub door. "But you never got that, did you?"

I grew up with other worries, he wanted to say, but stayed silent as his once-friend left. The slam of the door was a fist against the side of his head; a heavy boot to his belly.

Other worries.

***

Everything at the boarding house was boiled — eggs, ham, cabbage, mince, potatoes. Except the toast, which was the sallow colour of geriatric skin. He imagined the landlady's frustration at not being able to boil the toast. It was easy to tell that Mrs. Oliver was a local. She fussed between the only two occupied tables at dinner, peering at her guests occasionally. It was the time of year for those with a certain purpose, she clearly knew that much.

"Remembrance Day," she said brightly. "Always good to remember. Mr. Oliver, you know, he was in the army, before he died."

Christopher looked up from the limp toast. Why would anyone serve toast at dinnertime?

"He died in action?"

"In Bradford. He was hit by a bus."

She didn't seem terribly bothered about it. The only other guest, a scarecrow of a woman in a worn tweed skirt suit and lumpen pullovers, was trying not to laugh.

He went up to his room and opened the single window, paint flaking off the sash cords as he tugged at it. There were the night and the sea, right where they should be. He wasn't going to welcome them in. A container ship was crossing the bay, the movement so slow at this distance that you couldn't be sure it was actually going anywhere unless you could measure its lights against something else — a beacon, a fishing boat. The tide had come in, and gone out again. There, by the gleam of a dog walker's torch, was the cormorant, on its solitary rock.

There were no dreams, no nightmares. He slept without more incident than needing to go to the toilet at three in the morning. The day's beer came out much as it went in, and afterwards he knew nothing until the clink of breakfast plates from below.

The world outside was made of wet steel — hard and grey, but so whelmed by November dank that it might as well have been raining. He would have gone inland, to the villages where he was raised, but he'd seen the maps. Most of the area was now holiday cottages and caravans; chic pottery shops and coastal trails. Even had it been the same, what would it have held? Slivers of momentary happiness, bludgeons of far worse memories.

The parish church in town held his mother tight in its shadow, the stone over her hardly weathered. He owed her that one visit, the first since she died.

"I came back," he said, dropping garage-bought flowers by her head.

She didn't answer.

Twenty years. Twenty years since his father drowned in the long waters which stretched to Norway and beyond. A distinct blessing for her, one which left her with a Merchant Navy pension and far less bruises. The body came back, torn by rigging and bloated by the sea, but Petty Officer Mainprize was no longer there.

Christopher and his mother knew where he was, and knowing that, had rejected custom, heritage, whatever you wanted to call it.

"I won't do it again," she said. "I'll stay here, but not for that. Not for the harvest. I couldn't bear it."

"I'm leaving, Mum. I need to try and make a life somewhere," he said.

And she'd been pleased for him. There wasn't love between them, but there was family, familiarity. Both of them knew that she could have been stronger, and so could he.

She only lasted four years after her husband's death. The funeral had been a small affair.

"I'm sorry, Christopher." The vicar, ten generations of the coast in him, stood close but not too close. "Your father...he was a complicated man."

But he wasn't. They used that word for a man who had friends and kept down a steady job, and then hit his wife, shouted abuse at his son.

A man who could shake your hand and lend you a fiver, then threaten you when he was in his drink, large frame rolling as if he was out there on a heavy sea.

That wasn't complicated.

"And will you be coming home, to keep up..."

"No." He'd kept to that snapped response until his life had turned — a loveless, childless marriage, well away from the coast, and then the certainty which came with middle age. He was no better than his mother. Little better than his father, maybe, though he'd never lashed out at Mary.

He stood over his mother's grave. He could do nothing for her, but there was always the sea, and its needs.

A hurried sandwich and a scalding coffee got him down to the shore below the town. The cormorant — *a* cormorant — kept its watch; three children screamed on the edge of the outgoing tide, observed by bored, shivering parents.

He stood and wondered, letting all his childhood years coagulate into this one view. Grey waters, grey skies, and a vast fingernail of sand.

"It steals the land."

He turned, clutching the pocket with his wallet in. City instincts.

The woman was tall, and he recognised her from the boarding house. The Tweed Woman.

"What?"

"The sea. It steals the land."

She pointed to the cliffs.

"You know that they crumble further back each year, don't you?" She stamped one foot on the sand. "This was farmland once, good growing for wheat and barley."

"I was...I was brought up around here."

"So was I."

She was older than he was, carrying the last of her fifties on narrow shoulders. They stared out over white-caps and an uneasy swell. He drew in the sweet rot of seaweed; the mothball sharpness of her clothes.

"My son is out there." She was closer, though he hadn't noticed her move.

"A fisherman?"

"Drowned off the point ten years ago."

"Oh."

Her right hand gripped his shoulder, a firmer, warmer grip than ever Mary had.

"There are fewer of us each year."

He stared at his shoes, at the scuffed, salt-stained leather.

"I don't know what you mean."

Her laugh put paid to that idea.

"I live in York these days," she said. "But I come back each year, and do my duty."

"I never have." It was the admission he needed to make. "My mother did, but she stopped when...someone died."

She nodded, as if this were perfectly normal. A dog barked, gulls screeched. The family was packing up, leaving litter across the sands. Plastic coffee cups and crisp packets, an unwanted bucket and spade. An empty cigarette packet was examined by a herring gull, and found to be wanting.

He had a question, one easier to put to a stranger.

"Do you ever... Have you felt him, your son?"

"No. He may have come to others, but not to me."

"Does that bother you?"

"Not so much. As long as we keep him, safe with us."

He felt awkward at that. She was what his mother would have called a "handsome" woman. Clear brown eyes, and hair that did what it needed to do. He offered to buy her a coffee, and they walked to the only outdoor stall on the promenade which was open at that time of year.

"The eleventh day of the eleventh month." She was looking at two old men by the stall, red poppies against faded brown overcoats. "It's like an echo, isn't it?"

He'd not thought of that before. His blank face drew another laugh from her. His wife Mary was one of those people who only smiled, carefully. He didn't know women who laughed.

"I'm Christopher."

"Corrine. Stupid name, but at least I'm not a 'Mary' or something dull like that." She took out her purse. "I'll pay for these."

His mind tumbled through nonsense, the thought that this woman had met him before, knew who he was, knew his wife's name...

"Did I say something wrong?" She pocketed small change from the girl at the stall.

"Uh, no." He spilled sugar into the coffee she handed him, trying not to squeeze the takeaway cup so much that it scalded his hand. He focused on what she'd said before.

"It's not like they would have thought of it. When they signed the Armistice, I mean."

"Things have a way of seeping in. Perhaps they felt it, rather than knew it."

"Martinmas." It was the first time he had used the word aloud in decades.

One of the old men looked up, frowned, and went back to the muttered conversation he was having with his companion. All Christopher could see was that the man had only shaved one side of his face, leaving a weak stubble across the other cheek. It absorbed him so much that he stared as the two men wandered off.

"I will be there," she said. "If you decide to take part."

He wanted to explain — about his life, his failed marriage to Mary, his mother, everything. He couldn't.

"I don't know."

He thanked her for the coffee, feeling that his smile was imbecilic, and retreated in disarray, pleading a forgotten task. He put purpose in his stride into town, as if to prop up his words, but he had no idea where he was going.

Caffeine and the cold flushed his cheeks. There were shops, but he had nothing planned. Toothpaste, that would ground him. Buy toothpaste, maybe something for lunch from the supermarket, and a couple of pairs of thicker socks. A book, although there were books at the boarding house...

"Now then, Chris, mate."

Steve Rhodes, waiting by the front doors of the small supermarket in the same torn anorak. He was guarding half a dozen shopping bags.

"Wife's inside. Forgot something," he said, awkward.

Steve hadn't mentioned being married when they talked in the pub.

"Oh. Who..."

"Helen Sacker. Remember her?"

He did. A short blonde girl with a habit of wearing tight jeans and no knickers. You could tell.

"Good for you. I mean, I hope so."

Steve shrugged. "We rub along okay." He abandoned his position, coming closer. "Are you going to...be there?"

Christopher couldn't keep saying he didn't know. It was more stressful than the alternatives.

"I don't think I can do it." That came out in a breathy rush.

Something of anger crept into the other man's face. "I've had to. And Helen."

"Look, it's not like you need me to—"

"Says you, who left it to us, to carry it all. Fewer of us each year, you know."

The words of the Tweed Woman. Corinne.

"Is it that bad?" He realised that curious shoppers were watching by the doorway.

Steve drew in a long, deep breath. When it came out, he sagged like the forgotten shopping.

"Oh, just piss off," he said.

A short blonde woman was coming towards the exit. Christopher knew her for who she was, another unwelcome fragment of the past. He fled.

***

In his room, the names were on his lips, passed down from his mother. Auburn, Monkwell, and Ringborough. The litany was still in his head. And the ships, though he hated those names. Dinghies and fishing cobles, trawlers and warships. Coal-barges. Far too many to keep safe inside, unlike the drowned villages. His mother had known the names of a hundred and seventy-two ships, all lost. She said there were others in the town who could do better than that.

To drown on this coast was different.

There was always the eleventh day of the eleventh month, and on that day, there were always those like his mother, Steve, Corinne...

The celebrants.

He went downstairs to see if he could get a cup of tea. Corinne was in the small, shabby lounger, eating biscuits from the packet.

"Caramel." She held the packet out to him. "Caramel flavour, at least."

"No thanks."

But he sat down in the armchair next to her. The television opposite them had no plug on it.

"So, tomorrow," she said. "I can't imagine you came back here by accident, not at this time."

"I had nowhere else to go."

He took his wife, Mary, and laid her out in words. He wove her in and out of his failing job in light engineering, and a marriage which no engineer could have fixed, no matter how many tools he had to hand. Unable to stop, he wrung himself dry of anything which mattered except...

"Who did you lose?"

"My father."

"You don't sound fond of him." The biscuits had gone. She put one slim hand on his knee, the slightest of connections.

"Will it...hurt?" he managed to ask.

"For a while."

Corinne rolled back her pullover and showed him her left arm. White scars ran across the inside of her arm. There'd been a girl at the factory who cut herself, but her marks had been haphazard, a pattern of distraction. These were orderly, and well away from the wrist.

"I...I didn't mean that part."

"I know you didn't. But you can use this..." She traced one raised weal. "To bear the other. If you need to."

He heard the front door click, and Mrs. Oliver peered into the lounge, missing everything but the empty packet.

"I bought digestives," she said. "I do hope that's all right?"

They smiled, and accepted the offer of a pot of tea.

He did dream that night, but only of Mary having sex with the man next door, writhing and arching her back, coupled on a bed of rotting seaweed. Wish fulfilment. The wish that his marriage, his life, had been broken by something real, not just time and tide.

***

The town was divided the next day. The bulk of people chattered, kept shop or shopped, did what they did. Bank tellers looked blank at bags of mismatched change, and traffic wardens crept along the streets, hyenas waiting for a badly parked car on which to chew. A few tourists ate candyfloss in the drizzle while their minds visited Paris and Honolulu — or simply somewhere dry. But there were others, and he knew those few from the quick efficiency they showed, the sideways glances to each other.

At ten in the morning, he walked the beach again. The cormorant was absent, but there was wrack from the previous night's tide to distract him — the spherical jewels which were floats from fishing nets, and great brown blades of kelp tugged up by a squall. He'd decided to miss the sad Armistice ceremony at the town Cenotaph, and the annual parade of bedraggled Cubs, Brownies, and Sea Cadets, shovelled into some sort of order by anxious parents.

Back in town by three, he saw discarded poppies on the streets. With a doner kebab rebelling inside him, he watched buses leave for Hull and York. Their passage only told him that he wasn't on them.

They'd been warned that dinner at the boarding house would be early.

"I'm off to my sister's in Hornsea for the night," said Mrs. Oliver. "I can trust you two to keep things in order, I'm sure." She clucked and fussed more than usual. "I've laid out everything for breakfast, and I'll be back on the 9 a.m. bus, so leave it all for me to clear in the morning."

He moved mince and potatoes around on his plate, knowing that Corinne was watching him from the other table. When the landlady's taxi arrived and the door slammed behind her, he abandoned the effort.

"He was a bastard," he said.

She put down her fork, waiting.

"My father. He worked the freighters from Hull — had done so since he was in his teens. Merchant Navy. Sometimes he was away for a month or more. That wasn't so bad. He came back with money, and then we had it all for a few days — presents and hugs, trips out, whatever we wanted."

She moved her chair nearer. "And after the excitement died down?"

"He drank. Bought rounds for everyone, a man with a hundred mates while he had the cash. Then the long nights. Waiting for him to get back, lying in the dark and listening to my mother cry as he shoved her around — or hit her." He looked up, angry. "She tried to keep it down, she told me after he died. Can you believe it? She tried not to cry out too loud, in case it woke me."

"You were always awake, though."

"Yeah."

"He's only one of so many. He isn't the point, the focus, of what we do."

"I know." Christopher looked away. "But if he were there, I don't..."

He couldn't finish. Couldn't express his sullen anger, the poison that lay in his thoughts. He told her more, searching out fragments of his parents. An incident which ended in the Casualty Department. A night when his father gave him a drunken hug and said he loved him — but the next morning, breakfast was on the floor and his mother was crying in the bathroom. And how she had told him about Martinmas, the year before his father died.

"I thought it was her one lie, a sort of escape from where she was. Her fantasy, some way of separating out what might still be good in him. Maybe she wanted him to drown. I certainly did." He paused, replaying what he'd said. "Uh... I'm sorry about your son, though. I didn't mean..."

"It's all right."

She took their plates into the kitchen at the back, and when she returned, she held a briskness, a purpose. He knew why. It was almost seven in the evening, and there would be people gathering on the long shore below the town, well away from the closed amusements and the shuttered ice cream stalls. Away from casual eyes.

"I'll be leaving tomorrow," she said. "A bit of a lie-in, and then I'll catch the train. But it's been good to meet you. You need to be kind."

"To him?"

"To yourself. There's a quarter-bottle of whisky in my room. Have a couple of glasses, and try to sleep."

When she'd gone, he was alone in the room with an aching head and a grease-spattered tablecloth. He followed the history of mince across the thin cloth, and knew that whatever was done, whatever was to come, neither of them would ever be wholly clean again.

He went upstairs. With the door open, in the half-dark from the landing, his room was the sea. The cry of a night gull, the low throb of waves, the smell of the wide waters. At the open window, he saw lights down on the far beach, strewn like a handful of bright dust.

It was beginning.

By the bedside lamp — frayed cord and yellowed shade — he read the letter that had come that morning. Mary must have written it as soon as she got back. She was at her mother's house in Surrey. She didn't think she wanted to be with him again. No blame, simply resignation. He understood, had expected it. He had done nothing wrong, she wrote. The problem was that he had become nothing.

In the gathering dark, a lone seabird shrieked emptiness across the bay...

***

Whisky laced his boots, and tugged on his jacket. The flowers dying on his mother's grave thrust him out into the night, and along the low seawall, towards the lights. The front was quiet. Locals knew what night this was, and chose to be in the pubs, or at home with the television turned just that little bit louder. Nothing would change for most of them.

He was stumbling on the sands, trying too hard. The gathering was far down the shore, by the mouth of Auburn Beck. Lost Auburn, a village taken back by the North Sea and held tight to its breast, like it held his father.

The lights were closer, his heart pounding. Once there would have been torches of tar, and great ship's lanterns on poles — now it was mostly flashlights, even mobile phones, which lit the water's edge.

He tried to count. More than twenty, less than thirty. People were moving, weaving in and out, but there were far less than he'd expected. These were the last few celebrants of something older than he liked to think.

His mother had told him, again and again.

"Chris, love, we're not bloody Morris Dancers, and we don't make corn-dollies. This is life, not a history lesson."

He edged closer to the group of people on the beach. On his left, one real torch sputtered and flared, held by a tall figure standing ankle-deep in the water. Someone he could cling to, or who would tell him he need not be there...

"Corinne!" he shouted.

She turned, as did the man nearest her, and Christopher recognised the vicar who had presided over his mother's funeral. Others looked in his direction, and a flashlight shone in his face, making him wince. He heard a muttered apology, and when his vision cleared, Steve and Helen were there, only a few yards away. Steve's face struggled between relief and doubt.

"Are you..."

"I'm here," said Christopher.

"So you are," said Corinne, handing him her torch. It was heavy, a length of wood with the end a mass of twisted rope and pitch. The smoky orange flame confused what he could see, creating more shadows than there should have been.

"The tide comes," said the vicar.

They ushered him into the line which was forming, a straggle of some two dozen people side by side. Men and women stood with their boots soaking up the saltwater, a cold wind on their faces as they faced the sea. He remembered his lessons, and was sure that the breeze should be flowing off the land, not towards it.

"Auburn and Hartburn. Owthorne, Monkwell, and Ravenser Odd." That was the vicar again, reciting as if he spoke the names of saints. "Lost to us now, but remembered."

"Great Colden and Ringborough," called another.

"Newsham and Turmarr." Corinne's voice, followed by the names of ships, so many ships. Dutchmen floundering on the sands; trawlers driven onto the rocks.

"The St. Ninian, the Falmouth..." The last lost to a U-boat off Hornsea. He'd read about that once. The recitation grew — a rowing boat which sank fifty years ago, and a coble which broke open in a storm last year. Christopher found himself adding those he could remember from his mother's list.

"This is our Old Hallow, our last harvest of the year." An old man spoke up, his voice cracking, and Christopher recognised him as one of the men from the coffee stall. He was still wearing his poppy. "We bring them in, we offer them remembrance."

The man bared one arm, and cut quickly into the wrinkled flesh with a small knife. There was little blood, but he shook his arm over the incoming tide, letting the water take it. Christopher saw others around him do the same, and hesitated, but Corinne was there, holding out a thin blade.

"For the harvest."

"For the harvest." He cut into his own arm, wincing, and she led him closer to the water, so that the dark red drops were shared with the sea. Her own blood followed.

The list of settlements and ships was over, and the heart of Martinmas began. The names of men, women, and children were spoken over the tide, people calling them out in turn at first, then together in a jumble of voices. He shivered, listening to the litany of the dead. Though it was darker than before, there were gulls above, echoing the names.

"We bring you in," cried out the old man. "We are refuge and remembrance..." He broke off, coughing, but the vicar took it up.

"We are here, before the year's turning. A haven for the drowned."

Christopher felt them then, heard the whispers from the sea. He knew them as they came, each as named. The pale host of fishermen, tangled in nets, torn by propellers, and the strong swimmers who found riptides which were stronger. Small children lost in two inches of water, ploughmen who dared the low cliffs too close to a storm. Those who took lifeboats out and never returned; sailors who felt the splinters pierce them, or fell under the rattle of machine gun fire.

And the hopeless souls, those who flew from clifftops to free themselves...so many, so very many.

"We call you back for another year and we are memory for you, who are not lost whilst we stand." Four or five of the celebrants spoke as one. "We bring you to the land, so that we may carry you all of our days."

Corinne slashed at her own arm again, flinging blood into the darkness, and he took the blade, doing the same to himself, for the whispers had become voices, counterpoints to the names cried out by the living.

The dead came with flashes of silver, borne on the flanks of fish. They closed on the celebrants in the quick clatter of lobster claws, and through the writhing of the kelp beds, their loneliness forgotten.

The gulls urged them in, the lost and drowned, and Christopher finally understood Martinmas from within. His body shuddered with memories which were not his, sheltering those who had passed. Some were angry, others shrouded in solitude, but there was no threat. The momentary pain of welcoming them was nothing, for each of them sought only remembrance, not control.

Eager, entranced, he called out a dozen other names. He knew them from his mother, and from the gravestones which surrounded her. He echoed them from others' lips, crying the name of Corinne's son as well. Blood flowed, and the drowned were brought home. A man in the water fell to his knees, sobbing, his arms outstretched. Steve and his wife were on the other side of the vicar, chanting and swaying with the impact of what came.

There was one more name, inescapable now. In the torch's flare, he saw the black rock which stood proud of the waves, the cormorant waiting, sinuous neck in motion. Corinne took hold of his free hand, whispering names as they looked out to sea, hearing the bearers of those names come back to them.

His father was in the myriad voices, only one of the many thousands, perhaps tens of thousands, who could be drawn from the cold, uncaring waters. He could hate his father, and yet hold him, safe.

"George Mainprize," he murmured, his throat tight. "Dad!"

The last, most intimate harvest of the year.

***

And there were beasts in the water, all manner of silvered fish and the deep pools of seals' eyes, witnesses to the drowned, yet unknowing because they were still beasts.

And Auburn had its Martinmas...

AUTHOR NOTES

The "drowned" Holderness coast is a real thing, and is where I grew up. All the names of places are genuine, as are a number of the other details. We have often run the dogs on the long sands where Auburn and other settlements used to lie, with only an isolated farm or two left to mark the hinterland of the villages under the sea. No bells tolling beneath the sea, but only low, eroded cliffs and the vast, lonely waters.

SHE IS RUNNING.

It is hard to find the green places, but they are there. Sad and railed, smog-ridden, in the centres of city squares. Fern-fronded and tanged with urine in small spaces behind the shops. Glimpses of a broken forest — a single ash tree, with graffiti sprayed on its trunk; an oak which sheds cupped children, only for them to die on paving stones insensible to life.

She dances through them, by them, drawing what she can from a single bold thistle or a tangled rose hedge. These are all she has. Thorn and spike, she borrows them, to be ready.

A busy road, avoided. A grid of houses, sterile traps which shine with a cold light of their own. She turns a corner, confused, only for a man to catch at her, trying to grab her shoulder for some unknown reason. The man's grasping hands shake with ferment, with their false brews.

She does not want to be touched like this, and makes this clear with her nails. He winces and draws back; she wild-smiles, and shows him the blood on her fingers.

Jump-Nancy keep me, if you watch,

And if you're gone, then come once more.

He holds his torn cheek and makes no move to come near her again. She leaps over a bent metal barrier and into the carpark wastes.

This is a poor land for her. Buckled concrete and oil stains, covered with a rainbow sheen. Hardly a dandelion between slabs of tarmac. Sliding into the lee of a truck, she sniffs the air. It holds the lifeblood of the city — semen and diesel. Both come from the other side of this particular wasteland, two people straining the springs of a rusting vehicle. A less-than man, a sort-of woman.

Somehow she knows certain things of this place. The words come and go.

Semen and diesel; cash and disgust.

And so she is running.

***

"I don't understand," the white-coat says.

But he is unknowing, a world away from hers. There is nothing to understand. They are the mystery; she is passing through. Or she had meant to...

The gleam of a metal box thundering forward as gases explodes within it, ice-white eyes that blinded as she hesitated on the great road into the city. No care what was in its path, and so she became chestnut-hard and oak; the glancing impact was less than the breath of moths to her. That's what she kept telling the driver when he finally staggered out, but he smelled of alcohol and sweat. She didn't like being close to him.

"What were you doin' there, stupid bitch?"

By the beaming eyes of his vehicle, then those of a police car, she stood upright.

"You walked, you bloody walked out, right into—"

A police officer gestured him back to his own vehicle, then bent over her.

"We're taking you to hospital, to get you checked out. All right, miss? What's your name?"

Random faces, unwanted. Words without value.

"Huldre," she said, to the far-off lime trees which were all she had sought.

Take care. Jump-Nancy had the Book of Trees, and understood. *This is a proper name to use, but not a safe one.*

"Right, uh, Huldre. Come with us. You might be hurt, uh...inside." For a moment his voice held a father's care.

There were slight cracks in her, it was true, though nothing that mattered. She saw determination in the officer's eyes, and wondered at the distance from the motorway to the nearest safety. Broken buildings loomed alongside them, an industrial estate. There was nothing there for her. Yes, motorway. That was what she had walked. She had dreamed of a Somewhere ahead, a place which held the lime trees in flower, but she had come too far from the true green places. Not paid attention.

She went with him, into his black-white vehicle. Curious, not alarmed.

It wasn't far. Red lights and blue, the scurry of importance on people's faces as they passed. They herded her further from her roots and into the desolation of a place where the air was lifeless, warm without warmth. Hospital.

"You must see a doctor," one said, and so here she was.

The doctor, stiff white body in a stiff white coat, feels gently at her wrist, her neck. She allows this at first, but does not know what he wants. Her throat starts to close tighter with every corridor they guide her down. He leads her to a bed by a window, where a woman makes her lie down. Nurse, that is another word. To nurture...

She looks around. A stunted cherry tree stands outside the building. A failed maypole in bloom. She clings to its presence and tries to ignore the worn shells which wheeze around it, drawing on their cigarettes and coughing like crows.

"You've been very lucky, miss. Miraculously so." The man shakes his head. "A few minor abrasions from a head-on collision? That's what they told me, anyway. Must have rolled with the impact somehow. Let's have a better look."

This is when Jump-Nancy comes to her again, head tilted wrong, arms all bent. Nancy is in the shadows, behind the things which wink and beep.

If they unclothe you, they'll see that you are hollow, Jump-Nancy whispers. *They will know you as huldre, inside as out.*

She hadn't thought. Already they are reaching to move her onto her side.

"No."

Their hands grow more insistent. She becomes alder, slick from the marshes, but they are reaching for pointed sticks, sharp metal needles, and it has to stop. If they see, if they know she is hollow and hidden, it will be bad.

She lashes out, slamming the nurse into a cabinet, and one horn-soled foot catches the doctor between the legs, hard. He falls to his knees, moaning.

Up she comes, up through the open window and to the cherry tree, scrambling but not yet running. The wheezing oners move, a slow scatter of drip-stands and dressing-gowns, but it is a trap — the courtyard is enclosed. She and the tree are captives in a garden walled by hospital, with a policeman and a porter at the only doorway. Cigarette ends and blossom swirl around her bare feet.

They take hold of her before she can appeal to the green places.

"Is she ill?" gasps the policeman, pinning her arms.

The doctor limps down the corridor, pauses.

"Maybe in the head." His thighs are tight together, protective. "Physically she's...strong as an ox. Fine. No obvious concussion, maybe a bit of bruising — not that she'll let me check the rest of her."

"Restraints?"

"We're not equipped. This is just a temporary assessment ward. I'll have to give her an injection while you hang on to her..."

She remembers the iron point. Hypodermic. No iron inside her. Ever.

Willow comes to her, cool as it weeps into the long waters, and she twists from the man's grip. She bends her slenderness round the doctor and the dazed nurse, sees real light beyond them down the corridor. Thirty paces, and there is real air as well. A metal box honks at her, but she remembers its kind now and slides round it. Ambulance — she can read the strange words. And cars, lorries, vans, all manner of horrids.

But there are people, uniforms in her way...

***

She is in a low place of rooms and cells. It is a hive of square places, like wasps gone mad. Concrete and plastic. There is nothing for her to become as they push her into one of these rooms, empty and cold, with the white glare of nothing on every wall.

"You need to tell us your name, miss," says a woman who is also police. "We want to help you."

"Huldre."

The officer shakes her head and takes a folder from the table in the middle of the room. Another man is watching, ready if she does anything.

"Look, love, we think that you're one of the patients who went missing from the Lowfields Unit, either Jennifer Davies or Nancy Wrightson. Do those names mean anything to you?"

Names again. There had been two women, two young women, once, far from here. And a meeting. Under the elm trees, when no one was watching. Mutter-time.

We can leave. There's no one on the gates.

That had been Jump-Nancy beneath the elms, picking at the beds of her fingernails. She had talked of freedoms, of many paths...

In this bright place, her captors watch.

"Do you know your name? Are you Jennifer, maybe, or Nancy?" The man speaks slowly, to a child. She is not a child.

"Huldre."

"So you're not Jennifer or Nancy? Those names don't ring any bells?"

Speak not, and keep the Within. Jump-Nancy is imperious, hiding beyond the corners.

The policewoman sighs. "There's a doctor coming, a special doctor to help you." She turns to her colleague. "There's been no sign of either of them for three days. Two blondes, similar enough. Early twenties, and both were supposedly on medication. They won't have any ID on them. Did a runner together in the night."

"Photographs on file?" He looks annoyed. "Fingerprints? Distinguishing marks?"

"They don't have a record. Nancy Wrightson was in for her own safety. Suicide risk. The other one, Jennifer, was just mad."

"Mad?" The man almost laughs. "That doesn't help a lot."

"I'm not a bloody psychiatrist. On the phone they said she talked about trees all the time. Someone's sending the details."

"She must be one of them, surely?" He frowns, as if he could identify her by staring hard enough.

"You'd think so. Don't know where she got those clothes, though."

"Charity shop? There's always stuff in the bin bags left outside the shops."

"Maybe."

This place is bad. She licks her lips.

"Water."

"I'll be okay with her," says the man.

The policewoman leaves the room.

"We're trying to help, you know." He scratches his neck, easing a tight shirt collar.

"Let free."

A shake of his head. "There's a procedure. You've no ID, you're wandering around barefoot and half-dressed — and you've been in a reported car accident. Add to that the fact that you assaulted a doctor..."

"No iron. Not in me."

He scratches again.

And she sees, through half-closed eyes, the way through, out. The doorframe and the boards which mark floor from wall. Not green, but the remembering of it. The tall pines, ripped into corpse-wood and drained of their resinous lives. This was how gods were sacrificed, pierced in the side and nailed up for a world's sorrow.

The policewoman returns, a notebook in her hands.

"Nancy Wrightson's dead. Topped herself, they think." She looks awkward, perhaps regretting her bluntness. "Uh, there was an incident by the rail line, out by Riggerton. Young woman seems to have thrown herself off the bridge. Positive ID on the body, from a Lowfields care assistant."

Jump-Nancy keep me, if you watch,

And if you're gone, then come once more.

They don't understand. She ignores their chatter and calls the pines, willing them into her.

"We think you're Jennifer Davies, love," says the man. "Does that ring any bells? Can you remember?"

He is trying to be kind. She can remember Nancy, remember Jennifer. She watched them, gathered between the elms, sharing their books and stolen chocolate bars, burying handfuls of tablets in the soft earth, scuffing the leaves over the grave. Small birds that would leave their cage.

Choices.

The memory of firs bends and sways, acknowledging her. Each knot in the boards weeps for her as she stands up.

"Huldre must leave."

They have not been bad, not forced things into her, so she will not punish them. The woman she pushes aside, the man she hits only hard enough to evade him. They cannot speak to the green places, and are unknowing. Sturdy pine lets her force her way from the room, towards the outside; the faint memory of willow slips her between grasping hands.

Again, she is running.

***

She feels the chase, and knows that they will come, the angry red faces she has left behind, as she heads back into their warrens of made things. For one mayfly moment she scents the lime trees, and almost has hope. It is a direction, at least, in a world without any other.

The day is waning when she enters more of their destruction. Places which grind life and stink the air. Factories. She sees islands of mock-homes between them, rows of houses each with a dusty patch of grass, a few tame trees. And a gathering place, where people drink and laugh brittle-like, draining down the sun in gulps of false fruit and ferment. Alcohol.

Her feet patter on gravel, concrete, hugging to a wooden fence so that she can watch. Jump-Nancy knows these people. Or their type. This is the ritual, breaking barriers with the drink, making plans of semen and diesel. They press close, sometimes to be thrust away. Laughter, scorn, and suggestion. *Not tonight. Maybe next time. He'll be waiting for me. She doesn't know about us. They'll still be awake.*

Part of her would be there among them, to feel flesh rather than concrete. Touching. Not her kind, though, and they would soon know her for what she was. She turns, but there are figures on the street behind her. They stare.

"Jesus, she looks a bit gone," says a large woman. "What is that she's wearing?"

"It's the distressed hippie look," says another. "I read about it."

"That's not distressed, it's bloody derelict."

Huldre drifts long fingers down her body, the soft dress of dandelion seeds and thistledown she thinks she has always worn, memories of the green places, dyed only with nettle, with madder and urine. Her sisters made it for her in the wildwood, even as they told her that the hollow should never go to the metal places. Even as she failed to listen.

"Mine," she says, not accepting shame.

"Oh my God!" The third woman, scrawny and hare-faced, shrieks. "It's the girl they're looking for, that one who attacked some cops. The mental case. I saw the newsfeed."

They huddle back, hard to the fence. One pulls a small cylinder from her bag, holds it up as if she were using a cross to ward off evil.

"Keep away. Cindy, phone the cops."

The hare-faced woman stabs thin fingers at something in her hand, a plastic thing that beeps like the hospital room.

She does not think that she likes these people. There is yellowed grass and ivy around her feet, the ivy smoke-sick or poisoned, blackened. She is tempted to hurt them, to take on tendrils, thick strangling stems, and punish them, though she does not. That is their pollution as well, the urge to hurt. She can feel it growing inside her, a poisoned seed.

She twists and is away, dancing the green places as best she can, from the sad ivy to a patch of lawn, a bush which someone has tended — anywhere. Garden to cramped garden, away from the shrieking women. The lakes of her past are ponds filled with captives. Fish which will never swim far or free; water-plants whose roots hit plastic liners, not the deep oozing mud of life.

A small boy calls out, not in wonder but in derision.

She is hurting.

***

Sirens roam the last light of the day. Some are for her, she knows. A police car drives her deeper into a maze of dead streets, and she grows tired, too tired. There are more gardens, but they are small and mean, with little on which to draw.

She runs jagged, slapping a hand against each roadside tree to find what comfort she can. A sycamore lends her life, reminds her what she is, and at last she catches the scent of blossom properly, not so very far away.

Not so very far away. The thought reverberates, revitalises. Two, three of the shrieking metal boxes are closing on her; a high wall of plywood sheets and corrugated iron blocks her path. Despite this, she is excited. There is a green place greater than any she has found here, in the midst of their wasteland.

Jump-Nancy speaks to her. *It is their conscience, a reminder of what they should be. A park, a place of healing. A Growing, by those who diminish all else.*

She can see what lies behind the wall, behind fluttering posters for events long gone. A half-constructed — or half-ruined — mass of glass and concrete stands between her and the pool of green.

A deep, unfettered breath. She smells lime flowers again, and hears the small makers in their thousands, their mottled coats brushed with the powder that brings forth wonders. Miner and cutter and bumble and more, returning as the sun sets. Why this thing is here, so ugly next to beauty, she cannot comprehend.

The men and women in uniform have left their vehicles, and are closing on her — some wary, some singing songs of false hope. The wall is hard, but the sycamore's blessing helps her over. Beyond is digging and making, the brutal holes, the empty pipes in disarray. Building site? Another set of their words, vaguely recalled. Tiring, she fails to notice the crouched figure until it speaks, a rasp of breath.

"They're always after you f'something."

The old woman squats in half-darkness, a bundle of worn coats and scarves.

Huldre pauses.

"I am not bad. Inside, outside."

"Shouldn't think y'are. I like your dress."

"Thank? Thank you." That seems the right thing to say.

The woman tilts her head at the sounds of the sirens. She has the face of yew trees, dark and peeling. Hard eyes, but with a glint of sweeter memories.

"What'll y'do now, girlie?"

Her pursuers will find a way round, or over, the outside walls, and she must choose, high or low. To bury herself in the tainted soil around her and wait, hope that they grow bored. Or to fly like Jump-Nancy. The choice is natural, instinctive. There are only the heights to seek.

"I will fly."

The old woman nods. "Good f'you."

Huldre climbs steadily, first on metal tubes and platforms, then up walls of raw brick and concrete. Her grip is good, fingers and toes, for she is ivy and mistletoe, born to cling and taste the air.

Shouts from below; alarm at her actions.

"Come down, love. It's all right!"

They are unknowing.

High on the crude scaffolding, she sees the world that is not hers, a glinting, over-lit unmaking of soft hills and deep, cold rivers. A death of grass, an attempt to manage the things they fear. In a sudden shiver, she is not without sympathy.

We must all choose, eventually, says Jump-Nancy. *You know that I did.*

The breeze is free of human voices, free of disgust or entreaty. And there, below her, on the far side of this constructed thing, the lime trees are waiting for night — and for her. She sees Nancy, sees Jennifer, as they plotted their escape, and she knows what they wanted. What they chose.

Spreading her arms wide, the wind catches at her hollow back and welcomes the truths within her. As she launches herself into the air, she smiles. She has become thistledown, to be borne down towards the green places. There will be freedom, of many kinds.

Jump-Nancy keep me, if you watch.

For she is falling...

AUTHOR NOTES

I have no answer as to who or what Huldre is in this particular case, or how this ends. I don't want one, really. I'm sure someone can work it out, but I'd leave it there, if I were you.

IN THE TIME of the Growing Cold, a finwife came to the Wolds. She came slow and silent, hauling herself from the seal rocks to the land, and she was not the finest of her kind. She was in fact a sadling, a runt of a girl with pearls of beach glass and dull hair which straggled on her shoulders. That she was there, so far from Eynhallow, could hardly stay unnoticed.

Charlie, the village's lengthman, saw her first. He was slicing his way down Odd Cows Lane, stripping back the summer's growth on the verges. He watched her progress around the gorse bushes, supposing herself unseen, and then he watched her slide into the mere. She didn't surface.

"Lunch," he said to his scythe.

The White Horse was quiet. Martha Grange leant on the beer pump and regarded the cigarette end floating in the slops tray. A tiny brown boat, bobbing on a brown ocean. She lit another one, and drew hard on it. Tuesday lunchtime. Four or five regulars, and a family passing through, two morose teenagers trying to sit as far away from their parents as possible. The father was muttering something about the taste of the beer.

Martha smiled. She didn't dislike strangers, she just didn't need them. Her worst fear was being put in some good beer guide and having people turning up, all notebooks, braces, and beards. With that in mind, visitors got the barrel ends and the slop tray.

"There's summat different come," said Charlie, propping his scythe by the door.

The tourists looked up. Martha scowled at the lengthman, beckoned him over.

"What do you mean, 'different'?" she asked, her voice low.

Charlie leaned right over the bar.

"Summat over Odd Cows Lane way. It's a lass. She went in t'mere, stayed there."

Martha stubbed out her cigarette.

"Best tell Harry, then."

***

The village of Gorse Muttering was not on any maps. It sat quiet and ignored in the folded landscape, not that far from the great chalk cliffs, not that far from the rolling farmlands of the Wolds. In the ramshackle glasshouse next to his cottage, Harry Cropton grew tomatoes.

He regarded Charlie with the calm that came from having managed to grow seven plum tomato plants from seed. The sea-frets and the cold inland winds were not kind to tomatoes.

"She's still there, I suppose." Harry, who was possibly eighty years old, sat on a stool outside the glasshouse, and considered. "Driven out, seeking summat, or just bringing mischief?"

Charlie blinked. He was far too close to Harry's aged cat, known locally as the Executioner. The Executioner didn't see that well, and didn't have the sense of smell he used to, but he'd never lost his touch. Anything smaller than a bullock was fair game if it strayed into his territory.

"I've Main Street to cut," said Charlie, edging back. "I saw nowt else, but they said I should tell thee, right away."

"Good enough. You get on wi'it."

Harry watched the lengthman leave, then kicked the cat. The Executioner sank his claws into the old man's foot, and found that Harry was wearing steel-toed boots, as usual. Disappointed, the cat staggered off to find something more penetrable.

Harry sniffed, wiping a dewdrop from his long nose, and set out for Odd Cows Lane. It was a ten-minute walk — for him anyway — along Main Street and round by Trench's Farm.

The mere was silent except for the sucking sound as Harry tramped through the reeds. A duck stared at him with distaste and paddled back into cover. When he was close to being ankle-deep, he stood and brushed the water with his stick.

"They say you're in there," he said conversationally. "Best come out and talk, or I'll find a way to send something in after you. There's more than one dog can swim round here."

Ripples, and then a sorry head. The finwife's hair looked better, but not much better, wet. Her large dark eyes lacked the usual shine. He was reminded of a seal with distemper.

"Sanc-tuary. I ask...sanct-uary," she said. Her thin lips struggled with the words.

"We'll see."

***

The kitchen of Cold Farm contained Harry Cropton, Jenny Mainprize, and one of the Misses Hetherington. Harry thought it was Miss Edith, but it was hard to tell.

"A finwife?" Jenny peered into the teapot, added another spoonful of leaves. "That's odd, isn't it?"

"Aye." Harry nodded, watching her bend over the stove in her tight jeans. He had his dear Elsie at home, of course, but Jenny Mainprize was a fine-looking woman. There was only fifty or so years between them, after all. Then he thought of Elsie's right hand clutching a kitchen knife, and decided to get back to business. "But she's shown no harm, as yet."

"Where did you put her?" Miss Hetherington was knitting. What she was knitting, no one dared ask.

"In Mike Trench's old barn."

"She's a long way from Finfolkaheim or Eynhallow." Miss Hetherington tutted as she tried to cast off. "But this is a time of changes..."

The others nodded. The Growing Cold. Things on the moors, even sniffing close to the towns. And the Children of Angles and Corners grew bolder with every year. All manner of hidden things were returning, and there were few people left who knew the old ways.

"Is this a matter for the cunning, then?" Jenny poured out more tea.

"Ten years ago I'd have let her be." Harry shook his head. "Now I don't know. If the finfolk want her..."

"She wants sanctuary from her own people. I don't understand that."

He took the fresh mug of tea from her.

"I reckon one of their elders has been pressing her. You know what happens — they get sent to wed a fisherman, or drag one down. It never ends well."

"Sanctuary, you said." Miss Hetherington looked up. "The Nazarenes used to like that word. We should put her in St. Michael's."

Harry and Jenny looked at the ageless apple-dumpling of a woman, surprised. It was a good compromise.

"I'll take her up after milking," said Jenny.

***

Gorse Muttering had been Ralph Townsend's escape from an inner-city church on a rough housing estate. He was in bad shape, physically and mentally, when the bishop made a tentative suggestion about St. Michael's.

"It takes a...a different sort of faith to minister in that, um, parish," the bishop said, peering over his bifocals. "You have to be somewhat, um, relaxed there."

Wary, and still nursing a broken arm from his last home visit on the estate, Ralph hesitated, but the bishop made it clear. It was St. Michael's, or a change of vocation.

After a year in the village, Reverend Townsend was not entirely thrown out by the arrival of Jenny Mainprize and the finwife.

"Can it...she...enter? Holy ground, I mean?" he asked, when the situation had been explained.

He looked at the nervous creature by Jenny's side. The eyes were too large and dark, the jaw too pointed, but she might just pass for a human girl, if they could find some clothes for her rake-thin body. At the moment, the finwife was naked except for a stained horse blanket.

"We'll find out, I suppose."

"So she's what, some sort of mermaid?"

Jenny gave him the sort of look you gave a slow child.

"Finwife. The finfolk didn't used to come further south than the Orkneys and Shetlands. The males are sullen, and violent."

"And the women, the females?"

"At the beck and call of their males, unless they find a way to escape."

Jenny urged the girl into the church porch. The finwife shivered but took damp steps forward, staring at the dark opening to the church itself.

"Well, we're very supportive of multi-faith initiatives these days," he said, and realised how stupid he sounded.

Jenny looked at him, supporting his self-assessment, but led the girl inside.

He was relieved to see that lightning didn't strike the steeple, and that none of the statues of saints started bleeding.

"Here, let's see what we have."

He opened a box of donated clothes inside the doorway. He found a long green dress and a cardigan, handing them to the finwife.

"You can change in there." He pointed to the small side door.

"I'll help her." Jenny and the finwife disappeared into the vestry, to come out five minutes later with the barefooted semblance of a teenage girl.

"How old are you?" the vicar asked.

Wide eyes met his. Jenny whispered in the girl's ear.

"Nine-teen," said the girl.

"And what should I call you?"

Another whisper followed.

"Kel-da."

The vicar frowned. "Can't she understand me?"

"Mostly." Jenny patted his arm. "Simple words, vicar."

"Come on, then. We should find you something to eat."

Stood behind the church, the parish hall was little more than a large shed, but it did have a sink and a toilet. Jenny Mainprize helped when it came to explaining the toilet, but otherwise he managed by gesture and the odd word to settle the finwife in. He brought a camp bed from the vicarage, a few blankets, and watched her crawl underneath the bed, still dressed and wrapped in the blankets as well.

"How long... I mean, what's going to happen to her?"

Jenny shrugged. "We don't know, vicar. We'll think on it."

He looked away. "Oh. I see."

Not that he did. The villagers were either kind or pleasantly indifferent to him. He could visit them, if he wanted. There was always a cup of tea, a homemade cake. He could even talk about the church, but it was pointless. The ones who weren't Christian were better versed in comparative theology than he was; the Christians didn't believe in the need for an actual church. Services were attended when it was raining or when they coincided near enough with a solstice. Apart from that, he was left to do whatever he wanted.

Ralph Townsend did not know what he wanted.

***

The presence of the finwife took up much of his time over the next few days. She would only eat raw food, preferably fish and raw meat. For want of ideas, he showed her round the church. She was the only person who had shown any real interest since his arrival.

"Time under you," she said, standing in the nave and looking down at the stone flags. "Many years gone, others in the earth."

He wasn't sure he liked the sound of that. He showed her the altar.

"Cross." She leaned forward, gingerly touching the brass cross on its dusty cloth. She seemed surprised when nothing happened. "Power inside?"

Her eyes were those of a wild seal.

"I don't know," he admitted. "Maybe. Yes."

A hissing laugh.

"Used to fear cross."

"There's nothing here to be afraid of, Kelda." He tried to think of something appropriately religious to say. "God is love."

The finwife looked down at her thin body, put one hand flat on her crotch. The short fingers were faintly webbed.

"Love," she said, rubbing at her crotch through the green dress.

The vicar reddened. "No, not sex. Um...love, care." He mimicked an embrace, a gentle kiss. She wandered off to look at the stained-glass windows.

They walked to the mere occasionally, so that she could shed her clothes and dive into the murky water. He tried to look away, but failed more than once. She had small breasts, a narrow frame. He closed his mind to that sort of thought, and whistled softly as she swam.

In the evenings, he left her in the parish hall, turned off the lights, and went to his own bed tired and confused.

***

Charlie brought Harry a newspaper most mornings.

"This is t'one," he said, leaning on the old man's gate. The Executioner was elsewhere, and Charlie relaxed.

Harry peered at the newspaper.

"Fishing coble wrecked off the Head. Last night, eh?"

"I know t'bloke what buys their crabs. One of them swears he saw hands grabbin' side of t'boat afore they went over." He drew on his pipe. "Teks a lot to turn a coble keel-side up."

"More finfolk."

"'Appen. Thought tha'd want to know."

Harry creaked his way up to the village shop.

A Miss Hetherington was sat behind the counter, round as an apple in a pinafore. He showed her the morning paper.

"There's a sale at Biltons," she said at last.

"No, the bit about the fishermen."

Mice explored a box of cereal which had fallen off its shelf. After some minutes, Miss Hetherington nodded.

"We need eyes, Mr. Cropton. Yes, eyes." She looked at the clock in the hallway. "September. Who can we beg, who can we beg? Ah yes, they don't need to be anywhere, and they do like the cliffs."

He could guess who "they" were. "Do you want me to—"

"I'll see to it."

"Thanks. I'll tell the others."

She settled back in a *whumph* of talcum powder and lavender which made him want to cough. He started for the door.

"The vicar's not a strong man, Mr. Cropton."

Harry paused.

"You mean it's a mistake to leave her up there?"

She pursed soft pink lips.

"I don't know. They won't enter the church though. Never a finman would dare that, not even in the Growing Cold."

***

He reached the parish hall by lunchtime, though he'd rather have been in the pub. The vicar was cross-legged on the floor, showing the finwife spelling books from a never-to-happen toddlers' group.

"Mar-y." The vicar sounded tired. "Jo-seph."

"Klok-folk," said the finwife, edging back from Harry.

"Everything all right here, reverend?" Harry leaned on his stick, catching his breath.

"We're making, um, some progress." The vicar stood up, brushing his knees. "She doesn't seem to be too sure of you, though."

"I'm not surprised. So, nothing unusual happened?"

Reverend Townsend looked at the half-clad finwife near his feet, then at Harry's carved blackthorn stick.

"No," he managed. "Everything's quite normal."

Harry decided not to mention the incident with the coble. He left the vicar and the girl Kelda to their lessons.

Down in the village, the White Horse was empty except for Martha.

"The jackdaws are up." She squinted at him.

"Miss Dorothy sent them."

They shared a quiet pint.

"I was watched, last night," said Martha, licking foam from the rim of her glass.

"Oh yes?" Harry held his own glass out for a top-up.

"It was them. The Children of Angles and Corners."

She might not have had the cunning, but the villagers kept nothing from her. She smiled. "I hammered a seven-inch nail into the roofbeam. They didn't half create."

"Good lass." He stared at his pint.

"How's the girl?" asked Martha.

"Still there. Klokfolk, she called me."

The landlady consulted her knowledge of the village, and added the encounter she had had with a Norwegian trawlerman last spring. The spare room still smelled of mackerel.

"The clever people." She nodded. "Close enough, eh?"

"Aye. I don't reckon a finwife ends up here by accident."

"And you think they're coming to get her back?"

"Mebbe."

Harry drained his glass.

If he went home now, he could still water the tomatoes.

Two walkers found a dead gull that afternoon. It was pinned to the side of a twisted hawthorn near the cliffs, its breast torn open and the small ribs spread wide. They had no idea what it meant, and so they left quickly to eat their packed lunches somewhere else. They preferred their countryside like their sandwiches, in small, tasteful bites.

A Miss Hetherington was sat outside the shop when the vicar came for supplies. She smiled at him and rolled her way inside.

"More pilchards, reverend?"

"I'm afraid so, Miss Hetherington. And do you have any cod-liver oil left?"

He filled his shopping bag and after a pointless pleasantry or two made his way back up to the church. He was slow today. His sleep had been broken, an odd night of dreams which he couldn't recall. He felt like he'd already walked five miles before he started.

St. Michael's stood to the south of the village on the rolling hump called Leatherman's Hill. Kelda was waiting for him in the church porch, wearing a soft blue wool dress from one of the donation boxes. Her white-blonde hair was combed, long and silky, and she smiled at him. The sight of her sharp little teeth seemed normal by now.

"Ral-ph."

She took the bag from him, handling it as if it were empty. He had been surprised at how strong she was. Though not as surprised when she admitted her true age. Kelda had been born, or spawned, he didn't like to ask, in the wild sea currents near the Orkneys, one hundred and nineteen years ago.

"We can have our lunch," he said, ignoring the way the wool stretched over her breasts. He struggled with two fantasies at night. One was that of Kelda coming to comfort him in his over-sized, creaking bed, the other was of converting a finwife to the ways of the church. Neither seemed likely.

They spent the afternoon exploring the churchyard. Kelda seemed interested, and he found the gravestones a sign of normality. Gorse Muttering had funerals and burials like any other parish, though he'd never conducted one here. Some of the stones were carved with unlikely ages.

"Crop-ton," said Kelda, tracing a name. "Cun-ning Folk. Like old man."

"Yes. Harry."

She pressed nearer to him, her thin body warm.

"He send me back?"

He put his arm around her. "No, I don't think so. He's a...good man."

After dinner she lay on the sofa in the vicarage while he tried to draft a sermon. It was getting close to the autumn solstice, a time when he could pretend to be a proper vicar.

He finished his notes a little before midnight. Kelda was asleep, her bare feet twitching. The soft webbing between her toes was almost attractive.

One swift whisky and he lay down, fully clothed, on his bed. He was searching for sense in the Gospel according to John when he drifted off.

The sea was a lonely place. Ralph Townsend dreamed of vast abysses under the waves, of a watery emptiness where he swam, lost, on currents which carried him away from everything he cared about.

And then there was warmth in his dream, like the night before. He imagined hands stroking his body, comforting him. He moaned as slender limbs entwined him, and two large eyes shone with pleasure...

Later, when the moon was dim, a particular chalk boulder near the edge of the village was moved. No one noticed.

Three days, and the jackdaws spoke of strangers between Gorse Muttering and the sea. Salt strangers. Harry failed to kick the cat that evening, only ate half of his over-cooked gammon. His wife, emerging briefly from her own slightly peculiar world, pushed cake into his jacket pocket and told him to walk the boundary.

"Why, Elsie love?"

"Summat's coming." She was a small woman, all pinafores and rubber gloves, as daft and as interesting as when they had married fifty-three years before. She had a touch of briar and rook about her, a gift with the wild. She was the only person the Executioner never went for.

"You mean the finfolk? Are they here?"

She lost interest. There was cabbage to be boiled, and Harry would know what to do.

He did. He gathered Jenny Mainprize along the way, drawing her from her cows.

"Our Elsie says to walk the boundary."

Jenny patted her prime milker, Hildaberg, on the nose and joined him.

They took the way past Cold Farm and onto the slopes, the village a clutch of buildings in the dip of the land below them.

"The Rook-Stones are all right," he noted as they passed a broken circle of boulders in the middle of a field. A rook tilted its head at them, and flew off towards Rail Woods, where the old station used to be.

The ward-post by Rail Woods was as it should be, a four-foot post with an eye carved into it. For the sake of any passing walkers, someone had added a yellow right of way arrow. No one knew where the arrow would lead people, but that wasn't the point.

They passed around the White Farm, and into the woodland between the White Farm and the north road. Crossing the road, east and onto open land, the mere lay below them. Jenny shivered.

"Something's missing," she said. "Harry, they've broken the boundary."

"Finfolk couldn't..."

"Something's missing," she repeated, and strode out.

He struggled to follow her, using his stick to keep his balance. Halfway up Odd Cows Lane they found the first breach. The ward-post lay on its side, kicked under the nearest hedge. The simple carved eye had been scored through. Three times.

"I ought to have felt it. The jackdaws should have said."

"Wasn't done by the Hidden or their kin," said Jenny, stroking the post. She was a good one for the Touch.

"An accident? Kids from town, ramblers?"

But he knew better. When they found one of the sea-stones further on, rolled out of its place and similarly marked with three knife scratches, they knew why Elsie had sent them out. Someone had known how to break the village boundary, open the way for those who might have little love for the people within.

"Who did it then?" Harry's face creased more than usual.

"Does it matter? If something's in, it's in."

"It matters," said Harry. "But as you say, summat's here. Suppose it's come for that girl."

Sea-stone and ward-post would need replacing, but not now. Gorse Muttering had granted sanctuary, and Gorse Muttering's word had to be kept.

They had to get to the church.

***

Ralph Townsend was praying, though he didn't expect it to do any good.

Three sinewy figures had arrived as he was showing Kelda back to the hall. Silhouetted against the sunset, they might have been men, but as they came closer they had a dark look which set them apart from any men he'd met before, even the worst of the thugs on the estate. Eyes as large as Kelda's, but full of ice.

They stood between the pair and the church, and he wished that he was wearing his cross. Somehow he'd lost it the day before. Their clothes were tangled with kelp and bladderwrack, like drowned sailors, and their long fingers moved in an unseen current. The girl cowered against the parish hall. Was this why she had sought sanctuary — the cold finfolk described by Jenny Mainprize?

"I'll protect you," he shouted.

The tallest of the figures laughed, the scrape of barnacle against rock.

"No need, God-man. Her part is done."

There was a rustle in the bushes by the graveyard. The finman looked, saw nothing, and turned back to the vicar.

"Our kin have seen you, calling your God. No one comes. This is the Growing Cold, our time again..."

"Not yet, mebbe."

Harry Cropton stumped his way around the corner of the vicarage, Jenny Mainprize in his wake.

"Thank God." The vicar ran to Kelda, tried to put his arm around her, but she thrust him away. The finmen hissed, and to Ralph's surprise the girl crawled towards the finmen like a whipped dog.

"What are you doing?" He reached for her, to pull her back, but found no strength in his hands or arms.

Harry nodded. "Reckon I see it now. You used her, she used him."

Thin laughter from the strangers. "Clever, clever. The sadling held him, made him pleased. Men do things in the night that they do not know."

The vicar remembered his dreams, the tiredness in the mornings.

"What did I do?"

Harry didn't look at him. "You broke the boundary. A stick here, a stone there. It wasn't your fault, reverend."

"But Kelda..."

"She was told to use you. I doubt she had any choice in the matter. They wanted to know what we had here, to see if they could come and go. They found a way."

"He is not klok...not wise. He does not even truly believe in his god." A finman hissed with pleasure. "So many children of men, so little cunning or faith. The Times Yet to Be will be easy, if even here we can walk."

The finwife was weeping.

"I think we will take this small God-man also. Drown him and make him dance on Eynhallow. He may be useful."

Harry and Jenny came closer.

"I don't think you will," said Harry. "This is our place."

The finman made a smile with an almost lipless mouth. One hand rose, and the vicar watched in horror as Harry and Jenny staggered.

"The Strength of Three is beyond you, Cunning Man," said the creature.

Ralph could see it now, a shimmer in the air between the finmen. They were bound together, working together. He tried to move, but was driven down by a single look from one of the finmen.

"Do something," he gasped at Kelda, but he could see that she was lost. A helpless girl, for all her years, under the thrall of the three.

The tallest of them nodded to another, who took the vicar's arm in a damp grip. He tried to fight, yelling at the creature which held him.

"In the name of Jesu—" An ice-glance silenced him.

"We go, with runtling and God-man. The testing is done." The finman gestured to Kelda, who stood up and came to its side, still weeping. "And we know what is here, now. We shall tell the Children of Angles and Corners, and others."

"You don't know as much as you think." Harry coughed, only upright because Jenny was supporting him. "He likes fish, by the way."

The finman frowned.

"What do you say?"

"He likes fish," repeated Harry.

The rustling noise heard earlier in the bushes became something large and vaguely ginger, if ginger had been smeared with mud, kicked around a bit, and run over by a lawnmower. With a screech, the Executioner launched himself at the leading finman.

The cat slashed great furrows in the creature's face, then sank his remaining teeth into its upper lip. It wasn't often that he got a chance to have a real go at something. Flesh tore, raw and oily, and the cat's hind claws raked its chest. The Executioner yowled triumphantly, his mouth full of something far more interesting than tinned cat food.

The finman screamed, a high gull scream which echoed off gravestones and church walls. It managed to rip the animal from its face, but some of its face stayed with the cat. The Executioner landed surprisingly lightly and swiped a large, disreputable paw at the legs of the next nearest stranger, his claws going deep...

The Strength of Three no longer held.

Harry came forward, his brown eyes shadowed.

"Uninvited."

Jenny Mainprize took his shoulders, steadying him.

"Unwelcome," she said.

There was a feeling in the ground beneath the vicar's feet, a sort of change that he couldn't describe, and the air was scented with hawthorn blossom, which wasn't possible on a September evening.

"Unlooked for." Harry took another step.

"Unwanted." Her words fell in the same cadence as the old man.

The creatures heard the bane words, saw that terrible animal crouched ready to spring again...

"You have made an enemy," said the unharmed finman, glaring at its wounded companions.

Harry Cropton's face was dark and angry.

"That's where you've got it wrong, lad," he said. He smelled of hawthorn and spring mornings, of tobacco and an old man's cardigan. "We had nothing in particular against the finfolk, 'til this." His right hand went up, fingers splayed, and the churchyard yews shivered, tips pointing towards the sea. "Now *you* have an enemy. Think on that, eh? Ask on Eynhallow, and see if your elders think you've done good. Ask in the deeps if it was worth this test."

The tall finman lifted its arm; the Executioner gave a preparatory yowl, and the arm went down.

"Our Drowned Word upon you," the finman snarled at the vicar, but Harry's hand held land rights and spring flowers; the cry of rooks and the first bleat of newborn lambs. The finman's Word was lost, and jackdaws circled above the yews, watching.

"Uninvited." A statement and command.

The finmen shuddered, their control lost. Stripped of power, they ran towards the cliffs, the girl limping behind them. Ralph thought that there had been a last backward glance from Kelda, but he found that he couldn't see so well. He seemed to be weeping.

The churchyard was quiet again.

Harry glanced east, watching the creatures head for their own sanctuary, the grey North Sea. The Executioner prowled through the grass, searching for pieces of finman that he'd missed. He seemed disappointed.

"Our fault," said Harry at last. "Never thought they'd go that far."

"The Growing Cold," Jenny said, and squatted by the vicar's side. "Cheer up, reverend. No damage done."

"Damage?" He looked up at her. "I was useless. I did nothing for her, couldn't protect her, couldn't protect myself."

"There'll be other days."

"What...what do you mean?"

"I'd ask God, if it were me." Jenny smiled, squeezing his hand.

Her eyes were not like Kelda's. They were grey and clear.

The old man tested his aching bones, and found most of them intact.

"No one comes to Gorse Muttering by accident, reverend." He patted his pockets to see if he had a mint. There was still a sour, seaweed taste in his mouth. "Not finfolk, vicars, nor cats."

The Executioner spat and padded off. Fish was all right, but Trench Farm had a new goat. Now there was a challenge...

AUTHOR NOTES

I grew up in a small East Yorkshire village where, when legends did not abound about a solitary boulder, a dark lane, or a body of water, we made them up. As children, we wanted the eerie and the strange. And then there was the long tradition of the Cunning Folk, which we did not make up, for it exists in many countries — the hedge-wizards, the witch-sniffers, the practitioners of small ways which benefit the community. Rarely grand magicks, but tricks, wards, and cures for common sicknesses and causes of strife. Small magicks appeal to me more than many grand ones.

I could explain some aspects of the above, but that sounds like hard work, so I'll just say that a lengthman is someone hired to keep the lanes and roads of the parish clear of weeds, over-long grass, and so forth, and my village had one.

IT HAPPENED, BUT it happened slowly.

First he lost his job when the machine-parts factory closed down. It wasn't a good job, but it made him talk to people. The more he was at home, the less he had anything to say to anyone but his mother, with whom he lived.

The following year his mother died, quite suddenly. A brief bout of pneumonia, and the house was empty except for him. He talked even less after that.

Then there was the subsidence at the end of the street. Old mine shafts, they said, empty snakeskins coiled under the road, waiting to collapse, and part of the street had to be demolished. The part with his mother's house on it.

So he had to move, and they found him a flat in Rowan Rise. It wasn't difficult. Rowan Rise would be next on the list for demolition, with or without collapsing mine shafts, and no one lived there if they had anywhere else to go. He didn't.

Names matter as well, not only jobs and homes. He had a name, obviously, but after a while no one bothered to use it, because they didn't need to. "Him in Flat Seven," they said. "That odd guy in the dump." And finally, as the other tenants left, one by one, he became nothing more than "that guy."

It didn't bother him, because he didn't notice the world outside anymore. He forgot to wash as often. His hair grew longer, began to straggle on his shoulders as it thinned on top. His fingernails thickened with age, harder to cut, and so he left them.

Money was tight. He'd had some compensation, but he didn't understand it. He bought cheap cuts of meat, stock bones and ham hocks, and learned to live on them. His jaws grew stronger, his teeth like yellowed pegs as he ground down the gristle and sinew. He tried marrowbones and fish-heads, all of which went down his gullet in a moment, pig's trotters and stewing steak. He grew, his shoulders wider than ever and his belly breaking open his pants. And yet he was always empty inside, somehow.

He wasn't seen much. When he did emerge, usually at night or in pouring rain, he moved in shadows, a bulk which no one wanted to approach. And even those appearances stopped eventually. It was rumoured that someone local did his shopping for him, but no one had seen them go in or out of the flat.

A few years passed. The flats were still standing, an ugly mass of bricks on the edge of the neighbourhood, and he was still there. While lawyers argued over land-law and zoning, office blocks and affordable housing, the kids found a new name for the one person left in Rowan Rise. They listened to their parents, and they remembered the nonsense that they had heard in bedtime stories.

They called him the Ogre.

***

Esme Carlito had almost gone in the place once, a few months ago when the front door of the flat began to hang half-open, one of the hinges rusting away. A dare, of course. She told her friends afterwards that the smell had put her off, a stench of stale sweat and meat. She told her dog Max, however, that she could hear the Ogre's breathing, a snorting in the darkness, and that she had been terrified. Max understood.

Her brother didn't want to hear Esme's stories. He was fifteen, two years older than her. The wrong age for bedtime stories, or for anything else. No love life, no skill at sports, and not particularly academic.

Daniel Carlito was a loner. Not because he wanted to be, but because he was edged out of everything that might have been interesting. The teams and clubs didn't want him, a mediocre boy with slightly too much weight around his waist. He was Hispanic, but not Hispanic enough to be considered hip. The others in his year derided him for his lack of sexual experience. He knew that most of what they said was made up, but he didn't tell lies very well. So he played computer games, read the odd crime story, and kept out of people's way.

That had worked, until Cresser noticed him.

"Whatya up to, Danny?" he would call out, cronies at his side. "Pickin' your zits again? Want a hand?" A half-empty can usually followed, spraying Daniel's jacket with flat Coke. Or a stone, a handful of soil. A schoolbook, and once a brick, which left his arm bruised for days. Fell over, he told his mother when she saw him wincing.

Daniel's mother said that Cresser had "anger issues" and "personal problems." But Daniel's mother worked all hours, keeping the family fed and clothed. She was guessing. Daniel had known kids who were bullied and lashed out in return. He'd known other kids whose parents fought a lot of the time, or whose parents were separated like his. He could cope with them.

Cresser was bad in the head, plain nasty. He always had been. He liked what he did, and he spread his nastiness, infecting weaker kids, drawing them into his circle.

It didn't get any better. Mrs. Carlito took one afternoon off to speak to the teachers, almost losing her position at the mini-mart. Then she spent an hour talking to Daniel about Cresser, bullying, and how to get on with others, and was late for her cleaning job. Daniel stopped mentioning it to her.

Fridays were particularly bad. On Fridays, Cresser would taunt Daniel with what might happen over the weekend.

"Ought to look out for that mutt of your sister's," he'd say. "Lot of gangs round here, they take dogs and make 'em fight together."

Or, "Thought I might hang out on your turf Sat'day, Danny. I seen which is your window, got me a BB gun now…"

It left Daniel waiting, and worrying.

On the Friday before the summer break, the wait was over. Cresser was there for him outside school, a few younger kids at his back. He had a corroded length of iron in his hand, twisted from the railings.

"Found this, Danny. Thought we'd hang out by the old flats, hit stones. Wanna come?"

Daniel put his head down, tried to walk past. Cresser tripped him and he fell, tearing one knee of his trousers.

"Thought you would."

They dragged him up and along the pavement. An old man walking by opened his mouth to speak, looked at Cresser, and carried on past in silence. Daniel wanted to shout out, but couldn't do it. If he struggled, yelled, it would get worse. Maybe he could take a few more bruises and get it over with. Cresser would get sick of the game eventually, move on to someone else.

The area around Rowan Rise was wildly overgrown, a mass of dog-roses and other thorny bushes which were thick with litter — torn newspaper, cans and bottles, plastic bags which were wet and might yet have something unpleasant in them. Every flat was boarded up except one.

"So, wanna meet the Ogre?" Cresser smacked the railing into the palm of his other hand, releasing flakes of rust. The smaller kids sniggered, urged Cresser on.

"Do him, Cresser."

"Yeah, smack him one, right here."

Cresser stood up straight, flexed his broad shoulders. He was heading for six foot tall, even at fifteen, and bulking up nicely. For him.

"Naah, I think he's gonna show us how tough he is. Go on, Danny, get in there..."

It wasn't a choice. His knee hurt, and the gang were waiting for him. Running was right out. He stumbled towards the Ogre's door. The uneven brick path didn't help, choked with thistles and other weeds so that the bricks had lifted here and there, almost tripping him again.

The plastic "7" was on its side, one screw missing. Daniel had to step round the door, which hung at a slant, stained and peeling. It had been green, once. His sister had been right about the smell. Rotting food and a sickly undertone, meat gone bad. Sweat and urine as well.

He tried not to gag as he edged into the debris-strewn front room. He could see the remains of a sofa in the gloom, and an armchair which had been ripped open, its springs hanging down to the remains of a carpet. There was no way of telling what colour it might have been. A television lay on its side in one corner, shattered. Torn curtains let in enough light to see, but behind the TV was another doorway, the darkness beyond that impenetrable.

He should have said hello, called out and asked if he could come in. He didn't. The fall, the whole thing with Cresser, and now this... Daniel felt his chest tighten, his stomach turn inside him. He leaned against the wall and closed his eyes.

"Nnngh." A deep sound, a voice of sorts, from the other room. Louder to him than the jeering outside, as Cresser yelled to see if he'd had enough yet, if he'd met the Ogre.

He turned towards the window, wondering if...

The impact on the side of his head was astonishingly painful, as if a baseball bat had been swung at his skull. Daniel took one choking breath, and blacked out as he fell.

***

Shadows, some caused by the pain in his head, some by the massive figure that stood over him.

"Bad." A finger, with greyish skin and a long, cracked nail at the end, more like a crocodile's claw. He'd seen them at the zoo. It was pointing in his face.

Daniel scuffled back against the wall, pressing himself to it.

"I'm sorry, I'm sorry." He cowered, wondering if there would be another blow. There usually was, with Cresser, but this was someone — something — else.

He'd never needed to come to Rowan Rise. Kids threw stones through any remaining windows on the first floor, sprayed tags on the outside walls. He knew that, but he'd never been part of it. He'd assumed that "that guy" was just another pensioner, trapped in trashy housing. The name the kids used meant very little to him. Maybe the guy was bad-tempered, a bully like Cresser? He knew that there was no such thing as an actual ogre...

Was there?

It smelled of meat and wet dogs, and it was big enough to block out most of the feeble light from the window. If it was a man, it had abandoned any pretence at looking like one. There were clothes, of sorts, but they were mostly rags around its waist. Wiry hairs covered its huge chest and shoulders, matted into the tangle of greyer strands which hung from an almost bald head, small in comparison to the body.

"Please, don't hit me again."

"Bad," it said again, but less harshly.

"I was...I was made to come in here, honest." Daniel waved one hand towards the world outside. "They made me, Cresser and that lot. I didn't want to..."

"Ngh." The thing stepped back, less threatening.

"I'm called Daniel, uh...Danny."

If there was any way he could get out of this, it would be through talking. His head hurt, his leg hurt, and this thing would have him well before he reached the door.

The Ogre appeared to consider this. He could see that it had two eyes, a nose, a mouth, but everything was exaggerated. It had lips like mottled sausages, the sort you threw in the bin, drawn back from teeth the colour of wet sand; the nose was pitted and flattened, too large for the face.

It picked up a framed photograph from a collapsing sideboard. He hadn't noticed the picture before. A cheap gilt frame, ridiculously small in those great thick fingers.

"Is that you? In the picture?"

But it wasn't. He could make out the features of a woman, a thin old woman with blue-rinsed hair like Mrs. Chester down Daniel's street. The Ogre threw the photo into the room behind it, a clatter as the frame hit something hard.

"Nuh. Gone, her."

"Oh." He tried to stand up, managed to prop himself on his feet, still shaky. "What's your name, uh, sir?"

"Nuh name," it grunted. "Furget. Hungery."

"They...they call you the Ogre." It came out, though he hadn't meant it to.

"Wass that?"

"An ogre? It's, I dunno, a sort of monster. Eats people."

There was a sort of surprise on the flat, pock-marked face. At least Daniel hoped it was surprise, not a sign that the thing was angry.

"Dunt know peepul. Dunt know nuh one."

Daniel couldn't detect any sadness or concern about this state of affairs, and he understood, in a way. Some things were what they were.

"Can I...can I stay in here, maybe for an hour or two? I won't bother you."

How he could have bothered someone, something like this, escaped him, but it seemed worth saying.

"Ngh." Indifference. The creature turned and shambled into the deep gloom of the other room. After a while, he heard the sounds of gnawing, grinding, the wet noises of something eating in the dark. Daniel sat down again and hugged his knees to his chin. Another half hour and maybe Cresser would get sick of hanging around, or assume that Daniel had found another way out.

Daniel would be patient. He knew how to do that.

***

Saturday was bliss in comparison to school — shopping for his mother, a couple of other errands, and a new detective book from the library.

Sunday brought Cresser, kicking pebbles into Daniel's front yard, waiting.

Daniel had to take the garbage out, and the bins were right next to his tormentor. Esme was away at a friend's, and his mother was in no mood for arguments.

He hauled the bag out, keeping the bin between him and Cresser.

"What happened to you, Danny boy? Meet the Ogre, did you?"

The tall boy's expression was one of amusement. It wouldn't last.

"No one there," said Daniel. "Must...must have left, or died, or something."

"So you sat there, all that time? Saw nothin', found nothin'?"

"Pretty much." Daniel lifted up the heavy plastic bag, manoeuvring it to drop it in the bin. A second before he had it in the right place, Cresser kicked the bin over. The bag burst on the concrete, spilling garbage across the sidewalk, a tidal wave of waste which stopped slightly short of Daniel's feet.

It was a moment to be angry, to let loose all his rage at Cresser's bullying and strike back...

Daniel was damaged enough from what had happened two days ago. Perhaps he would turn into a mad psychopath when he was thirty, or something weird like that, he thought, squeezing his anger down inside him. If he made it that far. He bit the inside of his cheek, and began to pick things up.

"Don't believe you," said Cresser, and walked away.

But it didn't end there. Cresser seemed bugged by what had, or had not, happened in Flat 7. Sly comments on the street, more threats, over the next few days. When Daniel saw Cresser and his "friends" walking down Main Street on Wednesday morning, he ran before they could spot him. He was not far from Rowan Rise at the time, and the thick bushes there were enough to keep him hidden.

The place looked exactly the same, deserted. No movement at the only window, one pane cracked but still in place. It felt as if he'd had a concussion, and dreamed the whole thing up. There was no ogre in that flat.

Daniel couldn't stand up to Cresser, but he could be brave on his own. He was on his own a lot. He edged towards the building, making sure that Cresser's lot were out of sight. Maybe he'd seen a tramp, got confused.

He stepped past the broken door as quietly as he could. The stench was the same — he hadn't dreamt that part. He listened.

There was breathing. The choked snorts of something very large breathing.

"Hello? Mr...er, sir?"

The blackness moved forward, becoming a dirty grey-brown mass that was exactly as he remembered it.

"Hungery," it said, but made no further move towards him.

Daniel felt in his pockets, came out with a bar of chocolate.

"Here."

Thick nails crinkled the wrapper, took it from him. The whole bar went into that mouth, went down with a gulp, foil and all.

"Any better?" asked Daniel.

"Hungery." The Ogre looked at him, red-veined eyes trying to focus.

"It's okay."

The fear had left him, though he had no idea why. If Cresser had turned up with his gang, he might have been wetting himself, but this...thing, this Ogre, didn't scare him. It was big, and it was "hungery," as it kept saying. That was all.

Daniel made himself smile, and sat down in a shaft of light. He opened his backpack, handed his sandwich to the Ogre. That disappeared just as quickly.

"All right if I stay here and read?"

"Ngh," said the Ogre, and slowly made its way back into the other room.

Daniel took out his library book, and began to read.

***

For two weeks, Flat 7 became Daniel's refuge. There was no noise apart from the Ogre's thick breathing, and the creature had no apparent interest in anything but food. It came more readily to see what Daniel had brought it as the days went by. The carcass of a roast chicken. Half a bag of raw, slightly green potatoes. A bag of sugar. Cereal. The Ogre ate them all, but at the end of every visit, "hungery" was still there on the pungent air inside the flat.

His little sister Esme had a load of idiotic stories about people befriending wild animals, monsters, even dragons, and how wonderful it was. This was nothing like that. The flat smelled, the carpet was dirty.

The Ogre said and did virtually nothing. It was, however, a safe place, away from kids like Cresser who were bored enough by the summer break to want a victim.

He'd almost settled himself into this routine when the worst happened. An errand for his mother, picking up dry cleaning. It meant a slow walk back home, the bags over his shoulder. Easy target.

The gang were by the corner, Cresser punching another kid's arm again and again as the others laughed. Five of them this time, including Lucas "Lukey" Santiago, who said that Daniel brought "his people" into shame by being so pathetic.

"Whatcha got there, Daredevil Danny?" Lukey sniggered.

"Dry cleaning," said Daniel, and kept going. He couldn't run unless he abandoned the clothes, and he knew that they were his mother's uniforms for work.

Cresser's large frame blocked the sidewalk.

"Ain't seen you for a while."

"Been away." He tried to edge around Cresser.

"No, he's not." Lukey swaggered closer, a wiry boy with fake tattoos on his right arm. One of them spelled out "Saten Ruls," showing Lukey's academic level. "He's been hiding out, up at the flats. I seen him, couple of times."

Cresser frowned. "Don't think you told me the truth, didya, Danny? You find somethin' in there?"

Had he found something in Number 7? Yes, though he didn't know what. He'd been in an ogre's lair, and had survived.

He was sick of this.

"Hit me," he said to Cresser, putting the rustling plastic bags down on the sidewalk.

"Uh?"

"Hit me. You're five inches taller than me, Cresser, a year older. You play football in the front row, and you get your kicks by beating up smaller kids who don't have a chance. It's pathetic."

Cresser gave a grunt, and slammed his fist into Daniel's belly, doubling him over. He managed to stay on his feet, despite the pain and the *whumpf* of air from his lungs.

"That's how tough Cresser is," he gasped, staring round at the others. "Ever see him pick on anyone his own size, or his own age? Anyone who might fight back? Bet you haven't."

Another blow to his belly, but Cresser's face was flushed, and some of the gang looked confused.

"You ain't worth it," said Cresser, turning away.

Daniel drew in ragged breaths, his hands on his knees, trying not to collapse while the others were still there.

"Better watch your back, Lukey," he said. "If he can't get it from me, you're the next smallest round here."

Santiago's look of puzzlement, then his quick glance at Cresser, told Daniel that he'd sown the seeds. It was the best he could do...or was it?

Cresser was muttering about going to the slot machines, but Daniel was hearing his own words again, in his head. He felt like he'd had a revelation. Anyone his own size...

"You were right about that flat, Cresser," he shouted after them. "There was plenty of stuff in there, but it's not yours, so tough!"

Another seed sown, he hoped, as he picked up the dry cleaning and limped home.

Maybe he was learning. One way or another, he felt that things would be different in the days to come.

***

Cresser went out the same night, back to Rowan Rise. That flabby waste of space Danny Carlito had been inside, stayed in there. He'd even gone back. What had he found? And Cresser knew that he needed to teach one or two kids a lesson. He hadn't liked it when Santiago had peeled away that afternoon, saying the slots were boring.

What if there really was something worth stealing in the old flat? His uncle knew where to get rid of dodgy goods. And maybe he could work out how to close the front door properly. Locking one of his gang in there could be a laugh. Control was everything.

"God, what a stink." He held his sleeve to his nose and mouth as he went in. He could see nothing but rubbish in the front room.

"Must be something in here," he muttered as he stepped into the doorway of the second room. What had that Carlito kid been on about? You didn't come here twice for a laugh.

Maybe there was more in the back, less wrecked than this stuff. He shone his torch around. It was a good torch, with a bright, narrow beam. It spotlighted the face in the corner of the room, showing every hair and pore on the dirty skin, reflecting in the two blood-shot eyes — like an animal in headlights, but larger, thought Cresser. He was too stupid to be afraid.

At first.

He hefted the iron railing in his hand. He'd meant it for smashing any locks open, but it would do as extra protection as well. He took a step forward.

"Whatya got in here, then? Silver, watches? Mattress full of cash?"

The figure gave an incomprehensible grunt, but there was a tone to it. It sounded like a question. Cresser saw large nostrils flare, drawing in his scent even above the stench of the flat.

"Nuh... Danny?" It lifted large hands, its eyes narrower. "Not Danny."

Cresser felt doubt, somewhere in his belly, but let it lie there.

"Danny? That loser?" He laughed. "So you're this Ogre, are you?"

"Hungery."

"Yeah, aren't we all, pal." The more he jeered, the braver he felt. "You live in this heap, do you? You're only an old dosser, probably pisses himself all day."

"Yuh not Danny. Yuh mean."

"I'm Cresser, and you'd better watch it. Unless you eat kids, of course." He laughed, and glanced around. He saw the glint of a picture frame. That could be silver, worth a bit.

The Ogre stood up.

Cresser's torch, focussed on the creature's head, had missed the sheer size of what was in the flat. It had been sitting or kneeling on the floor. Cresser blinked, and now his sense of humour had gone. The Ogre towered over him, its back bent but its head still scraping paint from the ceiling like huge flakes of grey dandruff.

"Hey, no, get back!" said Cresser, lifting up his rusty weapon.

The Ogre reached out with one gangling arm and yanked the railing from the boy's hand. It put one rusty end into its mouth. Cresser watched, paralysed, as the thing in front of him bit through an inch of wrought iron, then spat it out. The two halves of the railing clanged on the floor.

The Ogre came closer, a figure whose monstrosity had finally penetrated even Cresser's brain.

"Eat...kidss? S'pose...find out," it said.

Gnarled hands, each the size of a man's head, took hold of Cresser by both shoulders, drew him close. Spittle sprayed the boy's face. He saw broken yellow teeth with shreds of gristle between them, grey gums...

"Very...hungery."

Huge jaws closed.

Crunch.

***

Mrs. Jacobs arrived at six in the morning, whistling softly as she went to the fallen front door of Number Seven and reached underneath it. As usual, she found money in the broken flowerpot, but the note next to it puzzled her. Malcolm had never left her a note before. And there was far more money than she needed to get his shopping. She had promised Malcolm's late mother that she would always keep an eye on him, and she had. Whatever he had become in the last few years meant nothing to her. Promises were made to be kept.

She opened out the crumpled note, a large square of dirty wallpaper.

Kno wut to eat now. Not hungery no more. Thanc yu.

The writing was clumsy, and in what appeared to be dark red ink.

Why he had gone, or where, puzzled her. Nothing had changed as far as she knew. She blew out her cheeks, looked around. She always came at this time of day, to avoid nosy parkers and the neighbourhood kids, who used to shout names and throw stones at the flat. Ogre, they called him, that was the word. Stupid thing to say. Malcolm would never hurt anyone.

She went into the flat for once, to check he wasn't still there. Mrs. Jacobs had lost her sense of smell years ago, and her sight wasn't as good as it used to be. Her sister had booked her in for cataract operations, but she didn't fancy them much. So the flat was a mess. Single men, never did put the effort in.

He had definitely gone. She was about to leave when she noticed the trainers on the floor. They couldn't have been Malcolm's. He had always had big feet, even as a child. She picked one up, but it was stained and sticky, no use to her. That, on the other hand...

Mrs. Jacobs reached down and took hold of a large, fresh bone. There was a bit of meat left on it, despite the tooth-marks where it had been gnawed at one end.

"Do nicely for the dog, that will."

She popped it in her shopping bag, along with Malcolm's cheap bacon joint, the note, and the money.

And Mrs. Jacobs walked away from the Ogre's lair, carrying the last of Ricky Cresser to a better place.

AUTHOR NOTES

This was the first short story I wrote for money, when I decided that short stories might be my "thing." There had to be an ogre, so I made a proper one, without the fairy tale gloss. It sold immediately to a small American press I'd never heard of, which was surprising — but nice. So I wrote an awful lot more stories...

the horse road

DARK-MANED AND WARY, he waits. Crows creak on the edge of the moor, cotton-grass sways by the small tarns. The world is not as asleep as it should be. He is iron-shod and ready. Three nights he has been coming here, while the no-longer-child turns and murmurs in her bed. In the mornings she wonders why he is tired, and blames the grass, or the fodder from the high meadow. She grooms him, and whispers in his twitching ear. It matters — her concern, her...love. Something he would never say.

They say that he was born under a dark sign, changed in some way. They don't know, they only guess. They guess about most things because he is unique. He remembers drawing breath, a choke of fluid, and the gentle hands of a child. He understands their theories of bonding and imprinting, but he doesn't care. He chose what happened and why. He chose because the child held something different.

And now he waits, because old things are moving, and the world grows cold.

Chitter. Whispering down the past-ways, they slide through choices and out of the half-world, onto the bleak moor, snapping at each other's sides. Hungry for failure and hopelessness, thirsty for small pains. The Children of Angles and Corners are loose, and they must play...

He is an edifice, four pillars of taut muscle. There are some slivers of darkness which the girl should not have to face. She is courageous, and true. When the nightjacks skittered from the woods, she took her father's gun and showed them why they should leave. She argued with blasphemies, and took fire to certain shadows beneath the stones. But when the half-world opens, even he takes care.

Froth blew from his wide nostrils that first night in the barn, lit by storm-lantern and worried faces. Iridescent, blood-scented froth. There was thunder, somewhere, and a wind that tore at loose planking. The lantern swayed on its chain; rain spattered them from the open door. An auspicious night for some.

"I shall call you Mr. Bubbles," she said as she wiped his nostrils, his twitching limbs. "My first pony."

Even then he could have killed her with a single kick. It had occurred to him, in the early years. Her affection was a burden, a kind of debt that he owed her. Or it should have been. Instead he felt an uncomfortable warmth when she groomed him, a shudder in his massive heart when she was at risk. Humanity did things which were inconvenient. Her humanity, of course, not his.

Those days were strange, all blankets and currying-brushes. This field not that field, and a halter. When he tore the stake from the ground and shredded the halter rope, they got the message. Here, yes, and staying for a while but never tied here, never bound. She saw that, though her parents were less sure. Patting his muzzle, she threw the rope far away, opened every gate.

"This is your home, boy," she whispered.

Clinging to the cotton-grass, claws wrapped round stalks and stems, narrow heads lifting. Out of the half-world to play, soft pipes and changelings, curdled milk and torn bedsheets. The Children of Angles and Corners, as alike to the fey of folk tales as a cleaver to a butter knife...

He considers the world, and the half-world which is coming. These are bale-fire nights. More than the low moon lights the crags, flushing wings which should not beat from the burned heather. A dead fox stirs, unable to rest, its white bones gleaming in the tough grass. The owls do not call.

He knows these times, and is here because there are certain matters which he never shares with the girl. Sandra. This is a confluence of wrong places, the place she calls their home. A more sensible people would have fled, but these are Wolds-folk, centuries rooted. He has tried to explain it to her, but she has something called spirit, pluck. An old virtue, which stops her from seeing the worst, even when it claws at her face.

"Don't worry, boy. We'll see to it."

They did, mostly. But one day they might not, and he doubts that he will be the first to fall. Which worries him. Occasionally. Tonight is a night of questions.

He moves, a careful matter of one hoof then another, testing uneven ground. There are rabbit-ways and sheep trails, gullies where the wash from the crags makes iron-brown streams. Small beaches line the gullies, the glitter of fine sand by moon and stars.

Something calls out from the rocks above, and his ears lift, twitch. This is their time of sport. It isn't his only encounter with these things, not that the girl knows the half of it. They come to test and tease and feed. They slide through nowhere and into the world of people — soft, confused, stupid people. He has little love for humanity some days, but even less for the ones who come to prey on them.

And there is Sandra. Clear-eyed and best of breed. If they touch her, he will spread them, their thin limbs and their coppery blood, across an acre, a thousand acres of this land. He will break them in ways they cannot comprehend...

His own blood pounds at the thought, raising the red. He steps more quickly, wary for warrens and pits. For all his strength, a fetlock is a fetlock, easily caught in soft earth and twisted. The moor rises here in folds, beginning its broad journey to the horizon. There are spatters of light below and behind him, the farmhouse and then the village itself. His protectorate, by association. That's how the girl seems to see it, anyway.

Their music is a scrape on glass, a lost child's wail, forced through throats which do not quite exist. Their limbs twitch without sinews and bend where there are no joints. They see farmsteads and the flesh within, flesh that dances when plucked. Fat where they are lean, sweetmeats for their soured tongues...

A stretch of heather in purple fullness, lingering honey on the air, and he picks up his pace. They haven't seen him yet, because they long too much to slip into outhouses and worry the hens, set the dogs to running. There are memories and monstrosities in the woods far more dangerous than these, but they know their place, for the greater part. Even the nightjacks. Those who come tonight are older than most monsters, a land-memory for the northern Wolds.

By a peat-stained tarn, he gets their measure. The Children of Angles and Corners, many in number and fell with purpose. Wire-thin, heads held high above the heather. They stare at the village below as they creep across the moor, rustling the reeds. In the cold, gathering night they pause now and then to hiss at rabbits, or their companions. Even their own are prey, if they weaken.

And now they do see him. A few of those heads, almost triangular, turn. Scornful eyes regard him. A horse, a pony, a beast. Blind to their presence, surely, and elsewise powerless when the folk of the half-world come calling. Hoof and horn mean nothing to them. They turn back to snarl in pettiness, clambering one upon the other to be in the advance. Over rill and bracken, plucking ticks and beetles from the undergrowth, licking out the softness inside with tongues like blinded snakes.

A night of them, a wash of them to remind the village what elf-shot once meant. They will thrill to the ways which old folk shudder and sigh, brittle-boned and crack-jointed. They will feed on the shudder-dreams of the young. It has been a long time, and the Children must play...

He stamps on the soft earth, his breath a storm cloud. Are there too many of them? For a moment he remembers the girl's picture books, strewn across the barn as she read to him when she was small. Lords and ladies, fine robes for the fey folk on their white horses, and bells jingling from every halter. Fairy mounds and courts of soft laughter. She coloured in one of the pictures.

"Look, Mr. Bubbles." Her blonde hair fell across her eyes, and she giggled. "A fairy king."

And here they are in reality, with eyes of curdled milk, with tiny, needle teeth, a tumbling procession of hate and need. Crawling and leaping down off the moor, slit-nostrils quivering at the stink of tarmac as they come to the road. They spit and moan, but then they are on it and eager.

"Wouldn't if I were you." His words come from deep lungs, carrying on the cold air and wreathed in mist.

The spike-limbed mass before him pauses. A beast sees them. A beast has spoken.

"Horsey," hisses one of the Children, no more than twenty yards from him. "Clever horsey, learns the fat-things' words."

Their laughter is vinegar at his lips, sharp on his tongue. The girl does not know what "her pony" can sense, because he never tells her. He can taste her love, even now, and her loyalty. This is how he lives, how he survives pony shows, and village fetes. Ribbons in his hair, and half the prizes because they worry what might happen if he doesn't get that bright rosette. It makes her happy.

"Not your place, this." He tosses his head, mane black and wild, ribbon-free. "Best go back."

Laughter and menace, because they are the Children of Angles and Corners, and this is merely a beast with a trick or two. Nothing to them, for they have claws which shred, and they see no harm in practice...

He rears, tail swishing, and the red comes to him. She does not like such times, the girl, but she is not here and these things are. Born under an Elder Sign, fearless and far-sighted — and keen for the fight. He has always been like this.

They surge, a dozen, two dozen, chitter and claw as they come for him. If there is a fragment of sense in one or two of them — and there may be — it says that this animal, this pony, shows no sign of fleeing the half-world's hunger. And if they are a wrongness in human lands, then what is this which charges them, drumming the ground with its great hooves? The earth, which is not their earth, thunders under his coming, and the first of them, out from the pack, is...

Dead.

Cold iron, a horseshoe the size of two men's hands, slams into a narrow skull and makes it egg shell, broken egg shell. And another. Rear and kick, and he is in the middle of them. Their claws catch, drawing blood from his hide, but the cold iron drives down, shattering limbs, opening cramped chests. The Children of Angles and Corners shriek and caper, slashing out at him, and blood pours from one of his nostrils, spraying hot on their cold skins.

He takes a slicing cut to one side of his chest but wheels round and kills another of them with a backward kick which makes two of it. They pull back a yard, two yards, but no more. He is the core of battle, a blackness waiting to be washed by a grey tide.

"Go!" he says, hooves planted four-square, ready. "Not your place!"

They hiss encouragement, each to the other. He sees them creep, always encircling, and wonders how strong is strong. It must be done, though...

The initial blast splits the waiting; the second one tears the twisted legs from one of the Children on the edge of the pack. Iron shot, and salt, and the thud-click of a pump-action shotgun.

Hate-filled and hateful, the Children run, all small plans and malice abandoned. They cry and crawl, drive themselves into stands of bracken. They call to the half-world, and the half-world answers, opening for them.

Chitter. Slithering and weeping anger, they run for the past-ways, to swear vengeance and tear their own wounded as they go, knowing failure. Leaving the moors. The Children of Angles and Corners flee from a black-maned, iron-hooved monster...and another.

He snorts up blood, and turns to her. A slim girl with blonde plaits and an old combat jacket thrown over her shoulders, she peers into the darkness.

"Why did you come out here without me? And what were those creatures?" Sharp words. He hears anger; he tastes concern — and love. She comes closer, the gun in one hand and pointed always towards the moor.

"Oh. You're bleeding, boy!" With her free hand she pulls a torch and a cloth from her shoulder bag and examines him, tutting and dabbing at some of his wounds.

"Had worse." A sharp response. She fusses too much.

"Poor Mr. Bubbles. We must get you straight back to the barn, and cleaned up."

He turns his head to the moor, watching the flickers which she cannot see as the Children return to the half-world. She slaps his flank, demanding attention.

"Right now, if you please!"

The red has gone. He whinnies, lowers his head and follows the girl down to the farmhouse without argument. Far away, a dead fox settles and remembers how to sleep.

He is her first pony. She will never need another.

AUTHOR NOTES

This is the only completely serious tale of Mr. Bubbles, a slightly psychotic, unnatural equine who trots his way across East Yorkshire, protecting the Wolds from both resident and incoming horrors. It is in a sense an origin story, for what that's worth. Mr. Bubbles is huge, pitch black, and indomitable, and no one knows if he is a mutation, a monster, a demon, an eldritch spirit, or just a judgement on stupid people. I certainly don't. I know he likes parsnips, which is more to the point.

He is indifferent to most humans except his beloved Sandra, and inclined to kick first, ask questions later. He is also easily bored. Many of his shorter, more sarcastic (or ludicrous) outings exist somewhere on social media, and may or may not be gathered together one day. With a huge, bloodied hoof-print on them.

THE OX WAGONS creak and groan; a child is screaming, though the mother tries to stifle the sound with a stained rag; the soldiers' heads are lowered. The small column is a straggle of misery, alone on the veldt.

"We will see the hills soon, sir." Khumalo's voice is as flat as the parched lands around them. "Near Brandburg."

Lieutenant Redvers Blake looks up, startled.

"Ah, yes. The blockhouse on the Brandburg trail will have water, and feed for the horses."

"If it is not burned, sir."

Solomon Khumalo is not a cheerful man, but he is a good policeman; a Zulu and one of the *amaKholwa*, more Christian than most of the white men who trample his country. He and Khumalo have worked together since Blake was detached from his regiment, two months ago.

Blake lifts his hand and calls out. "Water!"

The column slows in a miasma of sweat, ox dung, and dust. The screaming has stopped, and Blake trots his horse over to the leading wagon.

"The child sleeps now, sir," says the native driver, hunched over the reins of the oxen.

Blake stares at the huddle of displaced women and children in the wagon. The woman whose son was screaming has a baby in her arms, a small thing which is too quiet, as if to compensate for the sounds its older brother has been making. She has a flat, dirty face, and her eyes are full of red-rimmed anger at the English officer on his fine horse. The officer who watched as his troops burned the family's farmhouse and took the cattle.

"Are you content?" she asks in Afrikaans. "They will be quiet, maybe, until I bury them."

"I did not want this duty, *mevrou.*" His horse moves restlessly, and he comforts it with one gloved hand. He has no such comfort for the woman, or for himself. "What is your name?"

"Andermaans. Hester Andermaans. My boy is Hansie; his little sister is Anya." She stabs at him with this knowledge, holding out the bundled baby. "She is sick."

"There's a hospital at Vrysfontein."

She glances at the silent women crammed in with her. They are all looking up at him now, thin children pressed up against them.

Blake tries again, in their tongue. His Afrikaans is passable, if no one speaks too quickly. "Give me a list of who amongst you is ill, in need. I'll do what I can."

"Need?" Another woman tries to spit, but her mouth is too dry. "We need our farms, our crops, our men."

"Your men went to war. This is what happens."

"How many of our husbands have you killed?" Hester Andermaans asks.

Khumalo has ridden up to Blake's side, looking worried. "Sir, this is not good talk."

"This is not a good war." Blake wipes sweat from his forehead. "See that the children receive an additional ration of water."

He has nothing else to offer, and turns his horse to inspect the rest of the column. The second wagon contains the old men and the boys almost of an age to hold a gun; that wagon seethes with anger. As Blake approaches, a native orderly is passing pannikins of water amongst them, the soldiers nearby ready for any sign of trouble.

"The bastards are quiet, sir," says Corporal DeVries, Anglo-Dutch from the Cape and decidedly venomous towards the Boer. DeVries is a big man, powerfully built, who rarely leaves the saddle.

"And the farmhands, corporal?"

The black workers keep to themselves at the rear of the wagons, unsure of their fate. They've been walking since they were taken from the fields they worked for the Boer, and are tired. Blake would have given them a spell in one of the wagons, but there would have been uproar – if not from the Rifles, then from the women.

DeVries looks at them, and sneers. "They are nothing."

Blake tugs on the reins and heads away from the stink of the column. He is a coward here, faced with the smoulder of women's eyes and the brutality of DeVries. Easier surely to be crawling across dry gullies, ready to risk a Boer's bullet...

***

The wrong stars fill the night sky, and the wind is cold. Not enough blankets or tents. A fourth wagon suffered a broken axle, and was abandoned; DeVries made sure that anything left behind was burned or broken, made useless to the enemy.

Scorched earth.

Lieutenant Redvers Blake does not like Africa. He is not sure it is a land for the British or the Dutch, however many towns, mines, and laagers they build, however many years they cling to the red soil. It belongs to Khumalo — to a dozen different peoples the colour of charcoal, ebony, or mahogany, not the scorched brick-reds and watery pinks of the Europeans. Blake does not greatly like empire, at heart.

"Duty," his father used to say. "Tradition. Honour..."

A Mauser bullet stilled those sentiments when it took off half his father's head at Magersfontein; his mother lost half her wits when she heard.

Duty, tradition, and honour are not serving the Blakes well.

"They are all quiet now," says Khumalo, offering him a tin plate of mealie meal and gravy. They squat together by a small fire, away from the wagons, away from the soldiers.

"We could ride off." Blake pushes his fingers into the stiff paste. "Leave the families and wagons here — say we sighted the Boer and went in pursuit."

"Corporal DeVries would not leave the wagons, sir."

"Not without shooting those within." Blake shudders.

The four black policemen under his temporary command don't care much for either side, but they have families of their own to support, to keep safe. He thinks of the Cape Mounted Rifles he's been assigned. Discipline and scowls on sun-scoured faces; Wolseley helmets and sweat-stained jackets. These men have lost comrades to the Boer; they would need little urging to kill the women and children.

"Give this to someone else." Blake hands his supper to the sergeant.

The woman who challenged him earlier is sitting on the edge of the wagon, one of the Rifles watching from horseback. She is staring at the jagged termite mounds which dot the veldt further south — irregular stalagmites which can reach twenty feet or more.

Blake walks over to her, making enough noise with his boots so she won't be startled.

"How are your children?"

"Alive." She knots her fingers. "They say many die in these camps of yours. Especially the young ones."

"I—"

"That there is not enough food — that we eat rice and potatoes, with little meat or fresh vegetables."

"Your men raid the supply lines. Even our own troops have short rations."

"Then let us go free, and you will have more food for yourselves." She squints at him by the light of the wagon lantern. "We should help each other. It is God's will."

For a moment his hand is pressed hard against the bare wood of the wagon, and he remembers too late that he took off his worn leather gloves to eat. The timbers are soaked with emotion from weeks of hauling the newly destitute away from their homes. Thin, drawn faces fill his field of vision, their expressions slipping back and forth between resentment and resignation — and he feels the wagon's other memories...

De Vries, red-faced and panting as he presses a Boer girl up against the empty wagon, dominance and dominion captured in a few desperate gasps of Afrikaans. A native policeman lashing out with his stick at other black men to get them onto the wagon. The constable's face is dark not only from his heritage, but from self-hatred.

An ox dying in its traces, only four days ago.

Blake shudders and pulls his hand back.

"God's will? No god watches what we do here."

He doesn't believe in his own cause any more than he believes in a deity. He is a soldier, nothing more, and will see his charges to their destination.

***

The following day they reach the blockhouse without incident, letting the horses and oxen rest for a couple of hours, and by pressing on, they manage to reach the main camp by dusk.

Vrysfontein. A fine name; a mockery of a place.

The long valley is damp and insect-blown; spring-water higher up turns to foetid stretches of marsh in the low places, assisted by the ordure from the camp. The rows — many rows — of tents are laid out between bare hills, canvas lines broken here and there by crooked huts made from scarce wood and stones dragged down the hillsides by native labour.

Blake has been on detachment here for six weeks, and he knows a graveyard when he sees it, without needing any talent to read the dank earth. He tells DeVries to lead the wagons down, and wanders up the slopes to sit with Khumalo and the native constables.

"Where are your own men now, sir?" asks the sergeant.

"The North Surreys? Up beyond Kimberley, seeking to engage the Boer in line."

"The Boer do not fight in line," says one of the constables.

"I know."

Blake has no illusions that these black men are his friends, but he has never had a feel for the officers' mess. Not that there is one at Vrysfontein, but he would still rather squat with Khumalo and chew grass — and from this ridge, he cannot smell the mortuary, the hospital, or the latrines.

The scattered watch-fires of Vrysfontein mock the unfamiliar constellations above. Once, such places were refugee camps and aid centres, kept for non-combatants and the Boer farmers who would not go on *kommando*. We must protect the civilians, the generals and administrators said.

Now Kitchener has his way. The farms are aflame, and these are concentration camps, Boer women, children, and their black workers crammed in places like Vrysfontein across the country, in order to break the enemy's will. Vrysfontein has one German doctor, and a handful of volunteer nurses from the Cape, but too many of the inmates still die — if not from dysentery, typhoid, and other sicknesses, then from malnutrition and despair.

The native constables must know what he is thinking as he stares down at the camp.

"The *mmabudu* comes each night, and takes them," says Abram, a lean man in his thirties.

Blake frowns. "I don't know the word. Zulu?"

Khumalo clears his throat. "Tswana, sir. It means the..." He thinks. "The small hyena which eats the ant, eats them in their hundreds, thousands."

Blake nods. "The *aardwolf*, the Boers call it. I've seen a few." He remembers the creature, like a small, striped wolf. "But they're hardly dangerous. Some sort of local tall tale?"

Abram shuffles closer. "No, sir. My father says this. He says that the *mmabudu* spirit was not seen here until the white men came. That he has grown because you feed him. He comes to each camp, and licks, licks. His long tongue takes those who are weak. But he does not come to the black camps. He does not eat our people. He likes only the *bosweu*, the white ones."

Blake gives a hoarse laugh, liking the irony. "You believe this, Abram?"

"I am a Christian, sir. But I am glad that my family and my ancestors need not fear the *mmabudu*."

The talk turns to matter of food, and drink, and women. Khumalo's men are both comfortable and awkward around him. He is not quite what he should be, which worries some of them.

"You like the kaffirs, lieutenant?" DeVries had asked a fortnight earlier, when they cleared a kraal and left ashes on the wind. The man's red face was smeared with contempt. "Want to find a black woman, maybe?"

"Do I like the natives?" Blake slipped his service revolver from its holster, and pointed it casually at DeVries, as if it were a toy gun. "I don't like anyone, corporal."

"You are mad, Blake. Sir," the NCO muttered, and walked away.

Blake is not mad, only tired. He nods to the constables, and heads down to the flea-ridden tent that is his home — until the regiment comes south again.

There will be the usual report to give in the morning.

***

Blake watches the superintendent's staff the next day, neat figures striding between the tents. Three women fight over a cotton dress, while their children stare, dull-eyed, at the hills. There are die-hards here who spit on *kakies*, their name for British soldiers — and there are families who would raise a Union flag over their farmhouses if it meant they could go back to the old lives.

More than four hundred men, women, and children are held in this camp; ten, fifteen people to a tent, and six latrine trenches for all of them. The families have never used Army latrines, and besides, they are used to squatting away in the scrub, a private affair. Faeces are splattered across Vrysfontein, polluting the marshy ground. Blankets are in short supply, and they are allowed few fires — timber is also scarce.

The women queue for water from a rusty tank on a supplies wagon. Some of them drink from the marshes, and are sick from it, but many are sick anyway.

Blake dodges a group of boys who are kicking a bundle of rags around, and heads for Major Gallagher's office. A ragged-trousered Boer wanders between the tents, shrieking "Piet!" repeatedly. He is ignored by all.

Khumalo says that in the blacks-only camps, the inmates must buy their own food, and are thus cheap labour for the railways. The railroad has been hit again by a Boer commando, and the tracks are up, meaning shortages. Still, Blake has messed down with his regiment in the Transvaal. British infantry eat what they can, when they can — and many civilians would revolt at the spoiled biscuit and maggoty meat the troops receive.

Major Gallagher has one of the rare huts, surrounded by lines of whitewashed stones. A tall, spare Scot, his command is a deteriorating rag-tag of unfit troops, detached officers like Blake, and orderlies who supplement their wages through corruption. The inexperienced, the drunk, and the insubordinate, for the most part. The major is interested in broad progress, not details. How many farms remain occupied? Did they see any trails which suggested Boer movement?

"Just hungry women, badly nourished children, sir."

"Little I can do, Blake. The superintendent here...he has no idea how to deal with so many refugees of—"

They both know that Cornwell, the superintendent, is a malaria-ridden alcoholic.

"Prisoners. Sir," supplies Blake.

The major shrugs. "Call them what you will. They're here until the Boer sues for peace."

That will come, thinks Blake, though not yet. Not until war and disease have slaughtered thousands more — and all to no purpose.

Dysentery is rife at Vrysfontein, and he hears that the red measles has taken hold. Some will die from that alone.

"You'll take the Rifles out again in three days. Dismissed, Lieutenant."

Blake tries to sleep through a burning noon, emerging late in the afternoon to check the wagons and then eat — mutton stew, mealies, and an apple. His sleep is fitful and unrefreshing.

There is nowhere to go but to the northern slopes, to what the white men call the Bantu *kraal*, a straggle of tents and lean-tos by the thorn bushes. Some scouts and servants sleep near their masters; Khumalo and others prefer to keep their distance from the camp.

"Sir!" The sergeant tumbles to his feet; Blake waves him back down. The native police are smoking stolen tobacco, which they know he will not report.

"Three days, sergeant. And then we ride."

These are decent men, and useful. They came up with him to assist with the clearances, and at least they can explain matters to the black field hands and other servants, avoiding unnecessary violence. It's not a task they should have to do, as far as Blake is concerned; more of their own people probably die in the camps than if they were simply moved out onto the plains and left to their own devices.

"The *mmabudu* came last night," says Abram. "Lick, lick. It stood above the doctor-place, and took ten, twelve children."

It is easy, looking down on Vrysfontein, to see it as a panic of ants — so many small figures, wandering aimlessly. There is no guiding intelligence in this broken mound, and Blake can almost imagine them prey to some terrible being, its long, wet tongue probing every tent, every hut...

But this is an Age of Science. Blake tries to explain the new sickness.

"It's the red measles, that's all. That's what's killing people."

The constables are polite, but dubious.

"It is said you have an *ngaka's* hand," says Joseph, the oldest man. "You will see the *mmabudu*, if others do not."

Blake has never heard Joseph speak before. Khumalo, his cheeks suffused darker than before, cuffs the constable on the side of the head; they argue briefly in their own tongue.

The sergeant will not look Blake in the eye. "Sir, one time only I told — of when you knew whose spear had tasted blood. You placed your hand on it, and it spoke to you. It is *ngaka* business, to know such things."

"Luck," says Blake. "A guess."

Again they do not believe him.

"It is a good thing, sir." Abram smiles, showing a broken tooth. "It is why I tell you of the *mmabudu*. Your ancestors have spoken to ours. I would not tell Mister DeVries this."

Blake lights a cigarette. His only ancestor out here is whatever passing breath remains of his father, what few atoms of skull, blood, and hair still stain the continent. Killed because he put his head up heroically — at the wrong moment.

"I know nothing of the *ngaka*," he responds.

The constables seem to feel they have said enough. He is an officer and a white man — and they must know from bitter experience that whites can be unpredictable, irrational. When Blake's cigarette is finished, he wanders along the slope, lost in sour thought.

Lanterns move to and fro from the hospital, the only building at Vrysfontein with stone walls. A sad, ululating wail rises from the camp and is lost on the breeze.

Children die — pale, dirty things which sicken away from their cramped homes. Children, he tries to persuade himself, who might have died anyway, malnourished and far from medical help.

There is a shadow, a slinking against the iron clouds.

The earthwolf will come...

Blake cannot afford such thoughts. He scrambles down to the camp, noticing that the sentry at the gates is half-asleep — a shooting offence. He kicks the man.

"If I were part of a *kommando*, you would be dead," Blake snaps, and the sentry begins to weep. He is muttering in Welsh, and Blake hears "Mam," "Mam," again and again.

Amongst the tents, die-hards creep out to beat or knife those they think are cowards, or acting as eyes for the British; older children steal from other families, and soldiers poke their sad members into the softness of Boer girls — also against regulations. The chill evening is crowded with victims of one regime or another. Vrysfontein is close to collapse.

Blake sees shadows by the back of the hospital, and lifts the flap of his holster. The Boer have been known to sneak in and take supplies and medicines — not that there is much here. He slides behind a water-wagon, moves closer...

It is DeVries, an unmistakable bulk, and the woman from the wagon, Hester Andermaans. Behind the plank wall of the hospital building, where children choke out their last breaths, the corporal is panting and thrusting, one broad hand over the woman's mouth.

"That's enough, damn you," says Blake. "You, *mevrou*, back to your tent."

DeVries pauses, then steps back from the woman, pulling his trousers over his suddenly flaccid member. Blake has his eye on the wrong person — it is the woman who launches herself at him, shrieking in Afrikaans.

"He promises my boy medicine!" She tries to rake him with broken fingernails. "He is taking us to the Cape, you *kakie* bastard—"

Blake struggles with her fury. "Your husband—"

"Killed." She drives a bony knee into his belly. "At Magersfontein."

The next moment she is on her knees, blood streaming from her cheek. DeVries stands behind her, and she lunges at him; his rifle butt drives down towards her head for the second time.

"No!" Blake tries to get between them, but he's too late. He hears the crack of a skull breaking, and the rattled gasp of a woman who will not rise again.

They stand over the body, both of them breathing heavily.

"Didn't mean to kill her." The big man is sullen, staring at the lieutenant. "She attacked a British officer. Christus, she was only a Boer!"

DeVries mutters that the body will need to be moved, and when Blake makes no attempt to stop him, he leaves to find a medical orderly.

Blake could have the corporal taken on a charge of rape, if nothing else, but Gallagher will hesitate, try to ignore it. Discipline at Vrysfontein is almost non-existent; Blake himself is paralysed by this place. There is something greater, something darker, looming above the camp, and he can almost believe that people like DeVries have drawn it here.

***

He cannot sleep. His watch — his father's watch — tells him it is three in the morning. He stumbles out into the camp, his jacket over his nightshirt, revolver pushed into his belt. A bloated moon hangs over Vrysfontein; the windows of the hospital block glow yellow, a fever-light. He follows the smell of the place until he is at the open doors.

Doctor Kauffman smokes a cheroot in the doorway. A squat Bavarian, who came to Cape Colony to study disease, and volunteered for the camps. Hard-working, but detached from the misery around him.

"Ah, *Leutnant* Blake. You are the one who brings me *die Masern, ja?*"

"Measles? No, *Herr Doktor*. Only dysentery and the like."

Kauffman has a skull of a face, with tight, parchment skin.

"It is not good, Blake. More die than they should, in the night. The nurses, they also become not well. Look."

The hospital block was built for a dozen patients, six on each side, yet there are forty or more children and young women in here. They rest on canvas sheets, camp beds, anything that is to hand, and the stench is dreadful. There is a shortage of bedpans, and of clean water — many have relieved themselves where they lie.

A Cape coloured woman moves between patients, letting them sip water from an enamel mug. Blake sees what Kauffman means. The nurse is unsteady on her feet, sweat gleaming in the lantern light.

"The mortuary is full," says Kauffman. "We should burn some of the bodies, *vielleicht?*"

There is one more corpse in there now — Hester Andermaans.

"I'll ask the major."

"*Danke.*"

A child, a straw-headed boy, lies near them. His legs are brittle sticks, his belly swollen; he clutches his groin, moaning. Blake sees raised red blotches over the boy's ribs and up to the throat.

"*Die Masern.* I think he will die — too weak to resist, *ja?*"

"Have you treated a boy, about seven years old?" asks Blake. "Name of Andermaans."

The doctor thinks. "*Ja*, he has gone to the women. He is not so ill. He may be more fortunate than his little friends. There is a wolf out there, *leutnant*. It waits until our bodies weaken, and then it pounces."

Blake stares, cold sweat at his neck. A wolf?

"What the hell do you mean?" he snaps.

The doctor looks surprised. "I speak *metaphorisch*, you know? You need a night's rest, Blake." He pinches out his cheroot, and with a nod, disappears into his terrible domain.

The moon seems close to the land, as if it will settle there, and it brings its own shadows, ashen blurs which cling to the hillsides.

Blake stiffens. Along the foetid watercourse, a presence comes closer to the camp, a hunger which has two low stars for eyes...

"I do not believe in you!" he yells. "Leave them be!"

The *mmabudu* pauses, slinks back.

It has each and every night to choose from.

***

In the morning, DeVries reports Hester Andermaans' "accidental" death. Blake listens in silence; Major Gallagher barely hears the corporal. A *kommando* has assaulted the blockhouse near Brandburg, killing four British regulars and three natives.

The major is jittery, his eyes slightly unfocussed. "Could you...could you arm your Bantu, Blake? Temporarily, I mean, of course."

Blake thinks of Abram, and old Joseph, of the youngest constable who keeps to himself. The major doesn't even know which of many peoples the black constables belong to. This was once called a white man's war, but the boundaries are crumbling. Promises not to arm the natives have been broken again and again on both sides.

"Sergeant Khumalo is sound; I believe the others can be trusted."

This is not a regulation move, but then Vrysfontein is sliding far from regulations.

Gallagher manages a weak nod. His face is pale under the tan, and he has a rash around his tight collar, extending up a neck which seems swollen.

"They'd better have the old Martini-Henrys from stores. Blake, I want you to relieve the blockhouse. Get the damage repaired — you can requisition workers from Brandburg." He scribbled orders out, ink spattering the paper. "You'll be there a month or so, and then the North Surreys will want you back, no doubt."

Blake looks at DeVries. "What of the Rifles?"

"Back to Cape Colony, other duties," says Gallagher.

For a brief second, as they meet each other's gaze, they seem to communicate.

"Yes, sir."

Outside the major's hut, he finds DeVries, waiting.

Blake removes his cap, wipes the sweat from his forehead. "You were never going to take Hester Andermaans and her son to the Cape, were you?"

"I don't know." The NCO narrows his eyes against the sun. "You are no better than I am, Blake; you take orders, you kill. The veldt does not care."

"Go away, DeVries. Go far away from me."

Blake wishes that DeVries might die tomorrow, that his horse will stumble and cause him to break his neck. Or that a Boer sniper takes him down. But wishes and prayers are futile; there is no God to make either happen, nor to stop them.

***

He is crouched in contemplation of nothing, not far from the "Bantu kraal," when he sees a medical orderly hugging his way up the slope.

"Lieutenant Blake?" The man is florid, and surprisingly overweight.

Blake stands up. "Yes."

"Doctor Kauffman's compliments, sir. He thought you would want to know, as you had been asking about the family..."

"Know what?"

The orderly pulls off his cap, squeezes it in his fat hands. "The Andermaans baby... She didn't make it, sir." Blake doesn't speak, the man twists the felt cap with more awkwardness. "Is there...is there a reply for the doctor, lieutenant?"

Blake draws in a deep breath, the breeze redolent of faeces and despair.

"Say that I appreciate being informed. Tell him...tell him to watch for the *mmabudu*. It has the taste, now."

Uncomprehending, the orderly struggles back down the hillside.

***

The tent in which Hester Andermaans was placed is the last in the line to the south. A large bell-tent, it has mould on the canvas, and ordure around it. The wet sound of his boots sickens him.

Inside, eight women and five children squat, surrounded by sour blankets and a few personal possessions. One old woman has a gilded clock which she hugs to her narrow chest; the woman next to her is turning a toy horse over and over in her fingers.

"Where is Hansie Andemaans?"

A wet cough; silence.

"Hester Andermaans' son. I want to know if anyone can care for him."

The old woman clutches her clock more tightly, and moans.

He is being stupid; most of these women speak no English. He tries again in Afrikaans; there is still no response.

"Hansie Andermaans," he says. "Does he have family here, in the camp? An aunt? Friends of his mother or father?"

These women have the look of DeVries about them — angry, unwilling.

Blake swears, and reaches, ripping the clock from the old woman's hands. She wails; the other women and children draw back. He presses one hand to the timepiece, a finely carved wooden shell around works which must have been made by a craftsman. He feels it, listens to it...

And tells them what he learns.

The long, sallow face of a naval captain, the seal of the Dutch East India company behind him. Lascars, struggling as ships founder; settlers drinking the salt sea, or choking on the sands of Cape L'Agulhas...

He feels the clock's generations-long progress as it makes its way to the Orange Free State — by hand, by ox, by cart...

"*Nie 'n soldaat nie,*" mutters the old woman. "*'N heks-man.*"

Blake is not a witch-man. He has a talent, a curse, that he does not want and that his father loathed. The father who died at the same battle as Hester Andermaans' husband. Chance and poor judgement rule over all.

The women pour out words now. They have the awkward expressions of Khumalo's men. "It is said you have an *ngaka's* hand." Now he is a *heks-man* too.

"There is an uncle, maybe, in Brandburg," says a jaundiced woman.

"*Ja, ja,*" says another. "A dealer in grain."

Their talk propels a shivering boy from behind dirty skirts. Hansie Andermaans.

"Hansie. I am going near Brandburg," Blake says, again in Afrikaans. "I will take you from this place, if you wish."

The boy looks blank; the women talk amongst themselves and nod their heads. This would be a good thing, they agree. The old woman holds out her hands, and Blake gives her back her clock.

"*Heks-man.*" A respectful smile of gums and spittle.

Hansie Andermaans follows Blake from the tent, because the women tell him to.

Khumalo and his men collect their rifles and a foil-sealed box of ammunition. Bandoliers for each, pull-throughs and gun oil — Blake makes sure that they have all they need.

They are not unhappy at this change of duty. There will be fresher food, supplied from around Brandburg; no more herding of shrieking women, children, and bitter fellow natives. No more of this squalid, disease-ridden camp. Measles and dysentery are spreading, and there is talk that both Major Gallagher and two of the nurses are sick now.

Blake explains that they will set out with the last of the day's light. The boy must know that his mother and his younger sibling are dead, but Blake believes Hansie has yet to grasp what has happened, or what might become of him. In that, he is little different from the men around him.

"God has called you to save this life," says Khumalo.

Blake does not argue — though he wonders how the *ikholwa* can maintain his faith under such conditions.

Unlike Khumalo, Blake feels no satisfaction at this most pitiful of gestures, this almost random largesse he has shown — to take a Boer child away from the camp, to an uncertain future with an uncle he does not know, an uncle who may well not welcome him. It is an act so small that it feels almost worthless.

One child.

***

A few miles from the camp, Blake turns his horse, reining it in so that he can look back on Vrysfontein for the last time — he hopes.

"Do you see it, sir?" asks Abram.

He sees it.

He would like to think he is looking at clouds and illusions, fuelled by campfire stories, but he is not.

The quiet, cautious earthwolf, its mane flaring, dips its head down across the camp. Evening stars glint in its eyes, and it has needs. Huge but light-footed, it slinks and bends its thick neck. A tongue of shadows flickers over the hospital...

Inside that low building, laid in pain, fever, and faeces, are the pale white grubs of children who will never grow up, and around them, the stricken workers and the damaged soldiers. Many who ought to recover, but will not. They are no better than the termites of the plains, a night-feast for that which hungers.

Hansie Andermaans shifts behind Abram, and the lean constable reaches back to pat the child awkwardly. The back of a callused black hand brushes the boy's dirty white cheek. Blake turns his horse to the Brandburg trail again, and they break into an easy canter, making the best of the cool night and the stars. Their rifles are loaded, and the blockhouse awaits.

Behind them, a darkness straddles Vrysfontein. The sick and dying have been exposed, and the *mmabudu* must feed. They — all of them — have drawn something strange, something hungry, to them.

Lieutenant Redvers Blake knows that neither the earthwolf nor the dead of Africa will ever leave him...

AUTHOR NOTES

As for this particular tale of the 2nd Boer War, it is sadly accurate to the times and conditions it describes, barring a few small liberties. Although I consider myself a relatively cheerful pragmatist, I find Redvers Blake a darker and more troubling character than almost any other of my 'regular' cast. His distracted egalitarianism, his atheism and his suspicion of authority... these make him few friends at any level. He is a troubled humanist, troubled because the humanity he would espouse is so often a disappointment, and he's not even that fond of himself. He keeps an oath he made to the dead Victoria Regina, the Queen in Black, and there are few 'happy' endings in his tales. But there are endings, of sorts.

I feel for him.

JOHN LINWOOD GRANT was raised on the cliffs beyond the Yorkshire Wolds by wild gulls, and still visits his relatives to beg scraps, but has lived nearer the Dales for the last few decades, attended by his pack of lurchers. He knows the true origins of the ghoul, the nature of subtle horror, and how to bake a good loaf of bread. He is old, sarcastic, and has his own beard. He may even have a family, somewhere around the house.

His published work over the last five years includes some seventy short stories, a novel, a novella and two collections, with more coming, and he has been in several award-winning anthologies. He writes dark contemporary fiction and period supernatural tales, both straight and queer. His novel *The Assassin's Coin* (IFD), features the feared Edwardian assassin Mr Dry, from the collection *A Persistence of Geraniums*, and the related novel *13 Miller's Court* (with Alan M Clark) won the 2019 Ripperology Books award. Otherwise, he writes stories of 1920s hoodoo, parodies, and tales of that slightly psychotic night-maned pony, Mr Bubbles.

He also happens to be the editor of *Occult Detective Magazine*, and a number of recent themed anthologies. He can be found regularly on Facebook, and at his eclectic website greydogtales.com.

Lightning Source UK Ltd.
Milton Keynes UK
UKHW010850190422
401707UK00002B/40